# His Name is
# Jacob Harris

by

## J.J. McFarland

with

## Wm. Francis Herlehy III

TURAS PUBLISHING
www.TursasPublishing.com

# His Name is Jacob Harris

A Confederate soldier whose love for intrigue, danger and espionage was exceeded only by his love for Lilly, a stunning southern belle whose greatest desire was to please him in every way.

by

## J.J. McFarland

with

Wm. Francis Herlehy III

His Name is Jacob Harris

by

J.J. McFarland

with

Wm. Francis Herlehy III

ISBN-13: 978-0-9982215-4-0
2nd Edition

www.TurasPublishing.com

# Contents


Preface........................................................................................vii

Acknowledgements........................................................... viii

Introduction.................................................................................1

Chapter One .................................................................................3

Chapter Two............................................................................ 11

Chapter Three...........................................................................17

Chapter Four ............................................................................25

Chapter Five.......................................................................,, 31

Chapter Six........................................................,, ....37

Chapter Seven .............,, ..............................................39

Chapter Eight ...........................................................................45

Chapter Nine ............................................................................53

Chapter Ten ..............................................................................61

Chapter Eleven.........................................................................71

Chapter Twelve ........................................................................81

Chapter Thirteen ....................................................................93

Chapter Fourteen...........................................................101

Chapter Fifteen...............................................................109

Chapter Sixteen...............................................................117

Chapter Seventeen ..........................................................121

Chapter Eighteen............................................................131

Chapter Nineteen .................................................139

Chapter Twenty .................................................145

Chapter Twenty-One .................................................149

Chapter Twenty-Two .................................................157

Chapter Twenty-Three .................................................167

Chapter Twenty-Four .................................................173

Chapter Twenty-Five .................................................187

Chapter Twenty-Six .................................................195

Chapter Twenty-Seven .................................................207

Chapter Twenty-Eight .................................................215

Chapter Twenty-Nine .................................................221

Chapter Thirty .................................................229

Chapter Thirty-One .................................................245

Chapter Thirty-Two .................................................255

Chapter Thirty-Three .................................................261

Chapter Thirty-Four .................................................269

Chapter Thirty-Five .................................................277

Chapter Thirty-Six .................................................285

Chapter Thirty-Seven .................................................297

Chapter Thirty-Eight .................................................305

Chapter Thirty-Nine .................................................313

Chapter Forty .................................................332

# Preface

A few years ago, while doing some ancestral research, I discovered my great-great-grandfather Jacob (Jake) McFarland and his brother Lorenzo were adopted by the McFarland family when they were 11 and 12 years old. Both served with the 51st Virginia Infantry during the Civil War and both survived the war. Believing this would be a great start for a book, I began my research and learned there is much about the Civil War that is still relatively unknown to most readers. I discovered that after 1863, Confederate leaders including the Confederate Secret Service began planning subversive activities in Canada to encourage the northwest states to secede from the Union and form its own Confederacy. I also discovered several well-known secret patriotic organizations like the Knights of the Golden Circle played critical roles in carrying out sabotage against Northern line-of-communication, transportation networks and national elections. The book describes in detail blockade activities of the Union Navy, the creation by the South of an ocean-going Naval threat against Union shipping, and the smuggling of arms from Liverpool to the Port of Charleston.

*J. J. McFarland*

# Acknowledgements

In nearly twenty years in the intelligence business I was privileged to work with many of the finest individuals in our intelligence community. When I decided to write this book four years ago, I relied on many of my experiences while attached to the 4078th Strategic Reconnaissance Weather Squadron, the 4080th Strategic Reconnaissance Wing and Detachment 32, Pacific Special Activities area, Seoul, South Korea. I would be remiss if I did not acknowledge their contributions to my thought process in this endeavor.

One particular individual I was stationed with at Bien Hoa Airbase, Vietnam, is Dr. William Francis Herlehy III, Professor Emeritus, Embry-Riddle Aeronautical University, who provided valued assistance with the book. Bill and I both taught at Embry-Riddle for more than twenty-five years and have much in common. Bill was instrumental in helping me create strong, dynamic characters, placing them in situations and settings that gave them greater meaning and followed the plot to its logical or emotional conclusion. He also helped keep me focused.

Thanks also to Ms. Sharon Sinner for providing me with original source material on our mutual great-great-grandfather, Jacob Jake Burris (Harris), the main character in this book. Seldom is an author fortunate enough to find a person who possesses enough original source material such as birth certificates, marriage licenses, military records, etc., to write a piece of historical biographical fiction spanning more than fifty years.

Thanks to Jillian Flaherty for her work on the cover sketch. Lastly, thanks to my book editor, Theresa (Terry) Marie Flaherty of Turas Publishing, who brought my book to life. Her editing skills brought full descriptions to each scene and her selection of just the right words brought emotion to each and every character.

# Introduction

This book not only speaks to the tragedy of the Civil War – it speaks to the heartbreak of loss on both sides and to the reality of history. It provided many lessons and introduced many great men on both sides of the conflict. Many of the Confederate officers, such as Robert E. Lee, were former Union officers and West Point graduates. Several, on both sides, fought together in the Mexican War. With the call of political leaders and protestors to tear down the statues of Confederate leaders and generals, many wonder where this will end and what the cost will be. This book was written to introduce the reader to elements of the war not often discussed in other books. There are surprises in its pages that might well challenge current thinking on the War Between the States and the brave men who fought it.

Figure 1.  Wolf Creek at Burke's Garden.

# Chapter One

## *The Attack*

JACOB and Lorenzo were barely eleven and twelve when their lives changed forever on that day in June 1841. The day began like any other in the rustic valley known as Burke's Garden, named after James Burke who first discovered it in the mid-1740s. The valley, nestled in the southwest ern corner of Virginia between Wytheville and Tazewell, is often referred to by its residents as The Thumbprint of God because of its unique shape and immense beauty. Deer, elk, and rabbits were plentiful, and bass and bluegills splashed abundantly in the streams, providing food year round for the settlers. During the summer and early fall, fresh corn, radishes, turnips, potatoes, and a plentiful supply of apples, cherries, blackberries, raspberries, and strawberries supplemented their diets.

James and Mary Burress, the hardworking parents of the boys, came to Burke's Garden in the spring of 1828 and finished building their cabin there shortly before the start of winter. In 1827, the Governor of Virginia awarded the three-hundred-acre tract of land to James Burress for killing three Indian braves while they

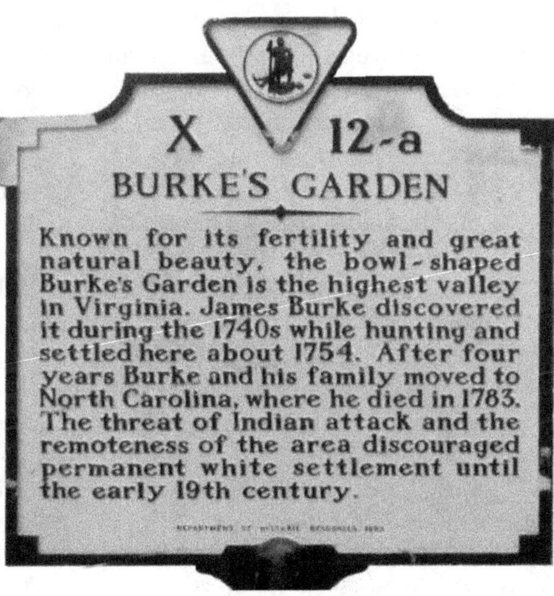



Figure 2. Burke's Garden, Virginia.

3

attempted to steal the entire supply of black powder from an unguarded munitions shed at Fort Gentry. James killed them in hand-to-hand combat as they loaded the powder into a stolen wagon.

In the first two years of their marriage they were blessed with the two boys, Lorenzo and Jacob. Then came William, Thomas, Rebecca and Margaret, who all enjoyed playing outdoors more than doing chores.

The tract of land belonging to the Burresses was adequate in size, but it had required a lot of work in the early years. James had bought Moses and Job for help in clearing the land, planting crops, and cutting firewood for his cabin and slave's quarters. As expenses accumulated, he withdrew more and more money from his family inheritance and savings. Periodic drought in the valley and the additions to the family made it increasing difficult to keep up with family expenses, and he could not afford to send the boys to Burke's Garden's one-room schoolhouse.

Early in the morning of that fateful day, Mary stepped into Jacob and Lorenzo's bedroom and called out, "Boys! It's time to get up! How about going down to Wolf Creek and catch us something for supper?"

Barely stifling a yawn, Jacob replied, "Okay! What do you want us to catch—fish, turtles, crawdads? What do you need?" The boys loved to fish and enjoyed splashing and swimming in the cool water afterward.

"Since you asked, how about bringing home some small mouth bass or bluegills. It doesn't matter much, but we have ten mouths to feed including our slaves Moses and Job."

"Do you want us to take any of the kids with us?"

"No," she said, "they all have chores to do and most of them still need a bath."

"I'll get a bucket to keep our catch alive till we get back," Jacob said. Then added, "What's for breakfast?" Although not yet teenagers, the boys always seemed to be hungry.

"I'll fry up some mush, and cook eggs if there are some in the hen house. Check under the hens and bring in what you find. I hope it's enough for everybody."

A short while later the boys returned with eleven large brown eggs that Mary scrambled for breakfast. After the meal was done, she said, "When you leave, don't forget to wash the tub out for the kids' baths. The kids are too small to clean it by themselves."

Lorenzo grabbed an empty five-gallon bucket and a jar of worms, and Jacob picked up two cane poles before heading out the door. As they approached Blue Spring, a free-flowing stream, their paths crossed with Joe, an elderly slave who lived in the slave quarters on the Lambert homestead not far from their property. Joe was also headed toward Wolf Creek. Lambert's wife Nellie had asked him to collect any small animals caught in the traps strung along the creek's edge four days earlier. The Lamberts helped the Burresses build their cabin and take care of their first and second season's crops when they first arrived in the valley.

Joe was a kindly old man with a halo of springy, thick, white hair and a quick smile. Every one in the valley enjoyed hearing his stories from the *good old days* when he claimed that he rode with Lieutenant Gadston, leader of the last official expedition into the valley in 1821. When the three reached the creek, Joe headed upstream to clean out and reset his traps. The brothers ambled downstream to deeper waters where the drop-offs were sharper and more rugged. After tying cork bobbers to their fishing lines and threading wiggling worms over the end of their hand-made hooks, Jacob and Lorenzo cast out their lines, dropping them quietly into a pool of still water. Jacob found a big rock to stretch out on, and Lorenzo rested his back against a nearby tree as they settled in to wait for a nibble or a strike.

As the sun rose in the bright sky and the boys grew hungry, they pulled out some hardtack, jerky and juicy apples. Lorenzo threaded his way through brush and trees the short way to the Blue Spring where he removed the canteen from his belt and filled it to the brim.

As the sun climbed higher in the sky, the temperature began to rise. The 3,100-foot elevation of the valley kept the temperature from rising too high. The fish continued to bite, and by noon the boys' bucket was overflowing with fish and crawdads. Although ready to start for home, the sparkling water in the creek enticed them to strip to their drawers and plunge into the cool water. Afterward, Lorenzo said, "Remind me to tell mom we took a dip in the creek, otherwise she'll expect us take baths later tonight. God knows we don't want to have to do that."

Meanwhile, back at the cabin, James thought he heard the children playing outside. Earlier the sound of clashing wooden swords filled the air as little William and Thomas battled each other. Rebecca and Margaret, anxious to find a frog or two or to catch some turtles, had been skipping along the path to a nearby pond. As Mary opened the door to peek out and check on the children, an arrow whizzed by her and struck a nearby chair with a thump. Terrified, Mary screamed to the children, "Take cover! Hide yourselves! Hide!"

Mary both heard Moses and Job rush for refuge in the shed that covered a spring in the back yard. Mary gasped when she heard Moses scream, "No! Please! Don't! Don't torture him!" An instant later, Job's blood-curdling screams reached them, but the screams soon morphed into agonized groans and stopped.

The tremulous voice of five-year-old Margaret begging the Indians not to kill Moses was like a knife in Mary's heart. Moses screamed, begging the Indians to leave the Burresses alone and not take the children. When Moses's voice crumbled into deep sobs, James and Mary knew the fate of their slaves was sealed.

James, pulling a poker from the fire with trembling hands, was shocked to see Mary running toward the kitchen. "For God's sake, Mary, where are you going?"

"I'm getting a knife."

Returning with a butcher knife in her hand, Mary cried out, "I'll use it if I have to." Suddenly realizing she had a better weapon in the house, she threw down the kitchen knife and rushed for the bedroom. The acrid smell of smoke quickly enveloped the cabin. Tendrils of flames spread down out of the roof, slowly torching everything in sight. In the distance, their children's terrified screams reverberated in their ears as the braves who snatched them rode away on horseback. Heat prickled their skin, and they knew time was running out. No matter what lay beyond the door, they had to leave the cabin. Mary reached inside the door of a clothes chest and pulled out a .45 caliber derringer she had purchased in Richmond before coming to Burke's Garden. Looking back at her with amazement, James asked, "For Heaven's sake, Mary, what are you going to do with that little thing."

As they were about to charge out the door, Mary grasped her husband's arm and whispered, "I just hope I don't have to use it, Jim. Promise me you'll kill me if it looks like I'm going to be captured. I'd rather be dead than a squaw in the arms of one of those savages."

James slipped out onto the front porch ahead of Mary. In an instant, two arrows pierced his chest, forcing him to his knees. In one quick movement Mary pointed the derringer at James' head and squeezed the trigger. Before he crumpled to the ground he heard a second shot. Mary had pressed the derringer's barrel to her temple and fired. She and her husband would once again be together.

Tom Long, the Burress' nearest neighbor, saw smoke rising from the Buresses cabin. Without a moment's hesitation, he grabbed his musket from its cradle over the fireplace and raced for the Burress homestead on his horse.

As Tom galloped towards the cabin, a young Indian brave bolted out the front door of the cabin, nearly tripping over the bodies of James and Mary. The brave, carrying two burlap sacks, sprinted off the porch onto his waiting pinto. Tom jumped from his horse and, with one smooth motion, pulled his musket from its homemade sheath strapped to the horse. The brave was not yet to the tree line. Dropping to one knee, Tom rested the musket's barrel on the top rail of porch and fired. He watched with grim satisfaction as the brave leaned awkwardly to the left and then tumbled backward to the ground.

Looking toward the slave quarters as he rode toward the downed Indian, Tom saw Moses and Job lashed back-to-back against a stake. Both were badly beaten and tortured in unspeakable ways. Job was partially scalped, but the cutaway section lay discarded in the dirt beside him, the talisman from a colored slave not worthy of the same status as a white man's scalp.

This savage attack on innocent settlers was not the first Tom had witnessed. His face was contorted with rage, and he was overcome with a burning need for revenge then and there. Mounting his horse, he rode quickly to where the Indian lay sprawled on the ground and noticed that his musket ball had hit him just below the ribs on his left side. Jumping from his horse, he grabbed the Indian roughly by his hair and stared at him contemptuously. The brave's eyes were wide with hostility and fear. Tom drew the fingers of his other hand across his own throat from ear to ear, to show the brave what he was about to do. With one swift movement, Tom slashed the Indian's throat with his Bowie knife, nearly separating his head from his body.

After tossing the brave's body on the back of his pinto, Tom mounted his horse and lead the pinto diagonally across a small trail that later joined the main trail leading out of the valley. About halfway across, Tom pulled the dead Indian off his horse and threw the body over the edge where it rolled more than five hundred feet into the trees and brush below. Calmer now, Tom vowed never to mention the incident to anyone. The revenge he exacted against one of the attackers who murdered and kidnapped the Burress family was one memory he prayed he could forget.

***

Before starting for home, the boys worked their way upstream to see if Joe was still clearing out his traps, but he was not there. They supposed that he cleaned them out and returned to the Lambert's homestead. Turning toward home, Jacob and Lorenzo saw smoke rising from the direction of their cabin. At first they thought a thunderstorm approaching and lightning might have started a fire. Joe would have seen a storm coming and started home before it arrived. In any case, Jacob and Lorenzo picked up their pace toward home.

Before cutting across the fields, the boys planned to stop at Blue Spring for a final refill of their canteens. As they approached the spring, the boys saw Sonny Boy, the family's draw horse, running back and forth along the crest of Robinson's Ridge, just east of the spring. Looking at each other in dismay, they knew this was an ominous sign. Because Sonny Boy was old, he was only used to pull wagons around the farm or to take the family into Jeffersonville to buy supplies.

Just before reaching the platform at Blue Spring, Jacob saw Joe and Trace Perry, Burke's Garden's Postmaster, hurrying in their direction. The boys had never seen Joe so distraught and somber, yet Trace appeared more upset than Joe.

Joe shouted, "Boys! Stop! There's been an Indian attack at your farm."

Confused, they looked at Joe, and Jacob asked, "What are you saying? Everything was fine when Lorenzo and I left this morning."

Joe replied wearily, "I know, but it was an Indian attack."

Shaken to the core, Jacob asked, "Where are mom and dad? What happened? Did they fight them off?"

"I'm so sorry! Your parents and Moses and Job were killed. Your neighbor Simon Bane and I covered them with blankets and will return tomorrow to bury them up the hill behind your cabin."

Lorenzo dropped his canteen to the ground at the horrific news and reached for his brother. With tears streaming down his cheeks and already knowing the answer, he could barely whisper the question out loud, "Did they take the children?"

Jacob stared into the distance, but he did not cry.

Trace had seen the braves ride away with the Burris children when he was delivering a package to a cabin near the Burris' home. Joe made a fist with each hand, then wrung them together again and again before answering softly, "Lorenzo, we looked for them, but they're gone."

"What will happen to them?" Jacob asked, but neither boy was sure they wanted to know.

Reluctantly, Joe answered. "Usually they raise the boys as members of their tribe. They'll teach them to fight and kill white men. After they grow up, the girls will be married off to one of the Braves who participated in the raid. They won't be physically abused, but they won't be free to decide who to marry or how they will live."

Jacob, listening intently, asked, "Do you know which tribe did this?"

"If I had to guess, I would say Shawnee. Several Burke's Garden residents have one or more Cherokee wives. I just don't see Cherokees attacking with so many of their kind around. There were no clues at the cabin.  I didn't see anything – arrows, hatchets or even so much as a feather – suggesting they were Cherokees.  The Indians pulled the feathers off the arrows that hit anything and stuck."

By now the enormity of what had happened nearly overwhelmed the boys.  With his head in his hands, Jacob sobbed, "Joe, what will we do?"

Trace replied, "For now, I'll take you to the Harris place. I'm sure they'll take you in.  They're good, decent people and they've helped other children in need.  Whenever the courts can't find families to temporarily care for poor children, they call Jim and Christina to help them out."

Joe interjected, "A year ago, they looked after a little girl who'd lost her parents until her aunt and uncle came to Burke's Garden from Indiana to pick her up.  Jim and Christina came here from Wilmington, North Carolina, about ten years ago.  There, he was a wagon maker, and Christina taught school. Jim came to Burke's Garden after receiving a portion of Colonel Steven Hart's Revolutionary War land grant for saving his son during an Indian raid near Roanoke.  As four Indian braves on horseback attempted to kidnap Colonel Hart's son, Jim charged the braves, killing two.  He grabbed Hart's son and took him back to his Regiment.  Colonel Hart's original 1500-acre grant included a 150-acre tract located at the edge of Burke's Garden original settlement.  This is the land that Colonel Hart gave to Jim. As of yet, they have not been blessed with children of their own."

With a comforting hand on each boy's shoulder, Joe said softly, "If you would like to stay with them, I'm sure Jim and Christina would welcome you into their home."

Still overcome with grief and conflicting emotions, Jacob and Lorenzo were relieved to be going to the Harris place.

Jacob and Lorenzo wanted to return to the farm immediately to look around, hoping to find animals, clothes or other useful items.  The first night, though, the emotionally exhausted boys bedded down in a small but dry barn near the Harris' main house.  Still agitated and too wound up to sleep, they talked late into the night, trying to come to grips with all that had happened. As the evening drifted into darkness, each heard the other's sobs of grief and despair over the loss of their parents and siblings.  They were devastated thinking about what the future held for their little brothers and sisters, and they agonized over what the future held for them.

Figure 3. Burke's Garden - Thumbprint of God.

# Chapter Two

## *Welcome to our Home*

EARLY the next morning Mrs. Harris, a vivacious woman with a no-nonsense air about her, knocked on the barn door and called out, "Are you boys awake?" When she heard the sound of feet hitting the floor, she added, "I thought you might want to get cleaned up. You'll find the spring and an outhouse on the other side of the house where you can wash up. I'll ask Miss Mary to bake you some biscuits and fry up some bacon and eggs. They'll be ready by the time you get back."

When Jacob and Lorenzo entered through the back door after cleaning up, they were surprised to find Joe in the little room just off the kitchen. Jim had added the room as a place where slaves could stay when it rained or when they had work to do in the house. Mr. Harris owned five slaves. Mary and Esther cooked their meals, washed the family's clothes and tended the vegetable garden. Micah, Tobias and Seth were strong, young field hands who planted seed in the spring, tilled the soil through the summer and harvested crops in late summer and early fall. The slaves lived in the corner of a recently converted barn. Between the house and barn was an enclosed kitchen where a stone hearth had been laid. All the food served at the homestead was cooked there. The slaves ate their meals at a long table and bench they had built themselves.

Joe's eyes lit up when the boys entered. He said, "I came over first thing to see if I could lend a hand in rounding up any animals still roaming the land near your cabin."

Jacob and Lorenzo were quick to respond, "Yes. That would be nice."

By now the boys were more at ease, despite their difficult situation. They were reassured that the Harrises would be able to take care of them. They had heard from others in Burke's Garden that Mr. Harris was a fair-minded man who treated his slaves with respect and did not harm them. This knowledge further reassured the two young brothers who had just lost everything.

When Mrs. Harris heard the boys, she came in and suggested, "Why don't you join the rest of the family in the main house for breakfast?" Joe told the boys he was returning to the damaged cabin with Tobias and Micah to make sure it was safe before he and the boys returned. Joe added that they would clear the area around the cabin so the boys could collect their personal belongings.

Mr. Harris told the boys after the area was safe for their return, Tobias and Micah would help them retrieve the boys' horses and buckboard from what was left of their homestead and return both to the Harris homestead.

Mrs. Harris led them into the dining area where Mr. Harris greeted them warmly. "We're so very sorry for the loss of your parents and brothers and sisters. There are just no words to express the sadness we know you must be feeling. We hope we will be able to provide a small measure of comfort," he said, then directed them to two chairs next to each other at the large table laid out with fine china and silverware.

As soon as they were seated, Mr. Harris asked them to bow their heads while he offered a blessing. Mary and Esther brought in trays piled high with plates of thick sausages and sliced ham, biscuits and cornbread, luscious fruit, and a large bowl of grits and a little pot of jam. The boys eagerly filled their plates and ate quietly, savoring the tasty food.

After the meal Jim stood up at his place at the head of the table. He was a tall man with a commanding presence. He began gently, "Jacob. Lorenzo. We sincerely welcome you into our home as members of our family. Sometime over the next few weeks, Christina and I will meet with the Tazewell County Sheriff and County Clerk to draw up a document granting us custody of both of you. We don't want some county official taking it upon himself to turn you into indentured servants that the county can sell to anyone willing to pay upfront for your services. We knew your parents, and I'm sure we can reach an agreement fair to the both of you, to us and to the county. Regardless of how the agreement is written, we intend to take care of you as though you were our own."

Lorenzo looked down at his plate to hide the emotions he was wrestling with. Jacob looked directly at Mr. Harris, but unshed tears glistened in his eyes.

Mr. Harris explained, "These agreements are called *bound out agreements* or *binding out agreements* depending on their purpose. Parents of the children and the family accepting children into their home usually sign, but in this case we'll need you to sign in front of some county official like the Sheriff or County Clerk. If you can't write yet I'll show you how to sign your names or you can make an X and I will witness it for you."

Jacob and Lorenzo both nodded their heads as they listened.

"The agreement," he continued, "will be pretty simple. It'll say you boys belong to Christina and me until you are eighteen. In exchange, I'll provide for all your needs. I'll send you to school and teach you a trade. When you're eighteen, I'll give each of you a lump sum of $200, a new suit of clothes and a good horse. How does that sound to you?"

Jacob liked what he heard. He rose, faced the man who would be their adopted father and answered, "Mr. Harris, I'm sure I speak for both of us when I say I think those terms are very fair. Lorenzo? Do you agree?"

"It sounds fair to me, Jacob."

Watching them closely, Jim thought to himself, *Jacob has demonstrated he will be the adventurous one. Lorenzo, on the other hand, is more quiet and methodical and will stay in the background and let problems come to him, examining them and solving most in his own way.*

Mrs. Harris rose as well and smiled reassuringly. She reaffirmed, "Our home is a God-fearing house where we say grace before meals. There's no shortage of chores to go around, but there's no shortage of love either. As of right now, official or not, this is your home. If there is anything else we can to do to help you, please, just ask."

Together the boys responded, "Yes, Mam!"

"For now," Mr. Harris added, "why don't you call us Jim and Christina." The boys nodded.

## *Return to the Cabin*

When Jacob and Lorenzo returned with Joe to the severely burned out cabin they wanted to look for any debris the Indians might have left behind. Earlier Joe had searched carefully for clues that might identify which tribe had attacked the family. Finding none, Joe knew the Indians had planned the raid and been methodical in carrying it out.

As the boys neared the scene of their devastating loss, both were overcome with pain and grief as despair and dismay washed over them once more. Drawing strength from each other, they took a deep breath to face the grim task ahead with determination. Satisfied with Joe's reassurance that the Indians had no left evidence behind, Jacob and Lorenzo searched for personal items. While sifting through debris in a corner of the cabin, Jacob overturned a tin cup and found his father's silver pocket watch and his mother's favorite pearl necklace. The tin cup had protected both from the fire. Tenderly, he placed the items in a trouser pocket. Outside, Lorenzo retrieved Rebecca's battered doll. In the front of the cabin he found a barely recognizable tattered remnant of a blanket William used in making a tent.  In a pile of ash, Jacob recovered the small pocketknife William used in whittling wooden whistles. The last treasure, one they discovered together, was a thin metal box filled with love letters their father wrote their mother when the two were teenagers.

***

It was not long before the Harrises decided they could afford to send the boys to school.  In fact, Jacob and Lorenzo's education became their primary focus.  When not in school or on the weekends, the boys learned carpentry and wagon making skills.  At the end of each school year, Jim sent the County Clerk's Office a letter with a list of the boys' teachers, the courses they took and the grades they received.  This letter was required by the courts to satisfy the Bound Out Agreement between Jacob, Lorenzo and Mr. Harris. In this letter, Jim asked the court to identify any associated costs so he could reimburse the county.

In the early years, the boys helped Miss Mary and Miss Esther do chores around the house.  They retrieved eggs, fetched water from the spring and made sure bridles, saddles, and other tack were cleaned and put away.  Whenever bad weather threatened, they brought the horses into the barn. Often Christina asked one or both of the boys to help Miss Mary with household chores requiring greater strength than she might have, such as carrying buckets of hot water into the house for cleaning and washing clothes.

Mary was younger than Christina, but older than the boys by nearly fifteen years.  Her light Mulatto complexion and soft facial features did not resemble those of slaves from West Africa. Unlike many of her peers, Mary was well educated, speaking both French and English equally well. When compared to other female slaves, she could best be described as exotic.  Sometimes, in conversations with other men, Jim described Miss Mary in terms that led others to think she was more to him than just a slave.  Although never openly mentioned, several Burke's Garden residents thought her large purchase price had more to do with her striking appearance than with her housekeeping skills.

It was rumored Miss Mary had been captured by Indians or pirates when she was very young, but Jim never shared such a belief.  Because he purchased her in Richmond, he assumed her owner had died, leaving her as property to be sold as part of the estate.  Most slaves auctioned there had been owned by wealthy merchants and plantation owners. On the auction block, she was identified as an orphan with no memory of her parents. Jim paid one thousand dollars for her but never mentioned the substantial sum to Christina.

To say that Miss Mary favored Jacob and Lorenzo would be a gross understatement. Their lingering sorrow brought back disturbing memories of her own from when she was captured.  Her empathy towards them was revealed in the little things she did for them. She doted over them, selecting the tastiest morsels for their plates and the softest linen for their beds. When Jacob and Lorenzo were helping in the field, Mary often trekked all the way to Blue Spring to fetch them fresh water. Sometimes she joined them on the creek bank while they fished and offered to clean their catch.  Before long, the three of them were comfortable enough with each other to discuss the secret things Jim had shared with the boys about love and intimacy. Mary's daily actions reinforced how much she loved them.

## Sojourn to Charleston

When Jacob was fourteen, Jim took him and Lorenzo on what would be their first annual pilgrimage to Charleston, South Carolina.  An experienced wagon maker, Jim preferred traveling to Charleston to buy sailcloth and canvas at the Rutledge Chandlery. These fabrics made the finest of covers for his wagons and easily identified them as being manufactured by him.  This brought him great satisfaction, as he was exceptionally proud of his wagons, knowing they transported much-needed supplies to factories along eastern tributaries emptying into the Atlantic. This same cloth was used for sails for ocean-going clippers, schooners, sloops and frigates, some carrying buyers all the way to China to buy exotic teas and spices at the peak of their freshness. Only the week before, Mr. Harris received a letter from the United States Army offering him a contract to build military wagons capable of transporting rifles, ammunition, and gunpowder from arsenals in the east to western outposts far beyond the Mississippi.

Sometimes on these trips Jim bought a slave or two, preferably a married couple, at Ryan's Mart in Charleston. Over the years he discovered that couples were easier to handle while being transported back to Burke's Garden.  As an expression of his love for Christina, Jim bought her imported fine linens, delicate chiffon fabrics and expensive perfume so she could enjoy some of the finer things of life only found in larger cities or major seaports.

Jacob and Lorenzo considered these trips an important part of their education. Whenever they stayed downtown, Jim took the boys to a fine restaurant followed by a play at Charleston's Dock Street Theater.  On this trip they saw The Recruiting Officer, a restoration comedy written by George Farquhar in 1706. The play described the social and sexual exploits of two recruiting officers in the town of Shrewsbury located in the Welsh countryside.

On these trips, Jacob and Lorenzo especially enjoyed taking boat trips up the Ashley River to the inland town of Summerville, known as Pineland Village when it was first settled in 1785. Summerville was a pleasant retreat from seasonal insects and swamp fever for affluent Charlestonians. On the way, the boys stopped by one of the plantations, Drayton Hall, Magnolia or Middleton Place for a meal and an opportunity to watch riverboats steam up and down the Ashley River between Charleston and Summerville. Nearly all the plantations had docks where paddle wheel steamers and other small vessels tied up to discharge their passengers who came to eat, rest and visit the lavish European-style gardens.

Sometimes, they attended one of the plantation-sponsored jousting tournaments where riders speared a small 4-inch ring with a long lance while galloping on horseback. After a set number of passes, the rider with the most rings on his lance was declared the winner.

## *Return to Burke's Garden*

The following year, when they returned from their pilgrimage to Charleston, all were surprised and dismayed to discover Mary was gone. Lorenzo noticed first, asking Christina, "Have you seen Miss Mary?"

Christina read the distress behind the question and answered, "Some members of her family now live near Bluefield and she asked if she could visit them. Because she has always been so kind, I just had to say yes. I signed freedom papers for her in case she was detained as a runaway slave, but she promised to come back in a few months."

"I hope she comes back soon," Jacob said quietly. " I miss her already."

"We all do, son - we all do."  Although Jacob tried not to reveal any evidence of his feelings, Christina recognized the characteristic set of his jaw as he clenched his teeth together tightly.

# Chapter Three

## *Millie and Annie – Love and Marriage*

BY THE time Lorenzo was nineteen, his education was complete and he was skilled as a carpenter and wainwright. As the older of the two boys, he was first to move out of the Harris home. As promised, Jim gave him a 20-acre parcel on the east side of his homestead. Micah and Tobias, and Seth when he could be spared, helped Lorenzo build his cabin and small barn. For nearly a year Lorenzo had been courting Miss Millie Bean, a bright, cheerful young lady who lived just east of the Harris homestead, very close to where Lorenzo built his cabin.

They met early in June at the picnic held every year by the Bethany Church in Ceres, a small town on the south side five miles away. Lorenzo mentioned to a small group that he was named after Reverend Lorenzo Dow, a circuit-riding preacher who spread God's word throughout Western Carolina and Virginia. Millie asked him timidly if he intended to be a preacher.

"Absolutely not!" he declared, turning his attention to the attractive brunette with a sprinkling of freckles across her nose. Before long, the two were deep in conversation, and before long they were considered a pair.

Most were convinced that Lorenzo's feelings for Millie influenced Jim Harris' choice in selecting the parcel of land he gave to Lorenzo. Burke's Garden was extremely remote. This isolation severely limited courting options for young men and women living in the valley. The only way into or out of the valley was a very small trail over a rugged mountain pass. Even a short trip to Jeffersonville, the county seat, took half a day by horse and buggy. Most young men in the valley grew up without ever meeting a woman their age from outside of Burke's Garden; consequently, they usually courted and married women from the valley.

Over the years, as the Harris homestead continued to grow, Jim, Jacob and Lorenzo traveled to Charleston where they bought slaves at Ryan's Mart, a sprawling auction gallery covering an entire lot between Chalmers and Queen Streets.  The slaves purchased at the auction were chosen to work the fields or do chores for Christina around the house. Sometimes, Jacob wondered how long the importation of slaves into the Commonwealth would last.  By 1850 changes were already taking place that would affect the future of slavery.

Jacob and Lorenzo had always been close, so after Lorenzo moved away, his cabin became Jacob's favorite haunt.  One day, as he rode up to the cabin, Jacob noticed a strange horse tied to the rail in front next to Lorenzo's mare and a sorrel he recognized as Millie's.  The horse was small and fitted with an English sidesaddle.  As Jacob dismounted, Lorenzo stepped outside and invited him in.  With Millie at his side, and a twinkle in his eye, Lorenzo said. "Jacob, you already know Millie, but please let me introduce you to her younger sister, Miss Emeline 'Annie' Bean."

Miss Bean was a strikingly beautiful woman with sparkling green eyes.  Her thick auburn hair was pulled softly from her face into a heavy braid coiled into a bun at her neck.  Tight little tendrils framed the delicate features of her face.  Jacob was dazzled by her sweet smile.

"Please, just call me Annie."

Lorenzo explained that Annie had lost her husband a few months before.  "He took a nasty spill off his horse during military training.  Millie has convinced her to return home for however long she needs."

"Annie," Jacob, distressed at her loss, said, "I am so sorry about your husband. If there is anything I can do, please don't hesitate to ask. I'm not far away."

Indicating that she had filled a picnic basket with fresh bread, blackberry jam, strawberries, and a few apples, Millie invited Jacob to join them.  Jacob readily accepted and escorted the girls to their horses. Lorenzo held the horses steady while Jacob helped Millie and Annie up into their saddles.  When Annie rode forward a bit, Jacob noticed how flattering her tight black riding pants and loose-fitting satin shirt were to her petite figure.

They rode for a while in pairs, enjoying the breathtaking scenery of Burke's Garden with its lush fields rimmed by low mountains in the distance, talking as they rode.  Lorenzo led them to a favorite large oak tree where the girls spread out a blanket, and they shared the goodies Millie had brought.

Lorenzo and Millie were obviously very much in love.  Lorenzo held one of her hands captive as she tried to open the basket to place two uneaten applies inside.  Laughing, she tugged her hand away from his.  He clutched his now empty hand to his chest in mock despair.

Jacob chuckled, and Annie lowered her eyes and tried to stifle the laugh that bubbled out anyway.

It was the first of many picnics over the summer. Jacob and Annie were often left on their own when Lorenzo and Millie found opportunities to go off by themselves.

Jacob was cautious, not wanting to move too quickly, but Annie had been married, and she was not afraid to show affection toward Jacob when she wanted to and thought it appropriate. By fall, the boys were ready to ask Millie and Annie's father, Mr. Uriah Bean, for their hands in marriage.

A few weeks before the wedding, Jim approached Jacob and said, "Son, it's time I make the same offer to you that I made to your brother when he moved out. The twenty-acre tract of land to the south of Lorenzo's place is yours. Micah and Tobias will help you build a cabin and barn. You and Lorenzo are members of our family in every way. We've worked hard as a family, and I consider both of you my sons."

"Lorenzo and I deeply appreciate all you have done for us," Jacob said. With some hesitation, he continued, "If I may, we have one request to make before the wedding. Lorenzo and I want to use the Burress name on our marriage papers as a tribute to our first family. But during the ceremony and afterwards, we want to use your family name because you and Christina have raised us since we were little. Would it be okay?"

"Of course," Jim replied with a broad smile, "I would consider it an honor. Christina and I filled out formal adoption papers with the Tazewell County's Clerks office several years ago. Those papers went far beyond the *Bound Out Agreement* we signed when you first came to live with us, so we've been your parents for some time now. Christina and I are very proud to have you as our sons and are honored that you and your future wives want to take our family name."

When Jacob and Lorenzo asked Mr. Bean for his approval, he suggested both couples be married at the Bethany Church in Ceres on the same day. Saturday, September 17, 1851, was the day both couples would take their wedding vows.

On the day of the wedding, both sets of brides and grooms arrived early at the Bethany Church in Ceres. The grooms wore black canvas pants and bib-embroidered white shirts. Their black boots were highly polished and the metal on their belt buckles shined. Everyone agreed that both grooms were exceedingly handsome. As a wedding present, Jim Harris posted two $150 marriage bonds for Lorenzo and Jacob. In 1851, for a similar amount, a slave field hand could be purchased. He also bought each of the two young men a new suit of clothes to replace the suits he purchased three years earlier as part of the original *Bound Out Agreement.*

The brides wore their very best long dresses. Small pink flames adorned the ruffled hem of Millie's white cotton and chiffon dress. The dress highlighted her long dark hair and slender figure. Annie's pale yellow dress was accented by blue and white trim at the hemline. Her stunning auburn hair seemed to glow as it fell across the low neckline of her dress and across her bare shoulders. The preacher wore a traditional black suit with a three-quarter-length coat and a stovepipe hat.

The double wedding was highly anticipated by everyone residing in Burke's Garden. Many had travelled over 30 miles to attend the festive occasion. The women installed themselves in the kitchen where each woman prepared her favorite dish. The September reception insured a fall feast featuring dishes made with the freshest ingredients, such as corn, apples, strawberries, blackberries and black cherries.

The men gathered outside near a storage barn and set up stakes forty feet apart where they could pitch horseshoes while the women were preparing a hearty lunch. The men spent the hour pitching ringers, leaners and close-enough-to-the-stake-to-make-a-point. Ringers were good for three points, leaners for two points and those attempts where the shoe landed within the side width of a single shoe received one point. The first person scoring twenty-one points was declared the winner. Some of the men stood outside near the cemetery comparing their animals and crop yields. Others discussed the merits of their slave holdings in terms of appearance, intelligence, strength and use as breeding stock. Still others described their female slaves more explicitly by their attractiveness, breast size, and how much they enjoyed pleasing their masters.

Jim, Jacob, Lorenzo and a few close friends discussed politics, the weather and plans for planting next year's crop. At 11 a.m. the first bell rang signifying time was approaching for lunch. By 11:30 everyone had assembled at the front of the church where the preacher offered the blessing, "Oh heavenly father, thank you for this beautiful day; a day in which two couples will be joined together in the holy state of matrimony; a day bringing us all together to witness this joyous occasion and in fellowship with one another. Bless all who are in attendance and all who need your guidance to attain eternal salvation. Lastly, Oh Lord, bless this meal for all to enjoy. In His name we pray, oh Lord. Amen."

He invited everyone to find a place at the long table covered with the delectable dishes the women had prepared. An hour of fellowship followed the meal, then everyone entered the church, found a seat and waited for the wedding ceremony to begin. The late September date assured the presence of beautiful fall foliage with a full complement of red, yellow and orange leaves revealed through green pines and evergreens. Together they provided a marvelous backdrop for the special occasion to come.

When the sweet sound of soft music began filling the church, the two beautiful brides, escorted by their proud father, strolled slowly down the aisle and stopped in front of the altar. Mr. Bean presented each bride in turn to her prospective husband. Each solemnly recited the vows, and the couples exchanged rings. At the end of the ceremony, Jacob and Lorenzo both kissed their brides soundly, to the delight of the onlookers. Both couples hurried down the center aisle and out the door of the church where they were showered with greetings of joy and wishes for great happiness. True to their word, the brothers used the Burress name on their marriage documents, but during the ceremony they used their adopted name, Harris.

For their honeymoons, the couples traveled to Richmond and spent a few days at a hotel downtown where they enjoyed a play and luxurious dining at both the hotel and in several other fine dining establishments throughout the city. The couples especially delighted in taking slow carriage rides around the beautiful southern city. Mostly, though, they spent considerable time ensconced in their suites exploring and enjoying the privileges of marriage.

## Slavery in the 1850s

Jacob was particularly observant, and he was a good listener. He often overheard interesting conversations about the future of slavery at the sawmill, the post office and inside the saloon in Jefferson. Whenever Jacob travelled to Jeffersonville to pick up needed staples for the farm, he made a point of visiting the local saloon to chat with local leaders while he enjoyed a shot or two of whiskey. Once several men, including the mayor, approached him about running for office in the state legislature. Jacob thanked them for their confidence in his abilities but replied there was no way he could leave his family at that time. Some of the things he heard troubled him deeply.

Jacob's concern about slavery was prompted in part by the passage of the Fugitive Slave Act of 1850, calling for the return of runaway slaves to their overseers or masters. Because many Northern states wanted to circumvent this act, Jacob began to realize that many people outside the South were against the practice of slavery. The thought of their family having to free the very slaves they had worked so hard to obtain did not set well with him at all.

Over the next few years, Congress passed other laws that fueled the differences between people in the North and South and highlighted the conflict over the status of slavery in the United States. Harriet Beacher Stowe's infamous novel *Uncle Tom's Cabin* was released in 1852, creating greater sympathy for the plight of slaves in the south. In 1854, the Kansas Nebraska Act granted the new states of Kansas and Nebraska the right to choose for themselves whether they wanted to be admitted to the Union as a slave or free state. In 1857, the Court handed down what became known as the *Dred Scott* decision. This decision held that even though a slave was living in a free state, he did not have status in the courts because he was not a property owner.  In 1859 came John Brown's raid on the Arsenal at *Harper's Ferry*, further stirring up fury between sympathizers on both sides of the slavery issue.

On a visit to Jim and Christina, he finally broached his concerns to Jim.

"Dad, do you remember me asking all those questions about using your name during and after the wedding?"

"Yes, son, I do.  I remember telling you it would be all right with me."

"Can I ask you another question?"

"Sure."

"About the slaves."

"What about them?"

"I hear they're starting to run away — some, all the way to Canada. Are we going to lose them?"

"Son, I don't really know.  I try to take care of mine, so they won't want to run away. Ten years from now who knows what will happen. This could be just one of those things God has to sort out."

"Thanks, dad."

"That's okay, son."

The decade between 1850 and 1860 brought many concerns to southern land and business owners regarding the survival of their way of life. Increasing numbers of slaves and their families were leaving farms and plantations for a different way of life far from the only homes they had ever known since coming to America.

Abolitionist and sympathizers helped many of them by arranging for them to travel north via several Underground Railroad networks dotting the landscape in Virginia, Tennessee, Kentucky and Indiana—all the way to Canada.  There were concealed stops all along the way.  One of the favored routes used by slaves ran north from Lawrenceburg, Indiana, near Cincinnati through the towns of Metamora, Connersville, Centerville,

Fountain City and Fort Wayne. Using this route, slaves could easily make it all the way from the Ohio River to Canada.

Part of this route incorporated paths previously used by horses pulling barges up and down the various canals traveling north and south through Eastern Indiana. These waterways were part of a canal system first built in the early 1830s by the state of Indiana. As trains replaced canal barges, the state was forced into bankruptcy. For many slaves, these abandoned paths provided their best chance of escaping their masters and black overseers, many of whom seemed to enjoy exploiting their own kind.

The slaves who had been treated well by their masters and family members chose to stay. They had no desire to travel north and seek work in the large cities with their unending noise and squalor. They took their master's last name and named their children after their owner's children. The slave population of Tazewell County was only about ten percent, but too frequently Jacob heard of another family losing a runaway. Jacob wondered if these escapes were signs of more ominous events to come.

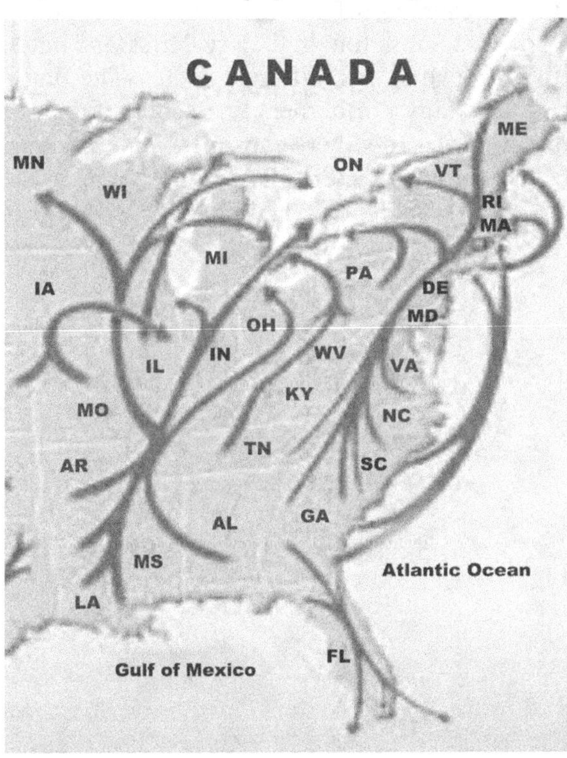


Figure 4. Underground Railroad Routes.

On November 6, 1860, Abraham Lincoln was elected the sixteenth President of the United States and sworn in on March 4, 1861. Nearly all of his support came from the North. He was not even on the ballot in ten southern states and won only 2 of 996 counties in the South. His election led to South Carolina's succession from the Union on December 20, 1860. Before Lincoln even took office, Mississippi, Florida, Alabama, Georgia, Texas and Louisiana followed South Carolina's lead and seceded from the Union.

The first shots of the Civil War may well

have been fired on January 10, 1861. That day, Confederate Batteries at Morris Island in Charleston harbor targeted the Union merchant ship *Star of the West*. The ship was sent to fill a supply request from Major Robert Anderson, Commander of Fort Sumter. The *Star of the West* had sailed from New York only a few days earlier with the supplies needed by Major Anderson's compliment of troops. Strangely enough, the Union military tried to recall the ship, but the semaphore recall message was never received on the *Star of the West*.

On February 9, 1861, The Confederacy was established with Jefferson Davis as its first Provisional President.

Most Civil War historians consider April 12, 1861, as the official starting date of the War Between the States.  On this date Confederate General P.G.T. Beauregard ordered his cannoneers at Fort Johnson and Fort Moultrie to open fire on Fort Sumter, located dead center in the middle of Charleston Harbor. Understanding the gravity of the situation, Major Robert Anderson surrendered the Fort the next day, April 13, 1861, to officers representing General Beauregard.

On July 21, 1861, the North and South fought their real first land battle just outside Washington, and is known by two different names: The Battle of Bull Run and First Manassas. Many northerners were so confident of victory that they brought along family members carrying picnic baskets, but after Union and Confederate forces death tolls and casualties rose, both sides realized they were engaged in a great, and bloody, Civil War.

# Chapter Four

## *The Call Up*

AFTER Bull Run, it was just a matter of time before the Confederacy needed more soldiers and leaders to command them. By early summer Confederate recruiting officers were deployed across the south to sign up volunteers for various militias sponsored by each southern state. On a trip to Jeffersonville to pick up needed groceries and carpentry supplies, Jacob and Lorenzo saw a Recruiting poster near the livery stable. It read: "Army Officers will begin recruiting in Hixville, on June 12, 1861."

Jacob thought, *That's only a few day's away.*

When they returned to Burke's Garden, Jacob and Lorenzo split up and rode to their own cabins, each thinking about how they would approach the subject of what they had seen and heard with Annie and with Millie. Both families so far had been blessed with three children. Jacob and Annie's two boys, Will and Sanders, were 7 and 4, and Jemina was 5. Lorenzo and Millie's son Ballard was 5, and their two girls, Barbara and Lucinda were 8 and 3.

As a mother Annie fretted and worried over every ailment and little scratch, while Millie was more relaxed and calm with all the children. The men, too, differed in their roles as father. Both men were often away from home; consequently, they were less involved in the daily events of the children. Lorenzo was always more eager to get home. He relished the noisy greetings and sloppy embraces of his little ones when he returned. Millie, too, was as eager to have him back in her bed as he was to be there. They were much more open with each other about all aspects of their lives.

Although Jacob loved his family deeply, he tended to tune them out when he was focused on a task, whether small or large. Annie was usually so absorbed in caring for her children that his inattention went unnoticed. But this evening after the children were asleep, Jacob surprised her when he began to talk about what he had seen in Jeffersonville.

"Lorenzo and I saw a recruiting poster in town today. Army officers will begin signing up volunteers in Hixville soon," he said. Dismayed, Annie looked up from her mending, but did not respond.

"Lorenzo and I want to enlist," he declared. The statement hung heavily in the air between them.

"Surely you don't mean that," she whispered. "You both have families!"

He reached over and lifted her chin with his hand so she would look at him. "All the more reason why we need to go. Our whole way of life is threatened. Everything we've worked for, everything our fathers worked for could be taken away."

Annie stood and turned away from Jacob. This was not a topic she wanted to discuss. "Let others do it," she sobbed. "Think of the children."

"I am thinking of them and what the future will hold for them if we don't go."

***

Lorenzo, too, waited till the children were asleep and they were lying in their own bed before bringing up what they had seen. He kissed Millie tenderly and held her as he spoke, "Jacob and I saw a recruiting poster in town today." Millie lifted her head to look at him. "Army officers will be coming soon to sign up volunteers."

"And you and Jacob want to sign up!" It was a statement said without emotion, although tears threatened to spill. "What will you do?"

"I'm not sure," he said gently. "Jacob and I need to talk to Jim about this." Both knew a difficult decision lay ahead. Millie clung to Lorenzo and let the tears fall as they found comfort in their passion for one another.

***

Early the next morning, Jacob and Lorenzo met and rode over to meet with their father. They relayed what they had seen and heard in town, but Jim already knew.

"Are you telling me you want to enlist," Jim said softly, "that's a big step—would you like to discuss this?"

"What is there to discuss?" Jacob asked, "We have to fight for what we believe in!"

"Of course, you do," Jim responded, "but we all need to think through the ramifications of this. You both have wives and family to consider. Nothing says you have to be the first to go."

"It's because of them we have to do this," Lorenzo insisted.

"I know, I know!" Jim shook his head in frustration. "But there are things to consider first. Think it through.  Why couldn't one of you join first and the other follow a little later? We have to consider Millie and Annie and the children."

Jim did his best to talk them out of it, but eventually they decided Lorenzo, since he was the eldest, would enlist right away. This way Jacob could stay behind and help take care of Lorenzo's family.   Lorenzo decided he would enlist in late June.  Waiting till then would give him a few days at home with Millie to prepare before signing up.

Lorenzo thought about what provisions he would need to go to war. They waited until the recruiters were seen in Hixville before riding over to see what regiments were signing up new recruits.  The brothers hoped observing the recruiters would give them an idea of what provisions Lorenzo should bring with him when he enlisted.

When Jacob and Lorenzo arrived in Hixville, they saw many new recruits entering the main tent to be interviewed.  Those who had completed their interviews were directed to an Army doctor who had set up shop under a large oak tree nearby for a physical examination.  The doctor gave each new recruit a thorough physical, checking his eyes, hearing, general strength, etc.  He also made sure the recruit had all his limbs, fingers and toes and was not a carrier of any serious disease such as typhoid or smallpox.

The Officer in Charge told Jacob and Lorenzo that recruits from Tazewell County were being assigned to the 51st Virginia Infantry Regiment, Army of Kanawha under the command of Colonel Wharton.

Several recruits brought weapons with them, old Kentucky or Harpers Ferry muskets.  Recruits from families of better financial circumstances brought with them Spencer or Sharp rifles.  At the beginning of the war, the Confederacy was issuing a .69-caliber smoothbore musket or an 1841 Mississippi muzzle-loading-percussion musket to new recruits. The 1841 Mississippi was named after the Mississippi regiment commanded by Lt Colonel Zachery Taylor during the Mexican-American War. The Mississippi musket was used by both sides during the Civil War, and Confederate marksman favored the 1841 Mississippi for sniping.

## Burke's Garden

The days passed far too quickly.  Lorenzo spent more and more time with Millie and his children.  Relieved knowing Jacob would be there for Millie when he left, he had no doubt the upcoming separation would be hard for her.  Jacob also tried to spend more time with Annie, since when Lorenzo left, she would be focused on comforting Millie.

Lorenzo and Millie spent the days with their children.  They made frequent trips to visit Jim and Christina, and the two families spent time together as well. Their nights were filled with passion as if to make up for the time together they would lose.  All the while Lorenzo tried to put aside thoughts about his upcoming trip to Hixville on the twenty-eighth.

The day before Lorenzo's departure, the brothers rode to the Harris place where Christina asked what she could prepare for them to eat. They assured her that any bacon or biscuits left over from breakfast along with honey and butter and perhaps some fresh milk would be just fine.  Miss Mary brought them everything they asked for including a fresh jar of blackberry jam. As they ate, Jim came in to join them at the table.

"I am so relieved new recruits are being assigned to the 51st Virginia Infantry Regiment, Army of the Kanawha," he said.  "The Kanawha region is close to home.  You're already familiar with the area it encompasses."  The region covered Southwestern Virginia, Eastern Kentucky, and East Tennessee.

"It's a relief to me as well," said Lorenzo.

They discussed the merits of the smoothbore .69-caliber black-powder muskets being issued to new recruits.

"Do you think you might need something better?" Jim asked.

Lorenzo considered the question, but he was sure a much older Kentucky black-power musket was the only weapon Jim kept in the house. He shrugged, but did not answer.

Jim rose from his chair at the head of the table, strode across the room and retrieved a Lorenz European rifle from behind a bookcase.  As he handed it to Lorenzo, he said, "Son, I think you might need something with a little more accuracy built into it."

A broad smile lit up Lorenzo's face as he took the Lorenz. "Thank you so much, Dad."  He stroked the stock and turned the rifle in his hands. "This is an excellent weapon.  I will be proud to use it."

As Jacob and Lorenzo returned to their cabins on horseback, both hoped this would not be their last ride together in the valley. After fording a shallow stream they saw Joe carrying five rusty traps, heading upstream to place his traps at water's edge.  Joe waved and called out, "Hello, Boys. How are you?"

"Pretty well," Jacob answered, "Millie is coming to live with me and Annie while Lorenzo is gone so we can see to it she's properly taken care of and not so lonely.  Mr. Harris has promised to lend us Micah and Tobias to help in tending the fields while Lorenzo is gone."

"That's good news!" Joe said, but a frown of worry creased his forehead. "You be careful now!"

On the other side of the stream Lorenzo and Jacob separated, each headed toward his own cabin. Just over the mountain, a vivid red sunset lit the sky, telling them tomorrow would bring cloudy skies and possible rain for their short trip to Hixville.  It was after 7:30 p.m. when Lorenzo arrived home.  Millie had already fed the children who were ready for bed, but waiting to say good night to their father.  After he had tucked them in, Millie asked him, "Who gave you the Lorenz rifle?  I couldn't help but notice it."

"It was dad. He pulled it out from behind a bookcase. I suspect it's been there for some time." Millie could see in his eyes how proud he was that his dad had given it to him. She sensed also that he didn't want to talk about it.  Instead of asking more about the rifle, she asked about the other goods Jim had provided for his trip to Hixville.  He told her, but she was barely listening.  Overwhelmed by the thought of him leaving so soon, she could no longer hold back the tears welling up in her eyes.

Through tear-streaked lashes she looked up at him.  "I love you so much, Lorenzo!" she cried.

"And I love you, Millie."  He smoothed her hair gently from her face as he pulled her slowly closer to him.  He devoured her with his eyes, wanting to remember everything about her.  When he kissed her, she was lost in his embrace.  Together they stumbled to their bedroom for their last night of passion together.

Early the next morning, they awoke to the sound of Jacob's horse's hooves as he rode up to the cabin.  Millie quickly shouted that she wasn't dressed and announced she would be in the kitchen in a few minutes.  Laughing, Jacob responded. "Millie, take your time, those people in Hixville won't be going anywhere any time soon.  It's grey outside, and rain's not far off."

"How do you know it might rain, Jacob?"

"You didn't hear thunder last night?"

Millie asked, "What thunder?"

"I wonder if you and Lorenzo were making a little thunder of your own!"

"Jacob!" Millie blushed as she said his name.  "Stop talking like that. You are supposed to be a God-fearing man."

"Yes, Millie, I am - but I'm not dead," Jacob laughed again.  "Where's Lorenzo?"

"He's getting dressed.  How about a cup of coffee while you wait?"

"No, thanks.  I'll wait out here."

Lorenzo kissed Millie soundly, then went out to join Jacob who was waiting by his horse.  He mounted his horse, then grabbed Lorenzo by the arm and swung him up behind him. Millie picked up Lorenzo's rifle and threw it to Jacob, who slid it into Lorenzo's hand stitched scabbard.  Both men noticed how easily Millie had lifted the rifle and tossed it to Jacob, and both remembered, too, that Millie's father had been an Army Calvary Officer. The brothers looked back as they rode down to the main trail. They saw Millie's struggle to keep from crying. Jacob called out to remind her, "Millie, I'll be back to take you and the children to our cabin."

# Chapter Five

## *Company F, 51st VA Infantry Regiment*

AS JACOB and Lorenzo rode toward Jeffersonville, Lorenzo repeated several times his request for Jacob to tell Millie he was enlisting to preserve their way of life.

"Please tell her I'll be all right," Lorenzo insisted again. "Promise me you'll look after her."

Jacob assured him over and over that he would.

"If something bad happens, you have to take care of her," Lorenzo insisted.

"You know I will. Dad has promised to send Micah or Tobias over to help in the fields, and Mom will let one of her girls help in the cabin. We'll be fine. Just be careful." Jacob replied.

Both brothers knew Lorenzo was nervous about what lay ahead. Lorenzo also knew Jacob would do whatever was necessary to protect his brother's wife and children and home.

Before long, just outside Jeffersonville, they came upon a small encampment of Confederate troops. They approached the largest tent, figuring incoming soldiers were processed there. As they slid down off Jacob's horse, a portly Sergeant in a uniform stained with an unknown substance hurried over and asked Jacob, "Are you here to sign up?"

Jacob answered, "No, Sergeant, I'm not, but my brother Lorenzo is."

Lorenzo confirmed Jacob's statement, saying, "Yes, sir. I'm ready— my brother's staying behind to care for my wife and children."

The Sergeant directed Lorenzo to the smaller of the tents to see a Doctor for his physical, "Please proceed to that tent over there for your induction physical."

Lorenzo found the Sergeant's formality a bit comical, considering his unkept appearance; nonetheless, he listened intently to every word. When Lorenzo finished his physical, the Sergeant guided him to another tent to sign enlistment papers. Once finished, he went outside to wait for further instructions with the other recruits.

The Sergeant returned shortly to tell Lorenzo he passed the physical, so he could pick up a full clothing issue and field gear, consisting of a canteen, ammunition, and a heavy Bowie knife.

"You'll also need two canvas bags. They're in those boxes over there under the dead tree. I recommend you keep black powder in one of the bags. In the other, you'll want to keep personal items – like food, matches, and perhaps a book or two. Personally, I'd recommend one of those books be a Bible or New Testament." Then he added, "Be sure to leave room for items you pick up off the battlefield, like ammunition."

The Sergeant glanced appreciatively at Lorenzo's rifle and complimented him on his choice of a Lorenz as his personal weapon. After collecting his clothing and field gear, Lorenzo joined twenty other recruits under a large canopied tree not far from the big tent. Within an hour the men were instructed to gather their gear, form up and be prepared to leave in fifteen minutes to walk to Wytheville. There, the recruits who had received the .69-caliber smoothbore muskets would be issued powder and ammunition.

This quick departure left Jacob and Lorenzo with only a few minutes to say goodbye. The brothers hugged each other and indulged in a little sibling jousting, slapping each other's back and punching each other on the shoulder as unshed tears glistened in both their eyes. Jacob mounted his horse, waved to Lorenzo, and turned away to hide his distress. Returning home without Lorenzo seemed so wrong. He wondered if they would ever ride together again.

The Sergeant strode into the Wytheville telegraph office when they arrived in Wytheville and telegraphed the 51st asking for exact rendezvous instructions for joining up with the main regiment. Once powder and ammunition was loaded onto wagons, the Sergeant instructed his troops to prepare to move out. When the courier finally arrived, the Sergeant read aloud the instructions from the 51st, "The rendezvous point will be just south of the bridge leading into Princeton." They were heading north toward Princeton.

***

Getting through the first few weeks was a struggle for Millie, not just because Lorenzo was gone but also because the Confederate Army was suffering heavy casualties across all battle lines. Every week lists of dead or missing Confederate soldiers were posted at train stations, general stores and telegraph offices across the South, and local newspapers printed casualty figures. The suspense was never ending for families on both sides. All dreaded receiving a letter from their son or husband's Company Commander telling them their loved one had died in battle. Even worse was learning the body could not be recovered because the terrain of the battle was too rough. Lorenzo wrote home saying almost every member of his unit had upgraded his rifle with one he had picked up from a dead soldier on the battlefield.

Eventually, things in the valley settled down and family routines returned to normal. Millie and her three children were living with Jacob and Annie and, as promised, Jim sent Micah and Tobias to help tend the fields and perform maintenance work around the house. Millie and Annie worked together well, and occasionally Christina sent Esther over to help them.

One day in the spring of 1862, Annie prepared a picnic lunch, rounded up all the children and disappeared, allowing Millie some time alone to write to Lorenzo. Millie heard Jacob talking outside and assumed it was with Jim. She supposed he had come to discuss a trip to Charleston. A week earlier Jim had mentioned he wanted to buy two more slaves at Ryan's Mart, the slave auction, and that he needed more canvas as well. Millie assumed he had come to discuss a date for the trip.

## Home is Where the Heart Is

Without warning the front door flew open and there stood Lorenzo in his Confederate uniform. Millie was stunned. At first she was frozen in place, unable to move. Tears of sheer joy streamed down her cheeks. As she rose, Lorenzo reached for her and lifted her completely off her feet. Taking his face in her hands, she kissed him tenderly. Then he kissed her again, more deeply, holding her so tightly she thought he would never let her go.

Because Annie was not expected to return any time soon, Millie let Lorenzo lead her straight to her bed where they were lost in the bliss and joy of each other's arms.

"Do Jacob and Jim know you're here?" she asked when she caught her breath.

Lorenzo smiled. "Yes," he answered. "How do you think I made sure Jacob and Annie wouldn't be home when I opened the front door? They're taking the kids to stay with mom and dad, and they'll stay at our cabin tonight, so we have the place to ourselves till tomorrow. We can visit mom and dad tomorrow around suppertime. I'd like to know what they think about the war."

Still holding him tightly, Millie asked, "How long will you be able to stay?"

"Only a few weeks at most." Brushing a strand of hair from her face, Lorenzo hesitated before continuing, "The fighting's been hell. My Commander, Colonel Wharton, sent some of us home to check on our families. There's going to be another call for able-bodied men in another three months or so to augment the diminishing ranks of Lee's Army. Colonel Wharton instructed us all to eat well to rebuild their strength. The Generals are having doubts about how long this war is going to last."

Millie chuckled, "I can feed you well, but I'm going to wear down your strength first."

"I'm counting on that," he grinned. "The colonel wants me to tell the family to expect solicitations from the Army for food and jewelry. Both will be needed in continuing the war effort. I need to pass the word that anyone with expensive jewelry or jewelry with sentimental value should hide it before the recruiters return to the Burke's Garden."

"I'll hide the pieces that belonged to my mother," Millie assured him.

"When I talked to Jacob earlier, he promised to go part way when I return to my unit." Millie was very astute and understood what Lorenzo was telling her. His Commander had given him a leave of absence to help with planting and to let them know the war was going to last longer than previously expected. Millie nodded, acknowledging what he had told her.

Changing the subject, Millie asked, "What would you like for supper?"

Before he could answer, both laughed, knowing neither was particularly interested in supper at the moment.

The following day Jacob and Lorenzo visited with Jim to discuss the current situation regarding the war in and around Tazewell County. Thus far, the county's residents who served in the Army of Kanawha had been most fortunate. Only a handful of fathers, husbands and sons had returned home injured. The families downplayed the nature of their soldier's injuries and deformities. Instead, they boasted about their loyalty to the Confederacy and their soldier's service to the Confederate Army. Even so, some of the families were beginning to weigh their southern pride against whatever return they expected from this ever-increasing long and brutal war.

Until now, Lee's Army in the east had been holding its own on the battlefield against the better-equipped Union forces. Time after time, General Lee's military tactics revealed him as the superior strategist. Nonetheless, his victories were not overwhelming. The body count in each battle seemed to show he had won only by a modest twenty percent or so. For the South to win decisively, General Lee knew he needed more troops, more money and more financial support from plantation owners, businessmen, and southern sympathizers in the North and South. Lee knew the day was rapidly approaching for him to issue a new writ for more volunteers for his depleted Army.

## The Recruiters

Confederate Army recruiters rode into Burke's Garden a few days after Lorenzo returned home. Notices were posted stating additional recruits were needed to continue the fight within thirty to forty-five days. New volunteers were advised to report to the officers of the 36th Virginia Infantry Regiment inside the Jeffersonville saloon. At the bottom of each notice was a paragraph instructing volunteers to bring with them their best rifle, otherwise, they would be issued a .69-caliber smoothbore musket. The notice suggested they bring with them a pair of brogans, a canvas bag for personal items, a canteen and as much ammo for their own weapon as they could carry.

On the first Sunday following the Recruiters' arrival, Jacob, Annie, Lorenzo and Millie attended a church social celebrating Burke's Garden residents who were serving in the Army of Kanawha. The political situation in Washington and Richmond was a topic of conversation, as were discussions about recent Confederate victories and losses sustained by both sides. A big concern to many was how the South would change if Lincoln freed the slaves. In spite of the overall military situation, a great deal of drinking and dancing lightened the tone of the gathering.

About halfway through the evening, two officers from the 36th Virginia Infantry Regiment stopped by and asked if everyone had seen the notices posted on the doors of the post office in Burke's Garden. They all nodded "yes." The officers then asked the ladies if any of them, especially widows, would donate their gold jewelry to the cause. The jewelry would be melted down and sold for cash and the monies used to purchase much-needed guns and ammunition from England and France. Nearly all the women removed their rings, bracelets and other pieces of jewelry and gave them to the officers.

The Recruiters then asked if the residents of Burke's Garden could provide food for their newly forming Regiment. In Western Virginia, Burke's Garden was widely known for its excellent quality fruits and vegetables. The valley was home to many varieties of wild game, including bear, deer, buffalo, quail and pheasant. The residents assured the officers they could provide the needed foodstuffs for their Regiment. In exchange for the food, the officers of the 36th pledged to give any excess game to the neediest families in the county.

Over the next few weeks, Jacob was consumed with thoughts of his family losing its slaves and way of life. Life would be very different. Slaves would have to be paid for their work or allowed to become share-croppers or indentured servants with guaranteed release dates. "Would such an agreement guarantee their full trust and loyalty?" he wondered as he considered how things would change for the slaves themselves. He grappled with question after question, "Could they adjust and avoid exploitation by those who would try to take advantage? Would they leave and move north to the squalor of bigger cities in the north? Would they die of illnesses and diseases unheard of in the valley?"

As the end of Lorenzo's leave time approached, Jim and Christina invited the brothers and their families over for a farewell dinner and fellowship. Jacob decided this would be the opportune time to tell everyone he was no longer willing to stand by as his brother went off to war without him. He breathed a sigh of relief knowing he would not have to tell Annie without family present. They would help her get her through this, and Millie would be the perfect person to comfort her and assure her Jacob would return home when the fighting was over. Jim would understand. Jacob was comforted knowing Jim would take care of Millie and Annie while he and Lorenzo were gone.

As the evening wore on, Jim and Lorenzo noticed how edgy Jacob was. They excused themselves, and led Jacob out to the back porch, presumably to enjoy a fine cigar. Lorenzo understood his brother all too well and recognized the changes that had occurred in him while he was gone. Lorenzo, too, had changed in subtle ways expected in a soldier with nearly a year of combat experience. He had fought in six campaigns. On September 10, 1861, he was part of Confederate forces engaged in a battle near the Gauley River. The next day his unit was forced back across the Carnifex Ferry. Five months later, in February 1862, he fought at Fort Donalson, Tennessee, where he and several other members of his unit were overrun and captured. Later, Lorenzo and six others were returned in a one-for-one prisoner swap.

On February 28th, he fought at Clarksville, Tennessee, and on March 6th he fought in Monroe County, Georgia. On May 17 and 18, he fought at Fayetteville, Tennessee, and Princeton, Virginia. Lorenzo understood all too well his brother's fear of losing the lifestyle he loved so much. For the past year, Lorenzo had fought like hell to preserve it.

# Chapter Six

## *Miss Mary's daughter*

AFTER about thirty minutes, Jim retrieved a second cigar from the inner pocket of his favorite vest and lit it.  Jacob asked Jim if he minded he and Lorenzo taking a walk around the homestead to reminisce about fond childhood memories.  Jim drew in a deep breath, held it, and as he exhaled, responded by saying, "You boys go ahead.  I know there are times you just have to revisit your past and catch up.  I hope you find things pretty much the same as before."

As the boys strolled the house and grounds, they recalled hunting small game nearby, fishing at Wolf Creek and exploring the caves just up the hill.  They remembered Miss Mary sometimes joining them and bringing sandwiches and a jar of fresh water retrieved from Blue Spring.

They remembered too well the day their first family was taken from them.  Over the years, the boys' sorrow had faded away in the loving arms of Jim and Christina, their caring family and, of course, Miss Mary.

Turning the corner of the house, slave children could be seen playing beside a pond where they could spear frogs and capture crawdads when it was too late in the day to catch bass or catfish in Wolf Creek.  There many of the slave children learned to swim and took their baths. As they came closer, they saw Janet, Miss Mary's teen-aged daughter, standing naked by the pond, holding a washcloth in one hand and a bar of soap in the other.  She was tall, statuesque and fully developed for such a young woman.  Noticing her light skin, Lorenzo wondered if she was a Mulatto. Since Miss Mary didn't have a husband, he wondered who might be Janet's father.  Lorenzo spoke first, "Jacob, isn't that Miss Mary's daughter?"

"I think so."

Hearing Jacob's voice, Janet turned to face them, revealing the full extent of her beauty and making no attempt to cover up any part of her body.  Looking at Jacob and Lorenzo, she smiled and put down her bar of soap before retreating to the other side of the pond.  She stepped onto a fallen tree trunk and dove in to rinse off.

Jacob declared, "She is absolutely lovely.  Look at her body.  She looks firm, soft and supple, all at the same time."

Lorenzo agreed.   "How old do you think she is?  Maybe 19 or 20?"

"Oh no—no way!  I'd say she's 16, or 17 at the most!  Actually, I know exactly how old she is.  She is 16."

"Wow—only 16—you think she does it yet?"

"Her mother did. Miss Mary was quite a treat."

"Jacob, tell me you didn't!"

"I did—when I was about Janet's age.  Miss Mary didn't say no or complain, in fact she let me know how much she liked it."

Lorenzo was amazed that he had not known about Jacob and Mary.  "I don't care how fine her daughter is.  You need to leave her alone.  If you don't, one of those big bucks might take offense and come looking for you with a pitchfork.  Don't even give it a first thought, let alone a second."

"I could never touch her, it just wouldn't be right.  But she does belong to us, just as her mother did."

"Jacob, are you trying to tell me something?"

"Can't say," he grinned.

"Is this why Miss Marry and her daughter just do chores around the house?"

"You'd have to ask mom.  She hands out the household duties."

"One thing's for sure. Annie would kill you if she ever found out."

"Heck, I'm more afraid of Miss Mary.  She has access to all the knives in the kitchen, and she can skin a deer with the best of them."

"Don't forget, Annie's first husband was an Army officer, and she knows how to shoot. She wouldn't have to bother with cutting your throat with a butcher knife."

"I was just kidding about Miss Mary and the knives.  Sometimes, when you see her lookin' at me, just look into her eyes.  There's no hate there.  She'd never hurt me."

Lorenzo concurred, then changed the subject, "Jacob, you know what was one of the things I enjoyed the most about living with the Harrises?  Our trips to Charleston—with the city's charm, majestic hotels, and magnificent restaurants.  It is truly the centerpiece of Southern culture."

Jacob agreed, "I guess that's why she's called the 'Queen City of the South.'"

# Chapter Seven

## *Charleston & Miss Lilly Cooper*

JACOB first saw on her in one of Charleston's finer eating establishments. A stunning young woman, she was seated at the bar as though waiting for a friend. Her pale alabaster skin contrasted sharply with shining brunette hair tumbling in ringlets to her shoulders, shoulders revealed by a low cut bodice of soft peach muslin embroidered with roses. An ample swell of smooth skin rose above the lace-edged neckline and, when she stood, the lines of the full-length dress flowed over the many colorful petticoats beneath. From her statuesque bearing, Jacob could see at a glance that she was very much a woman, wealthy and proud of it. He had to find a way to meet her.

As attracted as Jacob was to this beautiful woman, so, too, was she to him, for he was a handsome man. She liked what she saw the moment he entered the room.

Turning back to the bar, she casually summoned the barkeep and asked quietly, "Are you acquainted with that handsome gentleman just three seats over?"

"Yes ma'am, I am. His name is Jacob Harris."

"What can you tell me about him? I want to know enough so we can become acquainted. He intrigues me."

"Every time I've seen him in here, he's acted like a proper Virginia gentlemen. I've never seen him loud, boisterous or impolite. Sometimes another man comes in with him. I don't know the other man's name but they look so much alike, I'd bet they're brothers. They've been coming to Charleston for ten or more years now. Usually they're accompanied by an older man who buys sailcloth and canvas at a local chandlery. I once overheard him say he uses the material to make covered wagons."

"Go on," she encouraged when the barkeep paused.

"Occasionally, they purchase a slave or two at Ryan's Mart for their family homestead in southwestern Virginia. Jacob seems the more adventurous of the two; the other is quiet and more reserved. I suspect he might be a little older than Jacob."

"Thank you for the information," she said, slipping a bill discreetly across the counter.

"You're quite welcome, Ma'am."

She waited a moment or two before approaching Jacob, who had seated himself several stools from her. She asked him, "Are you enjoying our fair city, Jacob."

Looking up into her dark brown eyes, Jacob laughed, "Yes ma'am. But you have me at a disadvantage. It appears you know my name, but I don't know yours."

"You're quite right. The barkeep told me your name and said you've been coming to Charleston for some time. I'm surprised we haven't met before. My name is Lilly Cooper and, except for a few years when I lived in France, I've lived in Charleston my whole life."

If Jacob was surprised at her directness, he did not show it when she asked, "Do you have plans for the evening?"

"I have box seats for the Dock Street theater this evening, but I'm alone and don't like going by myself. Are you waiting for someone?"

"I think I've been waiting for you for a very long time," she chuckled. "Aren't you going to ask me to join you?"

"I most certainly am!" He rose, towering above her delicate form. "My name is Jacob Harris. Would you accompany me to the theater? Perhaps afterward we could take a carriage ride or return to the dining room at my hotel for a late dinner."

Lilly accepted with a nod. She was impressed with his tall, muscular frame, his chiseled face and infectious smile. He led her to a secluded table in a dimly lit corner far enough from the other guests to prevent them from hearing their salacious plans for the rest of the evening.

After attending the play, they rode through the streets of Charleston in one of the many horse-drawn carriages, admiring the many majestic homes built sideways to the street with beautiful courtyards in between. Most of the Charlestonian homes were built this way to avoid the window tax, a tax based on the number of windows facing the street. Lilly told Jacob about carriage drivers who often stopped in front of houses with gates left open so passengers could get off and walk through the beautiful European-styled gardens. Sometimes, homeowners even invited them into their homes and served them coffee, tea, and shortbread cookies while they discussed the war and worldly news of the day.

The couple returned to Jacob's hotel dining room for a late supper, drinks and dancing. At first he held her properly at arm's length, but by

Figure 5. Dock Street Theater.

midnight they were entwined in a full embrace. She offered no resistance when they stumbled into Jacob's room for she was as eager as he. For both, the night fulfilled their great expectations. By two a.m. they were exhausted, and drifted off to sleep. When the maid entered the room in the morning, she found them with arms and legs tangled together as they slept.

Jacob, who fancied himself a Virginia gentleman, felt his fantasy was fullfilled perfectly with Lilly on his arm. Likewise, Lilly enjoyed having Jacob next to her as they attended one dance after another celebrating Confederate victories across the South.

Although Lorenzo said nothing about Jacob's newly found friend, he did acknowledge that Charleston was indeed a charming city. On one occasion he mentioned taking a ferry to cross Charleston's northern river near the tidal basin to attend a party at a friend's house.

Jacob asked, "What river would that be, Lorenzo?"

"You know—The Cooper. I believe it's named after one of Lilly's ancestors."

## *Jacob's Departure*

After finishing their imported cigars, Jacob and Lorenzo returned to the living room to join Jim, Christina, Millie, and Annie. Jacob had delayed long enough. It was time to tell them he was joining in the fight to preserve their way of life. With glass in hand, Jacob tapped the side lightly with his spoon as he announced, "Tonight some of you commented on the weariness you've seen in me. I must confess my heart's been troubled ever since I saw the recruiting posters in Burke's Garden. I've always known I'd have to join Lorenzo in fighting for our cause."

Annie's mouth dropped in bewildered surprise. Jacob paused, took a deep breath, then continued, "When Lorenzo returns to his Company, I hope to get permission from the Army recruiters in Jeffersonville to join him. I know this'll be hard for all of you, especially Annie. But there'll never be a good time for me to leave home and join the Army."

Annie began to cry quietly. Christina and Millie reached out to her protectively, knowing she was about to lose a husband to military service for the second time. They could only hope and pray for the safe return of both brothers when the war ended. Jim was quick to assure them all he supported Jacob's decision and promised to care for Annie and the rest of his family.

"I don't have to leave for another week or two," Lorenzo said. "This should give me enough time to accompany Jacob to Jeffersonville when he enlists. Once he's got permission to join my unit, we'll ride out together and catch the 51st near Princeton. I've already telegraphed my regiment confirming a date of return and rendezvous point."

Jim was prepared for Jacob's announcement. He did the same for Jacob as he had done for Lorenzo. Instead of a Lorenz rifle, he gave Jacob an 1854 British Whitworth sniper rifle, often the weapon of choice for Confederate snipers. One of its main characteristics was the mounted brass scope running nearly the full length down the top of the barrel. Jacob, who considered himself an expert marksman, felt this weapon would give him a chance to prove it.

Jim and Christina announced they would host a farewell dinner for Jacob and Lorenzo and their wives the evening before the brothers left for Jeffersonville. Jim insisted on keeping the guest list short so the brothers would return home at a decent hour and not too inebriated to enjoy their last night with their wives.

Over the next couple of days, Jacob and Lorenzo spent their time with Annie and Millie. They planted large vegetable gardens and made repairs to their cabins. One day, they rode over to Blue Spring to fetch water and happened upon Joe washing off his traps.

"Jacob, I heard you're going to join the Army."

"Yes, I am. I just don't feel right staying here while Lorenzo goes off to fight."

Both filled their water bags, then tossed them over the backs of their horses. When they were mounted, Jacob pulled the reins gently to the right and tapped his horse's flank with the side of his boot. Lorenzo followed. They made a quick stop at the Harris home to pick up a special carriage, one Jim reserved for weddings, baptisms, funerals, and other special occasions. The brothers definitely felt their departure qualified as a special occasion, and they intended to make sure the dinner was a memorable one for their wives.

On the afternoon of their last day, Jacob and Lorenzo put the harnesses on the draw horses, then Lorenzo held them while Jacob attached the carriage. They picked Millie up first, then Annie. When the four arrived at the Harris home, Jim and Christina and the guests were lined up outside to greet them. As the brothers lifted Millie and Annie out of the carriage with what appeared to be little effort, all cheered and clapped. The women all wore their finest dresses for the occasion. Both brothers wore fine evening clothes they had purchased in Richmond on their last visit. After a lavish meal, the music began. Several guests provided entertainment by singing,

Figure 6. Lorenzo.

most danced and all enjoyed the free-flowing liquor provided. Any mention of the lovely city of Charleston and the time Jacob and Lorenzo had spent there was carefully avoided.

Jim and Christina could tell when both couples were ready to leave. Like a bride and groom at their wedding, they were the ones least likely to want the ceremony to drag on. The two couples said "goodbye" with many hugs and kisses for everyone. Jacob and Lorenzo once again thanked Jim and Christina for making the evening such a special one. Micah and Tobias drove them back to their cabins in the carriage, then returned with it to the Harris homestead.

Once inside, Jacob said to Annie, "Micah and Tobias were so polite to us. They know Lorenzo and I are leaving tomorrow to fight on the Confederate side. I wonder how they really feel about it all."

Annie replied, "Your father's always treated his slaves with respect. I suspect they want to show their gratitude. This could be their way of showing you they know he's a good man with a good heart."

Annie and Millie had discussed this night for several days. Each had selected an enticing negligée for the occasion. As memorable as the evening had been, they intended to make the night memorable as well. Jacob and Lorenzo would leave thinking only of them.

# Chapter Eight

## *Brothers in Arms*

NEITHER brother was eager to get up the next morning. After a late breakfast, each packed hardtack, dry beans, fruits, nuts, and fresh vegetables into their saddlebags. Two days earlier both had constructed new leather strap scabbards for their rifles and checked the stitching on their canvas bags, making sure they were tight enough to keep the contents dry. They also took with them bedrolls, extra sets of clothes, four pairs of dry socks, and gloves.

Lorenzo, having served a year already, knew exactly what was needed to survive. Each packed a Bowie knife for removing brush and skinning animals, and it would substitute as a bayonet if needed. On the way out of Burke's Garden, the brothers refilled their canteens at Blue Spring and began their exodus up the winding trail over Burke's Garden Mountain.

Just as they started up the first steep ascent, they noticed Joe sitting on a log at the edge of the trail. As Jacob and Lorenzo neared, Joe called out, "Lorenzo, I see you're heading out to return to your unit."

"Yes Joe, I expect to be there in a few days, depending on where my Regiment is located."

"Jacob, are you going with him?" Joe asked.

"Yes, after Lorenzo goes with me to Jeffersonville where I'm enlisting."

Lorenzo added, "I'm going to see if the recruiters will transfer him to my regiment. Since the 36th Infantry hasn't formed up yet, I don't think they'll object to transferring him to an active unit like the 51st, especially when they see the Whitworth rifle he's carrying."

"Take care," Joe responded. "I'll see you when you get back."

Jacob and Lorenzo dug in their spurs, and their horses began the long climb up the trail over Burke's Garden Mountain. In an hour or so, they reached Jeffersonville and made their way to the local saloon. As promised in the posted notice, recruiters were waiting to sign up new recruits. Jacob called out to a young Lieutenant, "Where can I go to sign up?"

The Lieutenant pointed towards the bar, "Sign your paperwork over there, then report to the doctor by the dice table. He'll do your enlistment physical."

While Jacob was getting his physical, Lorenzo approached Major Webster, the senior officer present, and requested that his brother Jacob be transferred to the 51st right away. He explained, "Our company is in desperate need of sharpshooters who have their own rifles."

The Major was well aware of the need and readily agreed. "Can he pick up his uniforms and other gear right away so he can accompany me to my regiment near Princeton?" Lorenzo asked.

The Major saw no reason why Jacob couldn't be transferred from the 36th to the 51st Virginia Regiment. "I'll prepare the proper paperwork as soon as Jacob passes his physical."

As they were about to leave to pick up Jacob's gear, Major Webster asked Lorenzo, "Do you plan to leave later in the afternoon or wait till morning?"

Lorenzo replied with a frown, "Why would anyone want to stay overnight in a tent rather than head out to their unit."

"Well, you see, we are in a town, Jeffersonville to be exact, and towns have whores – especially if they're camp towns. We let the new recruits entertain themselves before shipping them off for infantry training. In any case, Jacob is free to leave as soon as he passes his physical and picks up his gear. Good luck on your trip. I heard the 51st was garrisoned this side of Princeton. If Jacob passes his physical straight away, you might get out of here later in the day."

The Major and Lorenzo had just finished their conversation when Jacob returned, announcing to Lorenzo, "I just passed my physical."

After eating lunch with the troops, the brothers saddled up and rode out toward Bluefield where they planned to stay overnight. On the way to Bluefield, they talked about the Harrises and how fortunate they were to be adopted by Jim and Christina after the Indian attack. They spoke about their relationships with Millie and Annie and what good wives they were. Lorenzo brought up the last topic, one Jacob was not anxious to discuss. It was about Lilly.

Lorenzo began, "Jacob, I think it's time you told me why this relationship with Lilly is so important to you. You told me before that Annie is a great wife and you'd never leave her. You need to explain to me why your relationship with Lilly is so all-fired important to you."

Jacob replied, "Lorenzo, it's not what you think."

"Then what is it?"

"I do care for her, but she knows I'm never going to leave Annie."

"Then why are you still in a relationship with her?"

Jacob was not happy being interrogated by his brother. "It's kind of complicated."

"We have plenty of time – get on with it."

"Well," he said slowly, "Lilly's parents are very wealthy. They're in the shipping business and own several clippers, schooners and frigates. They smuggle guns from England and France into Charleston on their clippers. One of their ships is returning right now from Liverpool with Whitworth field guns and rifles for our Army. The clipper was loaded with many bales of cotton to pay for the guns."

He continued, "It's not easy for a woman alone to move in the inner circles in Charleston where she gathers intelligence on Union ships participating in the blockade. Lilly needs this information to guide her parent's ships through the blockade and into Charleston's harbor. My presence gives her the perfect cover to visit not only restaurants and bars, but places like chandleries, sail makers and slave markets as well where sea captains gather and discuss the locations of Yankee ships participating in the blockade."

"I get it, but you didn't exactly answer my question."

"Lorenzo, I care for her, and we enjoy our time together, but I have no intention of hurting anyone, especially Annie. Carrying out this role right now is vitally important not just to me. I promise you I'll walk away when its purpose is fulfilled."

Lorenzo nodded thoughtfully. They rode in silence for a time before Lorenzo said, "We'll soon be in Bluefield where we can stop and rest for the remainder of the day. The horses need to be fed, watered and brushed down. Before we stable them, we need to find a place to stay."

When they arrived in town, a sign just above a dry-goods store advertised "Rooms to Let." Inside an attractive young lady stood behind the cash drawer at the counter. They tied their horses to the rail in front of the store and walked inside to look around. The lady behind the counter asked, "Can I help you?"

Lorenzo answered, "Yes. Do you have any rooms?"

"By all means. They're a dollar each. The rooms are upstairs to your right. If you want a hot bath, it'll be an extra two bits."

"We'll take one, please. Send up hot water up as soon as it's ready."

After picking up a key and putting their things into the room, Jacob and Lorenzo took their horses to a nearby livery stable. They asked the young boy there, "How about you feed 'em, water 'em and otherwise care for 'em till morning?"  Jacob flipped two half-dollars to him.  "Boy, think this will cover it?"

The boy looked him in the eye, brushed his hand across his face and answered, "Yes sir!"

The brothers returned to their hotel, ate supper next door before retreating to their room to get some sleep. Early the next morning after finishing their breakfast, they saddled up and headed towards Princeton. Even though Lorenzo knew how important it was to get back to the 51st, the pace seemed to slow with every passing mile.

Lorenzo thought about Jacob and what lay ahead for them both. Once Jacob joined the unit, Lorenzo would look out for him until he was ready to fight on his own. Fortunately, both had already experienced being on their own, and knew they could count on each other.

Not far from Princeton, they came across a member of Lorenzo's Regiment. The man was considerably older than them, and his left knee was badly injured.  It was clear from the difficulty he had walking that his days as a fighting man were over.  As they crossed paths, Lorenzo asked the man, "Where are you headed."

He responded, "I'm being sent home to help on my farm not far from Wytheville.  Colonel Wharton told me I could still contribute to the Confederate cause by making sure our troops had enough food to last through the rest of the year."

When Lorenzo asked the man about his company, he answered, "I was assigned to Company F, 51st Virginia Infantry Regiment."

"You mean you were assigned to the Bland Tigers?

"I was."

"That's my outfit.  I was raised next door—so to speak—in Burke's Garden.  Do you know where the 51st is currently garrisoned?"

"They're up the road a ways guarding a large wooden bridge. You should be there in about fifteen or twenty minutes."  He added, "Today's password is 'Johnny Reb.' Expect to be challenged before you get there."

"Much obliged," Lorenzo said. "I certainly wish you the best with that leg."

As soon as Jacob and Lorenzo caught sight of the bridge, an armed sentry stepped out from behind a tree and shouted, "Who goes there? What's today's password?"

Startled, Jacob returned a hearty, "Johnny Reb."

"Why are you here?" the sentry asked, "and who are you trying to see?"

Lorenzo answered, "I am returning to my unit—F Company, 51st

Virginia. Next to me here is my brother Jacob. He just enlisted with the 36th, but I got him transferred to the 51st to be with me."

"Very well—you may proceed. I believe your unit's on the other side of the bridge, down about 100 yards on the right. Colonel Wharton was there early this morning. If you can't find him, report to your Company Commander."

The other soldiers promptly accepted Jacob. They quickly shortened his name to 'Jake.' Lorenzo was already known to his comrades by the nickname 'Rans.' Combat training began immediately. Once the Sergeant observed Jacob's skill with a rifle, he assigned Jacob as a sniper to cover one of the unit's flanks. Less than a week later the two headed north with a small contingent of soldiers to join the main complement of troops at Louisburg, Virginia. Just outside of town they encountered a rear element left behind to clear the area after a skirmish with Union militiamen. Within a few days they caught up with the regiment's main force as they were engaging two companies of Union troops ten miles south of Wheeling, West Virginia.

On the last day of May, their regiment engaged another militia unit at Seven Pines, just outside of Davisville. Both Jacob and Lorenzo were injured by light shrapnel from an artillery shell falling short and exploding. It struck their small band of soldiers as they cleared an advanced forward-firing position. Their orders were to move cannons forward in an alternating leap-frog maneuver, keeping some cannons at the ready, while the others moved forward with advancing infantry.

While recuperating from the wounds they received, they were camped not far from Colonel Wharton. He informed his troops that General Lee was reorganizing to be more aggressive in the field. But Lee needed his troops to rest before beginning attacks planned for the end of July or beginning of August.

General Lee confided to the Colonel that without more rest, the toll on his troops from the oppressive summer heat and disease would be more severe than initially anticipated. Lee instructed the Colonel to assemble his troops and send home as many as he could spare, especially land and slave owners, to help with late planting and early harvesting. The goal was to ensure enough food to get his troops through the coming months. The Colonel announced that a list of names would be posted early the next morning outside his tent of those authorized to go home. All would be needed back at the Garrison by August 20th.

The next morning Jacob and Lorenzo made their way down the worn path to Colonel Wharton's tent. A stack of wooden boxes containing dozens of new rifles shipped in from Richmond by train the day before blocked the entrance.  Nailed to the top box was a sheet of paper with the list of names.  Glancing down the list, they were surprised to see their own names, Jacob Jake Harris and Lorenzo Dow Harris, listed near the middle.

When one of the soldiers asked Lorenzo about his name, saying it sounded funny, Lorenzo explained he was named after Lorenzo Dow, a circuit-riding preacher well known throughout the states of Carolina and Virginia.  "I'm just one of more than 10,000 young men in Virginia and Carolina named in his honor."

Amused, the soldier quipped, "That's good to know, otherwise, I'd suspect he was a very busy man."  When the laughing stopped, another soldier asked Lorenzo about his nickname. Lorenzo explained he had taken the nickname 'Rans' after joining the Army, thinking it would be easier for his children to write the shortened name.

The man nodded his head in understanding and said, "You sound like you're a very good father."

Jacob and Lorenzo returned to their tents to pack up their belongings. Fortunately, their horses were boarded nearby.  The trip back home was much the same as when they first rode to their company's encampment. In Bluefield, they returned to the same rooming house after taking their horses to the same livery stable.  As they dismounted, the brothers recognized the stable boy who had cared for their horses. As Jacob and Lorenzo approached, the boy recognized them and called out, "Do you need me to take care of your horses?  The price is the same."

Lorenzo pulled a shiny new silver dollar from his pocket and flipped it to the boy who grinned broadly.  They dismounted and handed the reins of both horses to the boy.  He grinned once again as he led both horses to stalls.  No one was at the front counter when the brothers returned to the boarding house, so Jacob rang the small bell on the counter.  In response, a lovely young lady hurried out from a small room behind the front desk. She smiled sweetly and asked, "Are you gentlemen looking for a room."

Lorenzo replied, "Yes ma'am.  My brother and I stayed in a room upstairs on our last trip through Bluefield."

"My aunt recognized you when you rode into town. She just left to go to supper. Would you like the same room?"

"That would be fine. We'll take it.  Would you send up hot water for a bath?"

"Yes sir, the bath will be an extra two bits.  Anything else?"

"No, ma'am.  I don't think so."

"Well, if you need anything—anything at all," she said coyly, "I can always be found in my room—the first room behind the counter.  I was there when you came in."  She smiled suggestively and added, "While you gentlemen are here, I'll be sure to keep the door unlocked."

"Yes ma'am," Lorenzo answered, "but right now my brother and I need a drink."

Instead of going directly to their room, they stopped by the saloon to check on the current political situation in Washington and Richmond. Rumors abounded in both cities that President Lincoln planned to issue an Emancipation Proclamation on the first of January. This would mean slaves in both the North and South would be given their freedom and have to be paid for their work.  Jacob and Lorenzo were especially interested in how this would play out politically in Richmond.

As they listened to fellow customers, the consensus seemed to be that such a proclamation would have a seriously negative impact on commerce in the South.  Slave auction houses found it increasingly difficult to locate captains of slave ships willing to cross the Atlantic and run the blockade. Few were willing to risk the loss of an expensive, and illegal, cargo of negro slaves to privateers, pirates or Union warships.

It was no secret that the South was delaying major conflicts until shipments of new guns and ammunition arrived from Europe. Once they had heard enough, the brothers finished their drinks and returned to their room to consider what might be done to improve the situation.

As they stepped on the squeaking wooden sidewalk in front of the saloon, Lorenzo nearly fell over an old man sleeping soundly against a post. Jacob pulled the man up into a sitting position and asked, "Mister, are you alright down there?"

Shaken, the man shifted his weight from one side to the other as he looked up and said, "Sir, I could sure as hell use a drink."

Pulling a flask from his shirt pocket, Jacob handed it to him.  The old man took a large swig, swallowed, and apologized for his appearance.

"What's your name," Jacob asked.

"Sir, my name is Frank—Frank Cline.  I fought in the war 'til I was shot in the arse.  That's why I sit sideways on my hip."

Looking down at the man, Jacob laughed, "Don't you mean, 'ass?'"

"You can call it 'ass' but where I come from in Rich Valley we call it 'arse.'"

Jacob laughed again, "Sir, I'm not one to judge; feel free to call it anything you want."

Lorenzo then asked, "What's with the girl behind the counter?  Does she throw herself at every man staying at the rooming house?"

"Not everyone, just most of 'em—the ones she likes.  The whores working the camp towns around here use the rooms to ply their trade.  Are you going to see her later to find out if she's one?"

"Not likely, I'm on my way home to visit my wife and children.  Do you have a place for the night?"

"Not here, I have a brother about twenty miles west—I can stay there.  Perhaps I can get a ride tomorrow."

Seeing the bedraggled man was struggling, Jacob pulled him to his feet, slipped a couple of silver dollars into his hand and said, "You need some sleep.  Go inside.  Get yourself a room.  Who knows, perhaps the young lady will take a liking to you."

In the morning, after a quick breakfast at Maggie's, they mounted up and rode southwest towards Burke's Garden.  They rode in silence for more than an hour before Jacob finally spoke, "I've been thinking, Lorenzo.  Since Micah and Tobias do most of the fieldwork at home, I think I can better serve the Confederacy by returning to Charleston and to help Lilly's parents run the blockade and smuggle in guns from France and England. To pull this off I'm going to need an excuse for returning to Charleston.  I think dad can help me with that.  He's the only one who can give me a good reason for going back to Charleston now. What do you think?"

After considering the question, Lorenzo replied, "Jacob, I hate to admit it, but this time you're right. Besides, I can't think of a better plan."

Figure 7.  51st Virginia Infantry Flag.

# Chapter Nine

*James Reynolds – A Yankee Spy*

SHORTLY after the brothers returned to Burke's Garden, where their families greeted them with great enthusiasm, many hugs, warm laughter, and much love, Jacob arranged to see Jim at his home so they could speak privately.

"What a wonderful surprise to have both you and Lorenzo home again, Son.  You should be home with your family now."  Jim could tell by Jacob's expression and the way he clenched his jaw that something was on his mind. "Is something wrong?  Do you need something?"

"I would never lie to you, Dad. I need to ask for a big favor."

"What is it, son?  You sound so serious.  Does it have anything to do with that girl in Charleston?  We don't want to see Annie hurt!"

Jacob was stunned, but he quickly replied, "She won't be if you don't tell her, Dad.  The girl in Charleston—well, her family is wealthy and I do mean WEALTHY! They own a fleet of ships, mostly clippers, sloops and frigates. They're helping the South by selling cotton abroad and buying rifles and ammunition for the Confederacy.  Her parents just sailed from Dublin, and she needs someone she can trust to escort her to places frequented by sailors, sea captains and dockworkers. Lilly needs to visit these places to get intelligence on the location of Yankee gunships and ironclads roaming the approaches to Charleston's harbor."

Jacob took a deep breath and continued, "Lorenzo and I have been told the abolitionists are pressing Congress and the President to give slaves rights well beyond those found in the Emancipation Proclamation issued in January. Thank God we can still purchase them here in the South. Some auction houses are no longer accepting slaves from outside the United States.  Ryan's Mart has already posted notices saying they won't be selling any slaves shipped in from Africa after January 1st of next year.  If you could use more slaves, you might want to consider buying them now."

"I do need some, but if they are about to be set free, I don't want to buy more than two.  I could use one field hand and one housekeeper for your mother."

"Dad, I need you to play along, so Annie doesn't think this was my idea. I love Annie very much and would never leave her—so don't worry. My intentions in this matter are completely honorable."

The next day Jim came by their cabin so Annie would be present to hear him ask Jacob to go to Charleston for him. "My responsibilities with the local militia prevent me from going.  You know I trust you, Son.  I know you can negotiate the purchase of two more slaves for me.  Isaiah has been sick for more than a month, and he's getting old.  Ruth is expecting her second child, so I need another female to help Christina."

"But, Dad," Jacob replied, attempting a show of resistance for Annie, "I just got home."

"I know, Son.  But this is important to me.  I'm counting on you."

Jacob shrugged his shoulders and said, "Okay, Dad. I will." Annie picked up a basket of needlework and turned away.   The next morning, to Jacob's surprise, Annie told him she wanted him to leave the following morning, saying this would give them more time together when he returned. For the first time, Jacob wondered if he had taken Annie's love too much for granted.

## Charleston

As Jacob approached Charleston, the sun was beginning to set. He realized he had to pick up his pace to reach the Cooper Estate before dark. Riding up the long lane, Jacob saw all the signs Lilly was hosting another one of her fabulous parties celebrating recent Confederate victories across the South.  Carriages, with their drivers, were lined up around the large circle leading to the portico.  The orchestra's music consisting of southern tribute songs drifted outside where he could hear it.  Servants milled about with trays of beverages and hors d'oeuvres they offered to her guests.  As the warm afternoon light was turning to dusk, two servants lighted torches in the garden while others set up tables and chairs inside and outside for an evening meal. Jacob arrived at the door, looked inside and saw her coming down the stairs.  She held the skirts of her stunning pale yellow gown above her shoes, showing the colorful petticoats underneath.   The low-cut bodice revealed an enticing view of unblemished skin, pale as alabaster.   Jacob smiled, honored and proud that Lilly had chosen him for such an important role in her life.

As he strode across the room, she rushed to him, saying urgently, "Jake, please.  We have to go outside at once."  She took his hand and he

Figure 8. Cooper Plantation.

followed her.  Stammering slightly, Lilly cried out.  "Jake. I've been such a fool.  Can you help me?"

"Lilly, hold on!  What do you mean?"

"I think a man here is a 'Yankee spy.'  I saw him copying ship schedules from a log book Daddy kept in his desk."

"Lilly, how did this all happen?"

"Earlier today he stopped by and said he was a representative of an American company contracted to arrange delivery of French arms to the Confederacy. He wanted to talk with my father.  I let it slip that Daddy would not be in Charleston for another week or two.  He got all excited and said he would first have to contact his French liaison person before solidifying any arrangements. Believe me, Jake. He has to be a spy."

"Do you know his name?"

"James Reynolds.  At least, that's what he called himself."

"What exactly did he do to convince you he's a spy?"

"While we were talking about possible shipping dates, I pulled out a desk drawer in Daddy's desk and retrieved our ships' schedules.  When the book was out, Mr. Reynolds, if that's his real name, asked for some tea, so I left him for a few minutes. When I returned with the tea, he was looking at the book and scribbling cryptic notes on the back of his hand."

"Why is he still here?"

"I suspect he wants another look at those logs.  So far, I've avoided him by spending more time with my friends. Thank God, I have so many friends here in Charleston!  He appeared to be very nervous.  My guess is he's waiting for his carriage—I did notice he arrived in one.  Jake, what can we do?"

"The first thing is for you to go back to the party and act as if nothing happened.  I'll take care of Mr. Reynolds."

Promptly at eight-thirty a carriage came up the lane and parked under the portico. Mr. Reynolds, now sweating profusely, stepped into the carriage and instructed the driver to proceed down the lane, turn left at its end, then make a quick run for the Goose Creek docks.

Anticipating a quick departure by Mr. Reynolds, Jacob rode ahead to the end of the lane and concealed himself behind a large Azalea bush.  As the carriage left the house, Jacob pulled a spyglass from its case to follow the carriage's path until he was sure it was headed for the end of the lane.  Reaching into his scabbard, he pulled out his Whitworth Rifle as he scanned the area looking for a place where he could take his shot.  Even though the rifle had been credited with kills at 600 yards, its standard effective range was considered to be 300 yards. Jacob's preference was 200 yards; and, that's exactly where he set his scope.

When Jacob saw Mr. Reynolds coming into his desired range, he began counting off the number of fence posts to make sure his estimate was correct.  He then withdrew to the edge of a brackish pond where he set up for the fatal shot.  Jacob watched the carriage carefully as it approached the long uphill grade.  Under his breath, he counted off the yardage as the carriage approached the small hill, "Three hundred yards; two hundred seventy-five yards; two hundred-fifty yards."  At two hundred and twenty-five yards, Jacob assumed a kneeling firing position by resting his left elbow on top of his left knee.  He lifted his rifle, getting a good spot weld between the stock of his rifle and his right cheek, and leveled the barrel.  After lining up the cross hairs in his scope, Jacob squeezed his finger ever so softly until he felt the trigger release.  As the barrel lifted after the shot, Jacob felt a hard recoil deep inside his shoulder.

He saw the smoke rise from the barrel and watched Mr. Reynolds collapse into the seat. Jacob ran quickly towards the carriage, but the driver had jumped out and scurried down the lane before Jacob emerged from the woods. Jacob's shot had struck Mr. Reynolds squarely in the middle of his throat. Blood had spewed everywhere. He grabbed Mr. Reynolds by his boots and dragged him into the nearby stagnate pond. As he was leaving, an alligator on the other side of the pond slithered into the water in search of his next meal. Before riding off, Jacob looked back and saw that Mr. Reynolds' three-quarter length bloodstained coat was already in shreds and his right arm was in the mouth of the hungry alligator.

Once the deed was done, Jacob returned to the party and quietly whispered to Lilly he had taken care of Mr. Reynolds, assuring her that the man had no opportunity to share her parents' ship logs, schedules or any other stolen documents with anyone in his chain of command.

Lilly sighed with relief and asked, "Jake, how can I ever thank you?"

He grinned and said, "After this party is over, I'm sure you'll find a way."

The following day, a slave in search of frogs and crawdads found James Reynolds' unrecognizable body, half eaten by an alligator. Part of a note saying *James Reynolds – Yankee Spy*, was found loosely pinned to the lapel of his shredded dress coat.

Over the next few days Jacob and Lilly were inseparable, spending long days and even longer nights savoring each other's company. Knowing Lilly's role in helping her parents smuggle guns was both exciting and frightening at the same time. Jacob realized Lilly and her parents' lives would have been in danger if Mr. Reynolds had passed the ship schedules to nearby Union gunboats and ironclads. The *John Jameson* might have fallen prey to Union vessels patrolling the coast just outside Charleston harbor. If one of these ships had intercepted the *John Jameson* all on board could have been captured, tortured, killed or imprisoned. Any cargo on board, especially contraband, could have been seized and taken to a Union port like New York, Boston, Baltimore or Philadelphia for redistribution to the Union Army. More than likely, the *John Jameson* would have been burned to her waterline.

Lilly's father named his ship the *John Jameson* to discourage Union ironclads or gunships from boarding her. Her Captain, Joe Davis, spread the word his ship was nothing more than a contract vessel for *Jameson's Irish Whiskey*. He even painted the word *Dublin* under her name to indicate Dublin was her homeport, where *Jameson's Irish Whiskey* was distilled. This deception on the part of Captain Davis was conceived to reinforce the notion the *John Jameson* was, indeed, an ocean-going transport vessel of Jameson's Whisky. In spite of Captain Davis's precautions, the threat of being sunk by a Union ironside, sloop of war or gunboat remained a very real risk.

On Thursday, two days before the next slave auction, Jacob realized the time was approaching for him to tell Lilly this might be his last trip to Charleston for a very long time. Lilly, too, needed to share her family's future plans with Jacob should the South lose the war. Neither broached either subject until the night before the auction when they went for a long carriage ride.

At first they were both quiet, each dreaded bringing up what would be a painful subject. Neither could find the courage or the words to say what had to be said. Eventually, Jacob began, "Lilly, I'm a soldier now and it will be a lot more difficult for me to come back to Charleston. Even if I could get the time, I'm not sure what excuse I could use to return. Before, I justified my trips by saying I came to purchase sailcloth and canvas for our wagons or to buy a slave or two for our homestead. I've already heard Ryan's Mart is closing its doors to new slaves captured abroad, meaning they'll only sell slaves previous owned in North America or the Caribbean. Personally, I prefer getting them right off the boat so I can train them myself."

After hearing Jacob's comment, Lilly confided that one of the reasons her parents traveled to France was to look for a new estate near Marseille should the South lose the war. Lilly added, "My mother is part French, and both of us speak French fluently." Jacob realized that this was how Lilly was able to negotiate arms deals with weapons brokers, manufacturers and French government officials with such ease. Before the end of the ride Jacob and Lilly agreed they would take their relationship for what it was, for however long it lasted.

When they entered the Cooper Estate, Lilly dismissed the servants, telling them she would not need them until 10:00 in the morning. It was already just past 11:00 when they awoke the next morning. When they started down the winding staircase, the servants began stirring and headed for the kitchen. Breakfast was already on the table when Jacob and Lilly entered the dining room; although it was obvious the breakfast of ham, eggs, and biscuits had been there for some time. Miss Abigale approached Lilly and begged for forgiveness. Lilly responded gently, "Jacob and I were unusually late—so go ahead and fix another breakfast. You can take your time. In the meantime, we'll begin with hot tea."

Lilly reminded Jacob the afternoon session at Ryan's was scheduled to begin at 1:30 p.m.   After their late breakfast, Jacob let Lilly know he would be starting for home right after the auction. He hoped to find a hardy buck with a wife who could cook, clean and handle other chores around the house.

As he prepared to leave for the auction, Lilly put her arms around him and held him for a very long time. As they kissed, their fingers intertwined, sending an electric thrill through both of them.  They let go, not knowing whether this embrace would be their last. As he left, Jacob saw the tears in her eyes, but he turned away quickly, not wanting her to see the tears flooding his eyes.

At the auction, Jacob was fortunate. Even though he feared the price of slaves might rise because of the reduction in numbers available, Jacob found a large, muscled buck about thirty with a much younger wife.  Neither appeared aggressive and both spoke enough English to understand basic instructions. The large black man's name was Abraham and his wife's was Rebecca. With names taken from the Bible, Jacob was sure their previous owner was a God-fearing man.

Abraham and Rebecca quickly fit into life on the Harris homestead. Both seemed genuinely grateful for the kind treatment they received from the Harris family and their fellow slaves. Living there was a far cry from the cold, damp and dark cargo hold that had imprisoned them on their way to Charleston.

Jacob assured Annie when he returned that he would not be going to Charleston again any time soon.  "I heard the slave auctions there are scheduled to close in January. I am not planning on returning to Charleston for any reason."

Looking at Jacob lovingly, she said, "At the end of this war you need to be here.  I'm expecting again and the children and I need you, Jacob."

Figure 9.  Gettysburg Campaign Sign.

# Chapter Ten

## *Gettysburg*

WHEN Jake and Rans returned to the 51st, they learned they were among 240 soldiers that had been detailed to the 50th Regiment for an upcoming attack on the major elements of the Union Army. General Lee predicted the assault would take place just north of the Virginia and Pennsylvania border near Gettysburg, where ten roads intersected. Lee hoped an attack of this magnitude would force Union commanders to reconsider engaging Confederate troops on their own turf.

Arriving a day late, the brothers lost no time proceeding north to join the other 238 soldiers that had departed the previous day. Along the way, they passed numerous southern soldiers in tattered uniforms or civilian clothing, returning from the battlefield. Many suffered from wounds, lost limbs or disease; all showed signs of extreme fatigue. One of the soldiers, from Wilcox's division, handed Rans a battle map he had picked up off the road on his way out of the battle area. Looking at Jake and Rans, the soldier said, "It looks like you are trying to catch up with your unit. I picked this up about an hour ago. Perhaps it will help you find a staging area where someone can point you in the right direction."

"Much obliged soldier, I really appreciate your help."

Many soldiers had already ditched their obsolete muskets and replaced them with repeating rifles like Spencers, Sharps, or Henrys taken from dead or dying soldiers lying on the battlefield. Four men, returning from a reconnaissance mission led by Captain F. W. Kelly of Colonel Salyer's Regiment, told Jake and Rans the largest cluster of Yankee soldiers they had ever seen was bivouacked just a few miles north of their location.

The soldiers then directed them northeast to a small encampment used by the 50th as a staging area the previous night. There, a young officer in charge of supplies, brought them a battle map of the area adjacent to that covered by the map they had. He spread it out over a small folding table and fitted the adjoining sides together. After locating the main force of the 50th on the map, Jake and Rans realized reaching them would be impossible.  When Jake shook his head in discouragement, a senior commander approached, asking if he could help. Rans explained their predicament.  Pointing to a specific place on the map, the officer told them, "The 50th Virginia and five other Virginia regiments, the 21st, 25th, 42nd, 44th and 48th, are here. They will make the initial assault on Culp's Hill today around noon."  He then pointed to another spot on the map and said, "More specifically, the 50th is supposed to be here defending our field guns and advancing if reserves are needed."  Again, pointing to the map, he said, "You might be right about not being able to join up with your unit. Crossing that shallow creek right here and skirting the adjacent woods to reach your unit would be far too dangerous.  The 400 yards next to the woods is completely in the open."

Rans then asked the commander, "Sir, if there's no way for us to join the 50th, is there someplace we can join up with another regiment and be useful?"

Looking down at Jacob's sniper rifle, the officer said, "Young man, I know the perfect place for you, but I'm not sure about your friend."

Jake quickly spoke up saying, "He's not my friend. He's my brother, and we've taken care of each other throughout the war. We work really well together. Not only that, Rans can shoot as well as me anytime."

"Okay, boys. let me show you where to meet up with those boys from Texas and Alabama. Do you see those two hills over there?"

"Yes, Sir."

"The largest one is called Round Top Mountain. The other one to the north is a granite spur of Round Top.  We are already engaging the enemy on that spur." Pointing to his large-scale map of the area, he added.  "We could use you here, to the right of our main force, looking at it from this direction. The men out there are only one deep.  There are no reserves, and nobody is on their right.  A sniper or two here could prevent anyone from moving to our outside and outflanking us."

Rans acknowledged, saying, "I understand!"

Jake followed up with a resounding, "Yes, Sir."

"Knowing you boys are from Virginia, and they're from Texas and Alabama, it might be hard for them to understand you. But when they see your rifles, you'll be welcomed with open arms."  Grinning, he added, "Once in a while you might want to throw out a spurious Y'all to keep in their good graces."

Again, pointing to the map, the senior officer showed Jake and Rans how best to get from the staging area to positions occupied by the 4th, 15th, and 47th Alabama at the base of the spur. "We need to stop any attempt to outflank those Alabama Regiments trying to push those Yankees off that hill. A couple of snipers would go a long way toward accomplishing this goal.

After the senior officer finished his instructions to Jake and Rans, he mounted up and headed due east to the next visible staging area. A runner from the 4th Texas Regiment asked Jake if he knew the man who instructed them on how to get out to the three forward deployed Alabama regiments.

Jake responded, "No, Sir. I can't say we do."

"His name is Major General James Longstreet, and he's General Lee's right-hand man." The soldier then added, "I'm headed back to the 4th Texas, which is about twelve hundred yards north of where you need to be. Just follow me, and I'll get you there."

"Much obliged."

En route to the 4th Texas Regiment, Jake and Rans ran into injured troops being evacuated from the base of the spur. Most of the wounds were flesh wounds. Some wounds, however, were much more serious and had required the amputation of an arm, leg or other extremity. After the wounded were carried away, litters carrying dead soldiers followed. The dead were covered by tattered blankets thrown lengthwise over the bodies.

As they approached the hill, the sounds of guns and small arms fire became much louder. Occasionally, they heard musket balls pass by their heads and hit a tree nearby. One of the musket balls hit the young soldier leading them to the 4th Texas. He fell but was not seriously hurt. Jake picked him up and with one arm helped him forward to the 4th Texas' staging area.

Figure 10. Colonel W. C. Oakes

When the brothers reported in, the soldiers immediately saw Jake was carrying a Whitworth Sniper rifle. A young infantry officer, Captain B. A. Hill asked his Regimental Commander, Colonel W. C. Oates, "Sir, where do you want me to put these two?"

Jake immediately interjected. "Sir, General Longstreet said he thought it might be best if my brother and I were positioned east of here,

just to the right of the 15th Alabama. He said from there, we could
likely stop any attempts to outflank
us on that side.

Colonel Oakes replied, "He's
probably right, do you think you
can get down there in one piece."

"Yes Sir, we might have to run
a zig zag pattern most of the way
but if we can find a good spot, we
can make it real difficult for the
other side. Sir, do we know what
unit is on top of the hill?"

"Early in the engagement, one
of my troops was able to get a good
look at the unit's regimental flag
through a spyglass. It belonged to
the 20th Maine. Speaking directly
to Jake and Rans, Colonel Oates

Figure 11. Colonel Chamberlain
was on the Union side at Gettysburg.

told the brothers, "Once you get down there, move out as far out to the
right as possible. Just be sure to keep the main force in sight at all times."
He then added, "The last thing we need in this action is to be outflanked
by the enemy and cut to shreds by lateral fire."

"Yes, Sir!"

The two large rocky hills that had earlier been pointed out to them on
the map were easily recognizable. The surfaces of both hills were full of
imbedded granite rocks and tree stubble. After running a lengthy zig zag
pattern from the staging area to the base of the spur, Jake and Rans bent
over and placed their hands on their knees. They were completely out of
breath. They rested for a moment and began to look around. In front of
them, Jake and Rans saw a medium-height rock wall that should provide
them maximum protection from Union sharpshooters firing down from
dug-in positions further up the hill. They also saw a large black maple tree
standing less than a foot behind the wall. Looking at Rans, Jake spoke,
"Rans, that maple tree is large enough it should be able to provide at least
partial protection for our backs. I think if we hold up here we should be
able to pin down any Yankee sharpshooters trying to outflank us from our
unprotected side."

Throughout the day, the 4th, 15th and 47th Alabama charged the hill
five different times. Holding the high ground, the 20th Maine repelled

the attacking force taking only minimal casualties. At the end of each advance, bodies of fallen comrades lay strewn across the face of the rocky hill. Half way through the battle, Union soldiers remained hidden behind rocks and trees further up the hillside.  Jake and Rans were selective in the shots they took, taking careful aim at Union soldiers at the top of the hill. Not all found their mark, but many did.

During the first charge, Jake and Rans observed about thirty Union troops trying to slip around their position on the outside. They were nearly crawling trying to hide their presence.  Jacob was first to catch a glimpse of the small column.  Soon, he realized the brush between himself and the attacking force was too thick for him to take a shot. Looking back at Rans he whispered: "Why don't you climb up into the tree so you can get a clear shot?"

As he grabbed hold of a low tree limb, Rans spoke, "Jake, hand me my rifle after I get into position."

Once Rans had positioned himself in the tree, Jake handed him his rifle. Rans told him "I've got a clear shot.  You keep them busy thinking you're the shooter while I wipe them out – the more smoke the better. They'll never see me." A few minutes later nearly all the Union soldiers lay dead in front of them."

Shortly before Noon, Rans returned to the tree.  This time he took a spyglass with him.  Once in place, he popped the cover on his spyglass and started scanning a 360° arc.  At 25°, he noticed a group of eleven Union soldiers trying to work themselves between Jake and Rans and the 15th Alabama Regiment on their left. Soon, Rans heard the sound of rolling wheels in the vicinity of the troops. As the wheels rolled, Rans saw a small patch of tall grass separate and swing back further up the hill.  Before long he caught sight of a small artillery piece still working its way into position near the bottom of the hill.

Rans called down to Jake, "Jake, do you think we can pin those cannoneers down long enough for me to climb down and get some hand grenades?"

Jake answered, "I'm going to need some more ammunition. Let's see how many of them we can pick off before they realize we're out here by ourselves."

"Jake, how many hand grenades did you take off the field desk at the 15th? You know – the ones they used to hold down the large-scale map they had spread out on the desk."

"I took five.  What did you have in mind?"

"Behind us is a low spot that runs all the way down to that field gun they brought down the hill.  Off hand, I'd say the depression is a French drain.  I'll bet that field piece is an 1857 Napoleon Light, a 12-pounder. I read about it when I first joined the Army. It's the only gun light enough for them to get down the hill. Why don't we follow the low spot, and you can stop short when you find a good place to take some shots.  I'll take the grenades and see if I can take out the gun, its crew or some of the troops who brought the gun down the hill.  When they flee, they'll have to go uphill to get away and that's when I'll slow them down with my Lorenz. When they're out of my range you can pick 'em off with your Whitworth."

Within the hour, Jake and Rans saw the gun stop its trek down the hill and turn facing the 15th Alabama. The brothers knew they could not allow lateral cannon fire to hit troops preparing for another assault.  Rans removed 5 grenades from Jake's rucksack and placed them in his pockets. Jake ran ahead looking for a good shooting spot, preferably a dry one behind a large tree. Once in place Jake adjusted his scope for the proper yardage to reach just beyond the bottom of the hill. He pulled out his ammunition and laid it out in rows for quick retrieval.  By this time, Rans was within twenty yards of the field gun. He pulled out a grenade and let it fly. When the grenade hit, the gun's right wheel blew off and began rolling. One of the cannoneers quickly retrieved the wheel and started to place it back on its axel. With one wheel now off the gun, Rans tried for the left wheel, but the grenade missed its target, falling in the middle of the gun crew and killing three and injuring one. One of the soldiers accompanying the gun crew tried to destroy the gun but Jake shot him before he could pour gunpowder and shrapnel and mud down it's barrel. The soldier stood up screaming hysterically. His right hand had been blown off just below the elbow.

Realizing further efforts were futile, the rest of the soldiers fled leaving the gun behind. As they scattered up the hill, Jake picked them off one by one. Of the eleven soldiers with the gun, only three made up the hill beyond Jake's range.

Throughout the afternoon, the troops from the Alabama regiments continued their assault on the rocky spur. With each successive assault, Jake and Rans noticed fewer and fewer shots being fire during the encounter. They suspected that both sides were running low on ammunition. Before long, they, too, began restricting their targets to those they could see clearly and were within their kill range.  During the last two assaults, they observed more and more hand-to-hand fighting between the opposing troops, convincing them that both sides were indeed running out of ammunition—forcing them to mount their Bowie knives on their rifles and fight hand-to-hand. Near the end of the fourth assault, the hill fell into near silence.

The last assault caught Jake and Rans completely by surprise. In fact, the assault caught everyone by surprise. All day, the Alabama regiments had been on the offensive. Jake and Rans were suddenly awed when an incredible number of Union troops with bayonets came charging down the hill with reckless abandon. Most of the Confederate soldiers barely had a chance to fire once before the Union soldiers reached them. Many were slain with bayonets. When the two sides collided, the Confederate soldiers defended themselves as best they could in hand-to-hand fighting. The number of bodies strewn across the battlefield was astonishing.

Jake and Rans held their ground until they saw members of the 15th Alabama on their left preparing to withdraw. As Jake and Rans scrambled to join them, Jake's left foot caught between a large root and a rough spot under the rock wall. Wedged in so tightly that he couldn't remove it, it lodged in even tighter when he tried to free the foot—like a Chinese finger toy that grips the finger tighter the harder the finger is pulled, trapping it inside the toy. Alarmed at his brother's predicament, Rans called out, "Jake—what can I do?"

"You can get the hell out of here—that's what you can do!"

"No way, Jake! As long as you're here, I'm here."

Rans tried feverishly to free Jake's foot from the crevice, but nothing worked. Convinced he was about to be killed, Jacob stashed his rifle under some thick brush out of sight, knowing enemy soldiers were quick to take revenge on snipers who wrought so much fear and havoc on to the battlefield. Rans feared being captured and spending the rest of the war in Elmira or one of the other disease-ridden Union prisons. Looked wildly around, Rans glimpsed a Union soldier running directly towards them. *Should they fight or was it too late*? The fixed bayonet on the soldier's rifle suggested he was out of ammunition. In what seemed like an instant, the baby-faced Union soldier had jumped the wall and was holding the tip of his bayonet at Jake's throat. With shaking hands and sweat running down his face, the soldier looked at Rans in amazement. "Why didn't you run away like the others?" he demanded.

Looking defiantly into the soldier's eyes, Rans growled, "He's my brother. What kind of man would I be if I left him?"

The Union soldier, already weary with fatigue and dazed from all the carnage he had witnessed, could barely speak above a whisper, "Look! I have a brother too. We're at the very edge of this flank. I'll continue on my way if you promise to head away from the battlefield. Do I have your word?"

Jake quickly responded, "Sir, you have my word. There's been enough killing today. I just want to go back home to my wife and kids."

When the Union soldier slipped away, Rans used his Bowie knife to hack away at the tree bark just above Jacob's foot. After four quick cuts, Jake's foot was free. They gathered up their rucksacks and rifles and moved away from the battlefield. Jake's leg was throbbing, and he was limping badly. Rans had taken the lead and did not notice Jake's difficulty until he glanced back to see Jake leaning precariously against a tree. "What's wrong, Jake? We need to get away from here."

"I just need a minute," he said, rubbing the injured leg.

"Why didn't you tell me you were hurting? Let me look at it." He pulled Jake's trouser leg up enough to see the bruising and swelling, then looked around for small branches he could use to make a brace. Rummaging through what clothing he had, Rans pulled a shirt out and wrapped it as tightly as he could around the makeshift brace. Then he trimmed a larger branch with his Bowie knife for Jake to use as a cane to keep some weight off the foot.

After circling around, they came upon Confederate troops heading south towards Virginia. None were from the 50th, so Jake and Rans decided to go it alone to the 50th' Virginia's staging area where this had all begun.

After two grueling hours of walking, with frequent stops to realign Jake's splint, they stumbled into remnants of the 50th's primary staging area. The soldiers they found there were haggard, bedraggled and completely worn out. Many wore clothes that had not been washed in weeks.

Jake dropped down beside a soldier whose arm was swathed in bandages. Loosening his own splint, he asked the soldier if he was all right. Nodding, the soldier proceeded to tell them how he had scrambled from the battlefield after he was shot, leaving behind his canteen, rifle and ammunition, just as many others had. A few carried broken rifles and empty leather bags. He saw others throw down all their things and head toward the nearest road heading away from the battlefield.

They all knew Lee's Army had suffered a demoralizing defeat. For the badly wounded, the war was over. Jake and Rans wondered if unit commanders expected the remnants of their rag-tag units to have sufficient will to retreat to Virginia and start over again. For now, the troops needed rest and time to think of better times. The brothers thought of their beloved South and looked forward to returning home to heal and celebrate with their families the joy of being alive.

When Jake and Rans reported in, stories of their valiant efforts had already reached their Commanders.  The troops knew of the courage they displayed while keeping Union soldiers of the 20th Maine at bay for 5 hours while troops of the Alabama Regiments tried to advance up Round Top Mountain's spur. The troops were also told of Jake and Rans' last minute heroic efforts in holding off desperate Union troops as they tried to complete a lateral sweep across the face of the rocky spur near Culp's hill to end the battle. While swapping stories, the troops gathered their belongings and repaired what they could. Tears in shirts and trousers were stitched, boots re-tied, canteens filled and dry leather bags refilled with black powder and bullets.

A quick scan of the campsite showed Jake and Rans that some tents were now unoccupied.  Dry spots on the damp ground revealed where fellow soldiers had slept the night before. Nearly twenty percent of the regiment remained unaccounted for and were presumed dead, captured, injured or missing. The remaining troops scavenged through the personal effects of those who had not returned, hoping to find letters, pictures, orders or anything else to identify them so commanders could write letters of condolences to their families.  Most soldiers knew all too well that in the letters the commanders wrote they told the family how brave the father, husband or son had been in combat and attested to his solid character. They also searched for military items that might have been left behind, such as rifles, black powder, Bowie knives, etc. After everything was gathered, as much as possible was placed in wagons that would accompany Confederate soldiers to Richmond. When everything was loaded, the soldiers began their trek south away from the battlefield.  Like Jake and Rans, their hearts were filled with sorrow knowing thousands of their friends and fellow soldiers were not returning with them.

Soon after arriving at an overnight bivouac area, an officer ordered the soldiers to get some sleep. Another officer posted sentries around the encampment working in two-hour shifts. Jake and Rans were assigned the evening shift beginning at sundown. The next morning some of the older soldiers and those who were land and slave owners were told to evade capture and return to their homes until fall.  Since Jake and Rans had been assigned to the 50th for only a few weeks, their superiors were completely unaware the 51st had sent them home earlier to plant crops, tend to the fields and prepare for the fall harvest.  Although Jake and Rans experienced a tinge of guilt at being sent home a second time, they felt justified in going because the Army needed food and could go nowhere without it.

The first twenty miles or so they traveled slowly, avoiding the main roads.  Jake, still recovering from what he thought might be a broken leg, repositioned his splint frequently to reduce the pain in his leg. Both were unusually quiet, lost in thought.  Rans thought mostly of Millie and his children while Jake dwelled on the carnage he had seen and worried about what the future held for his beloved South.

Knowing their families were not expecting them, Jake asked his brother a perplexing question, "Lorenzo, what do you say we take a detour on our way home?"

"What kind of detour, Jake?"

"How about one last trip to Charleston?"

"Why?  Don't you want to get back to be with Annie?"

"Of course, I do!  But I don't know how we can explain all this—suddenly showing up after only a couple of months away. Someone might think we're cowards or deserters from Gettysburg.  Today is July 5th and by now word has gotten back to Jeffersonville and Burke's Garden about how badly we were defeated. We killed a lot of Yankees there, but we still ended up retreating back into Virginia. I heard one soldier from the 15th Alabama say that 150,000 troops were on the battlefield the second day and that as many as 20,000 were still lying there gravely ill or dead on day three."

"Though it's hard to admit, I have to agree with you, Jake.  Let's go to Charleston."

# Chapter Eleven

## *Return to Charleston*

A FEW minutes after crossing the Pennsylvania-Virginia border on July 7, 1863, Jacob spoke, "As soon as we come to a friendly rail line, let's see if we can catch a train headed to Richmond. From there we can grab another train headed toward Charleston." Before long they came across a freight train parked on a side spur. The train consisted of an old steam engine, eight drab and dirty boxcars, and a dingy, pale-yellow caboose. Lorenzo slid open a side door on one of the boxcars and climbed inside. He then reached down, grabbed Jacob's arm and pulled him up inside the boxcar. They changed into their own wrinkled clothes and sat down on bags of grain facing one another. Since many Confederate soldiers, especially volunteers, were never issued uniforms, they would fit right in with others trying to get a ride back home. Once seated, Lorenzo reminded Jacob to put his dirt-caked uniform and brogans into his rucksack.

After changing trains four times, the brothers arrived in Summerville, about 15 miles upstream from Charleston. There they booked two seats on a small paddlewheeler and rode it downstream on the Ashley River to Charleston. Once they reached the Ashley River docks, Lorenzo checked his inside pocket, making sure his "Letter of Credit" from the Exchange Bank of Richmond was still there. He and Jacob needed the money to cover their living expenses while they were in Charleston. After disembarking from the paddle wheeler, Lorenzo found a livery stable across the street and rented two horses for the duration of their stay.

While en route to their favorite restaurant on Meeting Street, Jacob tried to get a glimpse of Boyce's Wharf to see if the *John Jameson* was still docked there to see if Lilly's parents had returned to Charleston. If not, they were no doubt still crossing the Atlantic on their way from Europe. Since it was not in port, they stopped at the chandlery to find out if any ships from Europe were scheduled to arrive within the next few weeks. According to the storekeeper two Clippers were currently docked in port, and one was scheduled to leave by the end of the month. No one seemed to know if any ships were scheduled to arrive from England, France or Ireland in the near future.

They decided that Jacob would go to Lilly, and Lorenzo would stable the horses and arrange a room at the Rutledge House Inn. Thus far, they were pleasantly surprised to see Charleston had suffered little damage during their absence. Although Ryan's Mart was no longer trafficking newly arrived slaves from West Africa, they were still selling slaves brought to Charleston by slave owners residing in several Southern states. Occasionally, however, a slave ship made it through the blockade bringing slaves previously sold in Europe or the Caribbean. On such occasions, Ryan's Mart quietly held a special auction for their preferred customers.

When Lorenzo arrived at the Inn, he checked in, stretched out on the bed, and dozed. After enjoying a meal of fresh seafood in the elegant dining room, he went out on the town, expecting to take in the many charms Charleston offered.

Jacob, on the other hand, headed straight for the Cooper Estate. From the road, he saw a light in the upstairs ballroom and shadows of servants setting up the dining room for another festive gathering. A large orchestra was rehearsing the patriotic songs they would play later in the evening. Seeing life here in Charleston continue on as before convinced him that the city was immune to the horrid effects of the brutal civil war—a war Jacob felt had already lasted far too long.

Once he had climbed the steps from ground level to the mezzanine, he paused to gaze at Lilly standing outside the ballroom door as she worked the crowd as they arrived, soliciting donations to buy more guns and ammunition for the Army. The first sight of her always took his breath away—she was so beautiful. Lilly's dazzling smile and carefree attitude as she greeted her guests masked the seriousness of her efforts. Those who knew her well could tell she had found a cause truly worthy of her time and attention. She may have spoken of moving to France, but her true friends knew she was not anxious to leave her precious Charleston.

At first Lilly did not recognize Jacob, but once she did, she moved quickly to his side and began questioning him about the war. In particular, she wanted to know about Gettysburg. Seeing the splint on his leg, Lilly asked, "Jacob!  My love—where have you been?  What's happened to you?"

"I injured my leg at Gettysburg, but I should be okay in a week or two. The splint works just fine."

"I heard it was terrible, Jacob.  It's been reported that 140,000 soldiers were there, and as many as 20,000 didn't return to their units.

"It's more like 30,000 who didn't return. Many members of my regiment were overrun, and by the end of the day both sides were out of ammunition."

"How do you fight without bullets?"

"You snap a bayonet on your rifle and charge."

"How did you get hurt?"

"My boot stuck between a rock wall and a large tree root."

"How did you get it out in time?"

"I didn't."

"How can that be?"

"Lorenzo was trying to help me get my foot out from between the wall and a tree root, but before he could free me a large gruesome-looking Yankee soldier was standing over us with his bayonet pointing directly at me. The soldier asked Lorenzo why he had stayed to help me, and he told him, 'He's my brother.' The soldier said, 'I have a brother too. If you promise me you'll walk away from this, I'll walk on like I never saw you.'"

"What did you do, Jacob?"

"We did as we promised—after Lorenzo used his Bowie knife to cut away the tree bark, I was able to free my foot and stand. Then Lorenzo and I walked away and circled back to our staging area. After we returned, our Commander told us Lee had given the order to withdraw from the battlefield. Our first task was to round up any stray soldiers still fighting and get them back to the staging area. There, Lorenzo and I were told to go home and stay until Lee and his lieutenants could draw up plans to reconstruct new regiments with survivors of Gettysburg and replacements for those lost in battle. Instead we hopped one train after another until we ended up in Summerville. From there we took a steamer into Charleston."

"Where's Lorenzo?"

"He's staying downtown at the Rutledge House Inn. It's his 'new' favorite place to stay."

"I know the owners quite well. They are wonderful people."

"Where is your family, Lilly?"

"They're still at sea, returning from France and England. I'm expecting them any day."

"Are they still running guns for the South?"

"Of course."

"What have you decided about relocating to the south of France?"

"We're going to stay here until Charleston is threatened directly or until we can't get past the Yankee blockade."

"What are your plans for tonight?"

Lilly laughed and quipped, "Later I'm going to make a man out of you. You should take a nap." She sighed and added, "It seems as though I've already worked this crowd forever. They must be getting tired of my smile and solicitations for more money. Two hours after supper, I'll tell the guests it's time to call it a night and remind them of how much their donations are appreciated. I'll also invite them to another party celebrating the arrival of my parents when they get here. After everyone leaves, I'll have Miss Abigale prepare a bath for us. The hot days and humid nights here in Charleston make me feel sticky. I'm sure you must feel the same after such a long train ride."

After the guests left, Abigale prepared a warm bath for Jacob and Lilly and retired for the evening. Lilly, true to her word, came to the door and announced, "Honey, our bath is ready." Wiping the sleep out of his eyes, Jacob realized she was standing in front of him wearing nothing but a grin. She was absolutely stunning. Her body was smooth, supple and most of all inviting. Despite her lack of clothing, she was still every bit a lady. With grace, Lilly reached out with her hand, took his and led him to the bathtub. She washed him first, soaping him gently, then he did the same for her. When they kissed, they melted into one other's arms. Once the water cooled, she asked if he was ready and led him to her bed. They made love and wanted more. Fighting sleep, they continued their lovemaking. It was nearly 3 a.m. before they succumbed to a deep and welcoming sleep.

The next morning when Jacob awoke he found Lilly curled up next to him. Abigale was in the next room starting a fire to heat up bathwater. He slipped out of bed, grabbed a towel to wrap around his waist and went to ask Miss Abigale what time she usually set plates for breakfast. Smiling, she replied, "Eight o'clock, Sir—are you telling me you and Miss Lilly want to have breakfast before your bathe."

"Yes, Miss Abigale. I expect Miss Lilly will be quite hungry this morning."

Holding back a small laugh, Abigale responded, "I'll bake some biscuits and fry up ham and eggs. If you like I can also put on some grits. I know how this South Carolina heat can just sap the energy right out of you!"

"Take your time with the bath, Miss Abigale. She's not up yet, and I'm not sure just what her plans are for the rest of the day."

"Yes Sir, Mr. Jacob. I'll take my time. And—Mr. Jacob?"

"Yes, Miss Abigale."

"I'm going outside to make sure I have enough firewood to heat up the water."

"That sounds like a good idea, Miss Abigale."

Lilly was just waking up when Jacob returned to the bedroom, "Where have you been, Jacob?"

"Miss Abigale and I have been discussing whether we are going to bathe before or after breakfast."

"Jacob! Tell me you didn't have that discussion."

"She just wanted to know how much hot water she needed to heat to meet our needs."

"Honey, I'm starved. Let's see if breakfast is ready."

"Miss Abigale said she will bake some biscuits and fry us ham and eggs right away."

"You didn't turn down the grits, did you?"

"No, but how did you know she offered to make grits?"

"This is Charleston, and we always have grits for breakfast. I like honey and freshly churned butter on mine."

After finishing breakfast and a hot bath, Lilly and Jacob returned to the bedroom to discuss their plans for the rest of the day.

Once inside the room, Jacob asked Lilly, "What's next?"

Appearing a little coy, Lilly spoke up saying, "Aren't we going to finish what we started last night?"

"Finish! What do you mean, 'finish?' I seem to recall several 'finishes' to what we started last night. In fact, I seem to recall two or three."

"Jacob, the number was more like three or four. Let's stop talking about finishes and begin talking about starts. If we talk about starts, I expect the finishes will come on their own. Jacob! Oh! My God! Did I say that? That's funny! God will send me to hell for saying that."

"Have you been drinking, Lilly? You sound intoxicated."

"I'm intoxicated with you, Jacob. I love you so much."

"What now?"

"I'm going to bed, and you're coming with me. We are going to have lots more starts and finishes—till we're too tired to continue. Then we're going to take advantage of Miss Abigale's offer to prepare us a late bath. Afterwards, we are going to take a carriage to downtown Charleston where I'll buy you new clothes suitable for a Virginia gentleman. You can't wear what your wearing now in Charleston while you're with me. Laughing, she pulled at the towel Jacob wore, Desire blazed in her eyes as Lilly looked directly into Jacob's eyes and said, "I want you, Jacob—I want you now!"

Jacob and Lilly awoke, took a second bath shortly before lunch, then dressed. Their first stop after leaving the Inn was to purchase suitable attire for Jacob. After finishing their shopping, Jacob and Lilly stepped into their carriage and proceed down Meeting Street. As they approached the Mill House, Lilly out of the corner of her eye saw her longtime childhood friend Lucy Rutledge walking arm-in-arm with an incredibly handsome man at her side.

Lilly called out, "Lucy! Lucy Ann Rutledge, is that you? Who's that handsome man walking with you?'

"Lilly, is that you? Are you still here in Charleston?"

"I am. Would you care to introduce your friend?"

"By all means. This is Lorenzo Harris, and he's from Burke's Garden, Virginia."

More than a little startled to see his brother with another woman, Jacob reacted by asking Lorenzo, "Why didn't you tell me you had such a lovely lady right here in Charleston? It's obvious you've been holding out on me."

Appearing a bit confused, Lucy glanced first at Jacob, then at Lorenzo. "Do you boys know each other?"

Jacob answered, "Of course, he's my brother."

Lilly then explained, "Lucy and I have been best friends since we were little. Her family owns chandleries all the way up and down the east coast as well as the John Rutledge House Inn, here in Charleston. Her family's been staunch supporters of the ideals and lifestyle we are trying to preserve here in Charleston. Lucy, I am so glad to see you again, and Lorenzo—you're still a very handsome man."

Jacob suddenly interrupted, "Lilly, I seem to recall you calling me a handsome man several times last night."

"Jacob, please understand that when you're a 'wanting woman,' you're liable to say anything," she said in jest.

Gazing steadily at Lilly, Jacob responded, "Yes, especially when it's true."

Lucy reminded Lilly that her family's Inn had wonderful seafood as well as excellent food and drinks—and it was only three blocks away.

Lilly replied, "The Inn would be just fine."

Lucy said to the driver, "Take us to the Rutledge House Inn at 116 Broad Street. It's between Bay and Meeting Street."

"Yes Ma'am," the driver responded.

At the Inn, the foursome retreated outside to an eating area with a cobblestone floor generally reserved for private parties and meetings. The walls and ceiling were made of vines and flowers tied together with thin strands of leather. Of the ten tables in the area, only four were large enough to accommodate groups. The couples chose a secluded table located not far from the Inn's stone hearth. After ordering drinks, they discussed the recent battle losses in Gettysburg and Vicksburg. Jacob recounted their unit's alternating wins and losses across Tennessee and Northeastern Virginia. Lilly expressed her concern about the need to keep Charleston's harbor open for the impending arrival of her parents on the clipper *John Jameson*.

Lilly filled everyone in on recent actions taken by General Beauregard in defending Batteries Greg and Wagner, Fort Sumter, and the city of Charleston. Everyone present knew full well the Union believed that seizing Charleston would prevent large numbers of rifles, field guns, ammunition and other armaments from reaching Confederate forces across the south. They also knew closing Charleston's harbor would force blockade-running Clippers, Frigates, Schooners etc., to seek lesser havens elsewhere having fewer wharves, docks, and port defenses.

They discussed how the South had fortified their emplacements on Morris, James and Sullivan Islands during the previous winter and early spring by placing obstructions in the harbor and laying submerged mines called torpedoes to discourage Union ships from entering the harbor. The South also stationed the *Chicora* and *Palmetto State*, two Ironclads, inside the harbor to fend off attempts by the Union Navy to get their gunships and ironclads within firing range of Fort Sumter and Charleston.

While they were deep in conversation, a negro runner from Sullivan's Island burst in to tell Lilly the *John Jameson* had been spotted further up the coastline. He told her no Union gunboats or ironclads had been seen in the area and added tonight might be a good time to bring the Clipper into the harbor. Lilly instructed the runner to go to the port quickly and prepare for an evening arrival of the *John Jameson* at Boyce's Wharf. She also asked him to notify General Beauregard so his troops would be waiting to escort the weapons on board to the port armory across the street from the Wharf. Lilly then directed the runner to bring two torch stands to the wharf just before dusk. Lilly would use the torches to signal the *John Jameson* indicating the channel to use from the harbor entrance to the wharf. Fortunately, thus far, the Union Navy had not been able to sink enough ships to block all the primary channels used by blockade-runners trying to transit the harbor.

After the runner left, Jacob asked Lilly, "Is he one of your slaves? Do you trust him?

"His name is Solomon Brown, and I would trust him with my life. He protected me when I was growing up. I consider him a loyal servant and friend.  You must remember that here in Charleston many well-educated slaves perform essential work. Last year, one of them, a colored steamboat captain, took his boat out into the bay, dropped its eight passengers off on Sullivan Island and made a dash for a Yankee gunboat. He then surrendered the vessel to the Captain of the gunboat. The people who worked around the harbor had seen him piloting his steamboat so often, they forgot he was a slave.

Turning to Jacob, Lilly asked, "Can you and Lorenzo take the carriage back to the house and get into your uniforms? That way if there's any trouble on the docks, you won't get shot by any of General Beauregard's troops.  After you've changed, come back and join Lucy and me for an early supper.  Afterwards, we'll go to the wharf to light the torches needed to guide the *John Jameson* through the channels.  While you and Lorenzo are changing, Lucy and I will visit the port to make sure it's safe for the ship's return.  Sometime slave dockworkers aren't cooperative when it comes to unloading contraband like guns and ammunition. Even their negro overseers have trouble keeping them in line when they're asked to load or unload dangerous cargo."

Jacob and Lorenzo left to change into their uniforms as Lilly had requested.  Lilly and Lucy headed for the nearby wharf and, as they approached, they noticed an unusually large number of colored dockworkers in the vicinity of the wharf where the *John Jameson* usually docked.  As they walked around, Lilly heard two of them speaking French in what she suspected was a dialect spoken in New Orleans.  She also noticed several of them were wearing similar shoes and colorful silk scarves around their necks.

Lucy lowered her voice and said to Lilly, "I think New Orleans fell last spring.  When I was in Savanna, I heard the Union Navy was recruiting negro slaves to help man their ships. Some with seafaring experience were even made officers and given positions of responsibility on Union ships. Can you imagine!  I wonder if some of those men could have been sent here to Charleston to infiltrate the port and blow it up or burn the blockade runners to their waterlines while they are in port.  If so, I wonder if they might try to burn the *John Jameson* while it offloads its guns and ammunition. "

Lilly whispered to Lucy, "We need to leave now and get back to the Inn." They made their way back to the Inn as unobtrusively as they could.  Once inside the Inn, Lucy said, "We need to find General Beauregard immediately and let him know things don't look right at the docks!"  Lilly concurred, and both headed straight to the front door.

As Lilly and Lucy exited the Inn, Lucy saw General Beauregard leaving a nearby bar with one of his aides in tow. The General appeared quite upset at his aides' stage of drunkenness at this early hour. Waving her hands above her head, Lucy ran towards him, calling out, "General! Lilly and I need to speak with you at once! It's *urgent*!"

The General, looking intently at this very attractive southern belle, responded, "Yes, ma'am. May I be of some assistance?"

"General, there are a lot of people up to no good at the docks."

"What do you mean, young lady?"

"My friend, Miss Lilly Cooper and I were walking near Boyce's Wharf to see if her parent's ship was approaching the harbor entrance to make a run for the docks. While we were there, we saw several colored dock workers dressed differently from the others. Lilly speaks French, and she says they're speaking a French dialect spoken in New Orleans. General, things just aren't right. Colored dockworkers don't wear matching shoes and have colorful scarves around their necks."

"Young lady, I have known Miss Cooper for some time and have frequently attended some of the patriotic parties she hosts at her family's estate. You're quite right about her speaking French. I've heard her conversing with French emissaries about the availability of guns and ammunition for export to the Confederacy."

"May I ask your first name to make our conversation a little easier and less formal?"

"Certainly, General. My name is Lucy Rutledge. Feel free to call me Lucy. My family owns several Chandleries up and down the east coast. We also own the Rutledge House Inn here in Charleston."

"I take several of my meals at the Inn each week. It is indeed a fine establishment. I will personally check on the French being spoken by the dock workers. As I suspect you already know, I'm from New Orleans and can certainly recognize a New Orleans French dialect when I hear one. Before I head for the docks, I'll dispatch a courier to tell my troops, who occupy the warehouse at the end of Boyce's Wharf, to be ready for a frontal assault on the docks should your suspicions be correct. Knowing Miss Cooper and her parents as I do, I suspect you're right. Is there anything else?"

Lucy responded, "Yes, General. The ship we're expecting is the *John Jameson*. It's returning from England with guns and ammunition partially purchased with cotton grown here in South Carolina. Lilly's parents are on the ship, so please do be careful. Lilly and I will be meeting them on the ship as soon as they dock."

By now Lilly had joined the two. General Beauregard took her hand in welcome, but continued listening intently to Lucy, who continued, "Just one more thing, General! Two Confederate soldiers will be with us to help protect Lilly's parents as they leave the ship. Both are experienced riflemen and have been in combat. They will take up positions as high as possible on the ship near the main mast. After Gettysburg, both were sent away and told not to return until their unit is reorganized and replacements secured for those lost in battle. They're brothers—Jacob and Lorenzo Harris. You might say they are our 'beaux.' Both will be in uniform wearing kepis, so please keep an eye out for them should things get messy on the docks."

"You have my word, Lucy, I will tell my troops to keep them out of their lines-of-fire."

"General, you have my sincere thanks."

# Chapter Twelve

## *Attack on the John Jameson*

JACOB, Lorenzo, Lilly and Lucy met at the Rutledge House Inn for an early dinner to discuss their plans for boarding the *John Jameson* and safely removing the guns and ammunition from the ship's secure hold. Lilly suggested Jacob and Lorenzo board the ship with Lucy and herself, suggesting to onlookers they were visiting Charleston and accompanying their girlfriends in welcoming Lilly's parents back home. Jacob suggested Solomon Brown and his trusted dockhand friend board the ship first with a wooden box supposedly holding charts and other navigation supplies. In fact, the box would contain Jacob's and Lorenzo's rifles, black powder and ammunition. Lucy offered to obtain a wooden box from her family's chandlery stenciled with the chandlery's name on the outside. She would also bring back handmade semaphore flags Lilly had used previously to signal the *John Jameson* which channel to take from the harbor's entrance to Boyce's Wharf.

Lilly and her mother learned to use semaphores while in France, using the system developed there in 1790 by Claude Chappe and his brother. Initially, black and white flags were used to send messages from one outpost to another. Later, as methods became more complex, clocks, codebooks and telescopes were introduced. In the early 1800s, the maritime industry adopted semaphores as a fast method of communication between ships. To make her codes difficult to break, Lilly and her mother often sent their messages back and forth in French.

## *Boyce's Wharf – Charleston*

As Jacob, Lorenzo and Lilly left the Inn and walked towards the wharf, Lilly sent a courier ahead to tell Solomon and his friend to meet them at the entrance end of Boyce's Wharf. Lucy had left early to pick up the wooden box, an assortment of semaphore flags, a new sextant and torches from the chandlery. Before leaving the Inn, Lucy dropped a loaded double-barreled .45-caliber over-and-under derringer into her purse—one she once used to stop a mugger in Savanna.

Lucy's brother Henry, manager of the chandlery, had already set out the wooden box that would carry Jacob's and Lorenzo's rifles, ammunition and black powder to the ship. Before closing the box, Lucy placed the rifles inside. Henry closed the box and drove eight six-penny nails into the box at three of the corners, leaving one corner free for easy removal of the top.

Before leaving, Lucy made sure the box was stenciled with Rutledge Chandlery in large letters on top and two of the sides with Montreal, New York, Baltimore, Charleston, Savanna and New Orleans, in smaller letters underneath, so they could be seen easily. Henry then placed the wooden box into the Chandlery's delivery wagon and drove Lucy and the box to General Beauregard's warehouse at Boyce's Wharf.

By seven p.m. everyone had arrived in front of the warehouse. Lilly checked inside to confirm General Beauregard's troops were waiting should the negros try to attack the *John Jameson* or attempt to set it on fire. Peering inside the warehouse, Lilly saw Beauregard's troops finishing their meals, smoking cigars and cleaning their rifles in preparation for what might come later.

When Lucy and Henry arrived at the warehouse, Henry stepped inside to get some help unloading the wooden box. Meanwhile, Lucy took the torches, stands and lights out of the wagon and gave them to Solomon. The flags she handed to Lilly.

Once Lilly was in a good line-of-site position with the harbor's entrance, she instructed Solomon to give her a set of flags and two of the torches. Then stepping inside the warehouse Lilly asked one of Beauregard's officers if she could borrow his spyglass.

The older, heavyset Captain responded, "Yes, Ma'am." He removed the spyglass from its bag and handed it to her. She scanned the horizon with the spyglass, looking for the *John Jameson*. Two thirds of the way across her north-to-south scan she saw her parent's clipper entering the harbor. Not a single gunboat was in sight. She lit two torches and placed them in the pair of metal stands in front of her. Then she grabbed a black semaphore flag and a white one to signal the *John Jameson*. Raising her hands and crossing both flags above her head told the *John Jameson* the harbor was now clear of enemy ironsides and gunboats. Pulling the right flag down and pointing it to the ground while raising the left flag vertically over her head told the ship the most direct route to the wharf was via the

Figure 12. *John Jameson* at the dock.

first channel just south of Fort Sumter. As the vessel entered the harbor, the Boatswain acknowledged receipt of Lilly's message by holding both of his flags straight out in opposite directions.

Jacob and Lorenzo were amazed at Lilly's poise and confidence under pressure. They realized just how much they had underestimated her many talents. She was a true patriot working tirelessly for the southern cause. As the *John Jameson* dropped her sails, she reduced her speed significantly. Within minutes she was close enough to the wharf to throw two lines to waiting dockworkers who tied them off. Within minutes the ship drifted gently into the wharf, bounced twice and came to a complete stop. Lucy kept her eyes on the Negro imposters to make sure none moved in close enough to cut off Jacob, Lorenzo, Lilly, Solomon and his friend from the ship's docking spot. Once the *John Jameson* was docked, Jacob, Lilly, Lorenzo, Solomon and his friend began walking down the wharf toward the ship.

At the wharf, Lucy took up a position just outside the Boyce's Wharf warehouse. Should the Negro imposters gather to attack the *John Jameson*, her plan was to fire the derringer twice, alerting Beauregard's troops inside the warehouse to get ready to round up any imposters attempting to reach the *John Jameson* or to flee from the wharf.

Once the *John Jameson* was tied up, Lilly caught sight of her parents leaning over the rail waving to get her attention. She looked up at them and shouted, "Stay on the ship while Solomon and his friend bring aboard a box of charts and sundry items that will be needed for the return trip." Knowing the ship was not scheduled to sail for at least another month, Lilly's parents took the hint and immediately returned to their cabins.

Once the gangplank was lowered, Solomon and his friend picked up the box, walked it up the gangplank and boarded the ship. Solomon advised Lilly's parents that Lilly and her guests would join them shortly. Ten minutes later, Lilly, Jacob and Lorenzo boarded the ship, joining Solomon and his friend on the main deck. Once everyone was aboard, Solomon opened the box and withdrew the two rifles Lucy had placed in the box and handed them to the brothers along with ammunition and packets of black powder for their weapons.

Looking toward the cabins, Lilly called out, "Mother! Father! You can come out now. I'd like to introduce you to my friends. The two gentlemen standing next to me are Jacob and Lorenzo Harris. They are members of Company F, 51st Virginia Infantry Regiment. Lucy Rutledge is waiting for us near the warehouse at the end of the wharf."

Then she turned to the young men, "Jacob, Lorenzo. I'd like to introduce you to my parents Ray and Elizabeth Cooper. Daddy, at a recent party at our estate, a Yankee spy managed to get a look at our scheduling logs and fled before I could stop him. After Jacob arrived at the estate, I told him about the spy obtaining your schedules. He left immediately and was able to ride out and get ahead of the spy's carriage. Jacob said he took him out from about two hundred yards and left him for the alligators in a shallow pond. The spy's name was James Reynolds and General Beauregard said the Secret Service had been looking for him for some time. After Jacob shot him he pinned a note on his lapel telling everyone his name was "James Reynolds - a Yankee spy."

Mr. Cooper extended his hand and said, "Gentlemen, I am very pleased to make your acquaintance. I am sure you are both good soldiers and extremely loyal to our cause."

"Father, I brought Jacob and Lorenzo along because I suspect some of the colored dockworkers you see on the wharf are imposters. They speak with a New Orleans French accent. There appears to be about twenty of them. Earlier, Lucy reminded me New Orleans fell in April of last year. That's when the Union Navy started recruiting Negros to serve aboard their ships. Some were even given commissions and assigned leadership positions on Union vessels."

Ray spoke up, "I can't believe it. I just can't believe it!

Lilly continued, "Since all the Negros are wearing the same kinds of shoes and colored silk scarves around their necks, I suspect they're all in the Union Navy. If true, they're surely up to no good—no good at all. Before Lucy and I got here we checked with General Beauregard about their accents. Being from New Orleans, he confirmed our suspicions right away. His troops are now hiding in the warehouse at the end of Boyce's wharf."

After returning the torches, lights and stands to the delivery wagon, Lucy walked due north and stood behind a large tree about fifteen feet from the side door of the warehouse. This location afforded her an excellent line-on-sight view of Boyce's Wharf, the two adjacent wharves and the Negro imposters. Lucy's responsibility was to notify General Beauregard's troops should any of the imposters make suspicious moves toward the John Jameson. If too many of them gathered around the warehouse or made a break for the ship, she was to fire two shots from the .45-caliber derringer.

A few minutes after she put away the torches, lights and stands, the dockworkers began showing up in front of the warehouse two and three at a time. The first group brought with them two ropes, one ladder and two grappling hooks attached to ropes. The second carried torches and lamps that were already lit. All the Negros had Union standard issue .36-caliber, 1851 Navy Colt revolvers stuffed inside their waist sashes. As soon as the first two dockworkers broke for the *John Jameson*, Lucy stepped around the corner and fired both barrels one at a time. The shots alerted Beauregard's troops and those on the *John Jameson* that an attack was imminent. After firing the shots, Lucy quickly ran towards the warehouse side door. Seeing her running in his direction, a soldier opened the door and held it for her to enter.

Hearing the shots, Lilly turned and saw Jacob and Lorenzo on top of the ship's cabin where they had taken up prone firing positions behind some wooden boxes. She noticed, too, that wooden boxes were placed strategically on the main deck to provide them cover should the imposters attempt a breach over the side.

As the first ladder hit the side of the ship, Solomon Brown grabbed a long pole with a brass hook on the end and pushed the ladder backward across the gangplank. An attacker, holding on to the top rung, fell backwards hitting his head on a two-ton iron pulley sitting on the deck – catching the remaining attackers completely by surprise.

Moments later, a grappling hook landed on the main deck and began slithering toward the starboard side railing of the ship. As soon as it caught, one of the attackers hauled himself up the rope and pulled himself on deck. Looking for a target, the negro attacker saw Jacob loading his rifle for a second shot. As the negro imposter pulled his pistol from his waist sash, Lorenzo grabbed his Bowie knife, jumped from the top of the main cabin and slashed the imposter between his neck and left shoulder. General Beauregard's men, standing inside the warehouse, could hear the attacker's excruciating screams loud and clear.

He was still screaming when Lorenzo lifted him up and threw him overboard into the murky water between the wharf and the side of the ship. The body sank with barely a hint of a ripple left behind. Solomon's friend was now reloading for Jacob. None of the attacking negros in the second wave made it to within thirty yards of the *John Jameson*.

After Lorenzo tossed the dead impostor overboard, the rest of the initial raiding party fled in fear. Lorenzo shouted to Jacob, "They're fleeing and are almost out of my range. Get your scope set for a good range. Get as many as you can." Unbeknownst to them, the imposters' flight took them directly into the line-of-sight of Jacob's Whitworth Sniper Rifle. As each came into view, Jacob shot them one-by-one, dropping each where they were on the dock. By this time, Jacob could see Beauregard's troops leaving the warehouse and heading toward the wharf. Beauregard motioned for them to catch the fleeing imposters and provide cover for the two wharves adjacent to Boyce's Wharf.

Sighting some attackers more than half way down the wharf, Lorenzo clambered up the main mast to a cross arm where he had a better angle on those still within his range. Within minutes three more men were killed and another seven lay on the wharf writhing in pain. Beauregard's troops quickly surrounded the fleeing survivors and took them inside the warehouse for a harsh impromptu interrogation.

After the skirmish, Jacob, Lorenzo, Solomon and his friend joined Lilly on the main deck to welcome Lilly's parents back from their long trip. Solomon's friend excused himself saying he had important work to do at a nearby wharf. After appropriate greetings, hugs all around and some small talk, the group left the ship together and proceeded down the wharf.

At the warehouse, Lucy joined the party. Everyone agreed to go to the Rutledge House Inn to freshen up and meet at eight thirty for a late supper. Lucy assured everyone that the Inn, even in these hard times, had enough food for a first-class welcome-home meal. She also assured them there were enough rooms for everyone, should the evening run too late to return to the Cooper Estate. Everyone agreed it was a wonderful idea and thanked Lucy for the offer. As they left the wharf, Solomon ran ahead and grabbed three "hacks" for the trip to the Inn.

After arriving at the Inn, Lucy spoke to the chef to arrange a proper meal to be served by 8:30 p.m. The group had gathered in the sitting area near the front desk to wait for her. When she returned, Lucy handed each person a small piece of paper with his or her room number scribbled on it. She reminded everyone to reconvene in the foyer before supper. Nearly all admitted they were somewhat tired and looking forward to a lengthy nap.

By eight-thirty everyone arrived in the foyer. Neither Jake nor Lilly looked as though they had taken a nap. Lucy and Lorenzo looked a bit more refreshed, except a closer look showed several twisted buttons on Lorenzo's uniform and an unbuttoned one. Lucy's dress was more than a bit wrinkled. The Coopers, a distinguished-looking couple, were extremely well dressed, showing themselves to be exactly what they were—proud members of the Charleston Aristocracy. After a quick drink in the bar and a few minutes of small talk, everyone regrouped outside in the covered eating area where Lucy had reserved a suitable table for the group near the hearth.

Once they had taken their seats, Elizabeth Cooper spoke first, asking, "Lilly, what have your father and I missed since our last trip home?"

"Thus far, I think we have been most fortunate, Mother. Since the beginning of the year, those damn Yankees have been trying to land troops on the outer islands. They hope to gain a foothold and attack our island forts and shore batteries from there. At least so far, we've succeeded in holding them off and driving them back to their ships. As we saw today, some of the troops on Yankee ships are colored, so we must prepare to deal with future infiltration attempts."

Lilly continued, "You know that New Orleans fell last spring. A very good friend was there at the time. She said Confederate troops and gunboats were dispatched up the Mississippi to stop a large flotilla, leaving only 3,000 troops and a few ironclads and steamboats to defend New Orleans. On April 24th, Admiral Farragut's forces attacked and secured both Fort Jackson and Fort St. Phillip. My friend said Farragut brought 15,000 soldiers with him and a large fleet of gunboats and mortar boats. New Orleans surrendered on the 29th. She said local residents cursed and cried when the Yankees took down the Stars and Bars and replaced it with 'Old Glory.'"

"Stories in southern newspapers were quick to point out the Yankee victory was extremely costly to the Confederacy," Lucy added.

"Yes, it was," said Lorenzo. "With the Yankees now controlling the Mississippi, they'll have an open 400-mile navigable highway north all the way to Vicksburg."

Jacob agreed, "This will mean the North will have more men, equipment and ammunition to divert east to fight us in the Wilderness Campaign between Washington and Richmond."

Lucy described other events that occurred while Lilly's parents were away in Europe. "Last December the Union Navy tried to block channels in the harbor by sinking old or captured ships in the channels used by blockade-runners to enter or exit Charleston harbor. The *Mercury* called this effort the "great stone fleet" since granite stones were placed inside the ships to make them heavy enough to sink."

The conversation paused while a waiter delivered their drinks to the table. Just as the waiter began placing glasses on the table, General Beauregard appeared, tipping his hat to the ladies and extending a warm handshake to the Coopers.

"Ray, Elizabeth. I certainly hope you had a pleasant and successful voyage." Putting his hands on Jacob and Lorenzo's shoulders, General Beauregard commented, "I'd like to thank these men for the courageous efforts they displayed in defending the *John Jameson*. Their shooting skills were absolutely remarkable."

Ray Cooper pulled a chair out for him. "General, please join us. We're all on the same side at this table."

"Thank you, Ray. These young men did a masterful job of holding off so many attackers. Had they not been with you, it's likely the *John Jameson* would have been burned to her water line or lying on the bottom. You were very fortunate. By the time we confronted them on the pier, nearly all had tossed away their pistols and raised their hands." General Beauregard then asked, "Did you get a chance to see that property you were talking about before you left?"

Ray answered, "We had a lovely trip and, yes, we did get a chance to see the property, but as you know, this was primarily a business trip. We spent nearly all of our time in England and Ireland."

Jacob was relieved that so little was said about the property in Marseille. This suggested to him that the Coopers were not yet ready to leave their estate in Charleston. It also suggested that Ray was not insensitive to the strong feelings Lilly and Jacob had for one another. In his own way, General Beauregard also showed respect for the Coopers and Lucy Rutledge by not questioning Ray any further about them leaving Charleston. Realizing that he might have appeared to be insensitive, General Beauregard spoke up, "I'm so sorry, I didn't mean to pry. I just wanted to take a few moments to express my sincere thanks to these two fine men sitting with you."

Looking directly at Jacob and Lorenzo, the General continued, "Men, your actions today showed me how courageous and fearless you are. It's obvious you have many skills greatly desired by those in command, not the least being that you're both superior marksmen. That you are in the company of two of the loveliest women in Charleston tells me you both also have excellent taste and probably know your way around the dance floor. Those skills can be especially useful for working the party circuit in this fine city. Jacob, I'd like you and Lorenzo to meet with me sometime very soon to discuss new roles for you while you're in Charleston."

Lilly said to the General, "Are you aware that both these fine young men are experienced wagon and barrel makers?"

Jacob quickly added, "Yes, Sir. Before the war, we made wagons for the government under contract."

"You've made my day, Gentlemen. When do you report back to the 51st?"

"We were told sometime in late October or early November, but first we have to return to Burke's Garden for about a month to help with the crops and take care of things related to our finances and slaves."

"So, you own some slaves?"

"Yes, Sir. We bought most of them right here at Ryan's Mart. That's how we know so much about Charleston. We've been coming here for more than 15 years."

"I'd like you to teach my men to build wagons strong enough to carry heavy ammunition and turrets out to the gun batteries on the islands that ring the harbor."

"You mean Sullivan's Island, Morris Island, James Island, et cetera?"

"Correct. We just finished building Battery Wagner last month. It was named after Lieutenant Colonel Thomas Wagner, First Regiment, South Carolina Artillery, killed in action at Fort Moultrie." General Beauregard continued, "If you can build strong wagons it would be a big help. You know how to make barrels as well?"

"Yes, Sir. The government wanted supply wagons capable of holding enough water to last two men two weeks. We made six barrels for each wagon. The government seemed quite satisfied."

"Men, I have another task a General wouldn't normally expect of a private. I'd like you to work the party circuit with Lilly and Lucy to see if you can ferret out any more spies like James Reynolds. Having Lilly or Lucy on your arm will provide excellent cover. Lilly told me how you handled that Reynolds fellow. Pinning that note to his lapel saying he was a spy was a nice touch." He paused dramatically, then quipped, "However, next time I'd rather you just find 'em and not kill 'em. It's too hard to interrogate a dead man."

Turning serious again, he went on, "I will write your Commander and General Lee to square it with them for you to stay in Charleston a while longer. I'll provide you with a copy of the letters before you head for Burke's Garden."

"Jacob, Lorenzo, some of our most powerful and wealthy citizens meet regularly to discuss how we can react to any number of possible events. I want you boys there at those meetings. You're both smart, loyal to the cause, and have a lot of common sense. I want people like you in those meetings. We'll discuss this all in greater depth when we meet again later, but for now, enjoy your supper and savor the company of these lovely women—they are absolutely stunning! Good night, everyone."

The timing of General Beauregard's exit was perfect. The biscuits arrived at the table with delicious assortments of jams, jellies, apple butter and honey just as he was leaving. A large salad dressed with vinegar and oil was placed next to the biscuits. Later, a main course of baked ham, beans and collard greens was served, and sweet tea and coffee were brought to the table.

Lucy continued the previous conversation that General Beauregard had interrupted. "In late January, the North dispatched a ship called the *Isaac P. Smith* up the Stono River. As the ship sailed up the river, a young Confederate Lieutenant rode up and down the shoreline alerting our batteries to prepare for action. The ship's lookouts did not spot the guns at Grimball Plantation, and the ship suffered terrible damage. Twenty-five Union soldiers aboard the ship perished and the rest were taken prisoner. The next morning the Confederate steamer *Sumter* towed her into Fort Pemberton."

Lilly wanted to discuss what happened in Charleston on January 30th, 1863. She said, "It was reported in the *Mercury* a wooden Union Steamer named the *Mercedita* was rammed by the Confederate Ironclad *Palmetto State* and severely damaged. There were also confrontations involving the *Mercedita* and *Keystone State*. Altogether the Union suffered forty-seven casualties. No injuries were suffered by the southern Ironclads."

"After the confrontations," she continued, "General Beauregard actually took both the French and Spanish Consuls out to the bar itself to attest that the U.S. government had abandoned their blockade. Beauregard pointed out to both Consuls that under international law, once a blockade was broken, a thirty-day grace period had to be observed before it could be reestablished. He must be a very smart man to know that much about international law."

Lucy interrupted, saying, "Let me tell them what happened after the sinking of the *Mercedita*. In February, one of our spies told General Beauregard that Washington had dispatched 10,000 troops to Hilton Head to assist in operations against Morris Island. The spy said he heard Major General Foster was to command the force."

"On April 5th, a Federal Squadron of gunboats assembled off the Charleston bar. Beauregard, being prudent, ordered noncombatants to leave the city. Instead of leaving, Charleston residents flocked to the battery, rooftops, church steeples or any place else offering a clear view of Charleston harbor. Two days later, on April 7th, Confederate Colonel Rhett at Fort Sumter telegraphed the city that an attack appeared imminent. As the ships entered the harbor, they came under what could only be described as continuous bombardment from Fort Sumter and the many shore batteries strategically located on the islands surrounding the harbor. At four-thirty DuPont signaled all monitors to withdraw."

Lucy paused a moment to look inside her purse, and continued, "Here it is—I have a summary of the battle the *Monitor* ran a few days after it happened.  It says that those who saw the Union vessel *Keokuk* reported it looked like a colander.  When examined, it was discovered she had been hit ninety times with nineteen shots either piercing the hull or hitting below the waterline. The article also says Union monitors fired one hundred fifty-four rounds with only thirty-four hitting their target."

"It goes on to say Confederate Land Batteries and Fort Sumter combined to fire a total of twenty-two hundred and nine rounds with five-hundred and twenty hitting the Union ships. The attack did not continue for a second day. A month later, two Dahlgren guns from the sunken *Keokuk* were recovered and remounted at Battery "B" on Fort Sumter. On July 3rd, DuPont was relieved of command and replaced by Rear Admiral John Dahlgren."

Ray Cooper asked if anyone knew exactly how the Union had captured New Orleans.  He had several friends who lived there at the time and wanted to know if it had been a bloody battle or a peaceful turnover of the city.

Lilly responded, "After the surrender, I read a reprint of a *New York Times* article in the *Mercury*.  I kept it to show you when you returned. I must have read the article fifty times. From what I read, it appears this is what happened after Admiral Farragut attacked and seized Forts Jackson and St. Phillip with fifteen thousand soldiers. A fleet of twenty-four gunboats and nineteen mortar boats supported him. This attack opened up the river for the Union ships to cut right through eight sinking ships. After evaluating the situation, Confederate General Mansfield Lovell concluded that further resistance would likely lead to an unacceptable level of casualties of his troops. Lovell evacuated his forces, and Yankee soldiers began arriving on the 25th. The North couldn't land all of their troops until both Fort Jackson and Fort St. Phillip were secured. The city of New Orleans finally surrendered on April 29, 1862."

# Chapter Thirteen

*Confederate Secret Service & Knights of the Golden Circle*

LILLY finished bringing everyone at the table up to date, then Lucy asked Jacob and Lorenzo about Gettysburg and what they thought Lee's next move might be.  For everyone present, Lee's defeat had been a bitter disappointment.  Until then, Lee and his Generals had successfully fought off nearly every Union attack south of the Mason-Dixon line.

Jacob responded first by saying, "The Union Army lost nearly as many officers and soldiers at Gettysburg as Lee did.  We may have lost at Gettysburg, but it showed the North that the South is still a formidable foe.  Personally, I have to admit the loss has seriously impacted my perception of the war. I've been hoping the sabotage and subversion efforts being fostered by the Knights of the Golden Circle, the KGC, in the northwest states will bear fruit.  If they do, it could force the Union to negotiate a peaceful conclusion to the war.  Any resolution that preserves our southern lifestyle and dignity—including our right to own slaves—would be a victory as far as I am concerned."

Ray asked Jacob, "Would you be willing to join the KGC if it would help the Confederacy?  I'm a member!  What do you say?"

"Yes, Sir, if it would help.  I suspect Lorenzo would be willing to join as well, but I can't speak for him."

"No, Jacob, I only want one of you to join. We often operate outside of channels, so I need one of you to remain outside the organization to help with our communications, operations, and supplies.  We might even need Lorenzo to provide us safe havens should the situation warrant it."

"By the way, Jacob, are you a Mason?"

"Yes, sir, my brother is, too.  So was our father.   He was pretty high up when he operated his wagon-making and carpentry business back in Wilmington."

"I suspect you already know the KGC is a secret society.  Most people who know about it understand its relationship to Freemasonry. The Knights of the Golden Circle was formed in 1854.  Most of its current members are

Confederate officers and soldiers, plantation owners and southern sympathizers.  We even have a few outsiders out west like Frank and Jesse James, Cole Younger and renegades from Quantrill's Raiders helping us secure funds for our operations. When General Pike was stationed in the West Indian Territory; he commanded three Indian Calvary Regiments. While there, he recruited several tribal leaders into Freemasonry.  It's been rumored he handed out Masonic degrees and early promotions for their support against the Yankees."

Ray continued, "Later this week, General Pike is expected here in Charleston to accompany us on our trip to Montreal to attend a preliminary strategy meeting involving the Confederate Secret Service, the KGC, the Sons of Liberty, the Copperheads and the Order of the American Knights. As a Mason, I'm sure you've heard of General Pike. Over the years, he's been a very prominent fixture in the Southern Jurisdiction of the Scottish Rite. Since the beginning of the war, he's pretty much been the only active member of the Southern Jurisdiction."

Looking a little overwhelmed, Jacob responded, "Mr. Cooper, you've certainly told us a great deal, and we're grateful you trust us with such sensitive information.  I'm assuming Lilly and Lucy already know what you've shared with us?"

"That is correct."

"Am I also correct in assuming there's a reason behind all this—is there something you want us to do for you?"

Ray chuckled, "Yes, you would be correct in making that assumption."

"What do you need us to do, sir?"

"Lilly's told me you are scheduled to return home in a few days to check in on your families and see to it they're doing well.  While there, I want you to get plenty of rest. I have very important missions awaiting you when you return."

Addressing the rest of the group, Ray added, "Since we're all tired, the details can wait until tomorrow.  I want General Beauregard to be present so I can fill him in as well.  As I'm sure you've observed, he's a very detail-oriented person, and sometimes victory lies in the details. That was certainly the case for him at Bull Run.  He might well be the reason we won that battle.  Normally, he would be accompanying us to the meeting, but as you know, Union troops are very active in their preparations to take Batteries Wagner and Greg on Morris Island."

Although he had not been asked, Jacob interjected his personal thoughts about the General. "Sir, General Beauregard is both a patriot and a man with a good heart—exceptional qualities for a second-generation

Frenchman."

"Touché, very perceptive, young man. He is indeed both."

Still chuckling at Jacob's comment, Ray stood and reminded everyone of the lateness of the hour. "After you finish your wine, it would be a good time to retire to your rooms for the evening. The 'missus' and I are looking forward to a long encounter with a soft feather bed. We need our sleep. Somehow, I fear your encounters with feather beds might involve more strenuous activities than a good night's sleep."

Lilly, now blushing, looked sternly at her father and said, "Daddy, you were on that ship too long. Your language—you sound like a drunken sailor. I know we are all adults here, but please, daddy, someone might hear."

With Ray in tow, Elizabeth proceeded to the double doors leaving the foyer. Looking back, she asked, "How about getting together in the morning for a late breakfast or early brunch?"

Lilly answered, "Mom, whatever you call it, I don't plan on starting anything tomorrow morning before eleven."

Laughing so hard he could hardly contain himself, Jacob blurted out a little louder than he intended, "Lilly, honey, I'm sure as hell we'll be starting something a lot earlier than eleven o'clock."

Now, nearly red as a beat, Lilly glared at Jacob, "I'm not saying another word about any starts or finishes, especially when we are preparing to go to bed."

By this time everyone caught on to Jacob and Lilly's private joke. Ray, now tipsy, laughed raucously, nearly dropping the wine bottle he held. Swinging the wine bottle precariously in a great arch, he announced, "Way

Figure 13. Lilly Cooper.

to go, Jacob. I vote we meet at noon."

They all headed for their rooms.  Before entering theirs, Lilly turned Jacob around to face her and whispered, "Jacob, I love you. I want to belong to you."  In response, Jacob kissed her soundly. Opening the door, he lifted her off her feet and carried her into the room. As she slid to her feet he kissed her again. He felt her tremble. Her legs wobbled—she could barely stand.  Jacob reached around her waist to unbutton her dress as Lilly removed his shirt and caressed his chest with her fingertips.  When all the buttons were undone, her dress was loose, Lilly removed the hoops and petticoats.  Jacob slipped her dress over her head.  The material fell back, revealing her face.  He kissed her again, his hands capturing her ample breasts.  He stroked them firmly until they began to swell, heightening his senses and hers.  When he kissed each one tenderly, she was overcome with desire for him.

As Lilly released the many buttons on Jacob's uniform trousers, she thought, *buttons, why so many to be unbuttoned.*  When she tried pulling off his boots she wondered why they were so tightly laced, making them difficult to remove. They finally came off, and she tossed them towards the fireplace. Once his clothing was removed, she pulled him to her, holding him close for a long moment before they abandoned themselves to a night of blissful fulfillment.

In the morning, after knocking repeatedly on the door, the maid opened the door to find Jacob and Lilly wearing nothing at all, intertwined, and lying across the top of the featherbed.

Not sure what to do, she went directly to Lucy's room to ask. She knocked, and Lucy answered, telling her in a muffled voice to step in quietly.  What the maid saw was a large lumpy quilt rolled up on the floor with what appeared to be bodies inside. She was unsure as to which end to approach first. Suddenly, Lucy stuck her head out of one end.  Barely coherent, she managed to mumble she needed a strong cup of hot coffee. The maid assured her she would bring a fresh pot, then told Lucy what she had encountered in Lilly's room.  She reminded Lucy the hour was approaching eleven, and she was not sure what to do.  Lucy instructed her not to return to Jacob and Lilly's room until a little closer to noon.

It was nearly a quarter past the noon hour when both couples appeared in the dining room.  Ray Cooper welcomed everyone, adding that he ordered lunch to be served family style. Fresh coffee was on the table and sweet tea would arrive soon. He relayed both General Beauregard's regrets for being unable to attend and his instructions to Jacob and Lorenzo that after their trip home to Burke's Garden, they must return to Charleston by September 1st. This would give them one more week with Lilly and Lucy before they had to catch a train and head home.

Jacob asked, "Ray, how firm is that date?"

"I'm sorry to say, Jacob, but that date is very firm. You and I need to be in Montreal for a high-level strategy meeting between the Sons of Liberty, the Copperheads, the Knights of the Golden Circle and the Confederate Secret Service by Thursday, September 10th. A lot of important people will be there. General Pike will be there for sure because he's going with us. I'm also pretty sure C.L. Van Landingham, who is the Grand Commander of the Sons of Liberty, and Jacob Thompson, the KGC's money-man, will be waiting for us in Montreal. Thompson has a pretty good resume for someone referred to as a 'money man.' He was formerly Secretary of the Interior for the United States and is now the Confederate Army's Inspector General. Some people I've talked to think he might be the real architect behind the Confederate Secret Service's operations being run out of Canada. I was told Jeff Davis personally gave Thompson $600,000 to help fund the Canadian operations."

All were listening attentively as Ray continued. "I also expect Clement Clay to show up if he can. Sometime in the past Jeff Davis gave him the title 'Commissioner of the North,' but I'll be damned if I know what that means. I suspect they're just good friends and he's taking care of him. Major Culpepper, Captains J. P. Holcombe and Thomas Henry Hines of the Secret Service are likely to be there, although I haven't heard from them in several weeks. I haven't heard whether someone from out west might show up either. Usually, when they come they bring us gold or silver taken from Union Army payroll trains or banks."

Turning to Jacob, he said, "Since Charleston is the South's premier shipping port, I'm sure the attendees expect some input from us on the status of the blockade and how we intend to keep shipping levels up for the foreseeable future."

"How will we get there?" Jacob asked.

"We're going to take the *John Jameson*. It has always served me well. Do you think you can develop an Irish accent? I want to place you on the manifest of the *John Jameson* as a member of Captain Davis' crew."

"With my dad being Scotch-Irish, I think I can have the accent down in no time."

"That's good. I have Dublin listed as the *John Jameson*'s home port on the International Sea Registry. When you and your brother return, I'll have papers drawn up showing you as Irish citizens. That way you won't get hassled by the authorities should you be detained for any reason."

Ray relaxed once he had covered everything. "One last thing. Over the next week, I want both of you young men to enjoy yourselves and to take good care of Lilly and Lucy. They're both very special to me. Now, be on your way. I'm sure I'll see you both before you leave for Burke's Garden." Then turning to Jacob, he asked, "May I have a short word with you."

"Yes, Sir."

"Your Knights of the Golden Circle initiation ceremony is scheduled for three days from now at 8 p.m."

"Yes, Sir. I'll be there. Good night, Sir."

By now everyone had finished their meal, the table had been cleared, and everyone else was returning to their rooms. Jacob saw Lilly turn into the hall leading to their room. He called out, "Wait up, dear!"

Smiling, Lilly answered, "Don't worry, honey, what I have in mind will take both of us."

Over the next few days, Jacob and Lorenzo spent most of their days helping Beauregard's troops fix wagons, load ammunition, and transport needed supplies to the forts and gun batteries on Morris and James Islands. They spent their evenings with Lilly and Lucy attending charity events and parties in the homes of Charleston's aristocracy. With recent defeats of the Union Navy vessels still on their minds, Charleston's richest and most powerful residents continued to party and pour even more money into the nearly depleted coffers of the Confederacy.

When the time came for Jacob's initiation into the Knights of the Golden Circle it was completed in less than one hour. Because of the urgency of the situation only eight people were in attendance: General Pike, General Beauregard, Ray and Elizabeth Cooper, Lilly, Lucy, Lorenzo and, of course, Jacob. This was the first time Jacob met General Pike. He was an imposing man who radiated energy—six feet tall and wide of girth with shoulder-length hair and a beard that nearly reached his waist. General Pike officiated at the ceremony, and only General Beauregard, Ray, Lorenzo and Jacob were allowed take part in and observe the most secret part. Afterwards, everyone adjourned to the Inn for a late supper.

After supper, Jacob and Lorenzo excused themselves and went to the bar near the dining room for a couple of Hennesseys and to contemplate all that had transpired since they arrived in Charleston. Both men grasped the reality that in two days they would be saying goodbye to Lilly and Lucy for several weeks. They would take a carriage from the Cooper estate to the railway staging area west of Charleston and catch the first available train heading west to Knoxville. There, they would catch a train heading north on the Tennessee and Virginia Railroad. They knew all trains using this route stopped to take on water and firewood at a side spur just outside Wytheville.

The following day, the two couples toured the city by carriage, taking in most of the interesting sites. They revisited the wharf where they spent a few moments speaking with General Beauregard. He wished them the very best and said that he was looking forward to their return to Charleston and subsequent sojourn to Montreal.

On another day, the two couples boarded a small paddle wheeler at the Ashley River docks and headed upstream toward the plantations dotting the west side of the river en route to Summerville. They disembarked at Magnolia Plantation, where the four of them spent the afternoon touring the lavish gardens. Occasionally in the more secluded areas of the grounds, one couple or the other embraced or exchanged a sensuous kiss.

After returning to Charleston, the two couples chased down a carriage and proceeded to the Charleston Hotel where they enjoyed a delicious evening meal and a bottle of imported Champaign. As they left the hotel, they grabbed another carriage and headed to the Cooper Estate for the remainder of the evening. For both couples, this would be the last night they would spend together before the men departed for Burke's Garden. Although neither Lilly nor Lucy spoke of it, the realization that Jacob and Lorenzo were returning home to their wives and children weighed heavy on their minds on this last night together. Both were determined to make it a memorable one.

The next morning the couples arose early and enjoyed a hearty breakfast. As Jacob and Lorenzo were climbing into their carriage, a militiaman approached and handed them copies of letters General Beauregard had sent to Colonel Wharton and General Lee. The driver then snapped the reins and the carriage began its journey west to Quarter House, where Jacob and Lorenzo kissed Lilly and Lucy and said their goodbyes.

From there the brothers traveled southeast by horseback until they reached a familiar military staging area, referred to as 'the split,' where trains heading to North Carolina and beyond veered north off the main lines. The main rail line ran west from Charleston to Memphis via Atlanta, Chattanooga, and Knoxville. Because of its outlying location away from the city, this particular staging area was often used by Army Commanders to keep troop movements secret, away from the prying eyes of Union spies hiding in and around Charleston.

When they arrived at the split, Jacob and Lorenzo spoke with other soldiers about how things had been going in the west.  One older soldier, leaning against his rifle, responded, "It's been hell.  I don't know if you've heard, but Vicksburg fell and that's a terrible blow for us."

Curious, Jacob asked the beleaguered soldier, "When did it fall?  I thought we had things tied up pretty well out west."

The soldier replied, "It fell the first week of the month—about the same time we were fighting in Gettysburg."

"I didn't know—I was in Gettysburg, and it was hell there, too."

"Where are your rations?" Jacob asked.

"What rations?  We were lucky to have bread and a little stew.  Some days there was just hardtack or beef jerky, and that's all.  Where you headed?"

"Southwestern Virginia.  We need to get home and check on our crops, or it's going to be a long hungry winter for our troops.  Have you seen or heard about any trains headed west?"

"There's one about 300 yards down the track leaving around noon, I think. It's headed for Knoxville, and from there it goes on to Memphis. Near Knoxville, you can head north on the Tennessee and Virginia Railroad through Bristol.  That's the route I'd take. There's too much fighting up north to head directly for Richmond."

Jacob replied, "Many thanks.  Where are you heading?"

"Home—and I'm not coming back.  When this war started, it was all about the southern lifestyle and state's rights. Those ideals have been replaced by the four Ds: disease, desertion, death, and defeat.  My unit lost more men to disease than bullets or artillery."

Lorenzo said, "I fully understand.  Keep safe, my brother. Thanks for the info on the trains."

# Chapter Fourteen

## *Return to Burke's Garden*

AFTER boarding an empty boxcar, Lorenzo lost no time in saying to Jacob as he looked him straight in the eye, "I've seen for myself how attached you are to Lilly, and it's obvious she has strong feelings for you." When Jacob groaned and looked away, Lorenzo shook his head and said, "I have to say something, and I'm going to say it whether you want to hear it or not."

The two settled down on sacks of grain on opposite sides of the boxcar, and Lorenzo continued, "Look, Jacob. We both have families waiting for us in Burke's Garden. Millie and Annie have been wonderful wives. Both deserve the very best we can give them." Before Jacob could interrupt, Lorenzo continued, "I know! I know I've been enjoying this time with Lucy a lot more than I should, and I do care a great deal for her. But this is just a fling for us. We've agreed to take things as they come and be grateful for what we've had. We both know we have no future together. But you, Jacob! I worry that you've let yourself get in way too deep. You need to remember that when this war is over you're going to return home to Annie for good. That's where you belong."

Looking down at his boots, Jacob replied, "That's easy for you to say, Rans. But I don't think you and Lucy have the same kind of relationship that Lilly and I have."

"That's what has me so worried! Have your fun, but just remember what's waiting for you at home."

"Don't forget I still have KGC responsibilities to fulfill," Jacob protested. "And Lilly's very involved in that."

"You're not a spy yet," Lorenzo growled, "and the people back home are counting on us. Get your head out of your ass and accept the fact that we're on our way home. I'm not going to tell you again!" Jacob got the message, leaned back and said nothing the rest of the day.

Two days later the train pulled up a hundred yards short of a switching station just outside Knoxville. The two jumped from the boxcar, stretched their legs and walked down the track toward the platform, where they hoped to find out from the locals how the war was going in Bristol and north in Tazewell, Wythe, and Bland counties. While waiting on the platform, they saw a train destined for Memphis pulling out farther down the line. No additional troops, ammunition or provisions for units had been put on. Knowing that Knoxville was a key hub in the Army's supply chain, they wondered if the Confederacy was abandoning their operations out west in the favor of troops still fighting in Tennessee, Virginia, North Carolina and Georgia. The locals they spoke to on the platform confirmed their suspicions that the Confederacy was abandoning their operations out west.

Forty-minutes later, a military supply train heading north stopped at the switching station to pick up two boxcars full of ammunition destined for the 51st Regiment near Princeton. The brothers climbed aboard hoping the train would have to stop at Wytheville to pick up firewood and water.

Although long, the trip north was nonetheless uneventful. Eventually, they saw a small sign indicating the refueling and water stop in Wytheville was just ahead. Jacob and Lorenzo grabbed their rucksacks and rifles and prepared to jump. As the train was stopping, they leapt from the boxcar, making sure their rucksacks cleared the half-open door. Once on the rough wooden platform, they hoped to find a ride to the livery stable where they would rent horses for the trip over Burke's Garden Mountain back into Burke's Garden.

While they were looking around, George Cox, the owner of the small general store in Burke's Garden, spotted them, "Well, I'll be darned if it ain't the Harris boys! Ya'll headed home?"

"Hey, George," Jake replied. "We sure are."

"I'm heading thatta way if you need a ride."

After such a long trip, the only words Jacob and Lorenzo could muster were, "Thanks, George, much obliged."

George replied, "You being in the army and all, just tell me where you want to go, and I'll take you there."

"How about taking us to our dad's place, George. We need a bath and something good to eat. We haven't had a civilized meal in days."

"Boys, the Harris place it is."

As the brothers climbed aboard his wagon, George said, "I come down to Wytheville whenever I hear a train from Bristol is scheduled to stop for wood and water. I order a lotta things from Knoxville, Lynchburg, Richmond or Bristol, ya know, so I need to check to see if any of its come in."

Then he chuckled, looking a bit sheepish, adding, "Besides, these trips give me an excuse to stop at the saloon for some real whiskey—and I like to check out the newest crop of whores that stay in them rooms above the dry goods store."

"Just check them out?" laughed Lorenzo.

"You bet!" George responded as they left the station.

Christina was first to hear Jacob and Lorenzo step up on the front porch. As only a mother would do, she ran to each of them and held both ever so tight. After releasing them, she said, "Jacob, Lorenzo, I have a special surprise for you."

"What kind of surprise?"

"There are some folks here I know will want to see you."

Christina barely finished the sentence when Mary and her daughter Janet appeared, stopping just inside the doorway. Janet was now even more beautiful than when they saw her naked at the pond. Mary was struggling to find the words to express her feelings after seeing Jacob and Lorenzo. Her eyes welled up, and tears cascaded down her cheeks. She ran to Jacob, embraced him and said, "We've all missed you both so very much."

Janet stayed just inside the door, smiling shyly at him. As Jacob entered the house, Mary approached him and whispered, "Janet knows, but we promised never to tell anyone."

Jacob nodded and said, "Thank you, Miss Mary. That's very kind of you."

Once inside, the brothers wanted to know where Millie and Annie were. Christina told Jacob that Annie, Millie and the younger children went to Jeffersonville to buy staples and farm supplies Jim needed. Jim had gone to Wytheville to send a telegraph message to Colonel Wharton regarding bullets, black powder and foodstuffs needed by the local Militia. She added that he would be back tomorrow. The older children were out back near the spring catching crawdads. She sent Janet to tell them their fathers were at the house waiting to see them.

Christina looked them both over thoroughly and chided them both, "You two look like starved rats."

"We haven't eaten much for three or four days, Mom. All we had was some hardtack and jerky."

Christina asked Mary, "Why don't you cook these boys some food? There's plenty to eat around here—they're going to need some energy when Annie and Millie get back with the kids."

A bit embarrassed by his mother's remark, Lorenzo grinned sheepishly, "Thanks, mom—you, too, Miss Mary."

Later in the day, Jacob saw the family's horse-drawn wagon slowly working its way up the long 200-yard slope to the house. Barely more than a rough, unimproved trail, navigating it was especially challenging for unskilled wagon drivers. As the wagon approached, Jacob came along side and took the reins from Annie's hands and led the horse to the rail in front of the house.  Once the horses were tied to the rail, Jacob pulled Annie from the wagon and kissed her warmly and held her in a long embrace. Lorenzo helped Millie from the wagon and held her in his arms until all the children had jumped off the back of the wagon. Once on the ground, Lorenzo's children surrounded him, each competing for the most attention. He grabbed each one lovingly and kissed each one on the cheek. Jacob reached in and lifted Susan, his youngest daughter, from the rear of the wagon, squeezing her in a big hug and kissing her on her forehead before setting her on the ground.

Once inside, Christina told her grandchildren that their parents would be spending the night in their own cabins. As a plausible explanation for this, Christina explained that Jacob and Lorenzo needed sleep after such a long trip, and it would be better if Millie and Annie were there to fix them a good breakfast in the morning. Some of the older children, who knew full well why their parents wanted to be alone, found it difficult to keep from laughing. Nonetheless, for the benefit of the little ones, they said nothing.

As each day went by, new reasons were found for the two couples to spend additional nights alone in their own cabins.  When Jacob enlisted in the Army, Millie and Annie had moved their things from their cabins into the Harris farmhouse.  It was now much larger, because Jim put his slaves to work adding on two large bedrooms for the kids and an additional dining room.

The couples spent their nights in moments of passion followed by interludes of rest and quiet. Jacob did as his brother asked.  He put aside all thoughts of Lilly and concentrated on how to best meet Annie's needs. Jacob was comforted knowing that Mary and Janet had kept their word about his youthful indiscretion. Annie never brought up his all too frequent trips to Charleston while he was courting her and through their first year of marriage.  Jacob was extremely relieved by Lorenzo's pact with him never to reveal anything that took place in Charleston, especially his membership in the Knights of the Golden Circle.  His part of the agreement was that he would never mention their reassignment to Charleston nor Lorenzo's romantic interest in Lucy Rutledge.

While they were in Burke's Garden, Jacob and Lorenzo helped Jim with chores, changing axles, replacing wheels on his buckboard and shoeing horses.  With the help of Tobias and Seth, they constructed a new hearth with a spit to roast meat and built a new springhouse near the house.

They also dug a new well nearer to the livestock. Shortly after digging the well, they discovered it, too, was fed by an underground spring. The new well and springhouse assured that cold, fresh water would always be available on the homestead even on the hottest or coldest days.

As the days passed, Jacob and Lorenzo's relationships with their wives and children grew closer than ever. Both spent quality time with their families, doing everything together, long walks, swimming, playing games indoors and outside, and enjoying leisurely picnics. During their stay, neighbors frequently asked about how the war was going for the South. The defeat at Gettysburg was of particular interest, and they were often pressed for details. The brothers tried to reassure their friends and neighbors there was still hope of an eventual victory or a possible negotiated settlement ending the fighting in spite of their loss. Jake and Lorenzo listened intently to each and every question. They knew it was important for them to learn how the people of Tazewell County felt about the war. After only a few weeks in Burke's Garden, the brothers concluded many residents were already thinking about ways the South could end the war.

Before long, they began thinking of how best to return to Charleston. Since the Tennessee and Virginia Railroad passed through Wytheville only three or four times a week, they had to find a way to check daily when the next train heading to Bristol would stop at the Wytheville refueling spur. A few days before they planned to leave, Jacob sent Edward Stump, a sixteen-year-old militiaman, to Wytheville to check on southbound trains scheduled to stop at the Wytheville refueling spur to pick up wood and water. Edward thanked him profusely for giving him this unique opportunity to serve the Confederacy. Before the boy left, Jacob reminded him to tell the sentry in the tower to relay the message to him at the Harris home.

As the time for departure approached, it was difficult for them to tell their wives they would be leaving soon. Annie and Millie agreed to move back into the Harris home after they left. Since the war began and unrest in the area increased, they were afraid a slave or two might decide to run away and feared someone might be hurt. The brothers agreed and told their wives they would start helping them move needed items from their cabins back into the Harris home the following morning.

The following morning, Christina answered a knock at her front door. The young militiaman standing on the front porch held a handwritten note in his hand and asked, "Is Jacob Harris available?"

"No, Son, I'm afraid he's not," Christina answered. "He stayed the night at his cabin on the other side of our homestead. Do you have a message for him? I'm his mother, and I'll see he gets it if you can leave it with me. We're expecting him later this afternoon."

The young boy replied, "Ma'am, I just learnt to read. I'd like to read the message to you if that's all right."

"By all means, young man, go ahead."

"Yes, Ma'am. It was signaled to me from the Wytheville train station early this morning. Here's what it says: *Jacob Harris – Harris Home – Burke's Garden Virginia – next southbound – Tennessee/Virginia stops Wytheville noon tomorrow.*"

"You read the message well, young man. Come in. I'll scare up breakfast for you. You're skinny as a rail. When was the last time you ate?

"I 'ain't had nothin' since ten yest'rday morning, Ma'am. Yesterday I was in the tower covering for my neighbor, its hard to git vittles of any kind or even a cup of coffee when you're up in the overlook. Occasionally a civilian will climb up the ladder and bring us food when they're crossing over Burke's Garden Mountain."

"Well, we can't have our young soldiers going hungry." She called out, "Miss Mary, get this poor boy something to eat."

A few minutes later, Miss Mary brought out a plate. "What would you like to drink, young man?"

"Do ya have any milk, Ma'am? I ain't had none in a long time."

Janet was the one who returned from the springhouse with a tall glass of milk filled to the top.

The boy's eyes grew wide, and he grinned broadly, "That's the most beautiful thing I've ev'a seen."

Mary pondered his reply for a moment and then laughingly asked, "Are you talking about the glass of milk or my lovely daughter?"

Recovering well, he said: "Ma'am, they're both right purty."

The young man pounced on the plate as though he had never seen so much food on a plate in his entire life. When he was finished, he wiped his mouth with the back of this hand and sighed. After thanking Mrs. Harris, Miss Mary, and Janet over and over, he said, "I've gotta get back to the tower real soon." As he started for the front door, Janet smiled and handed him a few sandwiches, apples and biscuits to share with his friends in the tower.

After receiving the message, Jacob and Lorenzo agreed to let the grandparents keep the children overnight so they could stay in their own cabins and share their last moments of intimacy with their wives. The next morning was difficult for both of them. They had to say goodbye to Millie and Annie and prepare for their return trip. Jim had Tobias accompany them to the Wytheville water and refueling stop so he could bring the horses back once Jacob and Lorenzo boarded the Knoxville-bound train.

The trip back to Charleston was uneventful except for a fistfight between two regiments at an Atlanta staging area. Apparently both regiments thought newly arrived stores of food and ammunition were destined for their regiment. After the fight broke up, the Commanders of both regiments decided to divvy up the supplies and proceed to their planned destinations. Once again, Jake and Rans noticed that the railroad cars were moving more and more troops toward the frontlines with less food and ammunition accompanying them.

They also noticed large numbers of soldiers wearing only partial uniforms. Many looked sick, listless, and apathetic. Clearly, the momentum built up by early Confederate victories had evaporated, and the South no longer had the upper hand in this war—not even in the South.

Figure 14. A Parrott Gun and crew on Morris Island.

# Chapter Fifteen

## *The Parrott Guns*

FOUR days after leaving the refueling stop at Wytheville, the brothers pulled into Charleston's main railway station.  From the platform, Jacob and Lorenzo looked around to see if Charleston had sustained any major damage. They noticed right away that several homes and businesses near the port were seriously damaged, presumably by cannon fire.  After scanning the immediate area for additional damage, they hired a hack and asked the driver to take them to 116 Broad Street. Before long, they realized nearly all the city south of Calhoun Street had been heavily shelled.  Their first concern was the Rutledge House Inn.  As the hack turned onto Broad Street, they could see it had been hit by high explosive shells or incenderaries.  The brothers wondered how much damage the Inn had sustained. *Were Lilly and Lucy there during the attack?  If so, were they hurt—and to what extent?*  Figuring it was just as likely that Lilly was staying with Lucy as vice versa, Jacob and Lorenzo asked the driver to stop in front of the Inn and wait for them.

As they climbed from the hack, they were relieved to see that only the upper right corner of the Inn was damaged—all the other rooms remained intact. Inside, the staff told them that Lilly and Lucy were okay, adding Lucy now resided at the Cooper Estate. Wasting little time, they returned to their waiting hack and directed the driver to take them to the Cooper Estate right away so they could surprise Lilly and Lucy.

On the way to the Cooper Estate, the brothers discussed how difficult the past month must have been for Charleston residents, especially those within range of the Union Parrott Gun on Morris Island.  Lorenzo was overjoyed that Lucy was no longer in range of the Union artillery. Jacob, too, was glad that the Cooper Estate and Lilly, were out of range as well.

Lilly was first to hear the hack pull in under the portico. Realizing Jacob and Lorenzo were in the hack, she and Lucy rushed out the front door and down the steps before the hack had even stopped.  With Jacob's arms around her, Lilly felt safer than she had in weeks.  Lucy felt the same after a warm embrace by Lorenzo. Once inside the front door, Lilly sent Abigale to heat enough bath water for both couples.

Lorenzo remarked, "It'll sure be great to get the soot from the train off my body — and even greater to put on a clean shirt and a fresh pair of pants."

Jacob agreed, adding, "I'm looking forward to a good meal and time alone with you, Lilly."

After a welcome session of lovemaking, a good meal, a warm bath and a change of clothes, the men decided it would be best if they took a carriage downtown and reported in to General Beauregard at his headquarters at the *James Simmons House.*

Lilly quickly spoke saying, "I've heard General Beauregard is in the process of moving his headquarters to the *Aiken-Rhett House* north of Calhoun Street. It is out of range of that nasty Parrott gun that recently unleashed devastation on Charleston. The gun, referred to as the *Swamp Angel* by Union gunners, damaged many large and crucial buildings in the southern part of the city. With almost all of the businesses, governmental buildings and residents of the old city moving north it was the only logical thing for him to do. General Beauregard said his new headquarters is larger and substantially more secure than the *Simmons House.* Its location makes it easier and safer for him to get reinforcements via the rail switching yard, located just west of town."

Lilly added, "You might want to ask around to confirm the General's whereabouts before going straight to the *James Simmons House.*"

## *General Beauregard Headquarters*

After confirming the General's location with a militia member patrolling the street near the Inn, Jacob and Lorenzo asked the driver to take them to the *James Simmons House* at 37 Meeting Street. It was a formal Georgian, with a center hall plan. Over time it had been significantly altered with the addition of a pair of projecting bays flanking and an ornate balcony. As they alighted from the carriage, a sentry standing at the front door immediately challenged them. Jacob spoke up, saying, "We were told by General Beauregard to report to him immediately after returning from southwestern Virginia."

"Remain here!" the sentry ordered. "I'll check your story, and if it's true I'll let you in."

Lorenzo replied sarcastically, "That's fine.  I'm sure we'll see you real soon."

Five minutes later, the sentry returned, opened the front door and told Jacob and Lorenzo General Beauregard was down the hall on the right in a large office he called his war room. As they entered, General Beauregard apologized for taking so long. He chuckled as he explained that the forward sentry sometimes took his job a little too seriously.

Figure 15. General P.G.T. Beauregard.

Taking the lead, Jacob said, "Sir, it's good to be back—but what happened?"

Looking straight into Jacob's eyes, Beauregard responded, "You are quite direct. Strangely, that's what I like best about you. People always know where you stand, and you don't mince words."

Lorenzo nodded emphatically in agreement. After pausing for just a moment, Beauregard continued, "Jacob, the Yanks have managed to put a Parrott gun on Morris Island, and it's close enough they can now lob artillery shells into the city, at least up as far as Calhoun Street. Thus far, they've managed to hit the city thirty-six times. That was over a three-day period. The first shells hit Charleston at 1:30 a.m. on the 22nd. That first night was absolute hell. Looking at the impact patterns, it appears they used St. Michael's Church as their primary aiming point. Do either of you have any idea how big a Parrott Gun is?"

"No, Sir," both brothers answered as one.

"Well, it weighs around 16,000 pounds and fires a 200-pound shell. The gun carriage alone weighs 4 tons. For a normal shell to reach Charleston, it would have to be fired from within a five-mile radius of the city. Somewhere out there—in all that mushy sand and mud—the Yankees managed to find a chunk of land stable enough to hold a platform that can support 24,000 pounds. One of our spies on Morris Island says the artillerymen call this particular Parrott Gun the *Swamp Angel.*"

Pacing with his hands behind his back, Beauregard continued, "General Gilmore sent me an unsigned dispatch demanding the immediate evacuation of Morris Island and Fort Sumter otherwise, within four hours, he would open fire on the city from a newly constructed firing position on Morris Island. Since I wasn't here when the dispatch arrived, it was returned to Union lines for verification. That night sixteen shells hit Charleston; ten were incendiaries. My cannoneers tell me incendiary shells contain something known as *Greek Fire*. It's a jelly-like substance that spreads fire wildly on contact." General Beauregard stopped, picked up a piece of paper, and then added, "Immediately, I sent General Gilmore a letter."

Holding a copy of the letter in front of him, he read: *It would appear, sir, that despairing of reducing these works (Batteries Greg and Wagner and Fort Sumter), you now resort to the novel measure of turning your guns against the old men, the women and children, and the hospitals of a sleeping city, an act of inexcusable barbarity.*

Looking up at both men, he added, "I concluded my letter this way: *I am taking measures to remove with utmost celerity, all non-combatants who are now fully aware of what they may expect at your hands.*"

Reaching for another piece of paper, he grasped it in his hand and shook it. "A few hours later, I received the following reply from General Gilmore:  I am led to believe that most of the women and children of Charleston have long-since been removed from the city, but, upon your assurance the city is still full of them, I shall suspend the bombardment until 11 p.m. tomorrow."

He tossed the paper on his desk, "Fortunately, Lilly, Lucy, and their parents had a place to go to escape the bombardment. The Cooper Estate is too far inland for the Union Artillery to reach in future attacks. A few days ago, I learned from a resident of Morris Island visiting the city that on the 23rd, a gunner notified his Lieutenant after firing nineteen shots that he could no longer prime the Parrott gun. Later, however, the gunner fired another seventeen shots before the *Swamp Angel* burst and threw the barrel off its gun carriage."

Jacob and Lorenzo listened intently as the General continued, still pacing back and forth. "After the shelling, the residents, as expected, were unsettled. Here are just some of the comments found in the *Mercury,* one of Charleston's local newspapers." He picked up a clipping from the paper and read: "Resident Frank Vizetelly described the barbarity of the shelling this way: *It was now that, foiled at all points and smarting under his failures, the Federal General was guilty of barbarity, which has disgraced him as a soldier. Unable to capture the forts, he intimated unless they surrendered, he would turn his powerful guns upon the city. The threat was disregarded; disobeyed; no doubt, in violation of warfare proprieties, he turned his guns on unoffending women and children.*"

Tossing down that paper and picking up another, the General read, "Another Charlestonian observed: *the poor class sought refuge on the race course and other open squares in the upper city out of range. Businesses moved north of Calhoun Street, and the children in the orphanages were moved to Orangeburg.*"

He tossed aside that paper as well and grabbed another, "Jacob Schirmer, a Charleston diarist, wrote: *Our prospects are darker and darker every day.*"

Shaking his head as though to clear it, he looked at Lorenzo and spoke in a calmer manner, "Lorenzo, for the foreseeable future I'm going to need you to help my men fix and load wagons and carry ammunition to our batteries on the islands surrounding the harbor. I also want you and Lucy to continue attending parties and fund-raisers to glean what information you can from Charleston's residents. It's important to understand the mood of the city now that Charlestonians have had their first taste of artillery fire near their homes, businesses, and restaurants. Whenever Jake is tied up elsewhere with Secret Service folks, I want you to attend local defensive planning group meetings in his stead. I believe you can add a sorely needed element of common sense to those meetings."

"Yes, Sir. I can do that," Lorenzo said.

"As you know, my new headquarters is located at the *Aiken-Rhett House* at 48 Elizabeth Street. The defense council meetings will be held there on an ad hoc basis. The *Aiken-Rhett House* is a large, two-story home with a stacked porch across the front. The upper porch is supported by eight standing columns. Even though it is an older home, it's quite beautiful with the space I need for my Headquarters. Needless to say, the proximity of my current Headquarters to the area being shelled made it necessary for me to relocate further north. Rans, I see you have a bandage on your left hand.  Is that the same bandage you had when you reported in to me from Burke's Garden?  If you need care, I can have my personal physician take a look at it. Just let me know."

"Thank you, sir.  I will," Lorenzo replied.

Turning to Jacob, he went on, "Jake, I want you helping Rans with those wagons until just a few days before we sail. I also want you and Lilly attending as many fund-raising events as possible and, if you can, ferret out more spies—like Mr. Reynolds.  Right now, our departure date for Montreal is Thursday, September 3rd.  Our trip to Montreal should take no more than a week or two. I know the amount of time may sound excessive, but I've asked Captain Davis to loop around and enter the St. Lawrence River from the northeast, as though we were coming in from Ireland or England.  After all, we're supposed to be transporting fine Irish whiskey from Dublin.

"Jake, I want you and Lilly to look your best for our meetings in Montreal.  Have Lilly take you into Charleston and buy you a new set of gentlemen's clothes. The rest you can buy in Montreal. I'm sure Lilly and her mother will think it a marvelous idea to go shopping in some of Montreal's finest boutiques where they feature new fashions from London and Paris. For now, I want you and Lorenzo to take a few days off and enjoy some time with your ladies."

Both Jake and Rans relaxed and smiled as the General continued, "After the break, we'll need to get to work and see if we can prevent the North from firing any more shells into the city. I'll inquire to see if our batteries need additional ammunition to keep Yankee gunboats at bay while we are restocking Batteries Wagner and Greg.  I know I'll be seeing you before the *John Jameson* sails. By the way, do you have the letters I gave you before you departed for Southwest Virginia?"

Jacob answered, "Yes, Sir.  After you gave them to us, we read them and put them back in our pockets. They're in our other clothes at the Cooper Estate."

"Be sure to bring them with you on our trip to Montreal. Should any Confederate forces inquire why you're not with your unit, show them the letters. They explain why you're here and not garrisoned with the 51st. If there are any other questions, they can telegraph me here at my headquarters for confirmation of your story. Should the Yankees ever capture you, the letters might well keep you from the gallows."

The two had listened attentively to the General without revealing the inner turmoil they were both feeling. Seeing a portion of the destruction that had already taken place in Charleston was disturbing, but hearing the details about the intense bombardments the city had experienced added another level of distress. Both found it hard to come to grips with the ongoing dangers facing the residents of the city, but their overwhelming concern was for the safety of Lilly and Lucy. They planned to make the most of the few days off the General had given them to spend with Lilly and Lucy when they returned to the Cooper estate.

***

When the brothers returned to the estate, Lilly and Lucy helped them out of their clothes and joined them for a nap. Afterwards, Lilly and Lucy got up first and slipped into their favorite colorful frocks. Once dressed, they combed their hair, applied some light rouge and splashed on some enticing perfume. When Jacob and Lorenzo finally awoke, they joined Lilly and Lucy for supper in the dining room. With the North now observing a voluntary cessation of shelling on Charleston, the question now arose as to whether the couples should become adventurous and take a carriage ride through the city or return to their bedrooms and engage in more amorous activities.

Over the next few days, Jacob met with Lilly's father each day to learn as much as he could about large sailing ships. After all, he didn't want to get swept overboard on his first voyage. Mr. Cooper took the time to explain the relationship of wind speed and direction to the placement of sails and how these factors affect the ship's overwater speed and direction. He also explained how, with sound knowledge and preplanning, it was possible to sail even a large clipper ship against the wind for long distances. Jacob was genuinely impressed.

### September 3, 1863

Miss Abigale and her sister Barbara arose early to prepare breakfast for everyone heading to Boyce's Wharf for their departure to Montreal. Remembering Lilly and Lucy's fondness for hot, buttered cornbread dipped in milk, Miss Barbara prepared a pan to supplement their breakfast and a second pan for them to take on the voyage. At 5:30 a.m., she called everyone to the breakfast table. Mr. Cooper offered up thanks for the meal and asked that today's journey be safe for all on board.

Figure 16.  Damage after the Shelling of Charleston.

# Chapter Sixteen

## *Voyage to Montreal*

AT 6:30 a.m., Solomon Brown arrived at the Cooper's Estate with a carriage to take Ray, Elizabeth, Jacob and Lilly to the Port of Charleston.  As planned, Ray met with Beauregard inside the militia warehouse at the inner end of Boyce's Wharf where several wharves protruded from a wooden boardwalk into the water. He wanted to get the latest intelligence on the location of Union ironclads and gunships visible from observation posts on the outer islands. While they were talking, General Pike and Captain Davis joined in the discussion.  Both Generals were a bit disheveled, looking as though they had come from an overnight card game where far too much alcohol had been consumed.

During the discussion, General Beauregard told the group, "I received a dispatch from General Shelby saying he has not yet returned from his raid in Missouri.  According to the dispatch, his return date is uncertain.  He sends his regrets, but indicated he would sent a member of his Regiment to Montreal in his stead."

Turning to Ray, he said, "I am unaware of any Naval Order of Battle changes from yesterday." He paused then smiled broadly at Ray and Captain Davis, "I see you've brought along Captain Davis to skipper the *John Jameson*. He's the finest Skipper on the high seas.  You are most fortunate to have him."

Becoming serious again, the General continued, "Once past the blockade patrol area, I recommend you circle north and stay out of sight. Those three tall masts, large square sails and multiple jibs make the *John Jameson* easy to spot. I'd make sure I was out several hours before starting a sweeping turn to the left."

Jake asked, "General?"

"Yes, Jake"

"How did you learn so much about ships?"

"Son, when you're from New Orleans, you have to know something about ships."

As Ray, Elizabeth, Jacob, Lilly and General Pike turned to leave, they saw Beauregard's troops waiting to escort them to the ship.

"I'll be waiting for you when you return," Beauregard said. Then, looking at the *John Jameson*'s tall masts, extensive rigging and stretched jibs lines, he commented. "She just has to be one of the most magnificent clippers I have ever seen."

Hearing Beauregard's comment, Ray added, "General, at full sail, she might just be the fastest. She might even be faster than the *Flying Cloud*. The *Cloud* was built back in '54. I understand she's still sailing the tea routes from England to China and back. The *John Jameson* is much newer and her hull design is sleeker making for less resistance as she cuts through the water."

As the party began their walk down the wharf, Beauregard's troops grabbed their bags, carried them up the gangplank and then took them inside their cabins. Once the party returned to the main deck, they walked to the side rail and waved a fond "farewell" to Lorenzo, Lucy, and General Beauregard. After the deckhands untied the ship's tie down lines, Captain Davis let the *John Jameson* drift slowly away from her mooring.

Lorenzo then asked General Beauregard. "General, do you need anything else?"

"Let's have lunch around noon, Lorenzo. We need to discuss recent Union troop movements in and around Batteries Greg and Wagner on Morris Island."

***

Before boarding the ship, Ray had received the latest intelligence from General Beauregard on the two blockade squadrons patrolling off the coast. Yesterday's report had been quite good. No gunships, ironsides or monitors were visible from any Confederate lookout-posts on Sullivan, James or Morris Islands. One report from a Confederate spy in Port Royal did mention seeing several Union ironsides and gunships gathering in Port Royal Sound near Beaufort. General Beauregard suggested this might be an early indication the Union Navy might be preparing to support future attacks on Morris Island and Fort Sumter.

Once adrift, the passengers heard Captain Davis give his Boatswain the following order,

"Jack, heave a line to the *Blue Ridge* and tell everyone onboard to prepare for a rear tow."

After the *John Jameson* cleared the wharf, Davis ordered his Boatswain to have his seaman standing starboard to throw a line to the tug *Blue Ridge* and prepare for a 180-degree counter-clockwise turn. After the turn was complete, the *John Jameson*'s bow pointed toward the center of the harbor. The *Blue Ridge* came alongside and towed the *John Jameson* to within 500 yards of the Fort Sumter channel. After casting off all her lines, the tug made a complete circle, pulling up next to the *John Jameson* on its starboard side. The tug's skipper shouted, "Captain Davis, are conditions favorable for your ship to proceed under its own power?"

Captain Davis acknowledged, saying, "Conditions are indeed favorable to proceed." As the *Blue Ridge* veered away, he gave his Boatswain the following order: "Hoist all sails, jibs first."

The Boatswain acknowledged, "Aye, Sir," and shouted, "Men, raise in sequence all sails, jibs first." When the ship cleared the main channel, it was already under full sail heading southeast toward the harbor's exit at eleven knots. After exiting the harbor, Davis gave the order to set a new course north by northeast and put some distance between the *John Jameson* and the northern blockade squadron's patrol area.

Once beyond the patrol area, Captain Davis asked, "Mr. Cooper, are there any further instructions, sir?"

"Yes, Captain, once we're well beyond the same latitude as the St. Lawrence River, I want you to turn the ship left and approach the river entrance from the northeast. This will make it appear we are coming from England or Ireland. I don't want anyone to get the idea this ship is coming from a Confederate port. This will help us maintain our cover as a whiskey transporter out of Dublin."

Ray then added, "Upon arrival, I'll need you to check on hotel reservations for Mrs. Cooper and myself at the Hostellerie Pierre du Calvet. Its timbered ceilings, huge chimneys and large stone walls give it a downright rustic appearance. It's located at 405 Bonsecours Street, across the street from King Edward's Quay. You'll also need to get a room for Jacob and Lilly as well—preferably one close to a large bath tub."

Lilly found little humor in her father's comment about a large tub. Captain Davis, on the other hand, thought it hilarious. Captain Davis avoided looking at Lilly as he responded: "Aye, Sir. Will there be anything else?"

"Yes, Joe, get rooms for the rest of the party at the St. Lawrence Hall Hotel. This hotel is the most magnificent hotel in Montreal. There's no portico on the outside but a doorman is always on duty to escort guests from their hacks and carriages to the front door. Inside it's quite ornate and beautiful, and the lobby has an excellent bar and sitting area with long hanging drapes that enhance its beauty. It's located at the intersection of Great Street, James Street and Saint Francis Xavier. General Pike will be staying with his longtime friend, South Carolina State Senator William Bell, who lives just outside Montreal."

"Although the St. Lawrence is a marvelous hotel, be careful. Since the beginning of the war it's become a hothouse of international intrigue unmatched in Montreal's history. The Union has spies everywhere in the city but more can be found in the St. Lawrence Hall Hotel than anywhere else in the Montreal. Be sure to tell your men the St. Lawrence has been the birthplace of many intelligence operations being undertaken at this very moment by the Confederate Secret Service. Remember, it's important to keep our presence here in Montreal completely quiet.

Ray then spoke, "That's why my family and I are staying at the Hostellerie Pierre du Calvet. It seems like everyone in Canada knows the Confederate Secret Service is running operations out of the St. Lawrence. It's the worst kept secret of the war. Let's hope the operations we run out of the Queens Hotel in Toronto are not so widely known."

Turning to Jacob, he said, "Jake, as our newest player in all this, I want you to go over the paperwork I gave you establishing your new identity as Ian Jameson. Since Lilly will often be accompanying you, it is imperative you appear to be Ian Jameson, nephew of *John Jameson*, owner of Jameson's Irish Whiskey. Lilly will be travelling as your fiancé, Madam Marie Theresa De Conti; a student at the Sorbonne, who is observing first hand the influences of French culture on Montreal and Quebec. Be sure to carry your papers with you at all times. I don't want anyone arrested by local authorities or captured by Yankee spies or infiltrators."

"Ray, what happened to the idea you wanted me to have papers showing me as a member of your crew?"

"Initially, I thought identifying you as a member of my crew was best. However, when the Jameson family and the Mayor of Dublin offered to provide cover papers for both you and Lilly, it was just too good to turn down. The real Ian Jameson and Princess De Conti are on an extended honeymoon in Constantinople. At present, their plan is to continue their holiday for an additional six months in Cairo and Rome."

# Chapter Seventeen

### *Attack at Battery Wagner*

WHEN Lorenzo could no longer see the *John Jameson*, he returned to Beauregard's Headquarters, identified himself and asked the sentry standing outside if the General was available. The sentry replied, "The General is expecting you, but would like you to wait here for him." Minutes later, General Beauregard stepped outside and greeted him. After checking his pocket watch, he asked for his carriage. Beauregard and Lorenzo stepped inside when it arrived for the ten-minute ride to the Rutledge House Inn. After being seated, Beauregard told Lorenzo he would like to continue the conversation they began earlier in the day—and that the information they discussed was to be kept in strict confidence.

Lorenzo replied, "Yes Sir, I'm a good listener and not so good a talker."

Beauregard began by asking, "Rans…is it alright if I call you Rans?"

"Yes, Sir."

"How did you come up with that name?"

"Sir, I got that nickname because some of my little brothers and sisters had difficulty saying Lorenzo. Also, when I enlisted, everybody in the 51st seemed to have a nickname shorter than his given name. 'Rans' just seemed a whole lot easier to say than Lorenzo."

"Rans, our intelligence personnel just received a communiqué from a well-placed spy on the other side of the Potomac saying Lincoln has promised General Gilmore an additional 10,000 troops to capture Confederate shore batteries at Batteries Greg and Wagner. I'm quite certain Fort Sumter will be targeted as well. I'm going to need your help in training my troops to build new wagons and reinforce those we now have. We'll need them to carry ammunition and powder to outlying batteries surrounding the harbor. Should the Union troops have unexpected success on Morris Island, I want you to help my Militia defend their positions until we can evacuate. Your sharpshooting skills could prove to be invaluable.

Rans did not much like what he was hearing about the possible evacuation of Morris Island.  He knew well what abandoning the batteries on Morris Island would mean regarding Lilly and Lucy's safety. Evacuating Morris Island would give the Union additional gun emplacements at Batteries Greg and Wagner from which to fire even heavier artillery at Charleston and Fort Sumter.  Even so, Rans had a considerable amount of respect for General Beauregard's abilities. He knew General Beauregard would make the right decision regarding any evacuation Morris Island. Beauregard was highly thought of in Charleston and many Charlestonians thought him the smartest General in the Confederacy. He entered West Point at the age of sixteen and graduated second in his class at the age of twenty as an engineer. He ordered the shelling of Fort Sumter and was instrumental in the South's first ground victory at Bull Run. Before assuming command of the Charleston Defense Force, he also fought at Shiloh and Corinth.

The ghastly expression on Rans' face revealed to the General the grave concern he had for Lilly and Lucy's safety.  Understanding from that look on Lorenzo's face that he was upset with the possibility of an evacuation, General Beauregard quickly changed the subject, "Rans, I couldn't help notice that your left hand is still bandaged.  Did that happen while you were home?"

"No, Sir, It happened back at Fort Donaldson. When the Fort was overrun, I was captured after taking shrapnel in my left hand, wrist and ankle. While the Yanks held me, I managed to convince them I was left handed and no longer much of a threat. It must have worked because a few days later they included me in a swap for a like number of wounded Union soldiers.  Every so often a piece works its way to the surface and bleeds like the devil. "

"Sounds like you used your head."

"I tried to, sir."

"If your hand flares up again, let me know. I'll send you up to Chimborazo Hospital in Richmond—it's the best hospital on either side and you'll get the care you need. In the meantime, I'll have my personal surgeon take a look at it."

Returning to the previous topic, he continued, "Later this afternoon, I am going to meet with my Generals and Chief Engineers to discuss the status of the gun batteries on the outer islands. Afterwards, I would be most appreciative if you and Lucy would join me for dinner."

"Lucy and I would be honored, General. What time should we pick you up, sir?"

"How about seven?  That should allow you sufficient time to spend the rest of the afternoon with Lucy."

"We'll see you at seven, sir."

At 2 p.m., General Beauregard entered his War Room.  His generals and Chief Engineer had already pulled the area maps and began annotating them with the most recent Ground and Naval Order of Battle.  Beauregard told the invitees he had only five questions for them to answer. Hearing this, his Generals put away their pens, battle maps and "overnight" intelligence reports and returned to their seats. Before continuing, Beauregard took out one of his choice cigars, lit it up and took a seat in his favorite leather chair at the end of a large oak table. He then explained that the answers to the following five questions should give him enough information for him to make up his mind on the best tactics for defending the gun batteries on Morris Island.  Looking at those gathered around the table, Beauregard removed a paper from his vest pocket and read his first question, "How long can Battery Wagner be held without regard for the safety of the garrison?

His second question was, "How long can each battery be held with a fair prospect of saving its garrison?"

Then he asked his third question, "How long, after the loss or evacuation of Battery Wagner, can Battery Greg be held?"

Beauregard followed with his fourth question, "Can the heavy guns at Batteries Wagner and Greg be removed prior to evacuation without endangering the garrisons?"

He then asked his last question, "By landing three thousand men on Morris Island, can we mount an offense and attack the enemy?"

Beauregard told his Generals, Chief Engineer and others in attendance to discuss the questions among themselves and get back with him the following morning. After his subordinates departed the War Room, the General put out his second cigar, walked to his desk and drafted an order to prepare for the simultaneous evacuation of Batteries Greg and Wagner. If tomorrow's news was bad, he would sign the order and urgently dispatch it to the Battery Commanders on Morris Island.

Beauregard retired to his library, took a bottle of 1861 Chateau Lafitte from his wine-cabinet, poured himself a glass and sat down in his favorite leather chair. After placing the glass on a side table, he pulled out one of his better cigars, clipped the end and began a series of slow steady puffs.

* * *

When Lorenzo and Lucy arrived at Beauregard's Headquarters, the sentry, recognizing Lorenzo from earlier visits directed them to the library.

"Thanks soldier," Lorenzo said.

As Lucy and Lorenzo approached the open library door, they saw General Beauregard in his favorite chair with a crushed cigar butt on the floor and an almost empty wine glass sitting on a nearby mahogany table

Looking at Lorenzo, Lucy said, "Honey, I think you should let me take care of this."  She walked over to the General's chair, tapped him lightly on the shoulder, and ever so softly asked, "General, where would like to go for dinner?"

Sheepishly looking up at Lucy, Beauregard shook his head and blinked his eyes before responding, "I was just thinking about tomorrow when a nap came along and grabbed me. Let's just keep this between ourselves if that's alright."

"Yes General, I wouldn't have it any other way."

Beauregard then asked, "Is the Inn still open and operating?"

"Yes, Sir, it sure is, and even if it wasn't, we could still go there and have a nice supper.  As you know, I am on very good terms with the owners. Rans and I have a carriage outside waiting to take us there."

***

After seating the two men in the Inn's dining room, Lucy went to the kitchen and instructed the wait-staff to start the meal off with a nice Bordeaux, preferably an import or one shipped in from New Orleans before it fell.  She was well aware that shortly before the port's surrender, an employee of the Rutledge Chandlery in New Orleans purchased a significant amount of wine for the Inn. The wine was brought in from New Orleans on one of Mr. Cooper's clippers returning from Europe to Charleston via New Orleans. Whenever a genuine French Bordeaux was unavailable, the Inn substituted a bottle from New Orleans for one imported from France.

After Lorenzo, Lucy and General Beauregard worked their way through the first half of the bottle, the waitress brought their meal to the table and asked, "Will there be anything else?"

Leaning in her direction, General Beauregard smiled mischievously and asked, "A little later could you bring another Bordeaux to the table."

"Of course, General."

Looking at Lorenzo, Beauregard said, "Rans, after you left this morning, I asked my Generals a few questions I need answered before I can make any further decisions regarding gun batteries at Greg and Battery Wagner. I then told them I would need their answers by tomorrow morning. I want you to be present at nine a.m. when they give me their responses."

"That would be fine, General. After supper, Lucy and I plan on staying the night here at the Inn. That way, we can take breakfast here and either walk or take a carriage to your Headquarters. Lucy says the Inn has an extra room should you like to stay. For you, General, there would be no charge."

"Lucy, I would be pleased to accept your offer. The privacy of the Inn would give me a chance to consider some of the alternatives I expect the Generals to place before me tomorrow."

By the end of his meal, Beauregard had already finished his fourth glass of wine. As he tried to stand, the General found himself a little unsteady and asked Lucy and Lorenzo if they could help him up. They grabbed him by his arms and lifted him up out of his chair. Once his feet were firmly on the ground, Lucy and Lorenzo ushered him down the hallway to a room Lucy had already made up for him. After placing him in his bed, she and Lorenzo helped him remove his boots, saber, uniform jacket and pants. They laid him back onto the bed and covered him with a light continental quilt. A little later, Lucy looked in on him and found him sleeping comfortably.

Once inside their own room, Lucy pried off Lorenzo's boots and began unbuttoning his shirt. After a lengthy kiss, Lorenzo helped Lucy unlace her high-top shoes and the back of her tightly laced dress. Each then removed the rest of their clothing and crawled into bed under a featherbed comforter.

Lucy whispered to Lorenzo, "I instructed the staff to make sure a warm bath and a good breakfast awaits us when we arise in the morning. That means we have the rest of the night to fulfill our every desire without any distractions."

***

The next day, Friday, September 4th, the Generals entered the War Room ten minutes before nine. Some, those who had travelled to Morris Island and back, looked bedraggled from lack of sleep. Others wore clean uniforms with shiny insignia and highly polished boots. The news was not good. Union Forces were now almost close enough to Battery Wagner to launch their third assault. It was now clear that by tomorrow the North would be able to attack if so ordered.

Earlier this morning, several small bits of paper were delivered to General Beauregard in his War Room. A local fisherman found the pieces while dragging his nets just outside the harbor's entrance. In the net, the fisherman found what appeared to be a torn up copy of Union Special

Order 513 calling for an assault on Battery Wagner at nine a.m. on the September 7th, just three days away.  Edward W. Smith, Assistant Adjutant to General Gilmore had signed and distributed the order. According to the Special Order, the assault was to be in three waves. The first wave was to come from the seafront, the second from the beach and the last was to follow the second, ending with the deployment of Union troops between Batteries Greg and Wagner. Once he read the Special Order, Beauregard knew the answers to his five questions were no longer relevant or necessary.

Once everyone was seated, General Beauregard advised those present that recent intelligence makes it necessary for them to prepare for an expeditious evacuation of all Confederate forces on Morris Island. He asked them to coordinate with Lorenzo should they need help in moving troops or supplies before the evacuation. Then he asked Lorenzo to meet him at the Inn at noon on Saturday to discuss his role in the evacuation that would begin on Sunday, September 6th.  Beauregard instructed his Generals, "Gentlemen, I will need, by tomorrow, an accurate estimate of how many men will be required to evacuate all our forces from Morris Island. It is imperative our boys be off Morris Island no later than 3 a.m. on the 7th."

What General Beauregard did not tell his subordinates was that he already knew Union forces had orders to attack Battery Wagner at 9 a.m. on the 7th.

After dismissing those present, General Beauregard had Lorenzo meet with his militia commanders to determine the number of men required to remove all guns, gun carriages and powder from the Batteries Wagner and Greg and carry them off the Island. He whispered to Lorenzo, "I'm going to need those figures by tomorrow morning."

Changing the subject slightly, Beauregard added, "Make sure you leave sufficient ammunition for our rear guard in case they have to defend themselves during the evacuation. Should things not go as planned, you might think about being ready to fight if our forces become engaged or bogged down during the operation."

Rans interjected, "General, I would think the rear guard would be comprised of ten or fifteen men each at Batteries Greg and Wagner.  Since this is to be a quick withdrawal, I suspect each man should have enough powder and ammunition for five or six shots.  Regarding your question as to how many men and boats would be needed for the evacuation, I would say 4,000 men and around 900 boats. We currently have two ironclads in the harbor, two clippers tied up at wharves and six steamers at the Ashley docks we can use. The rest of the flotilla will be made up of small fishing boats and barges now used to move cargo to and from Fort Sumter. I'm pretty sure we have enough boats and men to accomplish the mission. Spies on Morris Island say the Yanks have somewhere between 1500 and 2000 men already on the island positioned to attack Battery Wagner. I think we should go with as many boats as we can in case residents of the island want to return to Charleston with us. I'll try to have better numbers by the time you meet with your militia commanders.

On the morning of the 5th, Rans met with the militia commanders at Beauregard's Headquarters. By the end of the day he had calculated the numbers of men needed to evacuate troops, remove guns from their carriages and carry the guns, their carriages and ammunition from the batteries on Morris Island to the coast. It was important this mission be accomplished in such a way the safety of the men removing the guns, carriages and ammunition would be insured. Rans also advised the commanders of just how many rifles, bullets, black powder, etc., he thought the rear guard would need to cover their withdrawal, as well as how many boats would be needed for the evacuation of personnel.

Rans took a few moments to review the most recent sketches of Ground Order of Battle provided by the militia. Once the locations were identified, Beauregard asked his engineers to select the best possible route for getting his troops from the gun batteries to the shoreline. The militia also provided him with the most recent tide and current information in the harbor between the port and Morris Island. After reviewing the information, Lorenzo reported his findings to General Beauregard and asked if he would need him further.

"Rans, you have done quite enough. Why don't you take some time to share company with Lucy. Tomorrow, after breakfast, I want you to report in here to get the latest on just what the Yankees are up to on Morris Island. After that, I suspect the Generals will need your help loading the nine hundred or so troops needed to evacuate our forces. Those poor souls on Morris Island have held those batteries now for nearly two months. It's time to bring them home. Now, get plenty of rest, and I'll see you on the wharf around 3 p.m. That should give us enough time to muster, get the boats ready and load up enough guns and ammunition to protect ourselves during the evacuation. You're dismissed."

## *The Cooper Estate*

Lucy was already up splashing her face with some cool spring water when Lorenzo awoke early the next morning. She walked into the kitchen, where Abigale was kneading some fresh biscuits for breakfast. Lucy asked, "Miss Abigale, would you like some help this morning? I can put on some French coffee and fix a few eggs to go with those luscious looking biscuits."

Initially, Abigale was going to decline Lucy's offer. However, after remembering Lilly's comments about Lucy's experience in the Inn's kitchen, she said, "Yes ma'am, I would be most appreciative."

When Lorenzo walked in, he was still in his summer underwear. Lucy, seeing him this way shouted, "Lorenzo!  The Coopers absence doesn't give you the right to walk around in your underwear outside the bedroom." Hearing Lucy's comment, Abigale laughed quietly under her breath.

Lucy demanded, "Miss Abigale, what's so funny?"

"Ma'am, you and Lorenzo are acting just like Miss Lilly and Mr. Jacob. When Lilly's parents were away in Europe, sometimes they would walk around for days with almost nothing on.  Whenever I mentioned it, all they would say was 'it's hot.'"

Later, after Lucy and Lorenzo had gotten dressed, they headed straight for the dining room where Abigale had set a proper table for a late breakfast of fresh ham slices with fried mush on the side. In the center of the table was a mouthwatering plate of buttermilk biscuits with strawberry marmalade and blackberry jam. The appetizing aroma of baked apples filled the room.

When they finished, Lucy asked Abigale, "Would you mind preparing a warm bath for Lorenzo and me? We're going to take a short nap, and it would be nice to freshen up a little before lunch. General Beauregard's asked Lorenzo to meet him at the wharf at two p.m. so there's no great hurry. Would it be a problem to have the warm water by let's say 10 a.m.?"

"Miss Lucy, no problem Ma'am, I might even have it done by nine."

"Miss Abigale."

"Yes, Miss Lucy."

"9 o'clock might not give us enough time."

"Oh my, I understand. Ten it will be. Enjoy your nap."

***

At one p.m. Lorenzo kissed Lucy goodbye and took a carriage to downtown Charleston. At two p.m. he met with General Beauregard. After exchanging pleasantries, General Beauregard showed him a dispatch he had received earlier in the day from Colonel L.M. Keith, Commander of Battery Wagner.  The dispatch was marked "Urgent."

*The whole Fort (Wagner) is weakened. A repetition to-morrow of today's firing will make the Fort almost a ruin. The*

*(Union) Mortar fire is still very heavy and fatal, and no impor-
tant work can be done.  It is desirable to sacrifice the garrison?*

After reading the dispatch, Rans asked General Beauregard, "Are you going to order Colonel Keith to hold the garrison?"

"No Rans, it's too late. The message said *there is no important work that can be done.* I take that to mean things are hopeless and they are sitting ducks for another attack. Those men have fought valiantly for nearly two months.  It's time to get them out of there. We need to get everything, troops and all off the island as soon as possible."

At nine p.m., Confederates soldiers began assembling their weapons and ammunition at the wharves in preparation for their complete evacuation of Morris Island. A large flotilla of many different kinds of boats began to arrive to take the waiting soldiers to one of two destinations on Morris Island. Most of the troops were to land on the east side of the island just south of Battery Wagner.  A smaller contingent would land on the north tip of the island near Cummings Point.  These troops would evacuate Battery Greg.  A rear-guard of thirty men commanded by Captain T.A. Huguenin maintained watch as the troops left by boat. Captain Huguenin's troops split into two groups, each boarding the last ship destined for a specific location. As General Beauregard looked on, the 900 boats quietly crossed the harbor in the direction of Morris Island.

During the evacuation, Rans rode in one of the rescue skiffs to help load troops for the return trip. The skiff was wide and shallow and the perfect boat to rescue soldiers or seamen who by necessity had to abandon their own ship. Rans' docking point was the beach one eighth of a mile north of Battery Wagner. Rans waited with the boat during the actual evacuation. He knew from the skiff he could provide suppression fire when the soldiers returned with their gear and weapons to enter the boat. After half of the soldiers had boarded the boat, Rans saw a large Union barge approaching at a much higher than normal speed. The barges intent was clear...it wanted to ram Rans' boat. Noticing armed troops aboard, Rans shouted for the Confederate troops already onboard to push the boat away from the dock and start loading their rifles. Rans grabbed his already loaded rifle, and started shooting at the troops on the barge. He saw four crumple on the deck and two others fell overboard. Once the Confederate troops onboard located their weapons and began firing, the Union soldiers on the barge quickly lost their appetite for a fight and gave up their pursuit. The 4,000 Confederate troops completed the evacuation by 1:30 a.m. During the evacuation, only two boats with forty-seven men aboard were captured by armed Union barges deployed between Fort Sumter and

Cumming's Point. It was nearly three a.m. before the evacuated troops and civilians returned to the wharves. It had been a long and difficult night. After a quick muster, General Beauregard released his men to return to their quarters. Before they left, he reminded them the gear they brought with them from Morris Island needed to be put away. Quickly realizing his error in judgment, Beauregard recanted, telling his men he saw no reason why the gear could not be stowed later in the day.

Rans did not return to the Cooper Estate until after 3 a.m., Even so, Lucy was waiting for him, anxious to hear every detail of his long night. He began explaining how the 4,000 soldiers boarded the 900 hastily gathered flotilla of ironsides, boats and steamers and began their round-trip journey to the Morris Island docks. He described the incredible effort needed in dismantling the guns and carriages and transporting them overland to the boats waiting on the shoreline. When Rans reached the part about the confrontation with the barge, Lucy stopped him saying, "Honey, I don't want to hear about that. You could have been hurt. I know that whatever happened, you were very courageous; but right now, I just want you here with me, holding me and saying only good things to me."

Rans, trying in his own way to release the tension, said, "Lucy, it wasn't really all that courageous. I'll tell you about it later when I have a larger audience."

Lucy chuckled and said "Honey, I think it's time to go to bed."

***

The Confederates at Battery Wagner held their position for fifty-eight days, fighting a Union Army force ten times their number. From 10 July to 7 September, Confederate forces fought off two frontal assaults and daily bombardment by General Gilmore's batteries, gunships, ironsides and monitors. In that time, they suffered only 641 casualties. The Union forces suffered 2,318 casualties in the Morris Island campaign. Over the same time period the Union Army and Navy fired more than 6,200 rounds of artillery at Fort Sumter. In all, only three southern men were killed and forty-nine wounded.

After the capture of two Confederate boats leaving the island, Gilmore was informed about the evacuation of Morris Island. The notification occurred just a few minutes after midnight. That morning, Monday, September 7, 1863, at 5:10 a.m. General Gilmore signaled to Admiral Dahlgren, "The whole island is ours, but the enemy has escaped us."

# Chapter Eighteen

## *Montreal*

ONCE the ship was docked at the port of Montreal, the party made its way down the gangplank. Captain Davis scanned the wharf for porters to assist with the trunks and bags brought along by Ray, Elizabeth, Lilly and Jacob. Soldiers sent to accompany General Pike boarded the ship and picked up his bags and those of Captain Davis and proceeded down the gangplank to waiting carts. The ship's crew carried their own bags down the gangplank and placed them on empty carts located up and down the wharf for public use. Once all the carts arrived curbside, porters removed the bags and loaded them on wagons destined for the Hostellerie Pierre du Calvet and the St. Lawrence Hall hotel. Confederate troops in civilian clothes then escorted the carriages and wagons to both hotels.

As General Pike left the wharf, he instructed his aide to send his bags to the residence of former South Carolina State Senator William Bell, where he would be staying until the meetings concluded. After the aide left, General Pike told Ray he was going across the street to a local pub, where he and members of the Confederate Secret Service would discuss the goals and likely outcomes of the strategy meeting. He invited Ray and Captain Davis to join him once they were settled in at their hotels.

Before hailing a local hack, Ray asked Captain Davis if he would check out his reservation at the Hostellerie Pierre du Calvet and tell the desk clerk his reservation was requested by mail approximately two months earlier. Ray handed Captain Davis the letter he had recently received from the hotel confirming his reservation and suggested that when he returned it might be a good idea to join General Pike at the pub across the street. Ray added, "Joe, I think it's important to keep an eye on all the major players, including General Pike, so we don't find ourselves blindsided by some previously hatched conspiracy, especially one designed by Albert Pike."

Joe immediately responded, "We are in complete agreement, Ray. I am well aware of General Pike's questionable activities out west. His actions with the Indians and suspected misappropriations of Army funds certainly indicate some level of scrutiny is warranted while we are here in Montreal."

"Joe, I think you're right.  Let's meet back here in an hour and join the General."

"An hour it is then."

## *Hostellerie Pierre du Calvet*

"Daddy, Daddy."

"Yes Lilly."

"What an interesting hotel.  It looks like a stone fort on the outside but it's very homey and cozy on the inside.  The rooms are incredibly beautiful, and each has its own fireplace."

"Were they able to get you a room near a bath, Lilly?"

"Yes daddy, Jacob and I are going to love it.  Realizing what she had just said, Lilly blushed, and her face began turning red.  "Daddy, I'm sorry, I shouldn't have mentioned Jacob in what I said."

"Dear, you're a woman now, and all I want is for you to be happy.  Does Jacob make you happy?"

"Oh, he does daddy; he truly does."

"Tell your mother Captain Davis and I are going to King's Pub not far from the King Edward Wharf.  General Pike is already there so I don't think this will take long.  When I return your mother and I are going for a short walk to one of the fine seafood restaurants on the waterfront.  Would you and Jacob like to join us?"

Although a short walk to the waterfront was not what she had in mind, she nodded and said, "That would be nice, daddy."

Ray said good-bye and reassured Lilly he would be back right after he and Captain Davis met with General Pike.

## *Kings Pub*

As Ray and Captain Davis entered the pub, General Pike stood up and shouted, "Over here, Joe! What'll you have?"

"As long as I'm sailing the *John Jameson*, I think I'll take a Jameson's."

"What about you, Ray."

"Since I own the ship, I'll take the same. "

"General Pike, do you think any of the attendees have agendas inconsistent with the objectives of the Knights of the Golden Circle, the Scottish Rite or the Confederacy?"

"I don't think so, Ray, but with so many participants it's hard to tell. Since I resigned my commission, I've been looking at things from a different perspective. To be honest, I'm here to make sure we don't do anything that could harm the Scottish Rite's objective to bring on new members."

"General, I think the Freemasons and the Knights of the Golden Circle have parallel goals. My role here is to provide input into the specific acts being planned to sabotage Yankee communication and supply lines in the Northwest states. Presently, we're talking about Ohio, Indiana, Illinois, and Missouri. The Scottish Rite enjoys considerable support in these states, and I want to make sure the Confederate forces attack only valid military targets and not facilities routinely used by innocent civilians. Unfortunately, the recent attacks by General Morgan suggest this hasn't always been the case. Don't get me wrong—I'm all for pursuing aggressive campaigns against those damn Yankees, but we must use some common sense and keep our soldiers from looting and pilfering items they don't need from local stores. I'm afraid some of the actions taken by Morgan's men during his recent raid might have cost us more in sympathy and future support than we gained. His men's actions appear to have hurt the very people we're trying to recruit to our side."

"General Pike, you have no idea how much I welcome your last statement. I, too, expect our officers and men to act like the gentlemen they were raised and trained to be. This goes double for those who graduated from quality military institutions like West Point, Virginia Military Institute and the Citadel.

"General Pike, have you heard anything about General Joe Shelby's raid into Missouri?"

"Only a Little. I understand he took 600 men and is making a sweep across the heart of the state. This raid also has me quite concerned with regard to hurting our cause. Missouri for many years has been a state where the Scottish Rite enjoyed great support. It also happens to be a state I've called my second home. I can only hope his raid doesn't screw things up for Freemasonry or the Confederacy."

"General, what are your reasons for attending these strategy meetings?"

General Pike smiled and nodded approvingly, "Good question. I'm here to represent the western districts. As you know, Frank and Jesse James, Cole Younger and renegade Confederate soldiers riding with Quantrill's Raiders have been busy robbing banks and trains to help us in the revenue department. I also heard Jacob Thompson, that lawyer from

Mississippi, previously brought $600,000 in cash from Jeff Davis to help fund the startup of our Secret Service operation here in Montreal. I understand there is now a question as to whether $600.000 will be enough. I guess some people would like to operate out of Toronto as well. I'm carrying $167,350 given to me by Frank James last month. I heard he and Jesse identified a couple of payroll trains heading west out of Fort Dodge and helped themselves to the proceeds. Frank pledged that he and his brother will continue to support our cause."

"General, do you have enough security for that money?" Ray asked.

"I'm not well known here in Montreal, and it's only a short trip to the hotel. I don't think I'll arouse any suspicion traveling from here to St. Lawrence Hall."

"General, if you're unsure, I can have Captain Davis round up some of his crew to make sure no one gets anywhere near you till the money is locked up in the hotel safe."

Turning to Ray, General Pike asked, "Ray, do you know where in the hotel we will gather for our meetings. I've heard there are a lot of Union spies in Montreal, and I'd like to be sure no one is listening to our conversations."

"I'm planning on having our meetings in one of their larger rooms upstairs used for gambling, General. The hotel installed heavy wooden doors at each entrance and exit to these rooms for security reasons. With the room so close to the kitchen, I'll make sure we have fresh coffee and croissants throughout the day. I'll also stop by the *John Jameson* and pick up some whisky to stimulate both the coffee and conversation."

"Captain Davis, is there anything you'd like to ask or contribute?"

"Yes, Sir. If any suspicious ships are seen coming into port, I'll have my men keep an eye out for any questionable activity till our meetings are concluded. We don't want any Yankee spies checking out the *John Jameson* to see if she can be scuttled, set adrift or burned to the waterline in port."

General Pike leaned toward Ray and Captain Davis and asked to be excused to meet with his host, Senator William Bell to attend a matinee at a local theater followed by supper at their favorite French restaurant just outside the city. After Pike's departure, Captain Davis asked Ray to join him on the *John Jameson* while he briefed his crew on his expectations of their behavior while they were docked in Montreal.

***

Once on board the *John Jameson*, Captain Davis mustered his crew to share with them the nature of their assignment and exactly how they would carry it out. "Men, we are here on a very important mission for the Confederacy. Over the coming days, General Pike, Mr. Cooper, his wife Elizabeth, daughter Lilly and her escort Jacob Harris will be attending meetings involving several agencies interested in preserving our southern way of life. Those of you coming ashore to help with supply efforts will be staying at the St. Lawrence Hall hotel. It is a very nice hotel, and you are to forget everything you hear or observe there. Likewise, if you see any members of our party at the hotel, or anywhere else in the city, you are to consider them on a mission and unapproachable. Should this occur, ignore the civilians and move on. Since it's not uncommon for a wife to accompany her spouse on short voyages; Mr. Cooper and his wife Elizabeth are traveling as themselves."

"Jacob and Lilly, on the other hand, are travelling incognito. Jacob is traveling as Ian Jameson, nephew of *John Jameson* owner of Jameson's Whisky. Ian is the heir apparent to the Jameson fortune. Lilly is posing as Princess Marie Theresa De Conti, a French university student, studying the influence of her nation's culture on Quebec. Any man caught revealing more than he should will be stripped to the waist, strapped to the foremast and administered twenty lashes by the strongest man in the ship's company."

"They'll be conducting counter-espionage activities at social events taking place at the St. Lawrence Hall Hotel. Later they will visit various locations in the United States to assess their suitability for sabotage and assassination attempts. Again, should you run into them on the street or at an event, consider them incognito and go about your business. Does everyone get my drift?"

"Aye, Sir."

***

As Ray entered the *Hostellerie Pierre du Calvet*, Jacob asked how things had gone at the meeting. Ray answered, "The meeting went quite well. In fact, it went better than I expected. General Pike said his principle concern was insuring espionage efforts originating here in Montreal are not adversely impacting innocent civilians, especially in regions where the Confederacy and Freemasons already enjoy significant support. I feel confident I can support him in this matter. It's not a sound military strategy to aggravate your supporters residing behind enemy lines. A day might come when you need them."

Ray continued, "Lilly and her mother told me earlier that when we returned we're all going out for a walk to see the sights, especially those near the wharves. I think what they meant was they wanted to end up at a fine seafood restaurant after our long walk. They also told me tomorrow they're going to visit some of Montreal's best haberdasheries and boutiques to pick up dress clothes for the Confederate Gala. Lilly said she wanted something very sleek and European; something everyone would call spellbinding. What do you think, Jacob?"

"I told her she doesn't have to wear anything special at all to keep me spellbound. In fact, I told her not wearing anything at all works best for me."

"Sounds like you have your priorities straight."

"Yes Sir," answered Jacob. "Are you planning on joining us when we pick out new clothes?"

"No, I don't think so. Elizabeth's always chosen my clothes, and she certainly has much better taste than I do. I suspect she'll try to find me something a little more refined and looking as though it came from England or somewhere else on the continent. Over the next few days I have a lot of work to do to prepare for the meetings so I might be hard to find. If you need me, ask the desk clerk at the St. Lawrence Hall. I'll leave word at the front desk as to where I can be reached. If I don't see you after supper, enjoy the sightseeing and shopping. I'll see you at King's Pub the evening before the meeting."

## *Haberdasheries, Boutiques and Furriers*

After a late breakfast, Jacob, Lilly and her mother hired a hack and headed for Montreal's shopping district located just inland from the port. Elizabeth first asked the driver to tour the area and point out some of the better-known haberdasheries, boutiques, furriers, cobblers and hat makers offering European styled clothes. After a few trips around the district, the carriage dropped them off in front of Wickham's, a well-known haberdashery. There, they began shopping for both Ray and Jacob.

For Ray, they bought a burgundy 100% wool Frock Coat, men's lace-up boots, a Klondike vest and Dorian-brushed cotton trousers. To accessorize they purchased black canvas braces, a black silk puff tie and a pearl tie tack. To top it all off, Elizabeth bought Ray a charcoal grey deluxe John Bull-styled top hat.

For Jacob, Lilly purchased a Highland styled frock coat, matching pants, a Tahoe-styled vest, brushed-cotton trousers and Tombstone White shirt. They also bought him black canvas braces and a silk puff tie with a pearl tie tack similar to Ray's. To complete his outfit, Lilly bought him a coachman's hat and a satin-plated finished men's premium pocket watch with chain.  As they were leaving the store, the clerk mentioned that he had recently received a quantity of high quality Derby canes from England. He followed by saying, "If one would help the gentleman with his slight limp, I would be most pleased to retrieve one and show it to you."

Lilly asked the clerk to describe the cane. He said: "Ma'am, it's made from a fine grade of walnut and has a solid brass tip and handle."

Lilly replied, "Sir, we'll take it."  Before they left, Elizabeth asked if there were any boutiques nearby that specialized in imported dresses from London or Paris.

"Oh, Yes, ma'am. If you turn right as you exit the store you will see at the first corner a boutique named *Exquis*. They have lovely dresses and nearly all are shipped in from Paris or London. The store is owned by one of the major European trading companies. Their local managers are well liked here in Montreal. The company trades Canadian furs for European finished goods to be sold here in Montreal."

Lilly nodded demurely to the clerk, and they left to find the boutique. As Elizabeth, Lilly and Jacob entered the boutique, the initial conversation began in French with the sales clerk saying "Bonjour, Mademoiselle." After exchanging pleasantries, Lilly asked if the sales clerk or someone in the store spoke English. The clerk immediately responded in English, "Madam, Mademoiselle, even though nearly everyone in Montreal speaks French at home, in the retail sector it is necessary for us to speak fluent English."

"My fiancé is from Ireland and speaks very little French," Lilly said. Smiling coyly at Jacob, Lilly then added.  "Ian is wonderful."

Responding to Lilly's smile, the clerk said, "Yes Ma'am, I can see that—where would you like to start?"

"Let's look at a few things for my mother."

"Yes ma'am. What kind of look would you like to portray?"

Elizabeth spoke up, "I would like to portray myself as a very successful Merchant's wife."

"But ma'am, you already look very much like a very successful Merchant's wife."

Raising her chin just a little higher, she said, "Then I would like to look like a very rich successful Merchant's wife."

"Laughing profusely, Lilly said, "Mother, I like your style.'

After nearly an hour they had selected for Elizabeth a pair of black short cut Veil Boots, a Bella blouse, a small hoop underskirt, Black Deerskin Dress Gloves, a Ruby flair-frame Taffeta Skirt, a premium silk handkerchief and cameo pin.  She then chose a small black coachman hat to complement her outfit.

Looking Lilly up and down, Jacob asked, "Ma'am, what look are you trying for?"

"I want something dazzling, beautiful and elegant."

"Go ahead and tell the clerk what might satisfy you."

"You satisfy me, Jacob!  I just want a dress that makes me look spellbinding."

"Let me bring you in a beautiful long-tiered dress without hoops," said the clerk. "It should fit your trim body quite well.  What is your thought about the neckline?"

Lilly contemplated her reflection in the full-length mirror for a moment.  "I want it low perhaps in a sweeping half circle."

"That's just wonderful, I have a dress that fits the description perfectly in Royal Blue. It will make you look like a Princess."

Glancing conspiratorially at Jacob, she replied, "I am a Princess, Princess Marie Theresa De Conti. I am studying at the Sorbonne in Paris. Presently I am exploring the influence of French culture on Quebec. May I see the dress, it sounds marvelous?"

Returning from the rear of the store, the clerk handed her the Royal blue dress she had described.  Lilly was delighted. "This is the most beautiful and elegant dress I've ever seen." Holding the bodice of the dress to her own, she spun around, "Mother, what do you think?"

"It's lovely, my dear. I think you should try it on and see how it fits."

The clerk added, "Alterations are included in the price, ma'am, but I doubt your daughter will require them. If you need the dress for the upcoming Confederate ball at the St. Lawrence Hall, I can assure you any necessary alterations will be completed on time."

"What accessories would you recommend to go with the dress?"

"Ma'am, the dress is so complete, I believe it needs only a few accessories. You will probably need a pair of Veil boots, a no-hoop underskirt, pearls or a cameo and perhaps a Black Battenberg-style lace fan.  With the low-cut bodice, you might want to carry a light shawl.  Did you want the merchandise sent to the St Lawrence Hall?"

"No, ma'am.  We are staying at the Hostellerie Pierre du Calvet."

"Oh, Congratulations, Ma'am. The Hostellerie Pierre du Calvet has very fine accommodations.  It's very hard to get bookings there this time of year. You obviously have excellent connections."

# Chapter Nineteen

## *Before the Meetings*

AFTER leaving the haberdashery, Jacob excused himself telling Lilly and her mother he wanted to check out the St. Lawrence Hall Hotel before his meeting with Ray at King's Pub. He wanted to get the lay of the land and see where the meetings were going to be held. As he entered through the front door, he saw Captain Davis sitting at the bar with a lovely woman next to him. Captain Davis immediately waved his hand and shouted, "Jacob, come on over and meet Mademoiselle Francine Du Bois. We met several years ago in New Orleans."

Mademoiselle Du Bois might have been a beauty in her younger years, but that beauty had faded and the years showed in lines around her eyes and brightly painted mouth. Her dress was very fine, although it revealed entirely too much sagging skin. Jacob found it difficult to conceal his surprise to see Captain Davis with a woman like her. He soon recovered; however, greeted her and asked, "Mademoiselle Du Bois, how do you like living in Montreal?"

"The city is absolutely wonderful, but it's terribly cold when compared to New Orleans." After just a few minutes of small talk, Miss Du Bois whispered into Captain Davis' ear, "Joe, honey, I need to leave for a few moments to take care of my customers."

"That's alright, dear, I understand."

After Francine left the table, Jacob leaned over and asked, "Captain Davis, is she a prostitute?"

"Not exactly. She is kind of self-employed—if you know what I mean. She has several employees, most of whom work right here in the hotel. As a matter of clarity, today she is not my prostitute, although I cannot say she hasn't been in the past. Let's just say, when I'm in town, she stays with me. She is lovely—don't you think? Please understand. When you're a seafaring man, you have two choices. If you're married, you keep a girl in every port. If you're not, you visit your favorite pub in the city and pick out the girl of your choice."

"Have you seen Ray?"

"Not lately.  The last time I saw him he was with Charlene, one of Miss Du Bois' best girls."

"Are you saying Ray is one of those men who keep a girl in every port?"

"Not every port.  Just some."

"Does Elizabeth know?"

"Probably, but she loves him and knows whatever he does, he doesn't do it to hurt her."  Then changing the subject, he said, "Jacob, did you know Ray was a former Sea Captain?  We sailed the tea route from South Hampton to Shanghai and back several years ago.  Between us, we've visited just about every port in Asia."

"Why did he quit?"

"I think it was his health. Those long trips take their toll on everybody. By the way, I see Ray and Charlene coming down the stairs right now. "Ray, Charlene. How about joining us for a drink. It's a little early, but what the hell. I've already told Jacob Charlene's name."

Glancing at Ray, Captain Davis continued, "Jacob just stopped by to take in a little of the ambience of St. Lawrence Hall Hotel. I considered asking him if he wanted one of Francine's girls, but I knew he would decline. When you're escorting the most beautiful woman in Montreal, you don't need to think about other women."

Ray quickly retorted, "Smart move on his part. When I asked Lilly if he makes her happy, all she could say was 'daddy he does, he really does.'  Needless to say, there will be no discussion about the goings on here in the hotel without clearing it with me first."

Jacob responded, "Aye, Sir."

Ray added, "Jacob, I'll see you at 7 p.m. at Kings Pub."

***

As planned, Jacob met with Ray at the Kings Pub to discuss the progress of the war in greater detail. In particular, Ray wanted to discuss recent Southern losses at Vicksburg and Gettysburg. After ordering a couple of ales, Jacob asked Ray, "Has the list of attendees had been firmed up?"

Ray replied, "I suspect you might know or have heard of only three or four of them, so let's wait till tomorrow for the details. Suffice it to say, there will be adequate representation from organizations like Scottish Rite, the Confederate Secret Service, The Knights of the Golden Circle, the Sons of Liberty and of course the Confederate military. I suspect, too, a few prominent people will be there who operate somewhat independently. I'll be sure everyone present is properly introduced."

"Jacob, earlier I saw Captain Hines in the lobby. I was surprised, since the last I knew he was with General Morgan on his disastrous raid through Kentucky, Indiana and Ohio. Needless to say, we're all hoping either Frank or Jesse James shows up with some of the gold they recently took off a Union Army payroll train heading west out of Fort Chafee."

"Let's hope they do," said Jacob.

"I'm going to meet with General Pike at 8 a.m. at the St. Lawrence Hall. I'd like for you to be there, Jake."

Figure 17.  St. Lawrence Hall.

***

As Jacob entered the hotel, he looked to his right.  Ray was sitting in a comfortable chair near the front window, casually puffing away on his favorite Meerschaum while reading a week-old paper brought in on an arriving frigate. Ray purchased the pipe in Constantinople a few years back while a Turkish tug boat captain piloted the *John Jameson* through the Bosporus and Dardanelles.

As Ray stopped to fill his pipe, Jacob approached and asked, "Am I early, Sir?"

"Not at all, Jake.  General Pike should be here any minute now."

Moments later, General Pike's bulky form filled the entrance to the lobby, and he began searching for Ray and Jacob. He soon spotted them at a window table enjoying a continental breakfast of pastry and French coffee.

"Ray. Jacob. It's good to see you.  I'm starved! What say we each order a large plate of ham and eggs and put down two or three cups of coffee."  Pike's eyes sparkled in anticipation.

"General.  You might have to settle for a croissant or two, juice and hot tea or coffee."

Patting his sizeable girth, he laughed heartily, "Then I'll settle for a couple of croissants with butter, coffee and some Irish whisky to make it more suitable to my pallet."

"I think you and I already know what we want to cover, General." Ray said.  "As I see it, it's going to be our responsibility *to separate the wheat from the chaff* with regard to operations already underway and new ones we want to plan and undertake."

General Pike responded, "Ray, I think I've already adequately stated my concerns about unwarranted military operations interfering with the long-term goals of the Scottish Rite and the Knights of the Golden Circle. From what I've heard I think we ought to bring up General Morgan's raid into Kentucky, Indiana and Ohio as a prime example. When General Morgan got permission to conduct the raid from General Bragg, I understand it came with certain conditions and restrictions.  The first condition was that he was to take no more than 1500 men. The balance of his Division was to remain behind to screen for Bragg should the need arise. He was also told to confine his operations to the state of Kentucky, staying close enough to his home base so he could coordinate with Bragg at all times.  Instead he took nearly 2,500 men and only 364 made it back over the Ohio River into West Virginia. At this stage in the war we can ill afford to lose a division of fine Calvary on such a foolish venture."

"General, I think we need to identify what topics we want brought up and in what order. I know we won't be introducing every topic but I do think it's important we try to control the discussion. Otherwise, extremists from some of those hate-mongering splinter groups might hijack the meeting and substitute their agendas for ours. I suspect tomorrow we'll get a chance to discuss the full range of topics covered in our agendas in greater detail. I have taken it upon myself to jot down a few of the specific topics I expect to be covered:

"The first topic is creating discontent in the northwest states of Missouri, Indiana, Illinois and Ohio. Hopefully, this discontent will encourage the populace in those states to secede from the Union and form their own Confederacy.

"Second, the participants need to lay out a plan to elect candidates sympathetic to our cause at all levels. I would expect such a plan to include the following:

"1. Intimidation of opposition candidates to discourage their entry into political races.

"2. Intimidation of opposition voters to keep them away from the polls.

"3. Bribing of police or elected officials to insure pro-south candidates are on the ballet.

"Third, I believe the kidnapping or assassination of senior government officials like the President, Vice President, Cabinet Secretaries, etc., has to be included as one of our topics.

"In light of General Morgan's recent raid, I believe identification of specific military targets for sabotage to include telegraph lines, trains, train tracks, and ammunition depots needs to be thoroughly discussed. It's imperative we attack only military targets.

"General, I think it extremely important we encourage our military forces not to loot, pilfer or otherwise destroy facilities needed by the local populace to survive and make it through the war. We need to make it clear to our military commanders, officers and men they are expected to act like gentlemen, particularly with respect to treatment of wounded enemy soldiers, prisoners of war and civilian non-combatants. Remember the objective of our acts in the northwest is to get those states to leave the Union. For us, this reduces the area we have to defend while undertaking more pressing matters further east. In clearer terms, our goal is to create allies not more enemies."

"Sir," Jacob said to Ray. "You gave a fine speech. I just hope you remember it when you give your opening statement. I jotted down a few notes just in case."

"Thank you for the fine critique, Jacob."

"You're quite welcome, Sir.

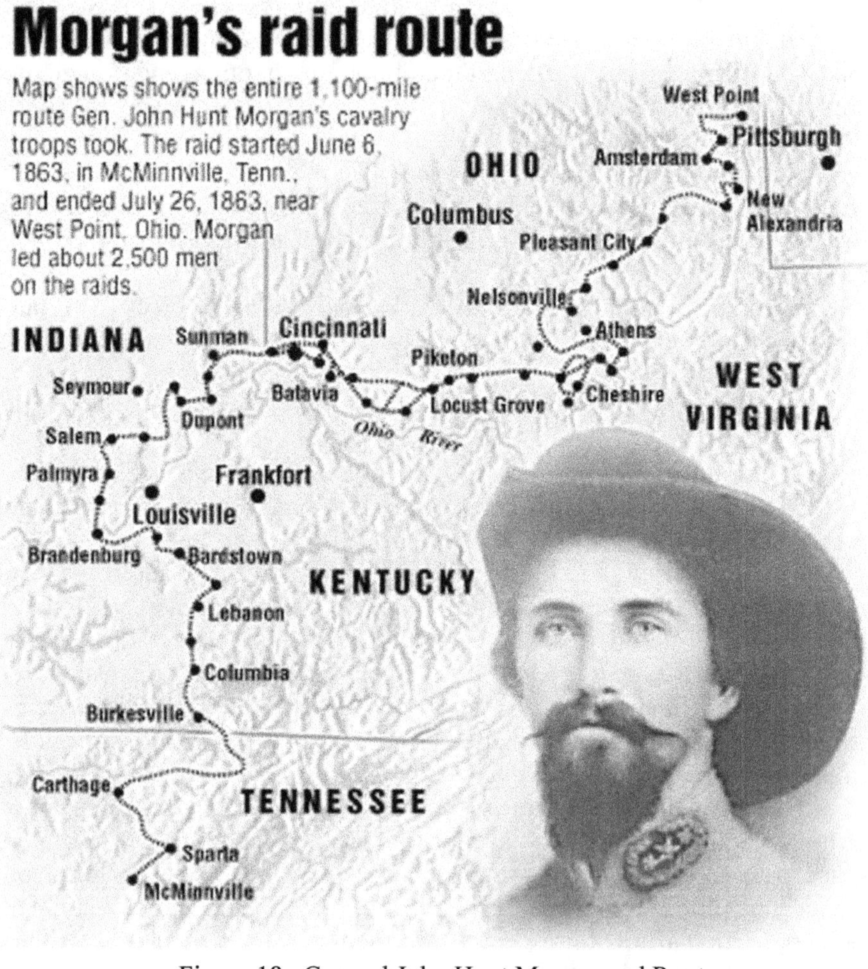

Figure 18.  General John Hunt Morgan and Route.

# Chapter Twenty

## *The Meeting Begins*

AT EIGHT a.m., a member of the hotel staff opened the door to a small alcove adjacent to the St. Lawrence Hall's dining room. Inside, laid out on several tables was a continental breakfast of coffee, croissants, crepes, and fruit. As each attendee entered the alcove, he was handed a plate and advised to help himself to any of the items on the tables and proceed to the dining room. Once seated, Ray immediately noticed a shot glass and bottle of Jameson's to the right of his place setting. Anticipating others would join them, Ian, Ray, Captain Davis, and General Pike seated themselves at one of the larger tables near the bar. Within minutes Clement Clay, Jacob Thompson, Clement Vallandigham and Major Thad Culpepper ambled into the dining Room. Thad asked, "Ray, do you have room for all of us at your table."

"Yes, Thad. It looks like we have plenty of chairs, so go ahead. Take a seat."

Moments later Captains Hines and Holcombe strolled in and made the same request. General Pike responded this time, "Gentlemen, as long as there are seats still open, feel free to join us. I'll ask my aide to bring more coffee, croissants, crepes, and Jameson's to the table."

Scanning the table, Ray spoke to the group, "I think I know everyone here, so perhaps I'd better make the introductions. I'll start with General Pike, here on my right. He's the Sovereign Grand Commander of the Scottish Rite - Southern Jurisdiction. He's here primarily to represent the interest of the Scottish Rite, but because of his former experience as Commander of Confederate Forces in the Indian Territory, he's also representing some elements of our military operating 'somewhat' independently out west. These forces include members of the James gang, Cole Younger and rogue members of Quantrill's raiders.

"Next to him is Clement Vallandigham, Grand Commander of the Sons of Liberty. For those unaware, they used to be called the Order of American Knights. The Sons of Liberty was formed when the 'Knights of the Golden Circle' and the 'Copperheads' combined forces. Right behind Clement I see Jacob Thompson who is referred to by his friends as 'that lawyer guy from Mississippi.' Jacob certainly has quite a resume. He was formerly Secretary of the Interior of the United States and now is the Inspector General for our Army. It's certainly worth mentioning he served with distinction with General Beauregard at Shiloh.

"General Beauregard is now responsible for defending Charleston, its harbor and the perimeter islands. He'd planned on being here in person but was busy upgrading battery defenses on Morris and James Islands. Before we sailed, he received a communiqué from a spy on the other side of the Potomac stating Lincoln had promised Union commanders in and around Charleston an additional 10,000 troops to take Batteries Greg and Wagner. Recent intelligence suggests an immanent attack as early as the first week in September is possible.

"In his absence, I will be representing General Beauregard's interests as well as those of commercial shipping and the Confederate Navy. On the other side of Ian, I see Clement Clay, Commissioner of the North. I understand Jeff Davis himself gave him that title. Clement, Congratulations. Just past Clement I see Captains Holcombe and Hines. I know Captain Hines was with General Morgan on his recent raid into Kentucky, Indiana and Ohio. I hope later he can share his experiences with us about the specifics of the raid. Captain Holcombe has been keeping us safe while we are here in Montreal. This task hasn't been easy with so many Union spies hanging out here in the hotel, and in all of the bars and restaurants we regularly visit. A colleague told me that there are so many Union spies in Montreal, it's almost impossible to get a dinner reservation at one of the finer restaurants when you want one.

"Lastly, sitting next to me is Ian Jameson, nephew of *John Jameson* and heir to the Jameson Distillery fortune. I'm sure now you know why my ship is named the *John Jameson*. What sailor in his right mind would want to attack a ship carrying good whiskey and send her to a watery grave? More than once I have been able to trade a few cases of Jamesson's for my freedom. I think I can assure everyone here we will not run out of Jameson's finest while I'm here in Montreal. Ian's lovely fiancée, Princess Marie Theresa De Conti will join us this evening at a Gala being held upstairs in the ballroom. Miss De Conti is a university student currently studying the influence of French culture on Quebec. Mr. Jameson and Miss De Conti have offered to help us reconnoiter targets for Secret Service operations in the United States and abroad if necessary. Their prominence and impeccable travel documents should allow them to travel unimpeded anywhere in North America.  Unless they approach you, I would recommend you assume they are on assignment and keep some distance."

At nine a.m. the Sergeant at Arms came in to escort the attendees down the hall to two large oak doors that served as an entryway into a large elegant conference room. As the Sergeant at Arms opened the doors, the attendees entered and each took a seat at a large mahogany conference table behind a brass nameplate that had been placed on the table earlier in the day.

To the left was a podium standing on a flat 10' square platform. Behind the platform hung two full-length velvet curtains with draw rods separating them. After the attendees were seated, the Sergeant at Arms pulled back the draw rods to reveal hand-carved logos, each two feet in diameter, of the Confederate Secret Service, the Sons of Liberty, the Knights of the Golden Circle and the Scottish Rite.  After the reveal, Clement Vallandigham, Grand Commander of the Sons of Liberty approached the podium, struck his gavel on a wooden base and took out his prepared notes.

Vallandigham, in his mid-forties, was a handsome man with dark, wavy hair and sported a sliver of a dark beard that surrounded his face, leaving most of his face clean-shaven.  Looking at the attendees, he spoke, "Gentlemen, even though we'll have the opportunity tonight to hear the Confederate National Anthem being sung in the Ballroom, I believe it fitting and proper we ask our resident troubadour, Ray Cooper, to sing the first two choruses at this time. The presence of those two magnificent oak entry doors should keep anyone outside from hearing our tribute to the Confederacy. Please stand while Ray sings his own rendition of our National Anthem, '*God save the South.*'"

Ray stood and said, "Clement, thank you for such a kind introduction."  Then, in a clear, impassioned voice, he sang the Confederate National Anthem, '*God Save the South:*'

*God save the South, God save the South,*

*Her altars and firesides, God save the South!*

*Now that the war is nigh, now that we arm to die,*

*Chanting our battle cry, "Freedom or death!"*

*Chanting our battle cry, "Freedom or death!"*

*God be our shield, at home or afield,*

*Stretch Thine arm over us, strengthen and save.*

*What tho' they're three to one, forward each sire and son,*

*Strike till the war is won, strike to the grave!*

*Strike till the war is won, strike to the grave!*

Clement paused a moment, then commented, "Ray, thank you for bringing such an important song to us on this special occasion." Turning to Mr. Thompson, he said, "Mr. Thompson, being a man of the cloth, would you present an invocation to open today's proceedings."

"It would be an honor, Clement." He bowed his head and began, "Our father, please bless this gathering of patriots who seek a resolution to this most bloody and painful war. Let us invite you into our hearts to help us find solutions to the senseless killing on the battlefield every day. Help us break the enemy's stranglehold on our brave people and let us persevere. We know you will give us wisdom and help us develop a plan capable of leading us to victory and bringing peace to ourselves and our enemies. In his blessed name, we pray. Amen."

Vallandigham paused once more. Then he said, "Mr. Thompson, what an inspiring message!" He paused again for a brief moment, then continued, "Before we begin the meeting, I would like to lay down a few ground rules. Normally, it has been our standard practice to conduct business meetings using parliamentary procedures used by the Scottish Rite and the Knights of the Golden Circle. In this case, however, it might be more appropriate to use a less formal format with rules allowing us get to the subject matter more easily and directly. There are several different agendas in this room, and I believe those agendas need to be discussed and even debated when necessary. Is there anyone out there who feels differently?" He glanced around the room. "Since I heard nary a nay, let's proceed. I don't know about you, but I would like to get policy issues out of the way today. This would allow the attendees to coordinate their planned operations with those scheduled to be carried out by our agents or our military over the next year. Are we all in agreement? Absent any objections -- let's continue.

"Since we have a General Officer present, I think he should be given the opportunity to start things off. For those who don't know General Pike, I believe he has the longest title in the room. He is the Sovereign General of the Scottish Rite – Southern Jurisdiction. As a Brigadier General, he commanded Confederate Forces in the West. He is also a member of the Knight of the Golden Circle. Are you ready General?

"Folks, it is my great pleasure to introduce to you General Albert Pike. General, the podium is yours."

# Chapter Twenty-One

## *Brigadier General Albert Pike's Presentation*

GENERAL Pike smiled as he rose quickly for so large a man, "Thank you, Clement. Captain Hines from General Morgan's Regiment is here with us. Before I proceed, I want everyone to welcome Captain Hines at this time. I understand he was able to escape the fight at Buffington Island where General Morgan's Regiment attempted to cross the Ohio into what is now West Virginia. Captain, how about joining me up here at the podium and tell us about your regiment's recent raid across Kentucky, Indiana, and Ohio. Captain Hines' comments will serve as a basis for my thoughts regarding the need to coordinate military actions taking place in the northwestern states with Secret Service efforts originating here in Canada. Captain, if I may, I would like to proceed in a 'question-and-answer' format. This format will help me align your comments to points I will bring up later. As you proceed with your description of the raid, I would, on occasion, like to ask questions regarding some of the specifics of what actually occurred, if that is alright?"

"That would be fine, General."

"Captain, the floor is yours."

The two, standing next to each other, could not be more opposite in bearing. While the General was a large bear of a man, Captain Hines was several inches shorter and very slender in build with a bushy mustache. He was a very important man to General John Hunt Morgan leading a preliminary raid into Indiana before General Morgan's fateful one. When he spoke, his voice was like a refined woman, only with a much higher pitch.

"General Pike's comments are quite correct regarding my escape from Buffington Island. When I clearly understood the majority of my Regiment weren't going to make it across the river, I rode across the nearby Portland Bottoms flood plain and headed north by northeast towards Pittsburgh. The first evening I stole some civilian clothes and ditched my uniform. I didn't want anyone to know I was a fleeing Confederate Officer. A couple of days later I boarded a train heading toward Canada.  Once across the border, I found the nearest train station and purchased a ticket to Montreal."

"That was very resourceful, Captain.  I compliment you on your escape and evasion skills. Did anyone ever tell you what you should do if your capture appeared imminent?"

"Yes, Sir. Our Commanders told us to flee to Canada. They told us most Canadians would help us get back to our Regiment or some Canadian port.

General Pike then followed, "I told my soldiers the same thing when I commanded our soldiers in Indian Territory. Let's go back to the beginning. Who authorized the raid, and how many troops were supposed to take part?"

"Major General Bragg first authorized 1500 men for the raid but somehow that number was raised to 2,000."

Figure 19. Brigadier General Albert Pike.

"Were there any other conditions for the raid?

"Initially, General Bragg told General Morgan to stay within consulting range and leave a residual 1,000 men in reserve, in case he—General Bragg—needed them."

"Ultimately, how many troops did General Morgan take with him?"

"Sir, around 2,400."

"Can you give me a brief synopsis of what happened on the raid?"

"Yes, Sir. On 1 July, as we crossed the Cumberland River we were spotted by local militia who began firing at us in the river. They were well hidden, so I doubt we hurt them much at all. They held two buildings on the other side including a mill, and for them it was like picking off ducks. We didn't finish our crossing until mid-morning the next day."

"Captain, why didn't you outflank them?"

"Sir, coming out of the water as we did, we just couldn't get up enough steam to pull ourselves up out of the river and climb the hills to get around them. On July 3rd, we faced as regiment of Federal troops at Tebb's Bend on the Green River. It was there that General Morgan's youngest brother Timmy was killed. After Timmy's death, General Morgan ordered the buildings around the depot destroyed and burned."

"Captain, how were you finally able to get across the Green River?'

"Sir, I hate to admit it, but it was numbers and experience. The other side looked as though they hadn't fought in combat. I saw several dead lying on the ground. They appeared to be no more than sixteen or seventeen years old. Since they were in uniforms, my best guess is that some of them might have been from a military school for high school students. Their tactics weren't very good either, and many of them seemed scared to pull the trigger."

"Is it fair to say that Timmy Morgan's death set the tone for the rest of the raid?"

"Not for everybody, Sir, but it certainly did for those closest to the General."

"Captain, let's move this along. What happened after Tebb's Bend?"

"Yes, Sir. On July 6th, Morgan's artillery let loose on a livery stable in Bardstown. I tried to tell the cannoneers' commander I didn't think a livery stable used by locals was a military target, but Major Shaw, their commander, told me to mind my own business and added it was his job to pick valid targets.

"On the 8th we married up with two steamers and crossed the Ohio into Indiana. The steamers, the John T. McCombs and Alice Dean, had been captured the previous day by the 10th Kentucky Calvary.

"Once across the river, the Alice Dean was burned to the water line. The John T. McCombs was spared since her skipper knew Colonel Duck. On the 10th, we reached the town of Salem. There we fired on a local railroad depot and burned every major bridge surrounding the town. Again, I tried to stop the burning but was told to stay away."

"Captain, did any looting taking place in these small towns?"

"Yes, Sir. Throughout the raid, our troops were guilty of wholesale looting and plundering of useless commodities from dry-goods stores and saloons. In addition, some of our soldiers beat some of the Union soldiers who surrendered. Again, local militia troops were not equipped to take on a 2,400 man Confederate Calvary Regiment. Plain and simple—they didn't have the numbers.

"Our next stop was at Sharonville, Ohio, about seventeen miles north of Cincinnati. While there the General handed us officers a glass of Brandy and some expensive cigars his troops had looted in Salem. Sharonville is a pretty little town with lots of storefronts. Here, we took whatever we wanted. Apparently, because of our swift crossing of Kentucky and Indiana the Yanks had not yet figured out where we were heading or our likely fording point across the Ohio.

"At 4 p.m. on the 14th, the Division encamped at Williamsburg, Ohio. It was there I realized we had just covered more than 84 miles in less than thirty-six hours."

"That sounds like quite an accomplishment, Captain."

"Yes sir, our officers were very proud of their cavalrymen."

"Were you able to keep your same mounts during the entire raid?"

"No, Sir.  As our horses wore out, we stole new ones to take their place."

"Where did you get the new horses, Captain?"

"We grabbed them from anywhere we could. Mostly we tried to get them from livery stables, but if it became necessary we took them from local farmers, residents and merchants.

"Captain, how do you think those local residents felt about losing their horses."

"I am sure they were quite angry, sir."

"Captain, what happened after Sharonville?  Did you have any military objectives in mind as you continued?"

"No, Sir.  The General just wanted us to create as much havoc and chaos as possible and steal as much stuff as we could."

"What exactly do you mean by stuff?"

"We often took items like clothes, boots, black powder and tobacco from dry-goods stores. Whiskey, of course, was usually taken from local bars and saloons. Buildings like warehouses, mills, telegraph offices and train stations were almost always burnt to the ground. The General and some of the officers said those buildings might be of use to the Union Army or local militias."

"Captain, did these businesses, mills, and other buildings you described belong to civilians?"

"Yes, Sir."

"Did anyone try to stop the looting and destruction of property belonging to civilians?"

"Some of the officers told their men to stop, but most continued looting.  Some of the troops even told their Commanders that General Morgan told them to burn everything?"

"Captain, were you one of those who told his troops to return the non-military items to those who owned them?"

"Yes, Sir."

"Why do you think there was so much destruction of civilian property on the raid?"

"Sir, after General Morgan's younger brother fell, he wasn't the same.  He was full of rage and didn't seem to care much about his objectives or the safety of his men.  To be honest, he made decisions I and other officers thought were careless and not in the best interest of our Regiment."

"Captain, to your synopsis. You said General Morgan didn't seem to have any specific military objectives in mind for Ohio.  What did he say about his overall objectives?"

"Sir, he didn't say anything about objectives. He just said we should look for a good place to cross the Ohio and get back into West Virginia. The General sent Lieutenant Dick Morgan with instructions to find possible crossing points where the river could be forded. The first possible crossing point was at Ripley, but gunboats and local militia were defending the crossing point. Dick rode on ahead until he came to a second possible place to ford at Portsmouth.

"While en route, a member of the main column's rear guard rode forward and told General Morgan that Union General Hobson was a mere fourteen miles behind in Mulberry. So, before continuing on, Morgan told his officers to have their men fell trees to fall across the road to delay Hobson.  He also ordered his men to overturn over any excess wagons they had in the middle of the road and set them on fire. Because of the closing troops, Dick Morgan chose to move on past Portsmouth to find the next possible crossing point."

"Captain!"

"Yes, Sir."

"Up to this point, how many soldiers were still with you?"

"Around 2,000, Sir."

"Out of 2,400… is that right?"

"Yes, Sir."

"Were most of the losses in major engagements or were our troops picked off one or two at a time?"

"One or two at a time, Sir, but there were times we lost more."

"Thank you for your candid answer.  Captain, were you able to cross the river at Portsmouth?"

"No, Sir."

"Once you realized you wouldn't be able to cross, what did you do?"

"The General directed us to head toward Eight Mile Island near Cheshire which he believed would be our last possible crossing point. En route we found local militias using the same delaying tactics we had employed earlier to slow down General Hobson's advancing troops.  As we continued along our route we found numerous obstacles lying across the road in front of us.  At our reduced pace, we continued to lose more and more soldiers from shots taken by enemy troops and militia along our path.   At Berlin Crossroads, we tangled with a large force of around one thousand militiamen.  Even though we eventually won the battle, it delayed our progress by an additional four hours. By the time we found the ford at Eight Mile Island, the rugged hills commanding our desired crossing point were crawling with Union troops. It was clear they had been alerted to our impending arrival.

"Within sight of the river, General Morgan saw two Yankee gunboats steaming toward Eight Mile Island and decided to proceed on to Buffington Island. Morgan said he believed the water level at eight-mile island was too shallow to be navigable. At one p.m., we arrived in Cheshire. Seven hours later General Hobson arrived followed by General Judah, whose troops had just been forced marched from Pomeroy to nearby Racine to joined Hobson.

"As our Regiment rode into a nearby flood plain aptly named Portland Bottoms, Morgan observed two Yankee guns defending the area. He decided the crossing would have to wait until sun-up the next day. That night he set up a perimeter around his troops and hoped contact wouldn't come until his troops had rested.  Early the next morning, Morgan found the river hidden in an early morning fog.  His first thought was the fog would help conceal the early arrival of his troops waiting to cross the Ohio River.  Judah's advanced guard ran squarely into Dukes brigade patrolling the Bottoms, and all hell broke loose. Judah himself barely escaped capture. Moments later, the Confederates were shocked to see a Federal gunboat, the USS Moose, at their flank accompanied by two armed steamers.

"Needless to say, when the gunboats opened up, Morgan realized his troops were cornered and in for the fight of their lives. Suddenly, the two Yankee guns spotted on the previous day began firing on Morgan's forces from opposite directions. One gun concentrated its fire on Chester Road while the other fired on the bottoms from an elevated firing position nearby. In the confusion, General Morgan escaped with about half of his men. With the few hundred men remaining, Colonels Johnson and Duke covered Morgan's retreat till they ran out of ammunition. During the battle, Morgan lost more than 670 soldiers killed, wounded or captured. After the attack, Morgan's remaining forces reorganized and set up an overnight encampment in a nearby woods. The following morning, the remaining cavalrymen headed out for the ford at Belleville Island.

"The next afternoon the remaining force arrived at the Belleville Island ford with hopes of a successful crossing. Meanwhile, the USS Moose arrived and soon found itself within range. The ship's Commander ordered his men not to fire on the Confederates in the water. Only about four hundred troops were able to ford the river into West Virginia. At this point, seeing some of his troops were still on the north side of the Ohio River, General Morgan reentered the water and headed back north to help his men. Although he was able to cross and keep fragments of his division together for another week, he was eventually captured on July 26th. Later, a colleague of mine told me he was 'tried' in Cincinnati, found guilty, and is now being held in a prison in Columbus, Ohio."

"Captain, how many men made it back across the Ohio into West Virginia?"

"Around 400, Sir. A few hid and were able to cross later.

"So, you lost about 2,000 cavalrymen in the raid."

"That sounds about right."

"Do you think the benefit derived from the raid was worth it?"

"No, Sir. I doubt it. Two thousand cavalrymen will be difficult to replace. I doubt if enough men can be recruited and trained in time to replace the Division and make a difference."

"Thank you, Captain. I am sure I speak for everyone here when I say we very much appreciate your candidness and willingness to share what you recall from the raid. Your comments reinforce my own conclusions about the raid. We need to limit our targets to military ones and not destroy private property used by local civilians to sustain themselves during these hard times. It's essential we not damage our relationships with civilian populaces who, by and large already support us. I readily acknowledge it's sometimes necessary to use every method possible to achieve our political, military or economic goals. I also understand, on occasion, it might be necessary to create as much chaos as possible to facilitate a victory. However, today, I ask each of you to pledge your

best effort in coordinating your operations with those of the Secret Service
and the patriotic organizations in this room. We can no longer sustain losses like Morgan took on his raid nor can we alienate those individuals we
are trying to make our friends."

Ray spoke up, saying: "General, I think you can take everyone's presence at this meeting as evidence we all feel the same way."

"Thanks, Ray.  Gentlemen, I've had my say. Clement, the podium is
yours for the next introduction."

Figure 20. General Morgan's Raid.

# Chapter Twenty-Two

## *The Private and his Princess*

CLEMENT Vallandigham rose and addressed General Pike, "Thank you, General.  Our next speaker needs absolutely no introduction, but it's my pleasure to make the introduction.  He is a former Secretary of the Interior for the United States and is currently Inspector General of the Confederate Army.  At this meeting, Jacob Thompson is representing the interest of our esteemed President, Jefferson Davis, and the Confederate Army."

Thompson, with an obvious air of authority, strode to the dais to address the group, "Thank you, Clement.  General Pike did a masterful job of articulating my exact thoughts on coordinating our efforts.  I'm well aware of the various agendas we have in this room.  I also know some agendas here are inherently in conflict with others. For example: The Freemasons, Knights of the Golden Circle and Sons of Liberty are all interested in persuading residents of the northwest states to secede from the Union and form their own Confederacy. Others, like the Confederate Army seek to destroy troop garrisons, train stations, supply depots and telegraph offices.  Still others, like the Confederate Secret Service, seek to assassinate or kidnap key military and political leaders and exchange them for large numbers of Confederate soldiers. They also seek to disrupt opposition political campaigns, thereby insuring election of candidates sympathetic to our cause.  Our presence at this meeting is a start in our efforts to insure the acts of any one agency do not interfere with the strategies of another.

"Tomorrow, in our individual planning sessions, we will share with one another the details of our individual missions so we will not hinder one another's plans.  Hopefully, knowing details of each other's missions in advance will improve everyone's planning efforts—making them more effective."

He paused, then turned to Clement, "Clement, I think it's time for you to call your next speaker."

"Mr. Thompson, you did a fine job of separating *the wheat from the chaff.* I see you've brought two colleagues with you. Would you mind introducing them to those in the room who have not heard of them?"

"I would be happy to, Clement."

"Gentlemen, Major Thad Culpepper is a long-time member of the Confederate Secret Service. He's here to give you some insight into future operations to be undertaken by his agents here in Canada. When I first met Thad, I asked him where he was from and he enthusiastically answered, 'Culpepper, Virginia, Sir.' I followed up with a short quip about how many members of his family were from Culpepper. He retorted, 'All of them, Sir …every single one of them… everyone who lives in Culpepper is a Culpepper.'" Those comments drew laughter and lightened the mood in the room for a moment.

Vallandigham continued, "Thad has a great deal of experience creating political chaos, stealing elections, sabotaging facilities like rail lines and ammo storage areas. He is also our resident expert on the use of Confederate codes and ciphers. If anyone here would like training in any of those areas, Thad has agreed to stay on after tomorrow's adjournment to provide whatever help you might need. Thad, why don't you come to the podium and tell everyone about some of the operations the Secret Service is considering for the rest of this year and next."

"Mr. Thompson, I want to thank you for inviting me to this very special meeting," Thad said. "Before covering our plans for this and next year, I'd like to make a quick comment about Captain Thomas Hines. Don't let Tom's youthful appearance fool you. He's been one of our most successful operatives and brought great credit to our service. He'll supplement my instruction by providing additional information on the use of Confederate Codes and ciphers in unusual circumstances and between naval ships and vessels. He'll provide this information after tomorrow's planning session to anyone interested."

Thad continued, "Gentlemen, the Confederate Secret Service Headquarters in Richmond has asked us here in Canada to assume responsibility for several ongoing operations in New England and the northwest states. Our most pressing operation is the kidnapping of Vice President Johnson while he is en route to President Lincoln's inauguration in mid-January. In the past, the Galt House has been the hotel of choice for past Presidents, military leaders and dignitaries visiting Louisville. We expect it will be the hotel of choice for this visit. The Galt House, located at the corner of second and main on the Ohio River has sixty rooms and an elegant dining area. Our operatives have told us Generals Grant and Sherman are expected at the hotel sometime later this year.

"Confederate spies traveling with Vice President Johnson believe he might be carrying instructions from President Lincoln to field commanders currently developing a strategy to take Atlanta and Savanna. With so many high-profile guests, we believe the hotel will be well guarded by frontline Army troops and local militia. We also expect numerous gunboats to be patrolling the river in front of the hotel to discourage any attempt to fire on the hotel from the water. For this reason, we're asking Mr. Jameson and his lovely fiancé to visit the hotel in advance of Johnson's arrival and collect valuable intelligence on security measures being taken to protect the Vice President.

"Another project we're examining is a deceptive attack on the state of Maine. We believe this feigned attack might distract Union forces enough to force them to dedicate troops to an illusionary threat. We've already sent French-speaking geological survey teams to Maine. If caught, members of the team are to tell the Yanks they're part of an expedition team sent to North America to collect scientific information on ocean tides such as tide times, water depth at each tide stage and seasonal water temperature.

"Our next project involves securing information on payroll shipments destined for Indian Territory and lands further west. It's believed robbing these shipments will create anger and discontent within the ranks. There's nothing like not receiving your $20 a month for serving your country. Frank and Jesse James and renegade members of Quantrill's Raiders will likely rob the payroll trains."

Thad paused as the room erupted in applause before continuing, "Another project assigned to our operation here in Canada is the robbing of banks along the Canadian border east of the Mississippi. Not long ago Confederate operatives out of Toronto robbed a bank in St. Albans, Vermont, and took more than $200,000 dollars. Frankly, we were surprised to find such a small bank holding so much hard currency. I think it's time we pay them a return visit and see if we can relieve them of such a burden. Since operatives out of Toronto did so well the first time, I say we give them another chance to do so." Once more the room erupted in applause, causing Thad to pause again.

"These next few projects are particularly sensitive and are not be discussed with anyone outside this room. Two of these missions are to take place on the east coast. This fall draft riots are scheduled to take place in New York City, Boston and Philadelphia. We need covert operatives at these locations to stir up the citizenry as much as possible. We hope these actions will discourage local youth from registering for the draft.

"The second operation involves intimidation of opposition voters during the upcoming Presidential election. Hopefully, keeping voters away from the polls will result in a change of voting patterns that result in the election of candidates more sympathetic to our cause. It's imperative the next President be willing to negotiate a peace settlement with the South that favorably considers the South's position on both states rights and slavery."

Glancing around the room, Thad saw many heads nodding in agreement. "Our last operation is a particularly sensitive one. Should Lincoln win reelection, it is our intent to support a proposed conspiracy to kidnap or kill President Lincoln, Vice President Johnson, Secretary of State Seward and General Grant. A thespian of note named John Wilkes Booth has already volunteered for the leading role. We believe the North would be willing to swap a large number of prisoners for any or all of these hostages. If anyone has questions or wishes to offer a plan of their own, I will be here in the hotel through tomorrow evening. Clement, who is our next speaker?"

"Thad, I believe it will be Ray Cooper. Since it's already one p.m. and we only have a couple of speakers left to go, why don't we break for lunch and enjoy a good cigar. Let's return around two thirty."

***

Clement returned to the podium. "Welcome back gentlemen, I hope you enjoyed both a fine meal and an even finer cigar. For those unfamiliar with Montreal, I encourage you to contact the hotel's concierge Mr. Baird for anything you might need. George, that's his given name, seems to be able to book reservations at any restaurant in the city, even when they are supposedly completely booked. He also knows where to find just about every type of entertainment one might imagine. Included are those types of entertainment we don't talk about when we go home. He knows what plays are being performed in Montreal's finest theaters and is equally familiar with the locations of seedy card games and gaming establishments in the darkest corners of the city. He is a fine fellow even if his name happens to be George." Quite a number of those present could be seen making a note of the name.

'Gentlemen," Clement continued, "our next speaker is someone we all know and love. He's our resident troubadour, and tonight he will sing a few tunes for you—to include patriotic songs about our beloved Dixie.

He's here to bring us up to date on the defense of Charleston and Confederate efforts to secure a second ocean-going sloop to compliment the *CSS Alabama*. Ray, come on up to the podium. The floor is yours."

Ray all but bounded to the dais. "Thank you, Clement. As Clement mentioned earlier General Beauregard intended on being here, but at the last minute he got word that attacks on Batteries Greg and Wagner are imminent. General Beauregard asked me to conduct this portion of the meeting for him. Although the Union Navy has on several occasions attempted to enter Charleston harbor, I'm proud to say as of this date their attempts have all been futile. Our gun batteries on the perimeter islands have kept them at bay and forced retreat on every occasion. I know General Beauregard would never say this, but I'm sure his exceptional engineering skills coupled with his field experience at Bull Run and Shiloh contributed greatly to our successes.

"Not all of you may know that last August 24, 1862, the Confederate Navy launched the newest of its ocean-going fleet, the *CSS Alabama*. It was built in the famous Laird Shipyard on the Mersey River in Liverpool. Her crew is mostly English. She is a wood-hulled 220-foot sloop of 1,050 tons. With two 300-horsepower steam engines driving one single two-bladed screw she can make 13 knots. In as little as fifteen minutes, her screw can be lifted and withdrawn making her an ideal sailing vessel. Although she has only 8 guns, they're strategically placed and highly maneuverable and are also of sufficient caliber to get the job done.

"Presently, the Confederate Navy is searching for a companion vessel to compliment the *CSS Alabama*. We are aware of such a vessel…the *Sea King*, which is currently moored on the Thames in London. The *Sea King*, built in Glasgow, is scheduled to begin sea trials in just a few weeks. Those trials will take her all the way to Wellington, New Zealand, Bombay, India and back."

"It's our plan, if and when she's purchased, to sail the *Sea King*, along with a tender, to the waters just off Cuba and refit her with armaments similar to those found on the *CSS Alabama*. After returning my family and guests to Charleston, Captain Davis will proceed to London to inspect the vessel and see if she can be purchased. In this case, I doubt President Davis will let cost get in the way of purchasing such a fine ship.

"Currently, the Union Navy has two squadrons of ships blockading Charleston, one north and one south of the harbor entrance. Thus far, I would have to say the Union Navy has achieved only marginal success in blockading Charleston's harbor. We believe three-quarters of the cargo formerly exiting Charleston is still getting through. Recent intelligence tells us some blockade ships have detached from their squadrons and are now anchored in Port Royal Sound.

"General Beauregard told me their presence at Port Royal might signal future actions against our guns on Morris and James Islands. If this is the case, we should try to ship as much cargo as possible out of Charleston between now and January."

Ray paused, looking down for a moment, "Thus far, my news has been in a positive vein. However, I also have some sad news to report from Charleston. At one a.m. on August 22nd, Union gunners for the first time unleashed a Parrott Gun on the city from a remote part of Morris Island. A report in Charleston's daily paper, the *Mercury* stated the crew and Unit Commander affectionately referred to the Parrott gun as the *Swamp Angel*. Over a three-day period, August 22nd, 23rd and 24th, a total of 36 shells landed in the city. The shelling began at one a.m., catching local residents completely by surprise. In all, sixteen shells landed in Charleston the first night, ten of these were laced with an incendiary chemical known as *Greek Fire*. Impact patterns tell us St. Michael's Cathedral was likely their primary aiming point. If it's any consolation, after firing 19 rounds on the 3rd day, the *Swamp Angel*'s barrel exploded killing three Union cannoneers."

After Ray's comments about the *Swamp Angel*'s barrel exploding, members of the audience began shouting, "Kill the bastards!" and "Put another one in his grave!" and "Serves 'em right!"

Once the room quieted enough for him to continue, Ray said, "After the initial shelling, General Beauregard immediately notified Union General Gilmore that civilians were still in the city. Gilmore sent a hurried reply saying he thought all non-combatants had been evacuated and added he would delay any further shelling until 11 p.m. the following night. After the 24th, no more shells struck Charleston, day or night. Thus far, I would assess the damage as moderate hit or miss, meaning some structures were substantially damaged while others remain unscathed.

"Nearly all the damage was south of Calhoun Street. The shelling caused many businesses, restaurants, banks and hotels to move further north beyond Charleston College. General Beauregard moved his headquarters from the *James Simmons House* at 37 Meeting Street to the *Aiken-Rhett House* at 48 Elizabeth Street, four blocks north of Calhoun Street.

"As most of you know, nearly all our ports have already fallen, making it even more important to keep Charleston's port open at all cost. Thus far, General Beauregard has been up to the task and done a masterful job of keeping ironsides and gunboats at bay while ensuring safe passage for Confederate and commercial ships wishing to enter or leave the Harbor.

He certainly deserves our gratitude. Before I ask Clement to finish out this meeting, I have one more item.

"After Captain Davis returns my party to Charleston, he will be sailing the *John Jameson* to London to inspect the sloop *Sea King.* The ship is 220-feet long and has a 850-horsepower steam engine. It was built for Alexander Stevens and Sons of Glasgow. The *North Britain Daily Mail* just reported she will soon be heading out for her sea trails to Wellington, New Zealand, Calcutta, India and back. Captain Davis will be joining James Dunwoody Bulloch, Confederate Chief Foreign Agent in Great Britain in London to look her over and see about purchasing her. We have been told she is currently moored on the Thames in London. The Confederate Navy has advised us once she is refitted, she will be renamed the *CSS Shenandoah.* Her purpose will be the same as the *CSS Alabama,* to roam the high seas capturing and sinking ships carrying cargo to and from the United States. Isn't the *CSS Shenandoah* a great name for our next ocean-going raider? We expect great things from her."

All heads turned as a man rose and started to leave.

"Sergeant at Arms. The gentleman now leaving is Captain Joe Davis, Skipper of the *John Jameson.* He has meetings to attend with Montreal port officials to coordinate our cargo deliveries and make sure the paperwork is in order for our return trip to Charleston. Sorry for the interruption. Clement, with those items out of the way, I'll relinquish the podium to you for your summation."

"Thanks, Ray. I have a few words to express on behalf of what is now called 'The Sons of Liberty.'"

Figure 21. *CSS Shenandoah.*

As Clement rose from his chair, he picked up some papers lying on the table in front of him and began walking toward the podium. About halfway there, he crumpled his notes and threw them aside. When he reached the podium, he began, "As most of you know the membership of the 'Sons of Liberty' comes primarily from members of the Copperheads Order and the Knights of the Golden Circle. In general, I believe everyone in this room is trying to achieve one or more of three long-term goals. The first is absolute victory. The second is a negotiated settlement, and the third is secession from the Union. I presume for everyone a negotiated settlement would be the preferred outcome. However, I suspect, too, there are many of you who would only accept a negotiated settlement if it allowed us to keep our freedom, our homes, our families and our way of life to include the keeping and holding of slaves.

"This meeting was put together primarily to see if we could bring about a negotiated settlement on terms acceptable to the South. I see three shorter-term objectives that must be accomplished in order to reach this goal. First, we need to create havoc and disarray during the election cycle in the northwest states of Ohio, Indiana, Kentucky, Illinois, and Missouri. We believe this chaos and dissatisfaction will lead to the election of candidates more sympathetic to the South and our causes.

"Our second objective is to sabotage communication and transportation lines wherever we find them. Lincoln relies heavily on telegraph communication to get intelligence to and from his commanders in the field. The Union also depends heavily on the railroads to deliver troops, ammunition and war supplies to the expanses of the Northwest states and further west into Indian Territory.

"Our third objective is to incite residents of the northwest states to riot causing them to revolt and form own Confederacy. Tomorrow, we will examine these objectives to see if we can come up with priorities acceptable to everyone. As we go into tomorrow's session, it's important to remember these missions might make the difference between winning or losing this war. Everyone knows the North enjoys many advantages. They have more soldiers, more food, more weapons, etc. What they don't have is the same dedication to their cause as we have to ours. We've been tested and won many battles even when seriously outnumbered and outgunned. In recent months, however, we've suffered major losses at Gettysburg and Vicksburg. It's now more important than ever that we convince the northwest states to secede from the Union and form their own Confederacy.

"President Davis has demonstrated his great faith in us by funding our operations out of Canada. It is now time for us to us to stop the bleeding. Next year, about this same time, I want us to return to the St. Lawrence Hall to evaluate our progress. I'm sure we all hope that by this time next year the North has either fallen or negotiated a settlement permitting us to return to our homes and families."

***

Clement paused as a member of the audience approached him and whispered in his ear. "Ladies and gentlemen, excuse me, please—I have an announcement! I've just been informed that one of our esteemed colleagues from the West has arrived at the train station. He's bringing with him a large valise containing an undisclosed amount of cash. I'm sure you've all read about his exploits with his brother Frank in your local papers. What some of you might not be aware of is that Jesse is a member of the Knights of the Golden Circle and a major contributor to our coffers here in Montreal. With someone from the west on their way here from the train station, this is a good place to end today's formal presentations. If anyone else wants to make a presentation to the group, let's take a few minutes before tomorrow's planning sessions and allow them to do so."

As Clement finished and was returning to his seat, a tall man dressed in a blue pin-striped suit appeared in the center of the twin oak entry doors carrying a large valise that he handed to the Sergeant at Arms. The man asked him to take the valise to the second floor and place its contents in the hotel safe. After scanning the room for a familiar face, he approached Ray's table and asked, "Ray, may I join you?"

"Anytime, Jesse. Anytime."

"Do you think I can get a drink?"

"What would you like?"

Jesse laughed, "After my train ride, how about something with lots of alcohol in it?"

"You're sitting next to the nephew of the owner of *Jameson's Irish Whiskey*; and I've got a shipload parked at the wharf."

"If he owns or operates a distillery, I think we need to get acquainted."

"His cover name is Ian Jameson."

"I see, what's his real name?"

"His name is Jacob Harris."

Looking at Jesse, Jacob inquired, "Sir, I think I'm operating at a slight disadvantage, what did you say your name was?"

"My name is Mr. James, but most people just call me Jesse."

Jacob extended his hand, "Pleased to meet you. I'm sorry I didn't recognize you. I guess I was expecting buckskins, a cowboy hat, and boots."

"This side of the Mississippi, a man dressed like you described draws a lot of attention, and when I'm carrying nearly $200,000 in cash, the last thing I need is more attention."

"Jesse!"

"Yes, Ray."

"Jacob will be at the Gala tonight. It'll start around 7:30 p.m. His lovely companion will be my daughter Lilly. Early next year, as part of a covert mission, she will be posing as a French Princess named Marie Theresa De Conti."

"Ray, if Elizabeth is her mother, and you're her father, she must be both stunning and smart. I look forward to meeting her."

"I am sure she'll be thrilled to meet you."

"At this sort of event we insist Jacob accompany her. Before General Beauregard grabbed him, he served as a sniper with the 51st Virginia Infantry. His ingenuity and marksmanship skills make him the perfect escort for her. He once killed a spy trying to get away with my ship schedules during a party. After he killed him, he pinned a note on his lapel identifying him as 'James Reynolds – a Yankee Spy.' The local paper had a field day with the note. The police just thought it was amusing."

Turning to Jacob, Jesse handed him a card, "Jacob, here is my business card in case you ever need me. Most of the people with these cards are members of the Knights of the Golden Circle, or close friends. Actually, it seems the only people in Missouri who don't know where to find me are the police and Pinkertons. If you're ever in Missouri, look me up."

As Ray was getting ready to leave, he asked Jesse, "How's Frank?"

"He's fine, but sometimes I get tired of hearing him quote Shakespeare all the time. He must have read every play the man wrote. He has copies of *Macbeth, Midsummer Night's Dream, Othello* and *Romeo and Juliet* scattered all over the house."

"Jesse, why don't you order something to eat and stay a while?"

"I'd love to, Ray, but Clement's asked me to make the rounds and meet some of the folks unable to attend the Gala. After a few handshakes, I plan to slip out, retire and have supper brought to my room. If I'm lucky, I might be able to take a short nap before the Gala. I want to make sure I have enough strength to have at least one dance with Lilly."

"You'll have to be very careful with my daughter. Jacob is her beau, and he can be very protective."

Jesse grinned at Jacob, "Jacob, I'll make sure I keep my Colt in its holster. A good rifleman can take a man brandishing a six-gun every time."

"That's okay, Jesse," Jacob interjected. "If Ray trusts you, so do I."

Ray added after Jesse left, "Don't forget, Jacob, tonight Lilly will be incognito. Her name will be Princess Marie Theresa De Conti.'

"Thanks for reminding me, I'll see you sometime after seven."

# Chapter Twenty-Three

## *The Gala*

AFTER the meeting, Jacob and Lilly shared a carriage with her parents and visited one of the finer eating establishments near the Hostellerie Pierre du Calvet. Once inside, they took seats in the small but elegant dining room. Lilly and her mother peppered Ray and Jacob with many questions about the upcoming sessions and Gala. Ray assured both ladies the prevailing attitude was still positive, in spite of hard debating about the relative benefit of General Morgan's disastrous raid into Kentucky, Indiana, and Ohio. Smiling broadly, Ray also declared that Jacob played his role magnificently, noting that not a single person challenged his new identity. Lilly was thrilled her dad's comments about Jacob were so positive.

Elizabeth was far more to the point. She sought more details on Morgan's raid and asked Ray if he thought the costly raid was worth it. She also asked about the rumors she'd heard from Charleston that General Beauregard was expecting more shelling now that Battery Wagner was under constant attack by Gilmore's troops.

Elizabeth was not at all satisfied with Ray's answers. She asked, "What role is Lilly supposed to play in Confederate espionage activities in the near future?"

Before either Ray or Jacob could answer, she added, "That includes Jacob as well. He makes her very happy. He and Lorenzo fought off those attackers in Charleston by themselves, and we likely wouldn't be here if they hadn't done so."

Turning to Jacob she said, "I regret I didn't say those words sooner."

Jacob took one of Elizabeth's hands in his, kissed it and said softly, "I was just trying to help Lilly, Ma'am."

Blushing slightly, but clearly touched, Elizabeth said, "Thank you, Jacob. Ray and I know you are a fine young man."

Thrilled and stunned at the same time, Lilly was pleased that her parents accepted Jacob and his brother so enthusiastically. Ray tried his best to answer Elizabeth's questions regarding Morgan's raid and Lilly and Jacob's role in future espionage activities for the Confederate Secret Service. Somewhat reluctantly, Ray admitted, "Morgan's raid went too far and was too costly. The South lost more than 2,000 well trained cavalrymen and gained nothing. The North lost less than a hundred militiamen, a few buildings, a telegraph office, and a few dozen horses. General Morgan's rationale for the raid seemed unclear from the start. Before the raid General Morgan justified the raid by saying he was going north to cut off Federal troops trying to advance into Tennessee; thereby, helping General Bragg. In any case, it appears Morgan's raid was a bad idea from its inception."

Ray's response to Elizabeth's second question certainly did not satisfy her. To reassure her, he said as soon as they returned to Charleston, he would check with General Beauregard and get a complete update. Ray's response did nothing to soothe Elizabeth. "Ray, you need to ask Beauregard how long he expects the shelling of Charleston to continue and how long he thinks it will be before the blockade ships anchored in Port Royal Sound return to their assigned patrol areas."

In a feeble attempt to reassure his wife again, Ray patted her hand and said, "Yes, dear! I'll make sure I ask General Beauregard every one of your questions."

Elizabeth's last question was, by far, the toughest for Ray to answer. He said, "I understand Lilly and Jacob will be reconnoitering hotels and military facilities in the United States and Canada for the Confederate Secret Service. I can reassure all of you that Jacob and Lilly's travel documents are impeccable. They will have no problems entering or exiting the United States or Canada. Although the missions are important ones, they will be infrequent and not particularly dangerous."

Unimpressed, Elizabeth spoke, "Ray, it's one thing for Lilly to take a whirl around a dance floor talking with various dance partners, but travelling into the United States and reconnoitering hotels for kidnapping or assassination attempts is quite another."

Ray could not think of a response for his wife's last comment.

Seeing the standoff, Lilly spoke up to quell the tension, "Mother, this has to be done, and Jacob and I are the right people to do it. We have impeccable travel documents, and Jacob is exactly the right man to protect me. I'm pretty sure we're both smarter than any old Pinkerton the Yankees hire to protect their dignitaries. I promise you our job is just to observe and take detailed notes on what we see. If it would make you feel better, I'll take the notes in French. I doubt if any of them speak French or know the

Confederate codes as well as I do.  I have already translated the codes into French, so I won't have to do that again."

Seeing her daughter's enthusiasm, Elizabeth finally said softly, "As long as Jacob is with you, I'm okay with it.  Do you know where the first location is they want you to canvas?"

Lilly responded, "I haven't heard anything official, but I recall hearing someone speak about the Galt House in Louisville."

Jacob added, "I seriously doubt they'll tell us the nature of the mission.  It's easier to be convincing when you say you don't know—especially if you don't."

"Do you have any idea how you are going to get to Louisville?" Ray asked.

"Daddy, I think it would be marvelous if we could take a paddle-wheel steamer from Pittsburgh or Cincinnati down the Ohio to New Orleans with a stop at Louisville. Completing the trip all the way to New Orleans would fit in with our cover of being tourists traveling across the United States.  It'd also give us additional time on the river to jot down the locations of gunboats and defensive positions along the Ohio and Mississippi rivers."

"Whoa! Young lady," Ray exclaimed.  "I'm sure the Secret Service has plenty of people tracking the flow of ironsides and gunboats down the Ohio and Mississippi Rivers.  I'm equally sure we know the strength of the defensive forces along those rivers and tributaries.  What we don't have is someone inside the Galt House taking notes on the locations of individual hotel rooms, dining rooms and meeting rooms and the specific security measures being taken to protect visiting dignitaries in staying in the hotel."

"But Daddy, I'm in this for the long haul. That's why I wanted to take the entire trip all the way to New Orleans.  With so many people there speaking French, I could polish mine. I've heard so many exciting stories about the city."

Ray grumbled, "So have I, young lady!  And they're not all good.  You can follow whatever plan Thad Culpepper gives you.  But remember, this is a package deal. You don't go anywhere on any operation without Jacob. Your mother and I insist."

While they were talking, a waitress stopped by and asked, "Should I bring hot coffee or tea to the table?"

"Yes please, both… with cream and sugar for the coffee."

"Does anyone want an appetizer of some kind?"

"Honestly, I don't think we're going to have time."

"I'll can see if the cook will expedite your order."

At this point, Ray gave the waitress a little wink, and she returned one in kind.

The waitress asked, "Are you going to the Confederate Gala at the St. Lawrence Hall tonight? I'm sure it will be a lovely event.  By the way, if you know anybody that's available, I'm still looking for an escort. I think it must be the worst kept secret in Montreal."

After they finished their meal, Ray and Jacob excused themselves to step outside for a quick puff on one of Ray's favorite cigars.  Once the men were outside, Elizabeth beckoned the waitress to come to the table.  A slight edge in her voice, she inquired, "Young lady, did I just see you wink at my husband?"

"Yes Ma'am," she said, grinning.  "Your husband's been coming here for more than twenty years. Back then my parents owned the place. Whenever he or Captain Davis returned from a tea junket to China or Japan, they'd stop by and say hello. A few years back I lost my husband when he fell off a schooner in a storm. They were trying to navigate the waters off Cape Horn when a gale-force wind blew white caps over the front of the ship, leaving me a widow with two children. Whenever your husband or Captain Davis docked in Montreal they stopped by and brought toys or games for my children. Ma'am, you're fortunate to be married to such a kind and considerate man. That's why we wink when we see each other."

Relieved, Elizabeth looked at the waitress and asked, "Honey, what's your name?"

"My name is Julie Jeffers."

"Miss Jeffers, I very much appreciate your honesty.  It's good to know that my husband is not trying to flirt with an attractive girl in front of me."

"Mrs. Cooper?"

"Yes."

"We were flirting… but it's been going on since I was eight."

"I'm so sorry.  I had no idea."

Miss Jeffers smiled at Elizabeth and beamed at Ray when he and Jacob returned to escort Elizabeth and Lilly to the Gala. Within minutes, they hailed a hack and returned to the St. Lawrence Hall Hotel. Once inside, Ray checked at the front desk for messages and asked where the Gala was going to be held.  The desk clerk advised Ray that the meeting room they had used for their gatherings was already converted into a ballroom. As Ray, Elizabeth, Lilly and Jacob approached the ballroom, they saw several couples already queued up to be announced.  When their turn finally came, the Sergeant at Arms, in a booming voice declared, "Ladies and Gentlemen, it is my great honor and pleasure to announce the arrival of Ray and Elizabeth Cooper. Mr. Cooper is a shipping magnet, owner of the finest fleet of clippers, schooners, frigates, and sloops found on the high seas. His wife Elizabeth is known to host the finest parties, dances, and charity events in the distinguished, and always beautiful, city of Charleston."

As Ray and Elizabeth were escorted to their table, Elizabeth looked at Ray and asked, "Dear, who was that man, and just how much did you tip him to make that splendid announcement?"

"His name is Paul Allen Schroeder, and I didn't have to tip him anything. He's the signalman aboard the *John Jameson*. Some people say when the fog is low and you can't see the signal flags, he just shouts his message to nearby ships."

"Let's look back and see how he introduces Jacob and Lilly."

In a whisper, Ray said to Elizabeth, "Dear, remember we can't use those names here."

"Sorry, dear."

As Jacob and Lilly approached incognito, Paul Schroeder opened the double oak doors and announced, "Ladies and gentlemen. It is a pleasure and great honor to introduce you to Mr. Ian Jameson and his fiancée, Princess Marie Theresa De Conti. Mr. Jameson is the nephew of the owner of the Jameson Distillery in Dublin Ireland. Miss De Conti is a graduate student studying at the Sorbonne in Paris. She is here in Montreal studying the influences French culture have on the Province of Quebec and the city of Montreal. Let me add, the striking style of her gown confirms her Paris origins. Let's give these two, who have travelled all the way from Europe, a warm southern welcome. For those of us who might be wondering what their role is in all of this, let me assure you—it is a very important one."

Delighted with the introduction, Elizabeth whispered to Ray, "Be sure you give Mr. Schroeder a very nice tip. I insist!"

When everyone was seated, Clement Vallandigham reestablished himself as the Master of Ceremonies and proceeded with a few formalities. He called Jacob Thompson to the podium to present the invocation.

"Clement, I would be happy to."

"Our precious Father, we give thanks for the meeting we have just completed. We ask you to bless all in attendance who seek peace for the Confederacy. This evening has been reserved as a time of fellowship; to allow us to develop greater friendships and trust in one another. Let it be your will that we are successful in achieving our lofty goals and may

God continue to bless the attendees, their home states and the Confederate States of America."

"Mr. Thompson, what a wonderful invocation."

"Thank you, Clement."

"Earlier today Ray Cooper gave us a rather subdued rendition of the Confederate National Anthem, 'God Save the South.' Before the Gala, I asked Ray to return to the podium after the Invocation and lead us in a hearty rendition of the same song—only this time he will be accompanied by our military orchestra."

When Ray finished his rousing rendition of the anthem and everyone was again seated, Clement thanked Ray. "What a marvelous job you did singing a song we all cherish so much! Might we hear another relevant to the South and its deep-seated heritage?"

"By all means, Clement. As I was looking through a book of patriotic southern songs suitable for this occasion, I came upon a song holding special significance to everyone in the south. It was sung at President Davis' inaugural. The song is entitled 'I'm Going Home to Dixie.'

Ray sang from the heart in a voice that was deep and full, touching all in the room.

*1. There is a land where cotton grows,*
*A land where milk and honey flows:*
*I'm going home to Dixie.*
*Yes; I am going home*
*(Chorus:)*

*I've got no time to tarry,*
*I've got no time to stay,*
*"Tis a rocky road to travel,*
*to Dixie far away.*

*I've got no time to tarry,*
*I've got no time to stay,*
*"Tis a rocky road to travel,*
*to Dixie far away.*

*I will climb up the highest hill,*
*And sing your praise with right good will*
*I'm going home to Dixie,*
*Yes, I am going home.*
*(Chorus:)*

*2. I've wander'd far, both to and fro'*
*But Dixie's heaven here and below.*
*I'm going home to Dixie,*
*Yes, I'm going home.*
*(Chorus:)*

*3. O'list to what I've got to say,*
*Freedom to me will never pay!*
*I'm going home to Dixie*
*Yes; I'm going home*
*(Chorus:)*

"Ray, I can't speak for everyone else here but my heart stirred with every note. Thank you so much for bringing us those wonderful words. Lastly, Ray, can I ask you to sing 'Dixie' for this special occasion? It's certainly my favorite song, and I have heard Mr. Lincoln is particularly fond of it as well. That's what I would call irony."

"Clement, 'Dixie' is a special song loved by nearly everyone. I want the audience to feel free to join me as I sing, this time accompanied by our fine military orchestra."

*I wish I were in Dixie*
*I wish I was in the land of cotton,*
*Old times there are not forgotten;*
*Look away! Look away! Look away! Dixie Land*
*In Dixie's Land where I was born,*
*Early on one frosty morning,*
*Look away! Look away! Look away! Dixie Land*

*I wish I was in Dixie, Hooray! Hooray*
*In Dixie's Land, I'll take my stand*
*To live or die in Dixie.*
*Now here's to the health to the next ole Missus*
*An' all the gals that want to kiss you*
*Look away! Look away! Look away! Dixie Land*

*And if you want to drive away sorrow*
*Come and hear our song tomorrow!*
*Look away! Look away! Look away! Dixie Land*

The hall reverberated with the sound of the audience clapping enthusiastically. "Ray, you might have just presented the best rendition of 'Dixie'

I've ever heard. Let's hear some more applause out there for the finest troubadour in the Confederacy.  I checked with the band and they've assured me they have a complete repertoire of southern music for tonight's activities.  To name a few, they included the following:  Ol' Dan Tucker, The Virginia Reel, To the Girl I left behind, Shiloh, Rock the Cradle – Julie, Bright Sunny South, The Arkansas Traveler, The Wearing of the Grey, The Southern Soldier, and for our friends out west—The Yellow Rose of Texas.  The band assured me they know many more.  If you don't hear your favorite the first time around, feel free to ask for it. The dance floor is officially open, so Mr. Maestro, begin when you're ready."

A few moments after the sound of the orchestra's music filled the room, a line of gentlemen formed at Jacob and Lilly's table, all wanting to ask Lilly for a dance. Her long deep blue gown was unlike anything else seen at the ball.  It highlighted her figure in ways she couldn't have imagined.  She appeared both elegant and graceful as she glided across the dance floor to the strains of the promised southern songs. After several dances, Jacob cut in and asked if she was ready for a drink.

A little breathless, she replied, "With you?  By all means!"

# Chapter Twenty-Four

## *Second Attack on the John Jameson*

IN A romantic mood, Jacob and Lilly strolled outside on the hotel balcony to enjoy the view. There was not a cloud in the night sky. Looking toward the dock from their high vantage point, they could see a strange gunship with lights out making its way upstream in almost total darkness.

"Jacob," Lilly said in a hushed voice, "Look! There—to your right. Do you see that ship running upstream with her lights out?"

"Just barely, dear. It's very dark out there."

"I think we'd better tell Daddy and Captain Davis to get down there and warn the crew." Lilly was becoming more agitated by the second.

"Lilly, I'm sure Captain Davis would post lookouts to keep anything bad from happening," Jacob said to reassure her.

"I know, Jacob. But I don't see any activity on daddy's ship. Something's wrong? I can just feel it. We have to do something."

Realizing there was cause for concern, he said to her, "Lilly, go fetch your dad and Captain Davis. In the meantime, I'll get my rifle and make my way down there to see if anyone is standing watch."

"Jacob, be careful. The ship coming upstream is only a half-mile away. After I tell daddy and Captain Davis, I'll notify the Montreal police and see what they can do to prevent the ship from approaching the wharf where the *John Jameson* is docked."

"Honey, dressed in that gown, I'm sure the Montreal police will listen to you. And once they find out you speak French, you'll have them eating out of your hand."

Minutes later, Jacob was on the wharf looking for the *John Jameson*'s forward lookout. As he approached the ship, he discovered the body of the lookout, Seaman Roger Sharp, lying face down on the wharf, an arrow protruding from his back—an arrow that could only have been fired from a nearby dock across the water. Uneasy already, Jacob's gut clenched when he saw Sharp had been scalped and his throat cut. Sharp had taught Jacob on the voyage to Montreal how to improve his chess game with moves he had learned from a book. As Jacob quickly scanned the area for intruders, another man dressed as a Mohawk slipped out from behind the mizzenmast and fired an arrow at him. In an instant Jacob dropped to the wharf's wooden deck, the arrow zipping by his head and landing with a thunk into the dock. He had performed this maneuver many times as a boy playing cowboys and Indians with Lorenzo behind the Harris' home. From his prone position, without a moment's hesitation, Jacob lifted his rifle and fired at the attacker. The man stumbled before falling back against the oak main mast.

By this time, Ray and Captain Davis had arrived and found the first intruder's body lying at the end of an adjacent wharf. Apparently after being hit by an arrow, Sergeant Sharp was still able to get off one shot, hitting the intruder in his spleen. Although the man's face was covered with Mohawk war paint, his facial features revealed to Ray and Captain Davis they were looking at a white man. Underneath his Indian clothing, the man wore the uniform of a Union Infantry Sergeant. Within minutes Ray, Jacob, and Captain Davis stormed up the gangplank to look for any additional Union attackers. They found crewmen John Stead, Robert Morehead, Stewart Tanner, and Raymond Churchill, all scalped, lying on the deck. Captain Davis' fourteen-year old cabin boy Tommy Sullivan was the only survivor. Despite an arrow in his leg, he had managed to crawl to the stern and hide in a box where unused folded sails were stored.

Observing five members of his crew stacked on the deck awaiting burial, Captain Davis was furious. Looking first at Ray and then Jacob he exclaimed, "Damn it, these were all good men…not just sailors…good men! If I didn't have to return to Charleston, I'd assemble my own war party and go after the bastards myself."

Placing a hand gently on Captain Davis' shoulder in sympathy, Ray said, "Joe, these were Yankee soldiers, trying to make this look like an Indian raid. You're right when you say these were all good men. We'll have a chance to tell everyone on board what kind of men they were when we bury them at sea with all the accompanying traditions."

After covering the bodies, Ray turned to Jacob and asked, "Jacob, what do you make of this mess?"

"I think the Yanks wanted to attack when the fewest number of people were aboard. I don't know whether they were trying to steal the whiskey, sink the ship or just burn her to the waterline; but it's evident they wanted to harm us. I just hope we find out who ordered the raid. Someday, I'm going to take out the bastard."

With the threat on board the *John Jameson* taken care of, Ray voiced his concern about the approaching gunship, "The question now appears to be how to stop the gunship before we come within its range. Jacob, what do you think?"

Right after Lilly pointed out the ship, she was going to tell Montreal police about the boat on the river steaming upstream without lights. "I'm pretty sure they'll figure out the ship is up to no good. I'll tell them we believe the *John Jameson* is their target."

"Smart girl! I don't think the Montreal police or militia want a Union gunboat operating in the river in front of the public docks."

Then Ray addressed Captain Davis, "Get the rest of your crew, arm them, and station them on the wharf in front of the ship. I'm not going to give her up without a fight. Once the Yankee gunboat crosses an imaginary line 400 yards downstream from the *John Jameson*, unleash a heavy dose of cannon fire on top of her. If the local militia hasn't already figured this out, I imagine they will join in and try to force the gunboat to retreat. They certainly don't want to have to explain an attack on a ship docked at a Montreal public wharf."

***

As the Yankee gunboat proceeded upstream toward the Port, Lilly was watching signal-flag conversations between Montreal's Central Police Headquarters and a militia gun emplacement on top of a hill overlooking the St. Lawrence River and the Port of Montreal. As the gunboat passed within 700 yards downstream from the port, the police station signaled the gun battery to fire if the gunboat crossed a line 500 yards downstream from Port of Montreal. When the gunboat did cross the mark, the militia began firing at the gunboat. After firing twenty rounds, it was clear the Canadians were not trying to sink the gunboat. Before the gunboat changed direction, the gun battery let loose another twenty rounds, only this time their aim was a lot closer. As the gunboat turned to head downstream, the gun battery released a third barrage of twenty additional rounds. The gunboat had no choice but to reverse course and head for the mouth of the St. Lawrence. Because of its small size, speed and substantial armament, the Union gunboat appeared to have sustained little damage. Nonetheless, the Canadian gun crews clearly demonstrated they were perfectly capable of keeping Union gunships from operating in the St. Lawrence River. After the shelling stopped, Lilly joined her father, Jacob and Captain Davis on the wharf. Ray took a moment and thanked Jacob for spotting trouble on his ship.

Jacob responded, "Sir, don't thank me. It was Lilly who pointed out the Yankee gunboat steaming upstream with no lights."

"You are indeed once again a modest man, Jacob. Thanks for your help."

The attack lasted less than an hour. When it was over, Ray, Captain Davis, Lilly and Jacob returned to the Gala as if nothing had happened. Once they were seated, Ray asked Lilly, "Did the Montreal police accept your statement about the gunboat without a fuss."

"Oh, yes, daddy. They were most helpful. They believed every word I told them and quickly signaled instructions to the gun batteries in the hills to fire on the gunboat if it came within 500 yards of the *John Jameson*, or opened fire on it."

"Where did the 500 yards come from?"

"It came from my head, of course. I figured if they were going to try to sink our ship they would fire from outside 500 yards. Coming in as they did, it was a dead giveaway they wanted to board her and take everything they could. Had they been successful, I suspect they would have torched her."

After listening to Lilly's rationale, Jacob gazed at her with admiration and said, "Honey, your estimate was right on. If the militia hadn't fired when they did, we'd have been goners. All but one of the crew left on board were dead. At that moment, only your dad and I were there to defend the ship. Captain Davis had left to get his men and bring them back to the dock."

When the Gala was over, Ray, Elizabeth, Lilly and Jacob stepped into their carriage. Ray asked if everyone would care to stop for crepes on the way back to the Hostellerie Pierre du Calvet. Everyone was both tired and famished, and acknowledged stopping for crepes was a great idea. When they finished their crepes, they climbed into Ray's carriage and returned to the hotel. Before going back to their rooms, all agreed tonight was one of those nights when sleep would be most welcome.

The next morning, the two couples met in the hotel lobby to discuss their plans for the day. Ray asked the doorman to summon his driver and carriage to take himself, Jacob and Lilly to the St. Lawrence Hotel. Elizabeth was going to take a hack downtown to shop for more accessories for the dresses she purchased a few days before.

In a few minutes the doorman approached Ray to tell him his carriage was waiting outside. The three of them walked outside and stepped into the carriage. Elizabeth waved to Ray and walked back into the hotel before asking the doorman to hail a hack.

At 8:30 everyone entered the alcove adjacent to the meeting room and selected breakfast items of croissants and fruits and coffee and tea to take to the dining room. No formal presentations were scheduled for today's meeting.  Instead, the organizations broke up into groups to plan, in greater detail, specific operations they wanted to pursue.  As each mission group formed, Ray met with them to coordinate their timetable with the projects of other groups so they would not be in conflict. He encouraged them to prioritize their projects in such a way the goals of the Knights of the Golden Circle, the Sons of Liberty, and the Confederacy would be preserved. Within a few hours, Ray was pleased to notice members of all the factions walking between rooms and discussing amongst themselves the best way to carry out their individual missions without interfering with the missions of others.

Jacob and Lilly knew the nature of their operation required them to meet with the Confederate Secret Service.  According to Ray the Secret Service office was on the first floor in an unnumbered, large conference room at the end of the east-wing hallway. The Secret Service had requested the location to make it easier for couriers to enter and leave their office unobserved.

To Ray's surprise, everyone in attendance agreed on the Secret Services' plot to kidnap Vice President Johnson. Everyone  hoped the Vice President could be exchanged for large numbers of Confederate troops held in Union prisons. All present also agreed that because of its importance, the kidnapping should be accomplished by the Confederate Secret Service.  By 1863, the Secret Service had already built a reputation for having the best people to gather intelligence and act on it.

Upon entering the unmarked room, it was immediately apparent to Jacob and Lilly that this was where the Secret Service had set up shop.  Thad Culpepper and Jacob Thompson peered down at street maps of Louisville trying to determine the likely route the Vice President would use to get from the main docks to the hotel. In his left hand, Thad held a hand-written train schedule. After reviewing it, he mumbled to Jacob Thompson something about an alternate plan should the original escape route be compromised or inaccessible.

Thus far, neither Thad nor Jacob Thompson had noticed Jacob and Lilly had entered the room, let alone had approached the large table where the maps lay unfolded.

Jacob spoke first, "Excuse me, can anyone get in on this session?"

Thad turned to acknowledged Jacob's comment, "I guess you caught us by surprise. Let's see, your names are Ian Jameson and Princess Marie Theresa De Conti.  Did I get that right?"

"Those are the names on our travel documents.  Our real names are Jacob and Lilly."

"Lilly, can I see those travel documents?"

"Yes, sir. Here they are."

Culpepper examined the documents carefully, turning them over several times. "These are real!  These are not fakes," he declared.

"We had a lot of help, Mr. Culpepper," Lilly said.  "The signatures are genuine—thanks to officials in the County Dublin's Clerk's office."

Jacob added, "Mr. Cooper's transported *Jameson's Irish whiskey* for several years and knows both the Sheriff and County Clerk personally."

"If he can get valid signatures like these, he and I have a lot to discuss. By the way young lady, how do you know Ray?"

"He's my father."

Nodding, Culpepper smiled and said, "Ah!  I should have known… forgive me.  You look like your mother."

Lilly was intrigued.  It was her turn to wonder, "How do you know my mother?  Did you meet her at the Gala?"

"I did, but I first met her several years ago when she did some work for us.  As I recall, it required a person who spoke French. I believe she negotiated a contract for Lorenz guns through a French manufacturer.  Ray picked up the guns in a schooner and brought them back to either Mobile or Charleston." Looking at the papers again, he said, "I see your papers show you are a French graduate student at the Sorbonne. How well do you speak French?"

"Well enough to negotiate with French emissaries in Charleston for the exchange of our cotton for French-made firearms."

Culpepper nodded approvingly, then said, "Talent and beauty! What a wonderful combination for espionage."

"There is one catch, however.  Daddy says I can't go anywhere without Jacob. He's my beau and he's saved my life on several occasions. In Charleston, he shot and killed a Yankee spy named James Reynolds after he stole some ship schedules from my daddy's desk while I was making drinks for my other guests."

"We're quite familiar with Mr. Reynolds. Catching or killing him was a high priority for us. He didn't look much like a spy, but I suspect that's why he was so successful." Turning to Jacob he said, "I hope you don't mind if I direct this next question to Lilly."

Jacob shrugged, indicating with a sweep of his arm toward Lilly for him to go ahead.

"Lilly, What can you tell me about Jacob?"

"He's a Confederate soldier and I've known him for some time. Currently he's with General Beauregard's militia. Before General

Beauregard acquired him, he was a sharpshooter with the 51st Virginia Infantry Regiment—and he has real combat experience that includes serving with the 50th Virginia at Gettysburg. Before coming to Montreal, he and his brother Lorenzo held off an attack from 20 coloreds posing as dockworkers in Charleston. They were attempting to board the ship with the intent of stealing her cargo and burning her down to her waterline. I can't imagine what they might have done to Captain Davis, his crew or my parents."

"How did you know what their intentions were—what led you to believe the coloreds weren't Charleston dockworkers?"

"Sir, my friend Lucy and I saw them earlier in the day, and they were all wearing the same kind of boots and similar silk scarves around their necks. Also, all of them were speaking in a French dialect. Lucy, whose family owns a chandlery in New Orleans, told me the dialect sounded like it came from there. Later in the day we asked General Beauregard, who's from New Orleans, to come to the docks and confirm the dockworkers were, in fact, speaking a New Orleans French dialect. During the attack, Jacob and Lorenzo killed about half of them. General Beauregard's troops rounded up the rest and interrogated them. Beauregard finished their interrogations himself. Being from New Orleans, they never had a chance. They said they were recruited in New Orleans after the fall of the Port. They were ordered to take the cargo, burn the *John Jameson* to the waterline and kill all the passengers."

Lilly shuddered, just thinking about it. "All of this happened while my parents were still on board. They'd just arrived from Europe with a shipment of guns and ammunition. As we walked down the pier to meet the ship we noticed the colored imposters gathering near a warehouse at the end of Atlantic Pier. This time we saw they were wearing side arms like those issued to Union Navy personnel. I'm sure Jacob can tell you the exact type and caliber."

Jacob interrupted briefly saying, "They carried 36-caliber 1851 Colt Revolvers—the weapon used by the Union Navy."

Lilly squeezed Jacob's arm, smiled at him, then looked at Thad, and said, "I told you he would know."

"Lilly, do you know anything about Confederate codes or ciphers?"

Lilly nodded, "Yes, sir. I use them myself a great deal when I work with our spotters on the outer islands. The spotter's job is to track the position of Union ships patrolling Charleston's coast. Sometimes when my mother was on board the *John Jameson*, I sent cipher messages to her in French; making it more difficult for them to be intercepted and deciphered. The last time I was in Paris, I had a cipher made similar to the Vigenere cypher designed by Francis La Barre. Generally, our messages contain information on the locations of blockade ships in the area, the best channel to be used to avoid obstacles in the harbor, and which wharf to use when they dock."

At this point, Thompson made his way around the table and introduced himself, "I'm  Jacob Thompson, and unofficially I'm in charge of the Secret Service." He had been listening intently, "I am absolutely fascinated by what I have just heard!  So, you know about cyphers, you speak French, and your personal bodyguard is an experienced sharpshooter. Is that about it?"

"Well," she said, pausing—not eager to boast about her accomplishments, yet wanting to be truthful.  "Whenever my parents are away, I run the family's shipping business and make the party circuit collecting information for General Beauregard."

Clearly impressed with her litany of talents, he turned to Jacob, "I take it you are Lilly's beau?"

"Yes, Sir.  His name is Jacob Harris," Lilly interjected before Jacob could answer.

"From what I have just heard, the two of you would be an ideal pair to canvass the Galt hotel in Louisville. Your impeccable papers will allow you to travel anywhere in the United States and Canada. Ray did a masterful job of obtaining them. We might have to call on him sometime in the future."

Thompson continued, "This operation will require a great deal of sophistication.  It's not the same as planting someone on the banks of the Ohio to count gunboats or search for enfilade mortar emplacements on the hillsides adjacent to the river.  With so many dignitaries staying at the Galt, security will be tightened up even further. Because they're close to the river, their security's always been strong.  Are you up to it?"

Jacob felt a tingle of excitement at the prospect of the mission, "Yes, sir."

"I'll get in touch after we steal a copy of the Vice President's itinerary for early next year.  Do you have any questions?"

"Yes, sir.  I do," said Lilly.  "Do you think we could get to Louisville via a paddle-wheel steamboat?  I've always wanted to take one of those trips from Cincinnati to New Orleans with a stop in Louisville, St Louis or Memphis."

"I assume you're going to say you want to do this to preserve your cover?"

Lilly raised an eyebrow as she looked at him,  "Sir, how did you even know what I would ask?"

He laughed at her response, "Because anyone in this game worth his salt would ask the same question.  For now, my answer is a resounding 'maybe.'" He glanced at his watch, then said, "I see it's time for lunch. Perhaps you can find your parents and enjoy a meal near the river.  Please tell them I said hello. I believe the mission will happen later this year. That's when the political parties send out their best speakers to the major cities to raise money. It's also a few weeks before the inaugural should Lincoln win the election. I look forward to seeing both of you then."

Jacob and Lilly shook hands with both men.  Lilly said, "Thanks to both of you. I just hope our efforts will contribute in some way."

In less than half an hour they found Ray and Elizabeth chatting with Captain Davis about the best time to return to Charleston.  Ray decided to allot a couple of days in Montreal for his family to rest and enjoy the city before returning to Charleston. Captain Davis thanked Ray for the extra few days. It had been several weeks since his crew had liberty in a major port with all of its temptations.

Ray said to Captain Davis, "Let's have the entire crew back on board not later than seven a.m. three days from now."

"Aye, Aye, Sir," Captain Davis answered.

During those three days, Ray met with the Montreal police and militia members responsible for manning the guns during the attack on the *John Jameson*.  As an expression of his gratitude he left them enough Jameson's to more than wet their whistles. In return, they told him anytime he needed such cover all he needed to do was ask. The Battery Commanders also relayed to Ray how much his men enjoyed watching the splashes around the gunship as their shells fell into the river. As Ray left, he thanked the crew again and added, "I know you missed the gunboat on purpose and could have sunk her in a Yankee minute if so ordered. Nonetheless, you did a fine job of chasing her all the way down the St. Lawrence River."

Three days later, the crew began gathering at 6 a. m. to board the ship. Clearly, the crew understood Captain Davis' orders to be there on time. Joe met Ray, Elizabeth, Lilly, and Jacob at the St. Lawrence Hall at seven for an early breakfast.  General Pike left a note at Ray's hotel telling him he had decided to stay a few days longer with his old colleague Senator William Bell with whom he worked in the Indian Territory.

After finishing his first cup of coffee, Ray asked Joe Davis about his plans for the trip.

"Once we clear the river's entrance and are in the Gulf of St. Lawrence we should keep a lookout for Cape North and Prince Edward Island. Once past those checkpoints, I think we should continue out another twenty miles or so to make sure we're beyond any Yankee gunboat patrol area. From there we should head south-southwest and keep a lookout for Yankee or British Navy vessels. That heading should give us a straight shot into Charleston."

Curious, Jacob asked, "Joe, how is it you never seem to get stopped?"

Ray rubbed his chin and chuckled. "Several years ago, the Captain heading up the patrol vessels was my First Officer. I bailed him out of trouble so many times he could never repay me. I think he told everyone on the high seas, all I ever carried was whiskey and to leave me alone. Occasionally, I send him a case or two to rekindle the memories."

A little after nine, the *John Jameson*, with all aboard, drifted away from wharf and turned sharply to the right. Joe had positioned local spotters in the hills overlooking the river and Port to make sure no gunships were present when he set sail.

Once the observer signaled the *John Jameson* the river was clear, Joe ordered sails to be hoisted and set a course for the mouth of the St. Lawrence River. After passing by Quebec City, Captain Davis piloted his ship to the mouth of the St. Lawrence, into the Gulf of St. Lawrence and continued east past Cape North and Prince Edward Island. After clearing Prince Edward Island Captain Davis ordered his helmsman to continue for another twenty-miles. There he gave the order to turn to starboard and pick up a south-by-southwest course that would take them to Charleston.

The next four days were uneventful except when they were stopped by a British 'Man of War' just off the coast of Cape Cod. Its crew had seen the name *John Jameson* on the side of the ship and asked if they had any Irish Whisky on board. Ray told the British Captain that he was not carrying a full load. As though in a spirit of generosity, he asked his men to enter the cargo hold and bring up twenty cases for the officers and men of her Majesty's Navy. The Captain graciously thanked Ray for the whiskey. As soon as it was loaded, the ropes were unhooked and the British ship drifted away.

A day out, Ray and Captain Davis met to discuss the next leg of Joe's voyage. Before discussing the next course correction, Ray asked, "Joe, did you ever get a chance to see the *Sea King* before her maiden voyage."

"No, Ray, I never got the chance. I must say sailing from England to Bombay and Wellington is quite a shakedown cruise. Now that she's back, I think we ought to consider buying her. We certainly need another war sloop to compliment the Alabama."

"You're right, of course."

"Joe, what's your role going to be in all this?"

Figure 22.  Setting sail.

"I'm going to evaluate her and negotiate a purchase price. Jeff Davis knows we need another good ship to sink commerce on the open seas. I can't believe he'll let money get in the way of this purchase."

"Where are you headed from Charleston, Joe?"

"I am going to London. The ship is moored on the Thames."

Ray gazed out over the vast expanse of water, took a puff from his cigar, gently released a steady stream of smoke, and said, "I've heard the Confederate Navy wants to sail an iron-screwed steamer the *Laurel* with the *Sea King* as her tender. I know the Confederacy has already contacted a local shipping agent named Henry Latone to make the purchase. If the *Laurel* becomes the *Sea King*'s tender, I imagine it'll accompany her to the waters just offshore Cuba and refit her with guns suitable to her purpose. If asked, I would recommend we pursue such a course. After the *Sea King* is refitted, she's to be named the *CSS Shenandoah*." Ray took another puff from his cigar, directed the stream of smoke away from Joe and said, "I can't think of a better name for her."

Figure 23. The Sea King.

# Chapter Twenty-Five

## *Charleston under fire*

SIX DAYS after leaving Montreal, Captain Davis asked his helmsman to make an arc to starboard and proceed toward the harbor entrance. When Charleston finally came into view, Lilly felt her heart fill with joy and hope. She knew most likely Lucy, Lorenzo and General Beauregard would be waiting to escort her, Jacob, Ray, Elizabeth, and Captain Davis from *Boyce's Wharf* to the *Rutledge House Inn.* Entering the harbor, Lilly saw several obstructions in the channels she had not seen before.

As the ship approached the row of wharves lining the Cooper River side of harbor, Lilly realized Captain Davis was not preparing to dock at *Boyce's Wharf.* Instead, Captain Davis floated the *John Jameson* gently into the center of South Atlantic Wharf, adjacent to *Boyce's Wharf.*

Lucy was first to notice two pilings of *Boyce's Wharf* were still smoldering and one had been sheared off just above its waterline. Charred and splintered planks lay everywhere. The carnage suggested Yankee cannoneers had hit the wharf with shells containing the incendiary *Greek Fire.*

Lilly shouted: "Jacob, come look at this!"

"All right, dear, I'm coming."

"*Boyce's Wharf* looks like it was hit. You can see it was on fire not long ago. We're docking at South Atlantic Wharf instead. I see Lucy, Solomon, and Lorenzo waiting for us on the boardwalk in front of the warehouses. Perhaps one of them can tell us more about the shelling Ray mentioned at the meeting in Montreal."

Before disembarking, Jacob put his arm around Lilly and said, "I didn't tell you before, but at the meeting in Montreal your father received an urgent telegraph from General Beauregard describing the attack in great detail. Your dad asked me not to tell you until we returned to Charleston. I think he wanted to make sure you enjoyed your trip."

Once Lilly, Jacob, Ray and Elizabeth Cooper and Captain Davis were on the pier, Lucy ran towards them, throwing her arms around each and every one.

Lilly spoke, "Lucy, I'm so happy to see you're safe and not hurt."

"It's rough, but somehow I made it through. I've missed you all so very much. I brought Lorenzo and Solomon to help with your bags. A couple of carriages are waiting curbside to take all of us to the Inn. General Beauregard had an emergency meeting so he couldn't be here but he sent some troops to help with the heavy trunks. We don't have to rush. I told them to prepare a nice supper and have it ready by six. It looks like you've arrived at just the right time."

The two brothers greeted each other with bear hugs and shoulder punches.  "You're looking fit," Lorenzo said, after looking Jacob over from head to toe.

"Thanks, Lorenzo—so do you!"

When Jacob, Lilly, Ray, Elizabeth, Lucy, Lorenzo and Captain Davis arrived at the Inn, General Beauregard called out, "Good to have all of you back—you must be exhausted. Please sit down and join me. The shelling has all but stopped so let's take advantage."

Around ten, after discussing the meeting in Montreal, General Beauregard asked, "Lucy dear, could I trouble you for one of your rooms tonight."

"By all means, General.  Room number six is ready should you decide to stay. In anticipation of your arrival, I had the staff stock the wine cabinet and fluff up the featherbed. It's a very fine room, but I must warn you the featherbed can be challenging."

"Lucy," the General said sternly, "I entered West Point at the age of sixteen and graduated number two in my class as an engineer when I was twenty. I made it through the Mexican War unscathed and you tell me a featherbed might be a challenge." Then he chuckled and said, "It must be one tough featherbed."

"When will you be needing the room, General?"

"I'd like to finish my dinner first and then have a bottle of wine before I turn in for the night. It's been a very long day." After finishing dinner and two glasses of wine, Beauregard asked to be excused for the night. Lorenzo helped him up and he and Lucy led him down the corridor to room number six.  General Beauregard said to them, 'Thank you both for helping me this far. I think I can take it from here."

As the General opened the door and peered in, he could see why Lucy chose this particular room for him. Beautiful Burgundy velvet drapes covered the window and glass teardrops sparkled from a crystal chandelier. The room was more like one would expect to find in a chic Paris bordello. The pink-flocked wallpaper was decorated with an unusual material reminiscent of Paris or Monte Carlo. On the walls hung paintings of

Napoleon, King Louis XIV, and General La Fayette. In the corner was a 16th century wine cabinet stocked with the finest imported wines available in Charleston. The centerpiece of the room was the huge featherbed Lucy had mentioned earlier. It looked both fluffy and foreboding at the same time.

After enjoying a second glass of wine poured from a bottle found in the wine cabinet, he removed a good cigar from his vest pocket and lit it. After finishing his cigar, General Beauregard hiked up his pants, stepped back and made a run toward the bed. He launched his body forward, intending to land somewhere in the middle, but he missed his target. Instead, he landed in a heap on the floor beside the bed. He pulled himself up off the floor, downed another glass of courage and primed himself for his next attempt. His second effort brought the same result as the first, only this time he paused more than ten minutes before pulling himself up off the floor. On his third attempt, he once again leapt toward the center of the bed, but this time he found himself thoroughly surrounded by a huge feather comforter. He had made it! Engulfed in the billowing down, he soon fell into a deep slumber and did not awaken until well into the middle of the next day.

***

The next morning General Beauregard was absent from the table. After serving everyone else a hearty breakfast of bacon, eggs, grits and fresh coffee, Lucy filled them in on the details of the shelling on August 22nd, 23rd, and 24th. Not wanting to delay because of the General's absence, she began identifying buildings destroyed in the attack and those left standing with little or no damage. She also described how angry General Beauregard was when he learned of the early hour of the first shelling—1 a.m.

Lucy pulled clippings from the *Mercury* newspaper from her purse and read every single detail to those present. Citizens were angry, but when word got out the Union gun crew manning the *Swamp Angel* had used St. Michael's Church as their initial aiming point for the shelling, they were furious and quick to express it. St. Michael's was located just a block down the street from the Inn's side door. The clippings also mentioned that the gun crew manning the Parrott gun had given it its name, The *Swamp Angel*.

Lucy was concluding her description of the bombardments when General Beauregard entered the room.

"May I join you?" he asked.

"Of course, General. Was the room satisfactory?  I see you must have mastered the featherbed."

"Yes, I did—on my third try. Might I ask who did your decorating?"

"I decorated the room myself. Many of the items in room six were brought here from New Orleans when we shut down our chandlery there. My brother Billy packed up the contents and shipped everything to Charleston on one of Mr. Cooper's ships. Since Billy arrived, he's been helping me inventory our stock and order items produced in France, directly from the manufacturers. Living in New Orleans, as he did for many years, he reads, writes and speaks French quite well."

Then, realizing the General would be famished, she asked, "Is there anything I can get for you?  Would you like some ham and eggs?  How about a beignet and a cup of New Orleans dark-roast chicory coffee?"

"Lorenzo, you better keep her tied down. She's a woman after my own heart. Lucy, where do you get your chicory?"

"General, the Army has its secrets; and, I have mine.  I am the only person, besides the maker, who knows where this particular blend can be found in Charleston."

"Smart Lady, Lucy.  Ham and eggs sound wonderful.  If this morning's blend of coffee is as good as what you served last evening, by all means, I'll take a cup."

***

Once the dishes were cleared away, General Beauregard looked around the table at everyone and remarked, "Lucy, why don't I give everyone a short version of how we evacuated Morris Island?"

When they all nodded, he began, "On September 3rd, the day you folks departed for Montreal, I shared with Lorenzo information I'd received regarding President Lincoln's promise to local Commanders to provide an additional 10,000 troops to take Morris Island.  I was told the information came from a very reliable southern sympathizer who was in Lincoln's telegraph office at the time the message was dictated. I had my staff provide me with options for defending the batteries at Batteries Greg and Wagner by the following morning,

"The next day, upon entering my war room, I was handed a copy of a special order signed by General Gilmore himself calling for an assault on Battery Wagner at nine a.m. on September seventh.  It detailed the three approaches they would use. The first approach was to be a full-frontal assault. The second was to be an attack from the flanks, and the third was to

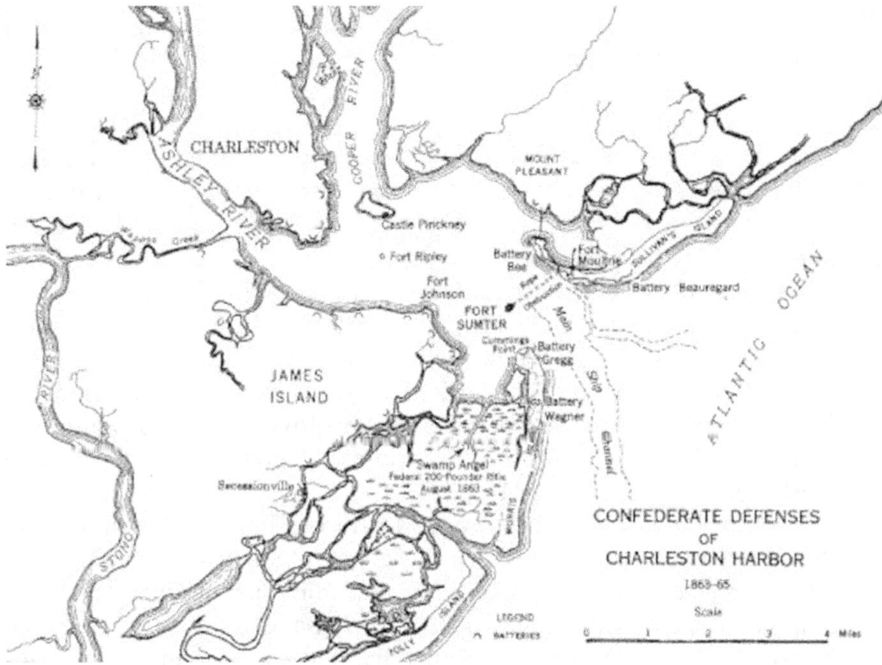


Figure 24. 1863-1865 Map of Charleston Harbor.

be another full-frontal assault following the path of the first. After verifying the reliability of the information with one of our spies on the Island, I ordered Morris Island evacuated by boat at least six hours before the planned attack.

"The evacuation started in the wee hours of the morning of the seventh. Lorenzo had already made sure we had adequate numbers of troops, equipment, boats, etc., and were ready to go. Considering the scale of the operation, I'd say it was carried out with near perfection. During the evacuation we lost only two boats containing forty-seven men. Both boats got lost in the fog and were captured. I pray General Gilmore's troops treat our men well and don't hand them over to Union prison camps. Just as some of our soldiers were jumping into Lorenzo's boat with their muskets, they began taking fire from the island's shoreline. When Lorenzo heard the sound of enemy musket balls striking his skiff, he grabbed the new Henry repeating rifle he picked up off the battlefield at Gettysburg and fired at an armed Union barge emerging through the early morning fog. As soon as the Confederate soldiers in the skiff began firing back, the Union soldiers on the barge were no longer interested in pursuing the fight."

Beaming at Lorenzo with obvious pleasure, he said, "Some of the soldiers who witnessed the encounter said Lorenzo was the best marksman they had ever seen.  Every single soldier assigned to Lorenzo's skiff made it aboard without injury."

Once Beauregard was finished with his description of the evacuation of Morris Island, everyone rose from their seats to congratulate Lorenzo on his courageous efforts. As each shook his hand he thanked them graciously for their kind words.

Looking at General Beauregard, Jacob asked, "What's next?"

Beauregard shrugged and sighed heavily before he responded, "Folks, I wish I knew. Captain Davis advised me this morning that most of the blockade ships formerly docked in Port Royal Sound have departed and are likely en route to their patrol areas. These moves might possibly foretell additional attacks on some of the perimeter islands or even on the city of Charleston."

"For now, he continued, "We need to ship as much cargo in and out of Charleston as we can. Eventually, those damn Yankees will build larger and stronger platforms for mounting bigger guns facing Charleston and Fort Sumter.  Of course, they can do this now on the platforms we vacated at Batteries Greg and Wagner.  I suspect that in the long term Charleston's future looks bleak unless we defeat the Yankees or force the North into signing some sort of peace agreement beneficial to both sides."

Two weeks later, Joe Davis stopped by General Beauregard's office to tell him he was leaving for London. Somewhat bewildered, Beauregard looked intently at Davis and asked, "London?  Who the hell is in London?"

"Henry Latone for one. He's a shipping agent. James Dunwoody Bulloch, Confederate Chief Foreign Agent to Great Briton, wants me to contact Latone about buying the *Sea King* and the *Laurel*. When I was in Montreal, a longtime friend and fellow Sea Captain John Spillman passed me an article that recently appeared in the *North British Daily Mail* on 18 August of this year. Spillman tore the article out of the paper while waiting to board his ship.  Let me read it to you.  It's titled '*Description of the Sea King:*'

*Yesterday, Messer A. Stevens & Sons launched, from their new shipyard shed at Kelvinhaugh, another one of their wood-and-iron-combination ships. The vessel is a superior steamship of about 1,200 tons.*

*The ship is named the Sea King. As we understand, it is the first 'screw' steamer built on the principles of iron frames and wooden planking. She is the first steamer specifically built for*

*'China' trade. She is built to compete with the fastest of ships. In the direct trade from China to London, she is expected to 'bring home the first teas of the season.'*

*The Sea King is a fully rigged ship with yards for square sails and has 21 working sails. She has a raised forecastle and a clipper bow stem head extended from the forecastle to the forecastle bulkhead. She has a poop deck extending about 30 feet, which contains a dining salon, staterooms, and the Captain and Officers' quarters. Under the poop is a well to receive the propeller when moving under sail alone.*

*Her crew is to be housed in the topgallant forecastle while a large deckhouse between the fore and main mast contains rooms for her petty officers and the galley. Her accommodations, with bathrooms and toilets, are up to date for a wooden vessel. Between the main and mizzenmast, space is provided for the auxiliary engine and boiler, which are surrounded by coalbunkers.*

*Her future armament consists of eight-inch 48 pounders and 12 pounders; all smoothbore: and, two rifled Whitworth 32 pounders.*

"In the summer of 1863, Bulloch was in Scotland with his assistant Lt. Robert R. Carter, when he discovered the *Sea King* anchored on the River Clyde. The crew told him the ship was designed by the firm *Alexander Stephen & Sons*. It was built by Clydebank Shipbuilders, who are known for hiring the very best skilled craftsmen in their trade, and they produce ships of the highest quality. Bulloch and Carter agreed the ship would make a fine addition to the Confederate Navy. At the time, however, she was preparing for her maiden voyage to India, New Zealand, and back and was not for sale. Bulloch and Carter were not alone in their assessment that the *Sea King* could easily be retrofitted and turned into a Confederate Sloop-of-War. Rumors are already circulating in Washington that Confederate operatives are already in Europe inquiring whether such a ship could possibly be available sometime in the future.

After carefully digesting the information, Beauregard looked at Captain Davis and remarked, "Joe, what do you think?"

"I think it would be a great vessel to complement the *Alabama*."

Obviously, what he wanted to hear, Beauregard smiled, then asked, "Do you have any idea how long it might take to buy her and get her outfitted as a sloop of war?"

"Well, Sir," Davis responded thoughtfully. "She's just getting ready for her sea trials. The round trip from London to New Zealand and back takes several months— even if all goes well. Then it will take time to buy, register, and insure her with Lloyds of London. When the sale is final, she'll be retrofitted somewhere off the beaten path. When we purchased the *Alabama* we took her to the Azores."

"Do you have any idea where you might take the *Sea King*?'

"Cuba, Sir! Cuba," Davis said decisively.

"Do you have a tender?"

"Yes, Sir. The *Laurel*. I want to buy both of them; my estimate is for late next summer for her to be ready."

"Joe, I certainly hope it's in time to do us some good."

"General, I understand the Union Navy has already dispatched Thomas Dudley, American Consul to Liverpool, to Glasgow and London, to report back to Washington whether a ship suitable for conversion is available in Great Britain. I believe his departure is in response to rumors circulating in Washington that the Confederacy has already found such a ship and is willing to pay top dollar. General, I think we just have to wait this out till the *Sea King* completes her seas trials. My crew just told me the *John Jameson* should be ready within the hour. If I see any ironclads or gunboats out there, I'll throw up some flags and tell you where they are. Also, if I can determine their speed and heading, I'll pass that along as well."

"Are you planning on stopping by Liverpool on your way back from London, Joe. The Whitworth field guns and sniper rifles destined for Charleston are being held there in an armory warehouse near the port." Pausing for emphasis, Beauregard said, "We could sure use 'em."

Davis replied, "Those are my plans for now. I don't want to have to make another trip later in the year."

"Have a safe trip, Joe. Be sure to fill her holds to the overheads for the trip back. Hopefully, your mooring space on *Boyce's Wharf* will be ready for your return."

# Chapter Twenty-Six

## *The North Atlantic Route - Fall & Winter 1863*

THE WATERS of the North Atlantic are often treacherous for vessels sailing from Europe to North America. Cold winds sweep across the deck at thirty knots or more, and the churning waters form whitecaps throughout the entire voyage. Whales and dolphins follow ships for long distances hoping to snatch anything edible thrown overboard. Despite nightly temperature plunges of more than thirty degrees, most sea captains still prefer taking the northern route to save time.

On this route, the distance between major land masses is significantly shorter than routes circling the earth nearer the equator. Once leaving the United States, ships proceed north towards Halifax and continue their voyage to the port of St. Johns where they stop and lay in provisions before crossing the longest leg of their journey across the North Atlantic.

After avoiding icebergs and floating ice lying in wait for the *John Jameson*, the crews' anticipation morphed into excitement as the *Emerald Isle*—their next destination—emerged from the mist. Once they had crossed St. Georges' Channel and entered the Irish Sea, the longest and most difficult part of their journey was over. Soon they would be in Dublin enjoying all the pleasures and excitement its nightlife has to offer. Within hours, the mouth of River Liffey came into view with the Port of Dublin to starboard.

Captain Davis shouted out his order, "Prepare for docking at the transit dock." As soon as the *John Jameson* made contact with the pier, a deckhand tossed a line to the dock where it was tied off on a mooring bollard by a dockworker. Within moments, Captain Davis ordered the gangplank lowered to the dock. Once firmly on the pier, Captain Davis proceeded to the Dublin's Custom's House to check in.

After notifying customs officials he had no cargo to declare, Captain Davis released some of his crew—those who had permanent homes in Dublin—to go home and visit their families. With a skeleton crew, he pulled away from the dock and proceeded east into the Irish Sea.

Turning south, he transited St. George's Channel and entered the Celtic Seas. From there, he first turned southeast, skirting the Penwith Heritage Coast, then turned northeast. He traversed the English Channel until he reached the Straights of Dover where France and England are separated by only 18 nautical miles. To port, Captain Davis and his crew saw the magnificent White Cliffs of Dover that guided him to the Thames River just fifteen miles beyond the cliffs. When Davis saw the Thames to port, he ordered his crew to enter its mouth and head west towards London. After tying his ship up at the London docks, Davis asked his first mate to make arrangements for himself and his crew to stay at the Wood Hotel. In an earlier communication with James D, Bulloch, the Confederacy's Chief Foreign Agent in England, and Henry Latone, an experienced Shipping Agent, both made it clear they wanted him to stay at the Wood hotel during his visit.

***

After inspecting the *Sea King* and the *Laurel*, Captain Davis contacted Bulloch and Latone to set a time for the negotiations, making it clear that he wanted to negotiate for both ships.

The next day, Captain Davis met Bulloch, his assistant Lieutenant Carter and Latone, in a pub near Piccadilly. Davis' impression of the pub was that it was too loud and far too gaudy, but the availability of strong whiskey and wanton women compensated for any shortcomings.

## The Negotiations

As an experienced agent, Latone kept trying to up the price, even though most of the pricing details had been agreed upon long before Captain Davis set sail for London. Bulloch, on the other hand, was more concerned with the level of secrecy in any financial transactions conducted to buy the ships and insure them through Lloyds of London. Only a few months earlier, the United States had threatened to sue Great Britain for damages for cargo lost to Confederate ships built and sold in England. Captain Davis' situation was quite different. Before the trip, Confederate President Jefferson Davis sent him a telegraph advising him to spare no expense in buying the *Laurel*. President Davis assured him the South had sufficient gold bullion waiting in a London bank to cover the transaction. The negotiations were completed and the preliminary paperwork drawn up in less than three hours.

Afterward, they celebrated with a bottle of good champagne and a box of fine cigars. Captain Davis invited everyone present to join him at a local nightclub that he won in a poker game a few months earlier. Before that card game, the owner told Captain Davis he was short of cash and needed to double his money overnight.

Henry laughed and asked Captain Davis, "What makes you think you're going to have any luck in a raunchy nightclub at four o'clock in the afternoon? You might be able to find a drink, but entertainment—I don't think so!"

"Not a problem, Henry. Remember, I own the establishment. Drinks and entertainment await us. Let's catch a hack."

***

Two days later, Captain Davis arrived curbside at the entrance to the Port of London. He sauntered down the steps to the pier leading to his beloved *John Jameson*. He strolled up the boarding plank and went straight to his office where he asked his second-in-command, "How long before the sails are unpacked and hoisted for the return trip to Dublin via Liverpool?"

"Not long, Sir. Perhaps an hour or two."

In just under two hours, the ship's cabin boy knocked lightly on the Captain's door and asked to enter.

"It's open, come on in," the Captain called out.

Once inside the boy spoke, "Sir, the sails are unpacked and hoisted."

"Well done, young man."

"Thank you, sir." The boy responded, but remained standing at attention.

"Is there something else, son?"

"Yes, Sir. I'm eleven now, and I wanna be more than a cabin boy. I wanna be part of your crew, Sir."

Captain Davis smiled inwardly, but directed a stern look at the boy. "Do you think you can do important jobs—like those too strenuous for a cabin boy?"

"Yes, Sir. I've already done some of those jobs, even when I was not told to."

"Well, then!" he said, pausing long enough to make the boy squirm. "This being said, I deem you qualified for a promotion. I hereby make you a *junior mate*. Moreover, I'll have the Boatswain instruct the crew to start calling you mate. Would you find this satisfactory?"

The boy straightened his back and attempted to suppress a smile, "Yes, Sir! You can call me mate straight away, Sir."

"Now, mate! Get out of here! I have work to do." The Captain chuckled to himself before turning his attention back to the ship.

The *junior mate* backed carefully out of the Captain's office, then made a dash across the deck to tell all of his friends about his promotion.

After sending the boy on his way, Captain Davis poured himself a drink and pulled a pocket watch from inside his jacket. Looking thoughtfully at the watch, he decided to give his crew another fifteen minutes. He removed one of his better cigars from a beautiful hand-carved humidor given him by a lovely young French woman named Elizabeth who sought passage on his ship to the island of Bali when he was sailing the tea route to China. Unexpectedly, he could not get her out of his mind. He leaned back remembering her dark brown hair, dark eyes, soft ruby red lips and voluptuous body. They had been lovers long before Ray came along. He wondered if Ray knew. As he lit his cigar, he heard a knock at his door. It was his first mate. "It's time, Sir."

Captain Davis carefully placed his cigar back into the humidor, cleared off his desk, unfolded a detailed map of the Thames and spread it out on his desk. After reviewing river and channel depths, he refolded the map, set it aside and advised the first mate that he would follow him to the main deck. Taking his place next to the helmsman, he checked to see that all tie-down lines had been returned to the ship and gave his first order of the return voyage. "Gentlemen, fore, center and aft, raise all sails in sequence, jib first. Our next stop is Liverpool."

Once the jibs filled with air, the *John Jameson* lurched forward, pulling away from her mooring. As additional sails were hoisted, the ship picked up speed and was soon cruising along at twenty knots. At the mouth of the Thames, Captain Davis ordered his helmsman to steer the *John Jameson* to a course of zero-nine-zero and to hold that course for approximately fifteen miles. An hour later, after passing the white cliffs at Botany Bay he ordered the helmsman to turn to starboard and point her bow southwest, toward the English Channel. Once through the channel, the ship navigated around the south of England and headed north toward the city of Liverpool on the Mersey River. There, he exchanged several hundred bales of cotton in his hold for Withworth cannons, field guns and sniper rifles being held in a Whitworth armory warehouse at the Port of Liverpool. After loading the contraband, Captain Davis took an extra day in Liverpool to give his crew some time for rest and relaxation. There, he visited several shipyards on the Mersey looking for more ships that might be of use to the Confederate Navy. This time he found none.

Early on the second morning, Captain Davis boarded his ship and took up a position next to his helmsman. He gave the order to hoist all jibs and pull their edges tight until the ship lurched forward and began a slow turn to port. After entering the mouth of the Mersey River, Captain Davis ordered the helmsman to strike out for Dublin on a westerly heading of 270 degrees.

## Dublin on the Liffey

Once into the Irish Sea, Captain Davis ordered his helmsman to steer to a course of two-nine-zero and head northeast for three hours. Three hours out, he told the helmsman to change his heading to two-five-zero and head west-southwest toward Dublin. Approximately three hours later, a seaman standing watch in the ship's crow's nest spotted the Liffey River dead ahead. As the *John Jameson* entered the approaches to the river, Captain Davis told the helmsman to take her into the mouth of the river. As the *John Jameson* entered the river, he looked through his spyglass and spotted the Port of Dublin to port. He veered starboard out of the main current and docked his ship at Albert's Dock near the center of the Port. Captain Davis then walked down the gangplank and proceeded toward County Dublin Customs House where he signed a declaration that he had no cargo on board destined for Ireland. He did give notice that in a day or two he would be picking up several hundred cases of Jameson's Whisky to be delivered to North America. He also told customs officials he would be setting sail for North America as soon as the whisky was brought to port and loaded into his cargo holds. After filing the necessary customs documents, Captain Davis asked for instructions to the Jameson Distillery Port Office.

On his way out of the Customs House, he ran into Jameson's shipping representative David Cochran on the front porch. Cochran told Captain Davis the whisky Mr. Cooper ordered the previous month was waiting in a warehouse next to the distillery. Although located just a few miles upstream from the port, many of the bridges between the Port and the quay adjacent to the distillery were too short to allow the *John Jameson* to pass under them. The only way to reach any of the quays beyond McConnells bridge was by river barge.

Captain Davis told Cochran the whisky would be used to cover the Whitworth cannons rifles and other contraband already loaded on the *John Jameson*. Davis added he thought it would be a good idea to load the ship under the cover of darkness to avoid suspicion. Cochran assured Davis the whisky would be loaded on barges, bought to the port by morning.

"Do you have a preference as to who should load the whisky on the *John Jameson*," Captain Davis asked Cochran.

Cochran replied, "It really doesn't matter to me. If your crew is busy, I can arrange for some of my workers to move the whisky from our wagons and place them inside your cargo holds on top of whatever contraband you have hidden there."

Before returning to the ship, Davis asked Cochran to send his regards to Robert Jameson, the Distillery Manager and added he especially wanted to thank Robert for his help in getting cover documents for a very important upcoming mission.

The day of the *John Jameson*'s departure, Robert Jameson visited the port to speak with Captain Davis. Davis asked Robert about the progress of Ian and Princess De Conti's honeymoon.

Mr. Jameson replied, "They are having a wonderful time and now want to extend their trip to take in Prague, Budapest, Moscow and St. Petersburg. I really can't think why they would want to do such a thing but they are young, in love, and it's summer time. Please tell Ray to feel free to continue using the cover documents I gave him. I do not expect Ian and the Princess back until sometime late next year. Perhaps on your next trip you will allow me to give you a tour of the city. I'm sure there've been many changes since you last visited. Have a safe trip back to Charleston."

An hour after loading the whisky and locking it in the hold, Captain Davis gave the order to cast off and hoist all sails. Ever so carefully he tightened the outer edge of the forward jib, turning the ship to port so it could pick up a reverse course and head out to sea. By the time the *John Jameson* cleared the mouth of the river, all sheets were either up or running up the masts and the ship was cruising along at twelve knots. Thirty minutes later, she was under full sail making a solid eighteen knots.

Captain Davis told his second-in-command to turn south across the Irish Sea and head for St. Georges Channel. After passing through the channel and entering the Celtic Sea, Captain Davis had to make his first real decision regarding which path to take to cross the Atlantic and return to Charleston. *Should I take the northern route—the same route I previously took, only in reverse—or should I take the southern route which runs parallel to the west coast of Spain and Portugal in Europe, Morocco in Northwest Africa and off the east coast of Brazil and Venezuela in South America? From South America, the John Jameson could cross the Caribbean using any one of several routes established over the last two hundred years.*

With November approaching, Captain Davis realized a twelve-day crossing of the north Atlantic would be brutal and should a late hurricane be encountered all could be lost. But he also knew the southern route presented many pitfalls of its own—the first being the voyage would require an additional five or six days to complete.  These additional days would expose the *John Jameson* for a greater length of time to pirates or privateers hoping to

Figure 25.  On dangerous seas.

relieve her of the liquid treasure. Additionally, there was a large section of the Caribbean, running from Florida to Puerto Rico to the Bahamas, where ships vanished without a trace leaving their crews and cargos missing or unaccounted for.

In the Caribbean winds are known to subside for weeks at a time, leaving ships at the mercy of the sun. Without fresh water an entire ship's crew could be lost to thirst in less than a week. The Caribbean also has an abundance of storms and sharks should anyone fall overboard.  Lastly, along the southern route scurrilous thieves, violent pirates and disease-ridden whores lurk in the shadowy streets and alleyways of cities like Kingston, Jamaica and Port Au Prince, Haiti.

Being a fair man, Captain Davis mustered his crew and told them, "I have a decision to make, but I feel the decision on which route we take home is too important for any one man to make.  There are only two choices—the northern route which is shorter but more brutal—or the southern route which will take longer and expose the ship to storms, pirates and privateers for a longer period of time."

After advising them of the risks and rewards associated with each route, he asked them to consider which route they preferred to take home.

"Captain Davis!" one of the men shouted.

"Yes, mate."

"What about women?  Are there women on the southern route?" The captain could tell from the burst of laughter this was a well-discussed topic.

"You mean those whores I mentioned?

"Aye, Captain."

"I'm pretty sure they belong to those pirates and thieves who lurk behind every door."

"Are there any women on the northern route?" another crew member called out.

"Some say beautiful women can be found behind every tree in Iceland.  Remember, the Danes settled Iceland."

From the crowd came a loud shout, "Mate, don't let him fool ya.  I've been to Iceland. They don't have any trees—or women."

Before the men could become too rowdy, the Captain said, "Gentlemen, in a few hours we have to commit to one of these routes. It sounds like the issue is time versus comfort.  Be ready to vote at our next muster."

### *Five hours later*

Shortly before sunset, Captain Davis asked his men to assemble on the deck to vote on which route they should take to Charleston.  As the men assembled, one of the riggers asked if he could address the crew.

Captain Davis answered, "By all means, Mr. Hoops."

"Sir, many of us have families back in Charleston and we miss them a great deal. I must confess when I was young the thought of a night in port with a bottle of rum and a beautiful woman tempted me beyond my senses and willpower. However, with guns and ammunition on board needed by our soldiers fighting this war, I believe we should take the quickest route home."

From the other side of the ship a deep voice boomed out, "I second John's motion. I want to get at home as soon as possible, too."

"Is there anyone else out there wishing to address the crew before we take a vote?" The crew was silent. "First Officer, give everyone a sheet of paper and pass your hat to collect the votes."

After the votes were counted, Captain Davis spoke again, "Mr. Hoops, your little talk must have been persuasive. We're taking the northern route. Sailors, let's bring her about and head west across the Atlantic. Charleston awaits us."

Five days out, the *John Jameson* encountered a United States Navy Man o' War with plenty of guns. She was looking for cargo-carrying frigates, sloops and clippers headed for or coming from Confederate ports. Seeing the *John Jameson*'s homeport *Dublin* painted on her side, the Navy Man o' War graciously accepted her identity at face value after receiving a generous gift of six cases of Irish whisky from Captain Davis.

Captain Davis stayed out about 200 miles as he sailed parallel to the east coast. When he started his turn west toward Charleston, he swung south to take a look for ironclads and gunboats that were anchored in Port Royal Sound when he left. The ships were now almost all gone. Their departure meant he might have to take a different approach into Charleston harbor should the gunboats be present just outside the entrance.

As he approached the harbors, Captain Davis used semaphore flags to send a message to one of Beauregard's men observing his ship from Kiawah Island. In response, the watchman signaled that he had not seen any gunboats patrolling north or south of the harbor's entrance. However, in a follow-on message, the observer signaled Captain Davis he had just sighted a Union gunboat heading north and advised him to exercise extreme caution when entering any of the approaches to Charleston harbor.

No sooner was the message received than a shell splashed into the water 200 yards to starboard. Captain Davis reacted quickly, shouting instructions to his crew to hoist more sails and prepare for a race. Once inside the harbor, Captain Davis knew Beauregard's gun batteries would either send the vessel home or to the bottom. As the *John Jameson* cleared the harbor's entrance, he heard the roar of four gun batteries opening up on the trailing gunboat. The batteries hit the gunboat eight times above her water line and stopped her dead in her tracks. Her pursuit was over. Fortunately for the gunboat, she was able to turn around and limp out to sea before she rolled over on her side and quietly sank into the ocean. Before she sank, another Yankee gunboat showed up at the scene and plucked her crew from the water. Shortly thereafter, Captain Davis received a message from the wharf telling him the main channel and his favorite docking spot on *Boyce's Wharf* were now open.

Captain Davis was first down the gangplank. He was well aware of Beauregard's fondness toward the Confederate Navy. He knew that General Beauregard had made a major contribution to the design efforts of the Confederate submarine *CSS Hunley*. Davis was anxious to reach General Beauregard's headquarters to tell him the news of his successful negotiations to purchase the *Sea King* and the *Laurel*.

He was also anxious to see Ray, Jacob, Lilly, Lucy and her parents who were still in Charleston. Over the past few years Captain Davis had grown quite fond of his many friends here in the Queen City of the South.

General Beauregard was pondering over navigation charts of the waters surrounding Morris Island when Davis entered the *war room*. Jacob, and Lorenzo, who had entered the war room a few minutes before, were bringing General Beauregard up to date on troop and equipment movements they had recently observed on nighttime junkets to Morris Island.

Captain Davis spoke first, "General, no matter how hard you look at those charts, Morris Island remains occupied. The only way we can win this thing is by putting more pressure on Admiral Dahlgren and General Gilmore, convincing them taking Charleston at this time would be far too costly to be beneficial."

General Beauregard was pleased to see him. His smile widened. "Captain Davis, I suspect you're right but right now I just don't know how our Army can put additional pressure on Dahlgren or Gilmore. Before we get down to business, let me welcome you back. It's a real pleasure to have you here in Charleston. How did the negotiations go?"

The two men, always comfortable in the other's presence, took seats to continue their conversation. "General, they went well. I think the Confederacy is about to be the proud owner of two new ships, one a sloop-of-war, the *Sea King*, and a tender called the *Laurel*. After we conceal the financial transactions associated with the purchase of the *Sea King* and *Laurel* and insure both through Lloyds of London, we'll take 'em to waters just off Havana and refit the *Sea King* with guns and other armaments befitting her stature. In other words, when we finish the refit, she is going to be another *Alabama*. After the *Sea King* is refitted she'll be renamed the *CSS Shenandoah* and turned loose in the North Atlantic. When the war is over, she will likely be used as an ocean-going war sloop or privateer. I believe she will complement the *Alabama* quite well."

"Joe, when do you feel the *Shenandoah* will be ready to join the *Alabama*?"

"I would have to say sometime next summer or early fall. You know how Europeans and Brits are about paperwork."

"It sounds like everything is going to our liking."

"Not everything, General. I made a point of swinging south to see if the gunboats and ironclads previously parked in Port Royal Sound were still there. Many had left. When I sailed for London, I put a spyglass on 'em and I counted seventeen. This time I did the same thing and there were only nine. I suspect they will soon be returning to their respective patrol areas.

Beauregard then asked, "Joe, what are your plans for the *John Jameson* for the upcoming winter?"

"I plan on giving her a rest. Since our next trip isn't until November, I think we ought to take her to someplace warm and out of the way where I can put her in dry dock. I'd like to take the barnacles off her hull and put on some new paint. On this last trip, the upper part of the foremast seemed a little weak so I might have to replace it. If any planks are split or broken I'll have them taken out and replaced. If they are still good, my crew can sand them, put them back where they came from and apply a coat of fresh varnish. I think Havana might be the best place to take her to keep her out of sight of the Union Navy. My crew has already gathered spare masts, yardarms, crossjack arms, and booms in case we run into bad weather.

"When I entered the harbor, I saw no ironclads patrolling north or south of our approach. However, one gunboat did make a run at us and fired one shot that landed 200 yards behind us. Once the trailing gunboat entered the harbor, our gun batteries on the Islands opened up on her and hit her several times above the water line before she was towed out to sea by a second gunboat. The second gunboat rescued most of the crew before the first gunboat listed to port and sank."

Beauregard then asked, "Joe, when do you think would be a good time to take the *John Jameson* to Havana?"

"I'd like to give my men some rest after our recent arduous crossing of the North Atlantic. How about the first week of February? I won't release the men until they finish the tasks they are currently working on at this time.

"Joe, your time frame sounds good to me.  I was just asked to take command of Confederate Military Affairs in the West, but I'll be damned if I know what that means. As I understand it, the west in this case, can mean anywhere between Georgia and the Indian Territories.  I think they want me to see what I can do about Sherman's advances toward the Carolina coast."

Jacob and Lorenzo were not surprised to learn that General Beauregard, in spite of his splendid performance in Charleston, was not being given a more deserving command. They were well aware of his frailty and digestive problems that required him to take along a cow for fresh milk during troop movements.

General Beauregard had a train to catch so he said his good-byes and stepped into his carriage and asked the driver to take him to the main train station.

Figure 26.  General Beauregard.

# Chapter Twenty-Seven

## *The Beginning of the End*

IN NOVEMBER 1863, the shells hitting Charleston fell more frequently, and Calhoun Street was no longer a dividing line between those who were safe and those who were not. Some stores and government buildings moved north of Calhoun Street while others relocated farther upstream on the Ashley to Summerville, far out of range of the Parrott Guns on Morris Island.

## *Defense Council Meeting - November 26, 1863*

Ray Cooper decided it was time to have the Defense Council meeting at his estate. General Beauregard, local businessmen, plantation owners and government officials were all invited. After consulting with interested parties, he decided the first Saturday in December would be the best time to hold the meeting.

The following morning General Beauregard stopped by the partially damaged *Rutledge House Inn* and asked Lucy if she could still cater the event. Cheerfully, Lucy answered "yes," and offered him several meal options depending on the time of day and kind of food he wanted to serve. Lucy also asked if he had a wine preference for after the meeting.

General Beauregard remarked, "Lucy, since I'm absolutely sure you have a much better idea of what would be appropriate for this occasion, I'll leave the wine selection to you."

"I appreciate your confidence, Sir. On his last voyage back from Europe, Captain Davis brought me a fine selection of French wine for the Inn. I'll see you get the best I have."

Ray had decided to hold the meeting at 2 p.m. For this reason, he asked Lucy to serve lunch at 11:30 a.m., and he told her not serve the wine till after 1 p.m.

Figure 27.  Rutledge House Inn.

***

After preliminary introductions, Ray called the meeting to order and began with an opening statement. "Gentlemen, we're here to discuss our recent losses at Batteries Greg and Wagner on 7 September. As you know, this attack occurred only a few days after my departure for Montreal. Before I left, General Beauregard told me he'd received several pieces of collaborated intelligence advising him an attack on Battery Wagner was imminent. Reacting quickly, he ordered his troops to evacuate all troops on Morris Island—thereby saving hundreds of lives.

"During the attack, Private Harris, sitting to my right, distinguished himself greatly by single-handedly holding off an armed barge until our soldiers could enter his boat, load their weapons and return fire. After our troops began returning fire, the Yankee troops on the gunboat decided they had had enough and turned around—avoiding any further confrontations. Private Harris is on loan to us from Company F, 51st Virginia Infantry Regiment, Army of Kanawha. He's been a frequent visitor to our fair city for more than fifteen years and is well acquainted with many prominent families here in Charleston.

"With regard to battles in September, I'm sure by now you've all heard we won the *Battle of Chickamauga* in Tennessee. Unfortunately, I've not been informed yet on who might've been killed or the number of casualties sustained by either side. Nonetheless, it was a victory, and we can all be proud of those brave men who fought and died so valiantly for what we believe in.

"It appears both sides were fortunate in October. Neither side engaged the other in a major battle. This, of course, means few casualties were sustained by both sides.

"This month the Union took Chattanooga. Again, I'm sorry I don't have the details. Although I hate to compliment the enemy, on November 19th Lincoln gave a masterful speech over the bodies of Union soldiers laid to rest at the Soldier's National Cemetery in Gettysburg. Even though his speech was more conciliatory than we expected, many southern plantation owners and farmers still fear he'll eventually bow to the pressures of northern abolitionist and free the slaves. This obviously would decimate our southern culture and destroy the very lifestyle we've come to love and appreciate. When I read the speech, it appeared to be most eloquent, showing genuine compassion for all who died at Gettysburg—Union and Confederate. It's nonetheless important to remember that at the same time Lincoln was giving his address, General Sherman was continuing his uncompassionate *march to the sea* burning everything in sight to include homes, farms, plantations and businesses. I would now like to read into the record Lincoln's Gettysburg Address:

*Four score and seven years ago our fathers brought forth on this continent a new nation, conceived in liberty, and dedicated to the proposition that all men are created equal. Now we are engaged in a great civil war, testing whether that nation, or any nation so conceived and so dedicated, can long endure. We are met on a great battlefield of that war. We have come to dedicate a portion of that field, as a final resting place for those who here gave their lives that that nation might live. It is altogether fitting and proper that we should do this.*

*But, in a larger sense, we cannot dedicate, we cannot consecrate, we cannot hallow this ground. The brave men, living and dead, who struggled here, have consecrated it, far above our poor power to add or detract. The world will little note, nor long remember what we say here, but it can never forget what they did here. It is for us the living, rather, to be dedicated here to the unfinished work which they who fought here have thus far so nobly advanced. It is rather for us to be here dedicated to the great task remaining before us—that from these honored dead we take increased devotion to that cause for which they gave the last full measure of devotion—that we here highly resolve that these dead shall not have died in vain—that this nation, under God, shall have a new birth of freedom and that government of the people, by the people, for the people, shall not perish from the earth.*

"Would anyone out there like to comment on the topics I have brought up thus far. If so, feel free to express your views on anything covered or not covered."

"Mr. Cooper."

"Yes, Jacob."

"Does this mean we're going to have to sit here and take the shelling whenever it comes?"

"We're not going to give up, Jacob, but with limited resources we might have to prepare for a protracted siege. I don't think the North can come at us from the north through the bogs, marshes and wetlands. For them it would be suicide. Due south is the harbor and I'm sure we can keep it clear. We also have control of the ground southwest of the city. Their only option appears to be taking the islands one at a time and shelling us from multiple locations. Over time I expect them to bring in bigger guns capable of reaching farther north in Charleston. When they're able to shell the entire city, each of us will have to make his own decision on when to leave or stay.

"Hopefully, an agreement of some kind can be reached to preserve the city before then. If not, all they'll find when they enter the city will be fires and burned out rubble. For those unfamiliar with war, the idea, when faced with this kind of situation, is to leave the enemy with rubble, fires and refugees they'll have to feed and care for and nothing else."

Aware that one gentleman was trying to get his attention, Ray said, "I see you have a question, Mr. Rodgers."

"Yes, Sir. How long do you anticipate being able to protect blockade-running ships carrying our cotton to England and the rest of Europe?"

"If the shelling picks up in January, I would suggest you halt any future shipments to Charleston until we have a better idea of how long the North intends to continue its siege. I'll be on the next blockade-runner headed to England and Europe to negotiate new arrangements for cotton deliveries."

"Is there anyone else with questions?"

Yes, Sir. I'm George Mathews, and I own several commercial buildings just north of Vanderhorst Street. How long do you think I have before I need to think about moving the businesses I own out of Charleston?"

"George, shortly after General Beauregard agreed to accept direction of Confederate military affairs in the West last October, he told me his

Figure 28. Parrott Gun on Morris Island.

intelligence suggested Union gunners on Morris Island are scheduled to get larger and more powerful guns to let loose on Charleston.  When those shells begin to fall, I'd strongly urge moving inland to Summerville or one of the other communities out of range of Yankee guns on the peripheral islands."

"Ray!"

"Yes, Emmitt."

"What's going to happen to Charleston if we lose the war?  Will carpetbaggers come in and try to buy everything on the cheap. What's going to happen to our slaves? To us?"

"Emmitt, I don't think we ought to be talking about our slaves right now. Even so, I'll answer your questions to the best of my ability.  Most of the big money in Charleston is old money, and I suspect many landowners have invested in or converted their assets to gold or silver. I believe they'll rebuild their homes and businesses and continue to live here. For that reason, I don't think carpetbaggers have much to gain by coming to Charleston. Regarding the slaves, I believe many of them will stay on if they've been treated well and work either as indentured servants or as sharecroppers. I know one of my slaves, Miss Abigale, has already asked if we could reach some sort of an agreement allowing her to stay should the South lose the war. I told her that she, Miss Barbara and the others were free to stay as long as they wanted."

Jacob then boldly asked, "Mr. Cooper, are we going to dissolve organizations like the Knights of the Golden Circle, Sons of Liberty, etc., who also want to continue the fight elsewhere should we lose?"

In response Ray said, "Jacob, I think we should discuss those organizations at a different time in a different place. I do know the plans we discussed in Montreal about creating disruption and chaos in the Northeast states are still in play."

"Yes, Sir."

"If there are no more questions, I will now adjourn the meeting and wish you all the very best. There are hacks outside waiting to take you wherever you need to go.  Thank you all for coming."

## *A Hard Day's Work*

Jacob was now routinely helping the militia reconnoiter Morris Island to see how successful the Yankees had been in placing bigger guns on the island. Tomorrow he would make the trip again using a whaler he had borrowed and dubbed "the Shrimp." Before leaving, he would once again lie and tell Lilly the mission really wasn't all that dangerous.  In fact, all missions to the Island were fairly risky since his boat was unarmed and not well camouflaged.  He told Lilly she could expect him back in three or four days and asked that she make sure Lorenzo was properly fed during his absence. When these reconnaissance missions became necessary, General Beauregard asked either Jacob or Lorenzo to accompany the soldiers selected for the job. Beauregard felt their combat experience virtually insured the mission's success. He always made it a point to send just one brother. The other was asked to stay behind and take care of Lilly and Lucy.

Lorenzo and Lucy had long since moved their belongings into the Cooper estate. Lucy was trying her best to keep the restaurant part of the Inn open until sundown.  After serving her last meal of the day she put away the dishes and took her carriage to the Cooper family estate. This time of year she usually arrived home sometime between 6:00 and 7:00 p.m.

Today, however, she and her longtime friend Solomon were taking a train to Savannah to see if anything could be salvaged from their Chandlery. Before leaving, she left Lorenzo and Lilly a note saying she expected to return in five or six days, provided no train delays were encountered en route or on the way back from Savannah.  She also told Miss Abigale the same thing and asked her to pass it on to Lilly.

When Lorenzo arrived at the Cooper estate, he was obviously worn out from a hard day of work. Since 7 a.m., he had been loading ammunition onto wagons for transport to gun batteries near Mount Pleasant. As he opened the door, Lilly called out, "Lucy's gone to Savannah for a few days. What would you like for supper?"

Lorenzo answered, "Lilly, anything you have in the house will be fine."

"Miss Abigale hasn't been to the market yet so we might have to get creative."

"What do you mean creative?"

"I mean we don't have fresh vegetables or fruit. We might have to settle for sausage, pancakes and fried mush. We do have some coffee to wash it all down."

"Lilly, everything you mentioned works fine for me."

After hearing Lorenzo's comment, Lilly turned toward the kitchen and asked, "Miss Abigale, did you hear what Lorenzo wants for supper?"

"Yes ma'am, you're lucky—cause those things are about all we have in the cupboard. If it's not raining tomorrow, I'll go to the market and pick up a few things."

"Thanks, Miss Abigale. If our rooms are made up, you can eat and go to your room. I'll wash the dishes."

After supper, Lilly and Lorenzo retired to the living room couch, and Lilly broke out a bottle of French Champaign. Puzzled by the gesture, Lorenzo asked, "What's the special occasion?"

"I've been hearing thunder a long way off most of the day, and whenever I hear it I try to find a pleasant diversion." Lilly glanced out the window, but the sky was clear. "When you're back in Burke's Garden, what do you do for relaxation and entertainment?"

"Well, Miss Lilly," he replied. "Mostly, the family sits around and talks about whatever they did during the day. Sometimes we play games, at other times I drink a little whiskey. I drink mostly when Jacob comes over. Whenever dad joined us we got out a box of good cigars and smoked one or two while discussing our past visits to Charleston. For about fifteen years we've been coming here once or twice a year to buy sailcloth or canvas to make wagon covers. Dad often bought a couple slaves to take home to the farm. He preferred to buy couples because he felt they were less likely to try to escape on their way back to Burke's Garden. I only saw him buy a single slave one time, but she'd been well educated by her English Master. Dad heard the auctioneer say her owner had died suddenly on a cotton-buying trip to Aiken, South Carolina, and his heirs in Europe needed to sell her to clear up his estate. Did I tell you she was both young and attractive?"

"No, but somehow I think you're about to."

"I think dad liked just about everything about her—if you know what I mean. He especially liked her British accent. I think when dad bought her, he was hoping she'd help educate Jacob and me and do household chores around the house. I do know mom was not pleased at first about how much money he paid for Miss Mary."

"How much did he pay?"

"Twice the usual price—more than $1,000. I must say though, she turned out to be a very good slave. Mom just loves her and her daughter Janet. After buying her, each time dad returned home from Charleston, he always made sure he had some expensive perfume and silk lingerie to bring home to mom. I think those gifts did a lot to help them sustain their marriage."

# Chapter Twenty-Eight

### *December 28, 1864*

AS THE NIGHT wore on, the effects of Lorenzo's fatigue and two bottles of Champaign were beginning to take their toll on both his mind and body. Lilly was feeling a sense of loneliness brought on by a warm glow and a need for comfort.

Suddenly, just outside the front window, there was a flash of lightning followed by the sound of thunder a few seconds later. Lilly reached out for Lorenzo, not unlike she had with Jacob so many times before. "Lorenzo, it sounded like artillery fire, and it's too damn close!"

Lorenzo pulled her close to soothe her and whispered calmly, "It's just lightning and thunder. When you see a flash like that, you know soon you'll hear thunder. If you count the seconds between the lighting strike and the resulting thunder, you can estimate just how far away the lightening is from you. We use the same principle in the Army. When we see a muzzle flash from a cannon, we count the seconds till we hear the boom and figure out just how many yards the cannons are away from us."

Lilly trembled and held tightly to him. "Lorenzo, I'm scared. Please come into my room and sit with me."

"Lilly, what would people say?"

"They'd say you're trying to comfort me. I'm sure Jacob wouldn't mind. He knows you're a perfect Virginia gentleman."

Before long Lorenzo and Lilly were sitting on the edge of her bed talking about how lonely everyone had become because of the war. Lorenzo told how some soldiers had gone mad after getting a letter from a beau saying she'd found another or just couldn't wait any longer. Some, of course, couldn't handle it and took their own lives—making it even more difficult for those still fighting. They talked of their futures and the future of the Confederacy. They also talked of the uncertainties surrounding them both. In spite of Lilly's efforts to paint a rosy picture of the war, they both knew it was just a matter of time before the end came, and the South would have to surrender.

As Lily began to cry, Lorenzo reached out and pulled her in close to his shoulder. He was not trying to seduce her. He only wanted to comfort her as she had said earlier. She looked up at him and kissed him, instinctively knowing it was wrong. The Champaign, the darkness and soft rain had created a dreamy sensual mood neither could resist. They no longer cared about excuses—they cared only about this moment and one another. This night would become a night to remember.

***

When Miss Abigale awoke the next morning, she began working on her daily chores as usual. First, she would wake up Miss Lilly and ask what time she wanted to take breakfast. After twice knocking on her door, she entered the room and was startled to see Miss Lilly stretched out completely naked across her bed. Miss Abigale knew that the love of Lilly's life was away on some God forsaken bog looking to see if more Union guns were being set up on Morris Island. Confused and bewildered, Miss Abigale expected Lorenzo would still be asleep. She opened the door to his room just far enough to peer inside. He was sitting on the edge of his bed, facing down, head in his hands. At that moment, she knew something awful had happened. She knew at once this was one of those moments she would have to forget and never tell a single soul.

***

As Lilly awoke, a cool breeze from the window skimmed across her bare skin. She quickly realized she was naked. Reaching for a sheet to cover herself, she tried without success to remember what had happened the previous night. She remembered Lorenzo's story about thunder and lightning, but she couldn't relate it to anything else they'd discussed or, more importantly, done the night before.

Lilly shouted, "Where the hell is Lorenzo? Has he left, or is he still here?" Her thoughts were jumbled, and her heart was pounding. *If he stayed, what did we do?* Then she thought, *Did I just betray Jacob with his own brother in a moment of intense passion?*

After getting up, she quickly looked for something to put on. She grabbed the first thing she could find, a long black free-flowing negligée with a lengthy slit up the side. When worn, the front tended to stay open when she was standing or walking. Lilly then thought to herself: *Where is Miss Abigale? What does she know about this?*

She then called, "Miss Abigale, I need you in here right now."

"Yes, Ma'am." Miss Abigale kept her eyes downcast and bit her lower lip.

Lilly asked, "Did I drink too much wine last night?  I want an honest answer."

"Yes, Ma'am. You did."

"Did you come into my room and try to wake me this morning?"

"Yes, Ma'am.  And since you asked, you were nekkid and laying across your bed."

"Was I alone?"

"Yes, Ma'am."

Lilly thought, *That's good.*  "Miss Abigale, Is there anyone else in the house?"

"Yes Ma'am.  Lorenzo is in his room. When I last saw him, his head was down and in his hands—he looked terrible."

"Miss Abigale, is there anything else I should know about last night?"

"That's all I saw, ma'am.  By the looks of you both, I can guess the rest."

Lilly lifted her head proudly. "Miss Abigale," she said sternly.

"Yes, Ma'am," Miss Abigale looked up and blinked.

"You are to take this and anything resulting from this to your grave. Do you understand?" Lilly was clearly distraught.

"Yes Ma'am—to my grave, ma'am.  I give you my word, ma'am."

"Did you say Lorenzo's in his room?"

"Yes, ma'am."

"You go ahead and fix us something for breakfast. I need to speak to Lorenzo about what may have happened last night." Lilly hastily retreated down the hall to Lorenzo and Lucy's room where Lorenzo sat on the side of the bed. Miss Abigale's description had been correct.  Lorenzo's head was down, and in his hands—he looked terrible.

"Lorenzo," Lilly said in a calm, clear voice.  "I can't recall a thing about last night.  I still feel a little foggy from the wine. I must have had too much to drink."  Then she laughed, a little too loud.  "All I can remember is waking up without any clothes on. Do you recall anything at all about last night?"

Lorenzo stood and walked to the window.  With his back to her, he said, "Not a thing. Are you sure you don't remember?"

"Lorenzo, I'm sure I could remember more, but I choose not to—for Lucy and Millie's sake."  Lilly took a deep breath, paused a moment to gain control of her emotions. "You're only going to remember what I tell you to remember. It must've been a special night because I don't ever end up naked on top of the covers unless I've had a wonderful time."

Lorenzo turned to look at her, and before he could say a word, she continued, "Neither of us did what we did with any intent of hurting anybody, so let's not be stupid and tell anyone. We don't want to lose our families or our lovers. I sure as hell will never tell."

After hearing the maturity and strength in Lilly's comment, Lorenzo knew another reason his brother loved her so much. "Lilly, does Abigale know about last night?"

"If she does, she'll take it to her grave. I told her never to tell anyone anything about last night unless I tell her it's all right. Lorenzo?"

"Yes, Lilly"

Tears glistened in her eyes, "I do remember everything, and it was wonderful. Last night was both truly remarkable and memorable. Right now, however, it's time for both of us to kiss, say good bye and say no more."

"Lilly," he said gently.

"Yes, Lorenzo."

"Did anyone ever tell you how great you look naked in the morning?" Then he added, "You might want to be wearing something less revealing when Miss Abigale returns."

***

Over the next few days, Jacob and Lucy returned from their trips, and Lilly and Lorenzo continued their lives as if nothing had happened. In the past, every year at this time, Lilly and Lucy could be found shopping for gifts for their families and loved ones and decorating their homes to create a festive feeling for Christmas. The Coopers and Rutledges also attended Christmas parties held at the Charleston Club, the Huguenot Society, the Scottish Rite and Ray's favorite, the Carolina Yacht Club. With many of the social clubs and fine eating establishments either damaged or destroyed, this year's Christmas dinner would be served at the Cooper estate for both families. However, this year the preparation and celebration of the holiday would be more subdued than in the recent past. The Coopers and Rutledges were all present, as were Jacob, Lorenzo and a few close friends. Miss Abigale and Miss Barbara volunteered to cook the special dinner knowing there would be more than enough to go around. At the ends of these special occasions, Elizabeth always told the help they we could take any leftovers home to their families.

## It started with a Loud Roar

December 27th began with a loud roar. The sound erupted while everyone was enjoying a simple breakfast of pancakes with maple syrup, bacon and hot coffee. Now trembling, Lilly asked, "Does anyone know what made that horrible sound?"

Jacob answered, "It sounds like something heavier than a Parrott Gun. I wonder if the gun crews are loading shells with larger loads of explosives. I saw some artillerymen load them heavy at Gettysburg. Tomorrow, Lorenzo and I will ride into Charleston to see if the damage has stretched father north than Calhoun Street or obliterated any larger structures." Jacob added, "Mr. Rutledge, Lorenzo and I'll be sure to check on the Inn and get back with you on what we find out."

## Checking on Charleston

Early the following morning, the brothers saddled up and rode south toward the city to assess the damage from the previous night's shelling. Even before they reached Calhoun Street, they saw random craters spread across the northern half of the city. Jacob and Lorenzo "All right dear, I'm coming?" knew their first priorities were to check on the status of the Inn, the *John Jameson* and General Beauregard's headquarters.

The Inn had been hit at least twice. One shell hit the second story just above the outside eating area in the courtyard. Another shell, likely an incendiary, hit the upper left side of the building scorching two upstairs rooms. Fortunately, volunteer firefighters were able to establish a bucket brigade using bay water to put out the fire. The brothers estimated the two upstairs rooms and the roof above the outside eating area could be repaired within a week or two using slave labor.

At the port the brothers were pleasantly surprised to see the *John Jameson* proudly docked at its usual spot on *Boyce's Wharf.* Unfortunately, the same could not be said for the wharf itself. Several seared pilings remained standing but many more were floating in the waters around the ship. This time it was clear the gun crews were trying to set the wharves and quays on fire in addition to sinking ships moored at the wharves. As the brothers scanned the harbor for gunboats and ironclads, all they saw were numerous small boats, with no one at the helm, bobbing up and down, drifting through debris.

Jacob and Lorenzo's last stop was General Beauregard's Headquarters. As they approached the *Aiken-Rhett House*, two sentries approached and grabbed their horses' reins and led them through shell fragments scattered across the street and walkway leading to the house. When the brothers dismounted, they took the reins from the sentries and looped them around the tie-up rail. As Jacob passed one of the sentries, he complemented him on his concern for his and Lorenzo' horses.

General Beauregard was standing at the door. He clipped the end of one of his better cigars, and invited them in to talk about Jacob's last mission to Morris Island. Both wiped the debris off their boots and stepped up on the porch. Looking intently at the brothers, General Beauregard said, "I am sure both of you heard those shells exploding last night. I'm also sure you noticed how much louder they were. It's obvious that they were larger and more powerful than previous ones. For now, let's keep this to ourselves."

Jacob spoke, "General, the last time I was on Morris Island, I did see guns positioned to be moved elsewhere on the island. One of our troops who has family on the island, told me his younger brother, age eleven, saw Union troops attempting to move guns across the Island in the direction of our abandoned sites at Batteries Greg and Wagner. However, the brother also said they were not yet set up nor ready to fire. When I was a kid, I remembered packing a little extra powder in my musket to make the balls go further. Perhaps the gun crew on the Parrott Guns has started doing the same thing. I'll bet that's why the *Swamp Angel* blew up on its third day."

"Jacob, are you sure what you told me is correct?"

Yes, Sir. I saw the guns in moonlight, and I was pretty close."

"How close?"

"Real close, sir. Maybe fifteen feet.

"That's certainly close enough," said the General. "I want to share with you some information about my comings and goings over the next three or four months. I've been offered command of the Department of North Carolina and Southern Virginia—probably to begin sometime in April. I believe they want me to stop advances being made by Grant's troops heading towards Richmond. Putting it another way, I think they'd like for me to trap Grant's troops somewhere between the James and Appomattox rivers. Of course, the Yanks might also try to attack Petersburg, which is the center for five different railroads used daily by the Confederacy. If they try to attack Petersburg, I might have to fight Grant's combat regiments nose to nose."

Lorenzo asked the General, "What do you want us to do next."

"Lorenzo, for now—we wait. Before we do anything, I'm going to need more information on the campaigns being fought north of us. I want to be sure Charleston is ready for a long siege should it come. For the next few months it's still my job to do whatever I can to preserve the harbor, the port and the city itself. In case we lose, I want to make sure the citizenry knows not to leave anything for the Yankees to use against us elsewhere."

# Chapter Twenty-Nine

## *Returning Home to Marseille*

A FEW days after General Beauregard's meeting with Jacob and Lorenzo, Lilly just happened to see General Beauregard outside the Inn and invited him to the Cooper estate for an afternoon drink. Knowing Jacob and Lorenzo were working with his troops at the warehouse at the end of *Boyce's Wharf,* Beauregard was somewhat surprised by her request. When he arrived, she asked him to sit down and brought him a glass of fine Tennessee Bourbon. She placed the bottle on a small table next to his chair.

"General," she said with just a hint of hesitancy. "I need a very special favor. Even though the request is personal; I can assure you it is in the best interest of the Confederacy."

He raised an eyebrow, his curiosity aroused. "Lilly, I'm sure you wouldn't make such a request unless it were beneficial for the Confederacy. What exactly can I do for you?"

She walked to a window and gazed out for a moment, before turning back to him. "I want you to send Jake and Lorenzo home for several weeks, perhaps even a month. Just enough time for me to join my parents on their next voyage to France a few weeks from now. We no longer feel safe here in Charleston. Every time I hear one those big guns, it scares me and I can't sleep. I need to get away."

"Child, I understand. But what about Jacob?"

"Soon this war is going to be over, and he and his brother will be going home to Burke's Garden. What am I to do then? I don't want him to see me boarding the *John Jameson* knowing we might only see each other one more time. I will, of course, continue to love him in every way before he leaves. I owe him that much, and it's the right thing to do. Right now, all he knows is that mom and dad are leaving Charleston. He doesn't know I intend to go with them. When Jacob and Lorenzo return, tell them Lucy and I left letters for them with Miss Abigale. In my letter to Jacob, I plan to tell him how much I love him and how truly special he is to me." Her eyes misted as she asked, "General, can you help me?"

He reached for her hand to soothe her, "Yes, I can help you. Please know, child.  There've been times when I felt you were my own daughter. What's next for you?  Have you told your mother and father you want to go?"

"Not yet, General.  I'm going there now to tell them it's time for me to return to Marseilles.  I also need to ask Captain Davis if he can get clearance from Admiral Dahlgren for us to pass through the blockade en route to Europe.  Since I'll be traveling as Princess Marie Theresa De Conti, I hope he's maintained his good relationships with all his seafaring buddies, especially Admiral Dahlgren. Captain Davis once assured me if we ever had to leave Charleston while it was under siege, he was sure Dahlgren would let him pass as long as he wasn't carrying contraband."

"Lilly, I believe the Captain's comments are true. Captain Davis and Dahlgren knew each of us well before the war. It's not the Navy's practice to sink ships just to kill people. When we do sink ships, we make every attempt to rescue those in the water. We bring 'em on board, we feed 'em and provide needed medical attention until we can drop them off at a friendly port."

After assuring Lilly of his support for her decision, Beauregard rose, walked over to her, lifted her hand and kissed it gently on the back. Pleased that he could be of service, he said, "Lilly, your presence has provided me with great joy through many moments of this disastrous war. Your incredible beauty is only exceeded by your superb intellect. I sincerely want to thank you for being the lovely young woman you are."

Grateful for his cooperation and his admiration, she kissed him quickly on his cheek.

"Would you mind if I finished my drink before I left?"

"By all means, General.  You may take the bottle with you if you wish."

"Thank you, Lilly."

"There's a carriage waiting for you when you're ready to go back to Headquarters—there's no hurry."

### *The General's Request*

The next day General Beauregard caught Jacob and Lorenzo on the pier and asked them to take a break and join him for a drink. One of the few hacks still operating was available and in just a few minutes they found themselves in front of the *Aiken-Rhett House*.  The General invited the brothers in and offered them a seat. Once inside, Beauregard poured

Figure 29.  Aiken-Rhett House.

each a glass of red wine, then turned to Jacob.  "Do you remember asking, 'What do you want us to do next the last time we were together?'"

Jacob answered, "Yes, Sir.  I do." Suddenly, Jacob broke into a series of hard dry coughs.

"Jacob, is that the same cough you had before you started scouting Morris Island for more Parrott Guns. Do you have any idea where you caught it?"

"I got it when I was at Gettysburg.  It's been getting progressively worse since then. When we left our staging area, we passed by several gun batteries en route to our final position on the right flank of the 15th Alabama.  The guns were trying to drive the Yanks clear off the hill we were trying to take.  Our whole regiment was covered in smoke and soot. We were there most of the day, and I'm sure we inhaled more smoke than we should have.  It seems like every hour or two I started coughing and couldn't seem to stop. Two weeks ago, I was coughing only once or twice a day, but now I'm up to three or four. I imagine rambling around in the swamps on Morris Island didn't help none either. If you want me go to see your surgeon, I'll take time to see him just as soon some of the shelling stops."

"Jacob, I appreciate your concern for our current situation here in Charleston but right now I want both of you to go home to your families and rejoin me here in late October to accompany me to Petersburg. We're currently in a defensive posture up there and, although we might win a battle now-and-again, we cannot win this war without the help of the Secret Service. We need them to kidnap someone of such importance the North will be willing to swap a thousand or more prisoners for his safe return—or sign a peace treaty ending the war on terms we can live with."

"You mean like the President or Vice President?"

"Exactly, that's why your mission to Louisville with Lilly is so important."

"When do you want us to leave, Sir?"

"Around the 5th or 6th of this month. I want you to stay at least a month."

"Jacob, if you haven't gotten rid of your cough by the time you return, I'm going to send you to Chimborazo Hospital in Richmond for treatment. We're going to need you at full strength this coming year—especially when you travel to Louisville with Lilly. Chimborazo is located high up on a cliff overlooking Richmond. For that reason it's known as the hospital on the hill by both sides. Since the Yankees know we also treat their prisoners there, it's highly unlikely to be high on their lists of military targets."

"Yes, Sir. Perhaps during the time I am at home, I can get over there and get fixed up."

The following day was extremely hectic. Before breakfast, Lilly informed Miss Abigale that she would be leaving soon and to have her clothes packed and ready for the trip—and swore her to secrecy. Miss Abigale began to cry and asked why she had to leave Charleston now.

Lilly replied calmly, "Miss Abigale, I have to go before my love for Jacob destroys me. He's become so much a part of me, I don't want to lose him. Even so, I know this war is winding down, and I have to look ahead. After the last shot is fired, I know I must give him up to his wife and children in Burkes Garden."

"Miss Lilly.  What about your house, the Cooper estate, and your slaves? What's going to happen to them?"

"Those damn Yankees can take the house if they want it. Miss Abigale, surely you've heard Mr. Lincoln has already freed the slaves."

'Ma'am, I wasn't talking about the other slaves. I was talking about Miss Barbara and me."

Lilly patted her shoulder reassuringly, "Miss Abigale, any or all of you can stay, if you so wish. You can stay here and tell those damn Yankees you're watching the house till we get back from an extended trip to France. Tell 'em my grandfather is quite ill and not expected to live. Tell them after his death, I intend to return to Charleston. I'll send you money every month to keep the place up and pay you a salary and living expenses. I've also left a will leaving you and the other slaves some money and permission to live here as long as you wish. If they take the estate, perhaps later I can petition the government to give it back to us. If they cannot find proof of what kinds of goods we were shipping back from Europe, I suspect they'll return the place to our family. If you have any problems, I've asked our family solicitor, Mr. Leonard Fry, to assist you. He's a long-time family friend and even attended my baptism. I trust him completely."

The next morning, before breakfast, Lilly tiptoed down the hall to her parents' suite of rooms in the east wing. She could hear their voices talking softly to one another. "Good morning," she called out. "Can I speak to both of you in the dining room before breakfast?"

Ray answered, "Yes, of course, dear." In a few moments, Ray and Elizabeth joined Lilly in the dining room and sat down with her.

Seeing Lilly's parents sitting at the table, Miss Abigale asked if anyone wanted anything special. She explained, "Unless someone speaks up, you're going to get a ham and cheese omelet, toast and coffee." After everything was served, Lilly asked Miss Abigale if she and her parents could have a few minutes to discuss family business.

"Yes, Miss Lilly. I have a pan of biscuits I need to take out of the oven."

Once Miss Abigale left, Lilly spoke, "Mommy, Daddy I have a request for you. It may very well require a great deal of understanding."

Ray and Elizabeth looked at each other in dismay. Ray spoke first, "What is it, dear? Are you and Jacob having trouble?"

"No, daddy. It's quite the opposite. It's like I need him every moment."

"So, what is it you need from us? When you're so serious and want to talk to both of us, you always have a request."

"When you go back to France, I want to join you, and I want to go soon—within a couple of weeks. I've already told Miss Abigale to start packing my things, and General Beauregard has agreed to send Jacob and Lorenzo back to Burke's Garden for a month's rest. Previously, Captain Davis told me he is pretty sure Admiral Dahlgren will let us sail through the blockade enroute to France provided we are not carrying any contraband."

"Lilly, it sounds like you have already thought this through. Whatever are you going to do about Jacob?"

"I am going to leave him a letter explaining everything; besides, I'll see him in November in Montreal when we plan out our mission in Louisville.  From what I hear, winning this war might well depend on the success of our mission. Afterwards, I intend to return to France. I suspect Jacob will rejoin his unit with his brother and continue fighting until the war is over. After our surrender, I expect Jacob and Lorenzo to return home to Burke's Garden."

"Lilly, your mother and I very much appreciate how difficult this decision has been for you. I imagine, too, you were surprised to learn Lucy and her parents will be accompanying us on the trip. A few months ago, her parents purchased a country home near Aubagne, a small inland community ten miles east of Marseille. Lucy plans on staying with them for several months and then traveling (probably with you) to Montreal to make a decision about whether or not her family should keep their chandlery there.  I did tell her after the war she might be able to petition the government for the return of her family's chandleries in the United States and the *Rutledge House Inn* here in Charleston. I'm quite certain the Inn was never used as anything other than a boarding house for the general public.  I also expect sometime in the coming years, the government will give us the opportunity to petition for the return of our estate here in Charleston. The government is certainly not collecting taxes on unoccupied homes and business properties."

"Daddy, this is just what I thought when I told the slaves they could stay if they wanted to and watch the place until we returned from Europe. This way the government can't say we abandoned our property. Perhaps someday Lucy and I can return to Charleston and start over."

"Lilly, what are your plans for the rest of the day?"

"Daddy, I told Captain Davis I would meet him this afternoon at the *John Jameson* to discuss our departure date and our route to Marseille. When he gives me our departure date, I'll let Lucy and her parents know so they can get packed up and be ready to go."

Lilly arrived at the *John Jameson* at 2 p.m.  The crew was diligently stacking extra spars in strategic locations on deck in the event one of those already installed failed.  Some members of the crew were busy repairing sails in preparation for hoisting.  Captain Davis' newly promoted *junior mate* was busy unfurling sails and spreading them out between the main and mizzenmasts to dry. Captain Davis was preoccupied taking practice fixes with his sextant to make sure it was still functional and in good working order.  When he saw Lilly, he asked if she wanted him to come down, or if she wanted to come up the boarding plank and join him in his office.

Lilly quickly responded, "I'll come aboard, Captain."

Once they were inside his office, Captain Davis asked, "Do you prefer hot coffee or tea?"

"Coffee, please, with cream and two sugars."

Captain Davis reached into his left drawer and pulled out a package of Italian biscotti cookies to go with her coffee. He sat down across from her and asked, "How can I be of service?"

"Captain Davis, can you tell me when the *John Jameson* is going to be ready to sail to Marseille."

"We could be ready in less than a week, but I understand you don't like difficult good-byes.  How about the tenth? I saw Jacob earlier today, and he told me he and Lorenzo were leaving for Burke's Garden on the sixth or seventh. The tenth would allow enough time for my crew to have a few days with their families before we sail."

Lilly nodded, "The tenth works fine for me."  Then she added, "Captain Davis?"

"Yes, Lilly"

"Have you written your letter to Admiral Dahlgren asking for passage through the blockade?"

"I just finished it.  Would you like to see it?"

"I've never seen a letter written to an Admiral before. I'd love to see it."

"Here it is, but be careful not to smudge the ink. It might still be a little wet."

*To: Admiral Dahlgren,*

*Although we find ourselves on different sides of this war, there are times we must apply reason to ensure innocent civilians are not hurt or overly burdened by it. This is one of those times. On September 10th, I would like to take my ship the John Jameson through the blockade en route to Marseille, France.  I am going to be carrying two French citizens and the American fiancé of one. I should also mention one of the women is a French Princess sent abroad to study in North America. Her name is Princess Marie Theresa De Conti. She is a student at the Sorbonne in Paris. I will also be carrying the Rutledge family who for many years owned the local chandlery and Rutledge House Inn, both of which lie in shambles.  The husband and wife (Ray and Elizabeth Cooper)*

*are long-time residents of Charleston and owners of my ship. I believe you know them. I shall not be carrying any weapons (other than those needed to fend off pirates in the Caribbean and waters off Tripoli should they attack). I shall not be carrying cotton or other goods frequently exchanged for guns and ammunition. A reply by September eighth would be most accommodating."*
    *Sea Captain Joseph Davis.*

"Captain Davis, you write quite well."

"Young lady, there is much about me you don't know. For the first five years after I graduated from Cambridge, I was a struggling playwright. I even had a few plays produced and presented in London's west-end theater district in Soho. After a few years, I realized writing and producing plays was not ever going to be my forte. Shortly after I stopped trying to be a playwright, I met Ray and joined his crew sailing the all the way to China. It didn't take long before I knew this is where I belonged. As a sea captain, you don't have a boss; it's exciting, and you get to see places others only dream about."

Lilly shook her head in amazement, "Captain."

"Yes, Lilly."

"Thanks for sharing your remarkable story. You're quite a man."

# Chapter Thirty

## *Dahlgren's Answer*

ON September 5th, five days before the *John Jameson*'s scheduled sailing date, Captain Davis showed up at the Cooper estate carrying Admiral Dahlgren's response to his request. Lilly saw it in his hand and asked: "What did the Admiral have to say?"

"Lilly, why don't you read it for yourself."

She took the letter from him and began to read:

*To: Sea Captain Joseph Davis*

*Joe, it is good hearing from you even though we, indeed, find ourselves on opposite sides regarding the blockade. Ray is very fortunate to have you as the Skipper of the John Jameson. Knowing you as I do to be an honorable man, I see no reason for not granting your request. I am sure you'll understand, I will have to board your ship and check for contraband. While on board, I might have to check for myself to make sure any whisky on board is up to snuff. As you leave the harbor, turn right and proceed as if you were heading for Port Royal. I'll instruct my second in command to pull alongside and toss you a line. Most likely, members of my crew can check the storage holds while we have a drink. When we finish, we can tap glasses and wish each other well. If Ray wants to join us, he is by all means welcome. After all, it is his ship. After our meeting, you will be free to plot a course for San Juan and points further east. I look forward to seeing you on the tenth.*

*Admiral John Dahlgren*
*Commander, South Atlantic Blockading Squadron*

## *Charleston - September 7th, 1863*

Jacob and Lorenzo's departure was quite different than it had been in the past. Eighteen sixty-three had not been a good year for the South.

Figure 30. Admiral Dahlgren.

The number of dead and wounded was downright disheartening. The North, too, had suffered significant casualties—especially in campaigns in and around Richmond and Chattanooga. Even so, it was clear the North had struck serious blows to Confederate forces with their victories at Vicksburg and Gettysburg. The victory at Vicksburg stopped the unfettered flow of Confederate troops and supplies up and down the Mississippi for the first time, thereby keeping the war from expanding further west into Indian Territory. The North's victory at Gettysburg was even more significant in that it shut down the South's advance into Union territory and forced them into a retreat that took them all the way back to Richmond. The victory brought to an end the South's much-needed momentum gathered only weeks before on the battlefield. There was only one question now remaining to be answered: *How can we stop the bleeding?*

In the days before Jacob and Lorenzo were to depart, the couples enjoyed several days of intense passion at a small hotel near Summerville. A small paddle wheeler took them to Drayton Hall and Magnolia Plantation where they visited the lush gardens that were manicured to perfection. They took afternoon tea and enjoyed assortments of cakes, cookies and biscotti biscuits under a large tree draped in grey moss reaching down from the tree's branches. They also watched jousting tournaments staged by local youth riding clubs. These trips meant, at least for a little while, they did not have to think about the rubble in the streets, the fires burning across the city and the empty ships floating away from their moorings.

***

On their return trip home Jacob and Lorenzo were both very quiet as they rode to the staging area near where two tracks veered north toward North Carolina. Their thoughts and memories were focused on Lilly and Lucy and the love they had shared. Both were comforted knowing when they returned in just three or four weeks Lilly and Lucy would be waiting for them.

When they arrived at the staging area, their thoughts quickly turned to the harsh reality that hopping several trains to Burke's Garden would not be easy. This time, however, they were fortunate, waiting only ten minutes before catching the next train heading west toward Knoxville. Several recruits on board were wearing only a few items of issued clothing. Most had been told they would have to wait until they reported to their regiments before getting the rest. Nearly all wore ill-fitting black or brown canvas pants, a butternut gray coat and black half chukka boots. They were told better boots and rifles awaited them on the dead soldiers they would find on the battlefield.

The brothers noticed the new ranks were filled with increasing numbers of older men. They spoke with several who said they were serving the enlistments of sons who had young families of their own back home. Far too many recruits were younger than the mandatory age of eighteen required for serving in the Army.

Over the next couple of days, the brothers jumped one train after another and, on one occasion, they walked seven miles between villages to catch the next train headed west toward Knoxville. On the fourth day, Jacob and Lorenzo boarded their last train at Rogersville Junction. The train's conductor said the Tennessee and Virginia Railroad train was headed for an undisclosed destination, just north of the salt and lead mines near Bristol. When asked if the train was headed for Tazewell or Bland County, the conductor said nothing but nodded his head suggesting it was. When the train arrived at Wytheville to load fuel and take on water, Jacob and Lorenzo jumped off and began walking toward the livery stable.

Seeing the brothers, Doc Thornberry stopped his buggy and asked where they were going. A short man weighing perhaps 130 pounds sopping wet, he was about fifty with a full head of silver hair. Jacob told him, "We're headed for Burke's Garden."

The doctor smiled and told them to jump in saying, "I'm headed there myself."

On the way Jacob asked, "Doc, do you know who you're going to treat?"

"Not really, I understand he is one of those soldiers—you know, the ones the Army's hiding in the valley to get rest. They try to fatten them up with fresh meat and vegetables before sending them back into combat. You can't live, let alone fight, on rations of hardtack and jerky."

Lorenzo    asked    the    Doctor,    "Who    sent    for    you?"

"I wasn't there when the young boy came in, but my helper said it was Will Harris. He said he looked to be maybe eight or nine years old."

Lorenzo asked, "Did the boy say how the soldier came to be staying at the Harris Cabin?"

"My helper said the boy told him the lady there and the officer had been friends for several years.  He said the lady mentioned the man had been stationed with her first husband at Fort Lee."

"Doc, do you have any idea what happened to him?"

"My helper said I should bring a splint or two—I imagine he broke something."

Jacob knew all too well what he hoped the soldier had broken, but he was laughing so hard he couldn't speak.

Trying to figure out what Jacob was laughing about, Doc Thornberry asked, "Where exactly are we heading?"

Jacob quickly answered, "The boy you described is one of mine. I guess we should end up at my cabin. However, before taking me there, can you drop Lorenzo off at his cabin down the road a bit.  It's not much out of your way."

Once out of the buggy, Lorenzo was flooded with hugs and kisses from each of his children.  Millie also wanted to show her appreciation for this unexpected visit but chose to wait till she and Lorenzo could be alone.

As Jacob and the Doctor arrived at his cabin, Annie quickly ran to Jacob and planted a passionate kiss dead center on his lips. Annie then coyly added, "Doc, excuse me—It's been a while."  Suddenly she realized Captain Robbins was still in pain in the next room.  She invited the doctor in and took him to the bedroom. "Doctor this is Captain Robbins, a long-time friend of mine. He took a nasty fall from his horse while I was giving him a tour of dad's place. The way he was trying to show off, he must have thought he was a Cavalry Officer instead of an Adjutant.

Looking sternly at Annie, Jacob spoke up, "Annie, what are you doing giving strangers tours of dad's place. It's enough to make a loving husband jealous."

"Jacob, shame on you.  Joe is a fellow military man, and besides I have known him since I was eight. When I was small, he was my protector. His unit was brought into Burke's Garden to rest and get medical attention. Since the boys haven't had anything good to eat in months, we try to give them some decent food. During the summer months, we try to put up as many fruits and vegetables as we can so we can serve the troops good food even in winter."

Jacob said sarcastically, "Annie, fruits and vegetables had better be the only thing the women in Burke's Garden are serving the troops.'"

Taken aback by Jacob's comment, Annie lashed out, "Jacob, you think I don't know! You think I'm naïve! I know right outside this valley there's a camp-town with all the whores a regiment could handle. Every night I see troops sneaking out to visit the bars and prostitutes shadowing the regiments. I see them washing up in Wolf Creek before returning to their encampments. I've been around. I know what's happening. Promise me if you ever must cheat, it will be with just one girl, and she had better come from a good family. I don't want to get any of those diseases the whores bring with them. Do you understand? I know we're losing more men to syphilis and gonorrhea than we are in combat." At the end of Annie's rant on syphilis and gonorrhea, Jacob had difficulty trying to take a deep breath and expelling air from his lungs. He was stunned. He had no idea of what to say. As it turned out, he said exactly the right thing—nothing at all—because he began to cough.

Annie asked him, "Oh, Jacob. Do you still have the cough from the last time you were here? I didn't mean to startle you with those accusations. I'm sure you're always going to do right by me."

Just then the Doctor came out of the bedroom and asked, "Do you have any whiskey?"

Jacob quickly answered, "Yes, we have plenty—perhaps even enough to quell the Captain's pain."

Annie was quick to counter, "I'll see what we have. We've been caring for quite a few of the wounded lately, so our supply is running low."

"Then we'll have to make do with what you have. Tell him to drink it slow and steady. I'll come back to align the fractures and set the leg in about ten minutes."

When he returned ten minutes later, Doc Thornberry asked Annie if Jacob could help him sit the patient up. Four screams were heard from the bedroom over the next 15 minutes. The first scream echoed through the house when Jacob and the doctor attempted to raise Captain Robbins to a sitting position. The second, even louder, came when they aligned the bones for the next step—to pull them apart and snap them together in place. When they pulled the bones apart and popped them into place, the third scream shattered the air. The final scream came when Jacob and Doctor Thornberry lifted him off the bed to measure his left leg and cut a splint to the right length.

Minutes later, the bedroom fell strangely quiet. The whiskey had finally taken effect, and Captain Robbins was now fast asleep. As the doctor grabbed his bag to leave, he instructed Annie, "Captain Robbins will require quite a bit of rest. Keep him as comfortable as possible."

As the Doctor stepped onto the front porch to leave, Annie said, "I'll follow your instruction to the letter." Then she handed him a few dollars. "Thank you so much for taking the time to come all the way over from Burke's Garden."

As the weeks passed, Jacob and Lorenzo settled into a routine they had long forgotten. They played games with their children, showed the slaves what improvements they wanted made to their cabins and took time to enjoy picnics, pitch horseshoes, and attend barn dances. To be sure, the presence of various regiments in and out of the valley reminded them both of the war but not as much as watching shells randomly fall on the Charleston landscape destroying its glorious architecture.

One afternoon, Jacob and Lorenzo decided to take the horse drawn wagon up the mountain behind the Harris home to cut a couple of cords of firewood for the winter. As Jacob was hooking up the draw horse to the wagon, Lorenzo approached and spoke, "A little while ago, Annie repeated your comment about being jealous over her giving Captain Robbins a tour of dad's place." Lorenzo saw Jacob's jaw clench, letting him know he was treading on a delicate subject, but he continued, "Someday you're going to have to choose between Annie and Lilly—and for God's sake—you better pick Annie. She loves you and has given you four lovely children. She's earned both your love and loyalty."

Lorenzo expected an angry response, instead Jacob sighed and said, "I know you're right, Lorenzo, but right now I don't know what to do about Lilly. We have to stay on good terms until our mission to Louisville is over in November of next year. Whenever I'm in Burke's Garden, I feel guilty as hell about my love for her—but it's hard to shut it off even when I know I should. With the war going as it is, I wouldn't be surprised if we get reassigned back to the 51st or some other unit when we return to Charleston, especially if General Beauregard takes command of forces in Virginia and North Carolina."

"Of course. General Beauregard could decide to take us with him, along with his cow, a few concubines and several cases of imported Champaign." Lucy once revealed to Lorenzo the General's many amorous activities inside the Inn. On occasion, members of her staff had approached her asking what they should do with articles of women's clothing, love letters, poems or expensive perfume found somewhere in his room.

"Jacob, it's good that you realize this thing with Lilly has to stop when you finish your mission to Louisville, but that doesn't change a thing with respect to Annie. You have a good woman right here that loves you deeply. You need to show her how much you care for her."

"I didn't know General Beauregard was such a lady's man. I guess his French accent, military education and formal appearance make him attractive to women." He paused, took a deep breath and added, "I accept your criticism regarding my relationship with Lilly, but what about you and Lucy? How is it any different?"

"Jacob, Lucy knows I'll never leave Millie and the girls. We're grateful for what we've had but when it's over—it's over."

After loading the wood into the wagon bed, Jacob climbed up into the seat and carefully drove down the hill toward the Harris farm. Lorenzo walked to the side making sure none of the wood spilled over the side. After unloading the wood and stacking it inside the barn, they washed up in the spring behind the house and entered through the back door next to the kitchen.

Hearing the commotion, Annie called out, "Jacob, what do you two want for lunch?"

Jacob replied, "Honey, I really wasn't thinking all that much about lunch."

"I know what you're thinking about, but first we have to eat something. Did you wash your hands in the spring?"

"I did."

"Did you bring in some fresh, cold water?"

"I did that, too."

"Go sit down and rest while I finish up here. Everything should be ready in about fifteen minutes."

After lunch, Lorenzo excused himself saying he needed to return to his cabin and help Millie with the chores.

After Lorenzo left, Jacob put his arms around Annie and pulled her in close. He whispered, "Annie, I love you. You've always been special to me. You gave me four wonderful children, and I'll always be grateful. How can I prove this to you?"

"Jacob, there's no one here—just love me."

***

Two days later, Jacob and Annie took the horse-drawn wagon over Burke's Garden Mountain to go shopping in Jeffersonville. After dropping off the horse and wagon at a livery stable, Jacob bought Annie some new clothes and took her out to dinner. When it was time for them to return to Burke's Garden, Jacob suggested they spend the night in Jeffersonville in the town's only hotel.

"Why in the world would you want to stay in town." Annie asked.

With a gleam in his eye, he responded, "Annie, I want you to remember how much I love you, and I want to make beautiful memories I can remember of you. It's been a long time since we had a night all to ourselves. Love means more when you're away from home. It adds to the excitement."

* * *

The next morning Jacob awoke with Annie's head resting on his shoulder. Yawning, she asked him, "Is it time to get up and get dressed?"

"No, Annie, it's time to stay here and make love till they chase us out of the hotel."

At ten someone knocked at the door and called out, "Mr. Harris, check out time is eleven. You might want to consider getting up."

Jacob answered, "Thank you for telling me. We'll be sure to check out before eleven."

At noon, Jacob and Annie left the hotel holding hands as they searched for a restaurant. They found one just two blocks away near a dry goods store. After lunch, they returned to the livery stable to pick up the horse and wagon and drove back to their cabin in Burke's Garden.

Lorenzo spent nearly all his time with Millie and their children. Whenever they wanted to be alone, they dropped the children at the Harris home with Jim and Christina. The closer it came to the time they would leave, the more often the children stayed the night with their grandparents.

A few days before they had to leave for Charleston, Jacob and Lorenzo met with Seth, Tobias, and Micah to explain to them what tasks needed to be done while they were gone. They knew they had to make the most of their time since only a few days remained before they would ride to the Wytheville refueling spur and jump the next train south toward Bristol. This time, of course, they knew their return to Charleston would be different. With General Beauregard leaving, they anticipated he would ask them to accompany him north into North Carolina and then stay or return to their unit to continue the fight. However, for now it was time to enjoy the company of Millie, Annie and their children.

### *Cooper Estate – September 10, 1863 – 7 a.m.*

The night before her scheduled departure, Lilly could not sleep. She thought about Charleston and the many friends she had there. Memories danced through her head about her childhood with a loving mother and father and Lucy, her very special friend. She thought of Lucy's somewhat older parents doting over her, granting her every wish. She remembered her first boyfriend, Tommy Martin, age fourteen, and how sad she was when he moved north to Philadelphia. She wondered, too, if he was in the Army, and if so, on what side. Then she met Jacob, and her life was never the same again. Before another thought could form, she heard Miss Abigale approach her door. In a waffling tone, she whispered, "Miss Lilly, everyone is already up, and breakfast is on the table. I'll look around to see if there are any stragglers."

At first, Miss Abigale thought there were two, but quickly remembered Jacob and Lorenzo had left for Burke's Garden a few days earlier. Lilly was not the only one who had experienced a difficult night. When Lilly, Ray and Elizabeth joined Lucy and her parents at breakfast, tears flowed as each one at the table tried to talk to one another. Even the staff was visibly upset—this meal would be the last the staff would share with the Coopers. They were eager to please and laid out a fine breakfast to show their gratitude for the Cooper's generosity.

After breakfast, everyone gathered their bags and moved toward the carriages and wagons waiting outside. General Beauregard, understanding how difficult this would be for Lilly and Lucy, dispatched twenty men to move their bags, wooden crates, trunks, and furniture onto the wagons. The soldiers accompanied the luggage all the way to *Boyce's Wharf* where they loaded trunks and sundry items on the *John Jameson*.

Captain Davis and General Beauregard met the party at the warehouse in front of *Boyce's Wharf*. They conversed quietly for nearly forty minutes while Beauregard's troops finished loading the bags and trunks onto the ship. Lilly and Lucy hugged everybody—many of them more than once. Lilly and Lucy and their parents strolled down the pier and up the gangplank to the main deck of the *John Jameson* and headed straight for their cabins. When Lucy asked Lilly if she wanted to take a last look at Charleston before they sailed, she said softly, "No, this is not the way I choose to remember her."

As the wind filled her sails, the *John Jameson* began moving. Once the lines were cast off, the helmsman took control of the ship and prepared for a rear tow by a side-wheel steamer called the *Brandywine*. Once out of her mooring the helmsman steered her through a series of maneuvers resulting in a 180-degree reverse turn. Looking at the young man holding the wheel, Ray smiled and said, "Well done, helmsman." As additional sails were hoisted, the *John Jameson* picked up speed, and Captain Davis began looking for an open channel to exit the harbor.

After exiting the harbor, Captain Davis noticed a gunboat approaching, signaling a desire to come aboard. The ship identified itself as the *USS Mohawk*. It also signaled that Admiral Dahlgren was on board.

Once alongside, Admiral Dahlgren, with an entourage of his second-in-command and five seamen, boarded the *John Jameson* to meet with Captain Davis and Ray Cooper. Once on the main deck, Davis spoke to Admiral Dahlgren, "Quincy, let's go to my office and have a drink. I have my very best Irish whiskey on board. If it's to your liking, I'll have my crew bring up a few bottles."

While Davis, Dahlgren, and Mr. Cooper were exchanging pleasantries, the rest of the boarding party began checking every hold to make sure there was no contraband on board.  Halfway through the visit, Lilly joined them, introducing herself to Admiral Dahlgren as Princess Marie Theresa De Conti, a French citizen studying abroad in North America. The Princess commented, "When visiting the United States, I expect the government of the United States to show proper concern for my safety."  Showing even greater spunk she added, "Even though I have impeccable travel credentials, I would very much appreciate your personal assurance in writing regarding my safety while I am traveling in the United States. Such a document would give me great comfort and alleviate any fears I might have should I travel here at a later date."

Stunned by her beauty and superb intellect, Dahlgren volunteered such a document and offered to sign it personally. Within minutes, Lilly had in her possession a letter signed by an American Admiral attesting to her identity as a French Princess traveling abroad to study French influences across North America.

Shortly after Admiral Dahlgren signed the letter, an aide stepped into Captain Davis' office to tell Admiral Dahlgren no contraband had been found on the ship—other than a few muskets for self-defense. Looking slyly at Captain Davis, Admiral Dahlgren asked, "Would you, by chance, happen to have any more Jameson's on board?"

"Admiral, as we speak, I am having several cases brought up on deck for you and members of your crew to enjoy. Let your sailing be as smooth as the whiskey you are about to take with you."

The Admiral shook Ray and Captain Davis' hands and made his way back to his ship. Captain Davis instructed his crew to cast off and change course to head for San Juan. After Dahlgren's departure, Lilly returned to the bridge waving the paper he had just signed for her. She then touted, "Daddy, Captain, I would say this has been a very successful encounter with the Enemy. It's not every day one gets a free pass to travel through enemy territory all the way to the Galt Hotel in Louisville."

Grinning, Davis responded, "Lilly, you are something else. I can't believe what I just saw. Even in these difficult times, you managed to talk a Union Admiral into giving you a free pass across the United States. I'm certainly pleased you're on our side. Is there anything you can't do?"

"Yes, Captain. I can't swim—and I can't keep Jacob."

## *Burke's Garden, Virginia*

A month after arriving in Burke's Garden, Jacob and Lorenzo saddled up and took the trail over Burke's Garden Mountain to Wytheville. Tobias rode with them to bring their horses back to the Harris homestead. At the refueling station, they boarded the next train south to Knoxville via Bristol. Between Bristol and Knoxville, Jacob thought about the past few weeks he had spent with Annie, realizing he was now caught between two worlds. The most difficult part to resolve was the reality that when he was in one world, the other was lost to him. The inherent danger of loving two women at the same time was becoming increasingly clear to him.

Inside the Bristol Train Station, Jacob talked to one of the troops he knew from Burke's Garden. The soldier told him earlier in the week that several segments of the rail line ahead had been attacked by a Union raiding party. Still, feeling this route would be the fastest way to Charleston, Jacob and Lorenzo disregarded the warning and boarded the next train headed for Knoxville. In Knoxville, they changed trains and proceeded to Charleston via Atlanta. The rest of the train ride was uneventful.

As the train slowed down to stop at the staging area west of Charleston, the brothers picked up their rifles and prepared to jump from the boxcar. Jacob jumped first followed by his brother. Neither were any worse for the wear. Once on the ground, they walked up the tracks toward a warehouse used to transfer supplies from boxcars on one line to boxcars on another. At the warehouse, they caught a ride back to Charleston from an arms dealer who had just dropped off a shipment of black powder destined for Macon, Georgia.

***

Once in Charleston, Jacob and Lorenzo had to decide where to go first. As much as they wanted to go straight to the Cooper estate, they decided their first stop ought to be General Beauregard's Headquarters. As they stepped into a hack parked curbside, Jacob asked, "Can you take us to General Beauregard's Headquarters?"

Looking back, the driver responded, "Gentlemen, can you tell me where it is?  I'm covering for my brother, and this is my first trip into the city for several years."

"Do you know where the *Aiken-Rhett House* is located?"

"Yes, sir.  I'm familiar with the neighborhood, and I'm free for the rest of the afternoon.  Would you like me to take you there?"

"That would be fine. After we finish talking to General Beauregard, I'd like to go to the port and see what ships are in. After checking the port, we'd like to drive by the *Rutledge House Inn* to see if it's still in business. After that we'll decide whether we'll need your services further."

As the hack entered the street in front of the *Aiken-Rhett House*, they noticed several columns lying on the ground that formerly held up the top porch.  Those still standing upright were supported by wood braces. A sentry on the front porch recognized Jake and Rans and asked, "Are you looking for General Beauregard?"

"We are, can you tell us where we might find him?"

"When I came on duty I was told he's in the *war room*—go on in." When they entered, the war room was a mess. Apparently General Beauregard had not been sleeping much over the last month. General Beauregard was not in his war room, so the brothers stepped into the hall to see if they could find him.  Hearing the brothers' footsteps coming down the hallway, Beauregard stepped from his library. When he saw that it was Jake and Rans, he smiled broadly and said, "Jake!  Rans! What a pleasure to see both of you.  How much rest do you need before we head to North Carolina and Virginia?"

"Good to see you as well, General.  We were hoping for a week or so to visit with Lilly and Lucy. We'd like to reassure them some before we mount up."

"Boys, did you stop by the port or check in at the Inn when you arrived?"

"No, Sir."

"If you had visited those places, you would know the Inn is no longer in operation. It was nearly destroyed by shells laced with *Greek fire* a few days after you left. Fortunately, Lucy was at the Cooper estate when this all happened.

"What about the port?"

"Boys, it's empty. All the ships are gone."

"Even the *John Jameson*?"

"It's gone, too."

"Are Lilly and Lucy staying at the Cooper Estate?"

"I'm terribly sorry, but no. They both left with their families for Marseille right after the Inn was hit."

Dismayed, Jake asked, "Who took them?"

"Captain Davis made a deal with Admiral Dahlgren to let him sail through the blockade en route to France. Miss Abigale has letters for both of you from Lilly and Lucy. Jake, Lilly said she's looking forward to meeting up with you in Montreal in November. I believe the kidnapping attempt is scheduled for some time in early January when Vice President Johnson passes through Louisville on his way to Lincoln's Inauguration. As I understand it, both of you are needed in Montreal sometime before November 15th of next year."

The brothers bowed their heads in disbelief. The day they knew would eventually come had come. Nothing was going to make them feel better. Jake and Rans looked helplessly up at General Beauregard. Jake said, "I guess this means we're heading out sometime this week."

"I'm afraid it does."

Jake asked, "What are the Coopers going to do about the estate?"

"Lilly told Miss Abigale and Miss Barbara, they could stay if they wanted to. She told the others they can stay, too. She told Miss Abigale, 'I do ask you to take care of the house until we return after the war.' Lucy, Lilly and their parents all said they had hoped to see both of you before they left. Ray, Elizabeth, Lilly, Lucy and Lucy's parents then stepped into two carriages waiting under the portico and started their ride to the port. After everyone said good-bye to the help, the soldiers of the Charleston militia grabbed their bags and loaded them into two wagons waiting to accompany them to Boyce's Wharf. By this time everyone was in tears, including Ray. After everyone got out of their carriages, Lilly ran up the boarding plank and headed straight for her cabin. She didn't even come back up on deck to take a last look at her beloved Charleston."

General Beauregard continued, "Jake, Rans. I think it might be good for you to visit with Miss Abigale for a few days before we head out for North Carolina. I'll send a couple of guards to the livery stable to retrieve horses for you so you can come and go into Charleston whenever you like. There is certainly nothing more for you to do here."

The lane to the house was the quietest Jake and Rans had ever seen it. There were no carriages parked outside nor servants grooming horses inside or outside the barn. The lights were off, and no sounds of patriotic music could be heard coming from the ballroom on the second floor. Most of all, there was no sight of Lilly or her best friend Lucy. When Miss

Abigale heard the familiar sound of Jacob's boots climbing the front steps, she ran to the door and said, "I'm so sad, I tried to get her to stay. She told me the sound of those guns was becoming more than she could stand."

Knowing Miss Abigale's last comment was probably a lie, Lorenzo played along. "She told me the same thing a week or so before we left, I saw her just sit and cry when she heard them. I think she just couldn't stand to see Charleston in rubble."

"Lorenzo, Lucy left a note for you. She told me I could read it. It said she would try to return to Montreal with Lilly in late November and hopes you can accompany Jacob on his trip there. She asked me to tell you she loves you and will miss you terribly."

"Mr. Jacob. Miss Lilly asked me to give you this letter and small box. Unlike Lucy, she told me not to open the box. I can assure you I did not read what she wrote or look inside the box." Peering up at both of them, she could see how weary they were. "You both look tired. Why don't both of you take a nap? The beds are already made up."

"Thank you, Miss Abigale. I think we'll take you up on your offer." Once inside his room, Lorenzo found himself weak and unsteady. He read the note several times, trying to read between the lines to see if he, in any way, had contributed to Lucy's departure. After accepting the realities of Lucy's elderly parents and the loss of the Inn, Lorenzo knew Lucy left because she truly felt it was necessary.

When Jacob entered his room, he felt lost and very much alone. His first thought was: *How could she do this to me? What possible reason was there for this strong, independent woman to board a ship and sail six thousand miles away to start a new life?* At first, he wondered if she or one of her parents was ill. If so, he had seen no signs or symptoms. He knew there could be no other man since he and Lorenzo had been with her virtually every minute. His last thought seemed inconceivable. *Had the flame burned out? Had she lost her love for him?* Certainly, their last night together did not reflect any loss of passion or love. Finally, he wondered if Jacob Thompson had asked her to participate in another Secret Service mission and asked her not to tell him anything about it. After hours of unrest, Jacob wept and fell asleep.

The next morning, the brothers awoke to the familiar sound of Miss Abigale preparing breakfast in the kitchen. As he rolled over to get out of bed, Jacob felt an object under his ribcage on his left side. Reaching back, he grabbed hold of the object and pulled it out from under him. It was the letter and a book-size box from Lilly. Jacob took a moment and called out, "Miss Abigale, how much time do I have before breakfast?"

She answered, "You have about 20 minutes—the biscuits just went into the oven."

When Jacob opened the letter, he was pleasantly surprised at what Lilly had to say:

*My dearest Jacob,*

*I know you are wondering why I chose to leave for Marseille at this time. Recently, I realized you have become part of me; and, my love for you has consumed me. I think only of you, and I cannot possibly do what I must do for the Confederacy in my present state of mind. Inside the box are two of the most precious and personal things I own. When I sat down to write this letter I wondered how I might express my most intimate feelings to you. Feelings, which at the time, were so intimate and sensual, I had to run home and write them down in my Diary in a very private setting. When I wrote this letter, I just couldn't find the right words to express the intensity of my feelings.*

*The first item in the box is a collection of hand-copied excerpts from my personal Diary. They are very explicit and express my feelings as they were in the intensity of the moment. Children should not see them. The second is lace from an undergarment I wore the first night we made love. I think it would make a nice bookmark for the excerpts I copied. You certainly made quite an impression. I hope you feel the same way about me.*

After reading the excerpts, tears flowed down Jacob's face. On the back of one of the pages, Jacob found a personal note written the day before she sailed for Marseille. It read:

*I am trying to pack but cannot remember where my clothes are. I cannot get you out of my mind and have no idea of how I am going to make it up the boarding plank to the ship's deck. I can only hope Captain Davis is there to help me. I know I cannot look back as we leave the harbor. However, I shall be thinking only of you. I have started counting the days until we reunite in Montreal and once again share our love.*

*With all my love,*

*Lilly,*

When Miss Abigale came in, Jacob asked for a minute or two to get ready. Lorenzo was already waiting for him when he sat down at the table. "Jacob, are we going to try to get General Beauregard to postpone his Change-of-Command Ceremony and take an extra day or are we going to leave tomorrow as scheduled?"

"As difficult as this is, I'd like to stay another day and reacquaint myself with the memories Lilly and I shared in this setting."

Once they had decided to stay, they sent Solomon to General Beauregard's Headquarters to make their request to stay another day. A few hours later, Solomon returned with Beauregard's response, "Jacob, Lorenzo. I can give you one more day."

Two days later, after accepting command of the Department of North Carolina and Southern Virginia, General Beauregard, along with Jacob, and Lorenzo, returned to the train station and boarded a train for Richmond. There, General Beauregard began concentrating his troops just outside of Richmond. On May 16, in a skirmish with attacking Union forces, Beauregard's troops first repelled and then pushed back attacking Union troops all the way beyond the James Rivers. Between June 15 and 17, Beauregard's forces were pitted against major elements of Grant's Army during his defense of Richmond's major rail center in Petersburg. Once Lee caught on to Grant's intentions, he quickly moved some of his troops to support Beauregard's.

Figure 31. Barbary Coast pirates chasing a clipper.

# Chapter Thirty-One

*Straits of Gibraltar – September 21, 1863*

IT WAS early morning when Elizabeth entered Lilly's cabin and told her the *John Jameson* was quickly approaching the Straits of Gibraltar. She asked Lilly to come on deck and take a look at the Pillars of Hercules. Lilly agreed and followed her up the steps to the main deck. There, her mother asked, "Lilly, why was it so important for you to leave Jacob now?"

Lilly answered, "Mother, have you ever loved a man so much you couldn't live without him."

"Yes, dear. I felt that way about your father."

"If I don't leave right now, I'll never go, and I must go."

"Why? Why must you go?"

"I'm not able to tell you, at least, not now. Give me a few months and it will become clear."

Once inside the straits, the crew knew they had to be on the lookout for pirates operating off the coasts of Tunis, Algiers, and Tripoli. In spite of the dangers waiting on the waters between Gibraltar and Marseille, Captain Davis felt secure knowing the *John Jameson,* under full sail, could outrun any pirate ship in the Mediterranean. After an uneventful first one hundred miles, Davis ordered his crew to be especially vigilant for any Barbary vessel or any suspicious ship approaching his ship.

Fifteen hours after entering the Mediterranean, a lookout perched high on the forward mast shouted, "To starboard, I see an unmarked Barbary vessel with two triangle-shaped sails hanging from her main mast. I see openings along her sides with paddles protruding into the water. It seems she is getting at least some of her power from slaves tending the oars."

Ray called for Jacob and Lorenzo to come on deck but quickly realized they were not on board. Fortunately, Lilly and Lucy were still below and didn't hear Ray's frantic call.

Looking at Joe, Ray said, "Skipper, let's head north by northeast and let out our sails. There's no way that Barbary vessel can catch us with all our sheets up." Before Ray could finish his sentence, a shell splashed into the water about a hundred yards behind his ship. Immediately Ray shouted, "Joe, let's get those sails up and trimmed. We need to be at twenty knots right away!"

After outrunning the pirates, Lilly asked her dad, "Where do you think that ship came from?"

"Algiers, I suspect."

"What is this thing with pirates from North Africa. What makes them think it's okay to hijack ships, ransom or kill their crews and steal their cargo."

"Lilly, in the very early part of this century pirates out of Tripoli, Algiers and Tunis were capturing American ships and holding their crews ransom. They told our government the only way to stop the kidnapping was to pay a tribute to the Moorish pirates or Muslim leaders who were sanctioning these acts. When asked why they thought it was permissible to kill unarmed sailors, the leaders said it was because 'Islam allows its followers to penalize, enslave, or even kill infidels in the name of their religion.' After hearing this, the American President sent Marines into the Mediterranean to change their minds. Even though agreements were signed to stop the piracy, it continues to a lesser extent to this very day."

### *Aubagne and Marseilles*

Three days later, the *John Jameson* entered the south approach to Marseille harbor. Ten miles out Lilly and Lucy came up on deck and scanned the horizon looking for the Port of Marseille. Soon they saw a large island and the Port of de Bank. As they approached the port's entrance, Lilly and Lucy looked starboard and saw Palias du Pharo, built by Louis Bonaparte—Napoleon III—for his wife Empress Eugenie de Montijo in 1858. Lucy commented, "Lilly, that's such a magnificent location for a Palace—at the very entrance to one of the most beautiful harbors in Europe." Once past the palace, Lilly and Lucy could see the Port and beyond the city of Marseille. When they docked, Ray scurried down the gangplank to run ahead and make arrangements for carriages and wagons to take both families to their new residences in Marseille and Aubagne, respectively. Meanwhile, Elizabeth was secretly hoping this vibrant port city would invigorate Lilly and help her get Jacob off her mind.

Lucy's personality had always been different from Lilly's. She had accepted from the very beginning that she and Lorenzo would never be together after the war. This laissez-faire attitude made it easier for her to leave Charleston and accompany her ailing parents to the south of France to live out their remaining days. Even so, this had not kept her from thinking about Lorenzo every time she had the chance.

A few weeks after his arrival at his new estate, Ray asked Lilly if she would like to go to a follow-up meeting to the one she and Jacob had attended last September in Montreal. To his surprise, she said, "No, daddy. I need more time away from Jacob. I don't know what I would do if I ran into him unexpectedly at the hotel or a nearby restaurant."

"Lilly, I understand, dear. I wish I could skip the meeting myself."

"Daddy, you could send an envoy to represent you—perhaps General Beauregard or Captain Davis. You're not getting any younger, and two trips across the Atlantic in four months are quite enough."

"Lilly, I'm pretty sure Captain Davis will be occupied getting ready to come here and take us to Montreal. I'll write General Beauregard and ask if he could find someone to cover the upcoming meeting."

A few days later while visiting Lucy, Lilly made a somewhat unexpected request. "Lucy, would it be alright for me to come and stay with you and your parents for a while?"

"Of course, may I ask why?"

"I can't tell you. I just need some time alone to put some of my memories in their proper place. I also need to put Jacob in his proper perspective as well. I'll always love him, but for now, I need to figure out how I can get him out of my mind. I need to be able to say good-bye to him after our mission to Louisville is over." After telling her mother and father her plans, she packed up and took the twelve-mile carriage ride to the Rutledge's new home in Aubagne.

## *Richmond*

Between March and October 1864, the South suffered significant casualties both on and off the battlefield. As many soldiers were dying of illness and sexually transmitted diseases as were dying of wounds received in combat. In March, General Grant became Commander of all Union forces. On April 12, the Confederate Calvary under the command of General Nathan Bedford Forrest overran Fort Pillow near Henning, Tennessee, and massacred half a regiment of Black soldiers after the fort surrendered. General Forrest claimed in his defense that he had given the Union soldiers three separate opportunities to surrender before attacking the fort. He also claimed once the attack was underway, he lost control of his commanders when they learned half the troops inside the fort were colored. On May 5th and 6th, both sides feverously fought in the wilderness between the

Potomac River and Spotsylvania, Pennsylvania. The results of this conflict could at best only be described as inconclusive. During this same time, the North also won the Battle of Yellow Tavern, which cost the South the loss of one of its best Generals, J.E.B. Stewart.

## Commissioning of CSS Alabama - Terceira, the Azores

On August 24th, 1862, newly promoted Captain Raphael Semmes of the Confederate Navy called his English crew to the quarterdeck of his new command, a 220-foot long battle cruiser named the *Alabama*. The ship was lying just off the coast of Terceira, Azores. While a band played Dixie, Semmes read aloud his commission from President Jefferson Davis. As the band played on, the Stars and Bars were run up the mast. Semmes told his crew their mission was to burn, sink and otherwise destroy commerce destined for or exiting the United States. He added the spoils of war would be divided proportionately.

The ship had been built at the famous Laird Shipyard on the Mersey River near Liverpool. The ship, a 220-foot sloop, had a wood-hull, bark rigged foremasts and rigged square-mizzenmast fore and aft. She weighed slightly more than 1,000 tons. With two 300-horsepower steam engines driving a single two-bladed screw, she was capable of thirteen knots. She was both a perfect steamer and sailing vessel.

The *Alabama* was constructed in such a way her propeller could be detached from its shaft and lifted sufficiently high out of the water so as not to be an impediment to her speed—and this could be accomplished in fifteen minutes. When this was done and her sails spread, she was, for all intents and purposes, a sailing ship. On the other hand, when her Captain desired her to be a steamer, he had only to start her fires, lower the propeller and, if the wind was adverse, brace her yards to the wind for the conversion to be complete.

Unlike a Napoleonic-type man-of-war, which carried more than 50 guns, the *Alabama* only had eight. Her six 6.4-inch, 13-pounder smoothbores were small when compared to her other weapons. Designed by Captain Theophilus Alexander Blakely of the British Army, her cast-iron barrels and breeches were wrapped in wrought iron or steel bands. Her guns were so heavy they had to be mounted inline directly amidships to keep her balance. For this reason, her guns could only be manhandled via a complex system of pivots and tracks to move from one side or another before battle. The aft 8-inch smoothbore fired a 68-pound shot or 42-pound shell; the forward 7-inch rifle fired a longer 100-pound shot or 85-pound shell.

The single-screw sloop *Alabama* roamed the seas for two years before putting into Cherbourg, France, on June 11, 1864, for dry-dock repairs. For nearly all that time, she was pursued by the armor-clad *USS Kearsarge*. In addition to being armor-clad, the *Kearsarge* had multi levels of chain-link armor covering the most vulnerable areas of the ship.

## CSS Alabama vs. USS Kearsarge - June 1864

On June 14, 1864, the *Kearsarge* caught up with the *Alabama* while she was in dry-dock being repaired. Five days later, the French ironclad *Couronne*, escorted the *Alabama* out of Cherbourg Harbor to ensure the upcoming fight would occur outside French waters. When the *Kearsarge* came within range (1,000 yards) of the *Alabama*'s guns, she fired her first shot.

Hundreds of people watched the battle from the French coast. An hour later, after being hit below her water line, the *Alabama* struck her colors and surrendered. In all, 40 sailors were lost by the Confederates during the battle. The *Kearsarge* picked up another seventy, and thirty crewmembers were rescued by a British Yacht named the *Deerhound*. After picking up the *Alabama*'s thirty crewmembers, the *Deerhound* broke away and set a course for Southampton. The *Alabama*'s Captain and three other officers were among the thirty rescued.

## The Sea King (Shenandoah)

With the sinking of the Alabama, the Union had freed up their global shipping operations to resupply the Union Army with war materials produced overseas. The sinking also insured the free flow of items used in the home and commercial establishments. In essence, the sinking of the Alabama negated much of the real impact of this war on ordinary Union citizens.

For the South, this sinking hastened the need to replace her with another quality ship suitable for conversion to a war sloop. In 1863, the previous year, the Confederate Navy learned of such a vessel when the launch of the *Sea King* was announced on August 18, 1863, in an edition of the *North British Daily Mail*.

In August 1863, Naval Officer James Dunwoody Bulloch was in Scotland when he and his able assistant, Lt. Robert R. Carter came across the *Sea King*, anchored on the River Clyde in Glasgow. The "beautifully modeled" and "excellently finished" ship bore the trademark of the justly famous Clydebank shipbuilders *Alexander Stephen & Sons*.

Their name was a virtual guarantee of quality and craftsmanship. Bulloch and Carter both agreed the *Sea King* would make a superb addition to the Confederate Navy and resolved to buy her. However, since she was preparing for her shakedown voyage to Calcutta, India, and Wellington, New Zealand, she was not for sale.

Bulloch and Carter were not the only ones aware of the vessel's potential as a ship of war. In the autumn of 1863, Union Consul Thomas Dudley reported the presence of such a ship in a letter to Washington. He also pointed out the ship might easily be converted into a cruiser and relayed rumors of its impending sale to the Confederacy.

Sometime after June 1864, Minister Charles Francis Adams Sr. advised Lord Russell British subjects were actively engaged in fitting out a vessel to resume the *Alabama*'s "dirty Work." United States Secretary of State Seward warned Great Britain: *they may be held justly responsible for losses sustained by Union ships as a result of attacks by Confederate war ships purchased in England and Scotland.*

After the loss of the *Alabama* in June 1864, U.S. representatives in Britain knew Bulloch would leave no stone unturned in his efforts to replace his beloved *Alabama*. He was well aware of the United States' interest in preventing the Confederacy from obtaining another ocean-going cruiser. This knowledge brought to the forefront the need for greater secrecy and deception in every phase of the negotiating and purchase process. Bulloch had learned his lessons well regarding the need for secrecy and, after purchasing the *Sea King* he refused to go anywhere near her and forbade the use of his name in connection with her.

Bulloch instructed Lt. William C. Whittle Jr., designated second officer for the new cruiser, to take a room at Wood's Hotel in London under the name of W. C. Brown. He was to appear in the coffee room with a white pocket handkerchief stuffed through a buttonhole in his coat holding a copy of the *London Times* in his left hand. He was instructed to wait for an agent to contact him who would identify himself using an array of signs and countersigns. Once satisfied, the agent would accompany the officer aboard the ship without attracting unwarranted attention. As melodramatic as the precautions were, they actually worked well.

Meanwhile other Confederate agents had purchased a tender for the *Sea King* and made arrangements for a rendezvous. The tender, known as the *Laurel*, was fully expected to recoup her purchase price and make a profit for the Confederacy as a formidable blockade runner.

Again U.S. officials took a keen interest in these activities. Thomas Dudley told Charles Adams, son of John Quincy Adams and U.S. Minister of the United Kingdom, that officers from the *Georgia* planned to sail on this relatively small ship even though it was carrying an unusually large crew. Even so, Dudley did have to admit he did not have enough evidence to seize the vessel. The Confederates meanwhile, advertised for passengers and freight to Cuba and, with a series of carefully planned moves, ensured the *freight* consisted of stores and armament for the new cruiser and that the passengers were in fact the officers and a few choice men selected to crew her.

The *Laurel* carried guns and equipment, originally intended for refitting the *Alabama*, including four 55-hundredweight, 8-inch smoothbore guns, two Whitworth 32 pounders, two 12-pounders, and a selection of small arms, ammunition, clothing, and coal.

Customs officials in Liverpool found no violation of any municipal laws and allowed the *Laurel* to slip away on Sunday morning, October 9th, 1864, the very same day the *Sea King* left London. James Waddell, the future commander of the *Sea King* was on board the *Laurel* when she sailed to rendezvous with the *Sea King* in Funchel Bay off Cuba. The total cost of the *Laurel*'s purchase and for the cruise, was 53,715 pounds ten shillings and nine pence, equivalent to $31,150 in U.S. dollars.

James Waddell, Commander of the *Sea King*, specifically requested George Harwood, who had served Semmes as chief boatswain's mate on the *Alabama*, to join the crew. He considered Harwood a superb seaman, an experienced "man-of-war" man, and one calculated to be influential in a crew composed mostly of Englishmen. Waddell appointed him acting boatswain as soon as the *Sea King* cleared English jurisdiction. At the same time, Waddell explained the actual purpose of the voyage to him.

The *Sea King* reached Madeira on Sunday, the 16th of October and anchored in Funchal Bay. There it waited for the *Laurel*. On Monday morning, orders were given to cease all on-shore communications except for the purchase of coal for fuel.

On the night of Tuesday the 18th of October, a black ship came in sight near the Funchal anchorage and began signaling with her lights. She steamed up and down the anchorage, but it was impossible for the *Sea King* to respond to her. Her appearance caused a stir among the crew who were still on deck. The phrase "that's her" could be heard all over the vessel.

Daylight came, and a messenger was dispatched to the custom's official requesting clearance. While the customs vessel approached, accompanied by all manner of fishing smacks and bum boats seeking trade with the crew, the black steamer came in sight again from the North, with flags flying at her mastheads, answering the *Laurel*. A great cry arose from the assembled Madeiran craft.

After the departure of the customs officials, Captain Waddell told the crew of the *Laurel* to weigh anchor at 10 a.m., and proceeded to follow her quarry, which had slowed her engines. Through his spyglass Waddell read the words *Sea King - London* on her stern in large white letters, and ordered his signalman to send the *Sea King* a message to follow the *Laurel*.

Both vessels then proceeded to the North side of the Las Desertas, where, in a calm sea with a good deep anchorage, the work could begin. Lt William C. Whittle Jr. then joined Waddell on the *Laurel* from the *Sea King* where he had been her purser. On the 19th of October 1864, the *Sea King* was commissioned as the *Shenandoah* and put into the service of the Confederate States of America.

On the quarterdeck, Waddell, now onboard the *Sea King* spoke with his crew, who were almost all English, explaining the true purpose of the vessel. As he described the forthcoming cruise, he attempted to solicit them to join the vessel's crew. Only twenty-three of fifty-five men signed on and the majority of those signed on for only six months. Thirty-two crewmembers were then transferred to the *Laurel*. With the Confederate flag flying gracefully, the newly renamed *CSS Shenandoah*, embarked on her great adventure accompanied by cheers and acclamations from the *Laurel*.

## *Marseille, France - Spring and Sumer of 1864*

By the middle of July, Ray received word President Davis had, in April, wired former Interior Secretary Jacob Thompson and asked if he would travel to Montreal to take over Confederate Secret Service operations in Canada. Davis also wanted to learn why so many of the operations planned at last year's conference had failed to achieve their desired outcomes. Davis decided it was time to send in a professional to stir things up and get operations back on track. Thompson quickly telegraphed Davis with his response saying, "Mr. President, when your President calls, it's hard to refuse. I will leave for Montreal at once."

By early June, it became apparent to Thompson the South's attempt to create chaos and discontent in the northwest states was failing. Although many of the businessmen, farmers, and merchants in the region were generally unhappy about how the North had treated them, seceding from the Union and forming their own Confederacy was out of the question.

The action officers assigned to the effort were James P. Holcombe, a University of Virginia law professor, and Captain Thomas Henry Hines, a veteran Confederate spy (even though he was only in his early twenties). Thompson, knowing these were two good men, wondered if a change of scenery was in order. Perhaps moving some of the operations originally scheduled out of Montreal to Toronto would be the right medicine to cure the recent ailment.

Why go to Toronto? By 1864, everyone had spies in Toronto and, not infrequently, they traded information among themselves. Thompson thought expanding Confederate spy operations in Canada would make it more difficult for Union soldiers to follow or otherwise track down Confederate operatives working in the United States when they returned to Canada to pick up new orders.

Hines and his fellow agents worked closely with all of the Copperhead organizations: the Knights of the Golden Circle, the Order of the American Knights, the Sons of Liberty, etc., in attempting to create chaos and discontent in the northwest states. All that resulted from this liaison was a great deal of inflammatory talks and no action. Captain Hines, in his youthful optimism, appeared to misinterpret the rhetoric on the streets and, far too often, believed it would guarantee the success of sabotage and espionage operations being conducted out of Montreal and Toronto.

During May, June and July of 1864, Maine coastal residents noticed about fifty artists sketching along the shore. They were, in fact, Confederate topographers sent to Maine to map the coastline. They were looking for coves and inlets suitable for use by armed steamers in a combined land and sea attack on Maine. The full attack never took place. Once again, another attack plan of the Confederacy was stymied by Union actions. Later, a similar, but scaled-back operation met an even more disastrous fate.

On July 14, the governor of Maine, Samuel Cony, received a telegram from the U.S. Consul in St. John, New Brunswick, Canada. It warned a Confederate party of 14 men was planning to land on the Maine coast. A later telegram advised the team was headed for Calais, in Maine, to rob a bank. It further indicated that a spy named William Collins led the team. On July 18, 1864, Collins and two other men, including famous Confederate courier Francis Jones, were captured on the Main Street of Calais walking towards the bank. When arrested and searched, Jones was found with a Confederate flag. He then openly stated he was a Confederate, claiming to be a Captain in the 15th Mississippi Infantry Regiment. The Maine police found no trace of the other reported 11 men. No real connection could be found between the intended robbers and the Confederacy in Richmond or operations in Toronto; therefore, the men were tried merely for *conspiracy to rob*. Each was sentenced to three years in the Maine State Prison.

Francis Jones, now a disenchanted Confederate, confessed not only to his part in the Maine plot but also supplied information regarding Confederate weapons caches in the North. He also provided the names of twenty of the most successful Confederate agents operating in Maine, Massachusetts, New York, Pennsylvania, Maryland, Illinois, Mississippi, Kentucky, Tennessee and Ohio. Based on these disclosures, arrests were made and weapons confiscated.

In the fall of 1864, operatives from Toronto traveled to St. Louis, Missouri, to destroy Union transport ships used to ferry Union troops and supplies up and down the Mississippi. They intended to use *Greek fire*—a Molotov cocktail, to attack and disable Union ships. The group managed to destroy or significantly damage five to ten Union transport vessels in port. However, with the Union still having seventy-five vessels, the loss was considered inconsequential.

In October 1864, the Canadian operation found itself in need of funds. Toronto operatives staged a successful bank robbery in St. Albans, Vermont, netting more than $200,000 in gold and currency. When the operatives returned to Toronto for debriefing, they told their superiors their greatest surprise was finding $200,000 in the small-town bank's safe. When pressed by the U.S. to return the bank robbers for prosecution, Canadian officials refused, indicating the operatives provided military orders from Richmond—proving they were on a military mission.

# Chapter Thirty-Two

## *Marseille to Charleston*

A FEW weeks after Lilly moved into Lucy's parents' home, Lucy and Lilly were having a cup of tea. Lucy turned to Lilly and asked gently, "I'm happy to have you here, but I don't understand why you felt it necessary to move out of your mother and dad's new estate."

Almost in tears, Lilly answered quietly, "Lucy, I'm pregnant. I need some time to collect my thoughts before telling my parents."

"When are you going to tell Jacob?"

"I'm not. And I don't want you to tell him either. That goes double for Lorenzo."

"What's Lorenzo got to do with it?"

Thinking quickly, Lilly responded, "You know how the boys are, neither one can keep a secret from the other. I just don't want Jacob to find out at all. I'm not even going to tell him when I see him in November. I love him and will never stop loving him. Nonetheless, when this mission is over, I'll be returning to Marseille to take care of my son or daughter. Until then, I'll continue to miss him terribly."

Looking at Lilly with sympathetic understanding, Lucy whispered, "Lilly, your parents love Jacob like he was their own son. They know you've been intimate. Won't they be suspicious about your silence?"

Knowing she could never tell Lucy there was a chance Lorenzo could be the father, Lilly continued, "Lucy, sometimes there are things you can't tell anyone, not even your best friend. This is one of those times. Right now, I just can't say anything. Please trust me."

Reluctantly, Lucy replied, "I'll try not to mention it again."

***

Two months later, Lilly confided to her parents that she was expecting. They were very excited. They asked when the baby was due, and she told them sometime in June. Remembering Jacob had spent time away from

Charleston before they sailed, Ray did not ask if she had told Jacob he was the child's father. Lilly was relieved when the question never came up again.

After Lilly returned to Lucy's parent's home, Ray told Elizabeth he thought it best not to inquire as to who might be the baby's father. Elizabeth raised an eyebrow, then asked, "Why not, dear? Do you think there's a reason she hasn't mentioned Jacob?"

"I suspect she doesn't want Jacob to know about the baby. Perhaps she doesn't want him to feel trapped or obligated to care for the child."

"Ray, if she wants to discuss it, she'll have to bring it up."

Once back at the Rutledge home in Aubagne, Lucy asked Lilly how it went. Lilly barely smiled, "My parents were very understanding and seem thrilled at becoming grandparents, but neither of them brought up Jacob in the conversation." Tears glistened in her eyes, but she wiped them away, "I guess I'm just confused as to why no one said anything about Jacob." All Lucy could do was shake her head.

Lucy then spoke up, "Lilly, if you'd feel more comfortable living here with me, you can stay however long you want to. There's a midwife who lives just ten minutes away."

"I would like that very much. I think we still have a lot to talk about our early days back in Charleston."

***

In the early morning on June 16, Lilly awoke with an excruciating pain in her lower back. No matter how she turned, the pain remained. When it finally subsided, she hurried down the hall and knocked hard on Lucy's door. "Lucy, "she called out. "It's time—we need to get a midwife at once."

Lucy threw on a robe and came to the door, "Lilly, there's a midwife not ten minutes away. Her name is Mme. La Blanc. Let me dress quickly and I'll leave at once to get her. But before I leave, I'll send my mother in to stay with you. You just go back and lie down till I get back."

Fifteen minutes later Lucy and the midwife rushed in the front door. Ray and Elisabeth arrived less than twenty minutes after being summoned and offered to help in any way they could. After eleven hours of some-times-intense labor, Lilly delivered a healthy baby boy. She held him tenderly when the midwife placed him at her breast. "What a beautiful baby he is!" she thought before drifting off from exhaustion.

Lilly's parents were overjoyed at the baby's arrival. They took turns holding him during those times Lilly was able to sleep. They doted over him, seeing to his every need.  They even hired a wet nurse to take on feeding duties when Lilly was unable to feed their grandson.

Everyone was very careful not to ask who fathered the child.  Eventually, however, it became time to put the father's name on the birth certificate. Ray told Elizabeth he would ask Lilly the identity of the child's father and explain to her it was necessary for the child's birth certificate. He also said he would ask if she had chosen a name for the baby.

"Lilly?" Ray asked when he went in to see her.  She was holding the baby kissing his tiny fingers.

"Yes, Daddy," she said, looking up at him and smiling.

"Sweetheart," he said.  "Can I ask you a couple of questions? I need some answers to fill out paperwork for the hospital and American Consulate."

"Of course, daddy. What do you need?"

"Lilly, I need to know the baby's name and the name of his father."

"Why, Daddy. I think you know Jacob is the baby's father."

"And what name have you given him?"

"His name is Jacob Harris—Jacob L. Harris! The L for his middle initial is there to honor his brother Lorenzo. Jacob once told me his brother named one of his sons Jacob to honor him."

"Don't you want Jacob to know he has a son?"

"No daddy, I don't want him to know. He's a good man, but when this war is over he'll be going home to his wife and family. It's going to be hard for him. He is a true believer, and I can only hope our mission will be successful and make a difference.  If we lose this war, he and Lorenzo will have to go back home and pick up the pieces from whatever is left."

* * *

Over the next few months, Lilly cared for her son and worked hard to return to the same dress size she was before she was pregnant. It was important for her to look her very best for Jacob.

## *Marseille - November 1864*

The day of their departure, Lucy and her parents took a carriage to Ray's new estate to have breakfast with Lilly and her parents. After a continental breakfast of pastry, fruit, croissants and hot tea, Lilly and Lucy said goodbye to Lucy's parents, and Lilly reluctantly handed her five-month old son to one of the servants brought along by her parents. As Lilly, Ray, Elizabeth and Lucy entered the carriage, Ray's heart ached to see the tears streaming down his daughter's face. Lucy, too, saw her parents trying to look stoic despite their tears as she stepped into the carriage with the Coopers before pulling away.  Lilly squeezed her father's arm and asked, "Daddy, how were you able to do it for all those years?  How was it so easy for you to say goodbye?"

Figure 32.  Map showing location of Marseille.

Ray put his arm around her, drew her close and kissed the top of her head, "Lilly, I promise you it was never easy. Seeing you with our grandchild, I know I've taken my last voyage."

At the wharf, Ray introduced Elizabeth, Lilly and Lucy to Captain Delgado. Although the Captain was a little portly, he was well dressed and appeared distinguished in his Captain's uniform. Ray had known Lou for many years and trusted him explicitly. For nearly three years, they sailed together to various ports in North America for the Hudson Bay Trading Company.

Captain Delgado told Ray and Elizabeth that soon he was going to have to board the *Portofino* and have his crew untie the lines holding his ship against the pier. The timing of his departure was critical because he had to catch the outgoing tides at precisely the right time. Lilly and Lucy gave Lilly's parents a big hug and kissed them on each cheek, European style. Captain Delgado invited them to join him as he leisurely strolled down the pier to board the *Portofino*. As they approached the ship, members of Captain Delgado's crew ran down the gangplank, picked up everyone's bags and took them to their rooms. Lucy and Lilly proceeded up the gangplank but remained on deck so they could wave goodbye to their families before the ship left. As the *Portofino* drifted away from its dock, Ray and Elizabeth adjusted their coats, returned to their carriage and headed home. Once the *Portofino* cleared the dock, Captain Delgado gave the order to hoist all sails, jibs first and veer to port to exit the harbor.

### *Charleston - Wednesday, November 1, 1864*

On the way to *Boyce's Wharf*, General Beauregard asked Jacob if he felt well enough to make the trip.

"Yes, Sir. While I was home, I took a trip to Richmond and visited Chimborazo hospital. The doctors told me I was suffering from Bronchitis and a skin rash. They said the coughing might have come from inhaling smoke from cannons on the battlefield. They said the rash probably came from bug bites when I hid in the swamps on Morris Island. They gave me two or three different medicines until one of them worked."

General Beauregard spoke, "To make your trip to Montreal a little easier, I've asked Captain Davis to pick us up here in Charleston."

"You mean Captain Davis is coming here? How is Lilly going to get to Montreal so we can plan our trip to Louisville?"

"Ray told me he asked Captain Louis Delgado to pick her up in Marseille and take her to Montreal on the *Portofino*. She's a fine ship, and Lou can handle any vessel on the high seas. He knows Marseille well and has sailed from Europe to Montreal many times. He sails in the tradition of his homeland, Cadaques, in eastern Spain—the sea is his home. I asked him, if possible, to dock in Montreal during the second week of November. Captain Davis told me Lucy might be coming with Lilly but don't tell Lorenzo just yet. I don't want to get his hopes up."

"Sir, I won't tell him a thing."

"Apparently, Lucy's family is trying to decide whether to keep the chandlery in Montreal or sell it. That's the primary reason Lucy is coming with Lilly. Right now, a friend of the family, George Willis, is running the store and has been since the beginning of the war. Jacob, if you would like Lorenzo to accompany you to Montreal, you certainly have my permission to bring him."

# Chapter Thirty-Three

*Reunion in Montreal - November 1864*

JACOB, Lorenzo and Captain Davis arrived in Montreal on November 5th, four weeks after Ray had made their reservations at the Hostellerie Pierre du Calvet by telegraph. He also made reservations for Lilly, another woman and Captain Delgado for the second week in November. After Ray, Jacob, Lorenzo and Captain Davis walked down the gangplank to King Edwards Quay, Captain Davis' crew quickly offloaded the bags from the *John Jameson* and carefully placed them into carriages destined for the Hostellerie Pierre du Calvet. After the bags were loaded, Captain Davis told the driver to take Ray, Elizabeth, Jacob and Lorenzo to their hotel. In front of the hotel, the party alighted from the carriage and entered. After checking in, Jacob, and Captain Davis asked to be excused to go to the St Lawrence Hall hotel bar for a drink. Ray and Elizabeth did not follow them—instead they proceeded to their rooms. Lorenzo also went to his room and took a short nap. After he had rested, he washed up, hailed a hack and rode to the St. Lawrence Hall. Ten minutes later, Captain Davis observed Lorenzo standing at the bar talking to a very attractive young woman. Before long she invited him to sit down next to her. Lorenzo ordered himself a drink and one for the lady. Observing Lorenzo's situation, Captain Davis thought this might be a good time to ask Jacob about sleeping arrangements at the Hostellerie Pierre du Calvet.

Looking at Jacob, Captain Davis asked, "Are you and Lilly going to be sharing a room on this trip to protect your cover? I never got a chance to ask her before we sailed from Marseille. If so, should I ask the Innkeeper to put you into the same room you had the last time you visited Montreal."

"Yes, Captain. Lilly and I will be sharing a room—and it won't be to protect our cover."

Laughing, Captain Davis replied, "I'll make sure you get the same room you had the last time—you know, the one near the large bath."

Figure 33.  Hostellerie Pierre du Calvet.

"Captain Davis, who did Ray ask to cover the meeting for him last September?"

Davis answered, "He was able to get Colonel William 'Hardin' Nuckles to cover for him. Apparently, he's a longtime friend of General Beauregard. Beauregard told me Nuckles had been a boxer at West Point."

Laughing, Jacob asked Captain Davis, "Surely you don't mean Mr. Nuckles' middle name is 'Hardin' do you?  Can you imagine having Hardin as a middle name as a child?"

"Jacob, I have to agree with you on that one. I understand it's a nickname—but one fitting his demeanor. He's awfully big, rough and looks like a bulldog. I believe his real middle name is Henderson but I wouldn't swear to it. I was told he's from New Orleans and, like Beauregard, speaks French. I have no idea whom he might be working for. Beauregard once told me he dealt in the collection of useful information and sometimes sold it to the highest bidder. Beauregard also told me he heard rumors Nuckles was helping with negotiations between the Copperheads and the Canadian government to get help creating chaos and discontent within the northwest states. I heard from another source the Canadians are also providing safe havens for Confederate spies trying to return to Montreal or Toronto after their missions. Apparently, they're also hiding Confederate soldiers who escape from Elmira Federal Prison in New York until arrangements can be made to return them to the south by ship."

Captain Davis asked Jacob, "What are your plans till the *Portofino* arrives from Marseille?"

"Actually, I plan on taking in the sights around Montreal. The last time I was here I didn't have enough time to see what Montreal has to offer."

With a grin on his face Captain Davis commented, "Time flies when you're sitting in a bath tub with a beautiful woman. I was surprised you managed to make it to both the meetings and the gala."

Winking at Captain Davis, Jacob said, "I seem to recall seeing you in the arms of a lovely young lass just a few months ago."

***

A few days later, while taking supper at the St. Lawrence Hall dining room, Jacob saw Mr. Thompson sitting at a table next to the bar. He picked up his drink, walked over to Mr. Thompson's table and asked if he could join him.

"By all means, Mr. Jameson."

"Mr. Thompson, I heard President Davis asked you to come to Montreal and make a few changes to get the Canadian operation back on track. Is that true?"

Not wishing to answer Jacob's question directly, Mr. Thompson leaned over and whispered into Jacob's ear, "I gather you want me to continue using your alias in this conversation."

"I think it would be prudent to do so."

"I agree. I just ran into a couple of gentlemen in the card room who I know are Union spies. A man can't go anywhere in this city without tripping over a spy or two. Where's your French Princess?"

"She's en route from Marseille. About a year ago, Ray and Elizabeth bought a new estate there, and she accompanied them when they made the crossing."

"I'm so sorry. I remember so well how much you loved each other."

"You could tell?"

"Everyone here knew. You were like two puppies. Is she going to accompany you on your trip to Louisville?"

"Yes, she's scheduled to arrive on the *Portofino* sometime around the fifteenth."

"So, Jacob. What are you doing in the meantime?"

"Just taking in the city and exploring the countryside."

"Would you like to conduct some Secret Service business for me. I need someone to courier some information to Toronto and bring back a saddlebag or two of gold bullion. I think it might take three or four days, at most. Are you with anyone?"

"My brother Lorenzo is with me. We were together in the 51st Virginia."

"It would be okay if you'd like to take him with you."

 "When would you like for us to go?"

"Tomorrow morning. You would be traveling by train."

"Thank God. I thought you wanted us to go on horseback."

"No, Jacob. The train is a lot faster."

"Who will I be meeting in Montreal?"

"Thad Culpepper for one. I sent him there right after I arrived. President Davis told me to do whatever was necessary to get our efforts up here back in order. Recently, we've had too many cases where we fell short of our mission objectives. I'm beginning to think Captain Holcombe and Captain Hines were overly optimistic about their ability to get the northern states to secede from the Union and form their own Confederacy. I think some of the tactics they dreamed up fall far short of what was needed to accomplish the task. What were they thinking when they came up with the idiotic notion we should invade the state of Maine? Jacob, have you ever been to Maine?"

"No, sir. But I have heard there's not a whole lot of anything up there worth defending."

"Your assessment is correct. What makes us think the Union is going to divert any major force up there to drive back a small contingent of Confederate troops invading from Canada? I think it's clear the northwestern states are not so dissatisfied with the North they're willing to leave the Union. Besides, the North doesn't look at slavery the same way we do. There's a strong abolitionist movement there, and I've been told there's a strong *underground railroad* secretly taking runaway slaves north through Kentucky, Indiana and Michigan all the way to Canada. It's my sincere hope that having a true professional like Thad Culpepper at the reins in Toronto will bring calm and insight into the picture. I've already asked the folks there to take a stronger role in our efforts, especially in the area of robbing banks to generate revenue."

The next morning, Jacob and Lorenzo boarded a train for Toronto, 335 miles away. They arrived some 8 hours later and were met by Major Culpepper on the steps in front of the train station. After tossing their bags into a hack, Jacob asked Major Culpepper, "Sir, is there a pub around here where we can get a good meal and a stiff drink or two?"

"There's one just around the corner. It's a little fancy, but not overpriced. The food is terrific. With regard to spirits, they have an excellent selection. You name it; they've got it." When they entered, Jacob and Lorenzo found a table near a warm and welcoming fireplace where Major Culpepper joined them. Jacob and Lorenzo both ordered a hearty stew with potatoes and carrots and hot coffee. Major Culpepper asked for the fresh catch of the day and chose red wine as his drink. Toward the end of the meal each brother ordered a glass of Canadian Club to drink while they discussed items brought up at September's meeting with Thad. After the brothers placed their drink orders, Captain Culpepper asked the waiter to bring him a Jim Beam on the rocks. As the night wore on, the topic shifted from the individual acts planned during the meeting to a more pressing concern—why were the intended results of the individual acts planned in Montreal not accomplished. After their meal, Major Culpepper gave Jacob and Lorenzo a short tour of Toronto's more interesting sights on the way to the Queens Hotel.

Before dropping the brothers off at their hotel, Major Culpepper told them to meet him in front of the hotel at 7 o'clock a.m. He added, "I'll have two or three saddlebags filled with gold bullion waiting for you. A man will be with me to escort you to the train station. Captain Holcombe will be waiting at the train station in Montreal to take the bullion from you and transport it to the second floor of the St. Lawrence Hall Hotel. He'll have armed guards with him to accompany him from the train station to the hotel. They'll stay with him until the gold is placed in the safe on the second floor. That safe is normally used for storage of cash and other valuables."

The next day when Jacob and Lorenzo arrived at the Queens Hotel, Major Culpepper handed them two saddlebags. They boarded the train and took seats in the second car behind the coal car. During the trip, Jacob started drinking from a bottle of Canadian Club and talking about seeing Lilly in just few days. Lorenzo sat quietly not saying a word. Jacob wondered why Lilly had not tried to contact him, not even once, since she left for Marseille. He wondered too, if she still loved him or if she had found a new love in France.

Eight hours later, they met Captain Holcombe at the Montreal train station and handed him the saddlebags. Both felt relieved when the guards placed the saddlebags inside a carriage destined for St. Lawrence Hall. Once curbside in front of the St. Lawrence Hall, Captain Holcombe picked up the bags and took them to the second floor and placed them in the Confederate armory safe.

The next few days, Jacob and Lorenzo spent most of their time in the St. Lawrence Hall hotel card room playing five-card stud. They spent their evenings drinking at local pubs and talking about Jacob and Lilly's upcoming mission to the Galt Hotel in Louisville. On November 14, as Jacob and Lorenzo were finishing up a card game, a young man poked his head inside the door and said, "Mr. Jameson, you asked me to tell you if I saw any ships coming upstream towards Montreal. Just now, I saw a clipper coming upstream on the St. Lawrence."

"Boy, how did you know it was a clipper?"

"It had too many sails to be anything else.  She was at full sail, and I couldn't count them all."

Teasing, Jacob asked, "You mean you couldn't count them without using your fingers and toes?"

"Sir, I don't need my fingers and toes to count the sails on a ship when I can see 'em."

"Thanks for telling me about the ship. Here's a dollar for your trouble."

Jacob's heart began to race. He quickly asked Lorenzo if he would like to go to the docks and verify whether or not the ship was the *Portofino*. He continued, "If the ship is the *Porofino*, come to the hotel and get me. I'd like to be waiting for her when she arrives."

Lorenzo responded, "Jacob, I'll go to the docks and check—if the ship is the *Portofino*, I'll come back and take you to the ship. After Lilly is on solid ground, I'll ask the driver to take both of you to the hotel. You have a lot of catching up to do. I'll catch my own hack back and see you at the Hostellerie Pierre du Calvet later this evening."

Jacob immediately grabbed a hack and returned to the Hostellerie Pierre du Calvet. He washed up and pulled out of the closet the finest clothes he had brought with him. He dressed and waited for Lorenzo to return. When Lorenzo stepped through the door, Jacob was brushing off his dress coat and hat. Lorenzo announced, "the ship now tying up at the dock is, indeed, the *Portofino*. The people at the docks told me the passengers should be ready to come down the gangplank in about an hour."

As Jacob and Lorenzo were exiting the *Hostellerie Pierre du Calvet*, Jacob paused and asked Lorenzo if he could return to the hotel bar with him for a last drink. Lorenzo replied, "Jacob, I know this is not going to be easy for you—It's been over a year. I know I'd feel the same if Lucy was on the ship. Lilly is a lovely woman and, regardless of what happens, she'll always love you.  I just know it."  After downing two Canadian Clubs, Jacob put down his glass and turned to face Lorenzo.

"Brother, it's time. Let's go," he said.

As they walked along the docks, Jacob reflected on his time with Lilly and the many adventures they shared together in Charleston. Lorenzo seemed more serious, wondering how Jacob would react when he and Lilly first saw each other again. They stood to the side on the wharf next to the gangplank while the luggage was brought down off the ship and loaded on carts waiting to take them to two carriages curbside. Suddenly Jacob and Lorenzo saw shadows of people stirring inside their cabins preparing to come outside on deck before disembarking. Soon, Jacob observed two young women shaking Captain Delgado's hand as they came on deck. He could tell they were thanking him for a smooth and safe crossing. After thanking Captain Delgado, the ladies began looking for the entrance to the gangplank that would bring them down safely to the dock.

Speaking to his brother Jacob said, "Let's stand back for a moment until we're sure one of the two women is Lilly. I wonder if she brought one of her servants to accompany her on the voyage.

Suddenly, a very surprised and excited Lorenzo spoke up, "Jacob, the second woman is Lucy! I swear to God. Those two women are Lucy and Lilly."

"Lorenzo, I think it's time we get out from behind these people waiting to pick up cargo and meet crewmembers coming off the ship."

Within moments, Lucy and Lilly saw Jacob and Lorenzo walking toward the gangplank. Once on the wharf, both women started to cry and ran to greet the men they loved so much.

Lilly spoke first, "Jacob, who told you our ship was here?"

"Honey, I paid a boy to watch the river and come get me if he saw anything resembling a clipper coming up the river. After the boy came and told me a clipper was coming upstream, I sent Lorenzo to the docks to verify the ship was indeed the *Portofino*. He returned to the *Hostellerie Pierre du Calvet* and told me the passengers were expected to disembark in about an hour, right after the bags were off loaded.

Lorenzo then asked Lilly, "What about Lucy? Why did she come along?"

Lucy interjected, "The government decided that since the Inn and the chandleries had nothing at all to do with the Confederacy, they would allow us to petition the government to get both back and reopen them if we wanted to. Since so many properties were destroyed, they said it might take a few months to complete the process. I suspect they are in need of the tax money the properties generate.

Looking at Jacob, Lilly commented, "Jacob, you damn fool, you still look so handsome." She glanced quickly at Lorenzo, "That goes for you, too, Lorenzo. Lucy is a lucky woman." Then she turned her attention back to Jacob, "How many days do we have before we have to board the steamship headed to Louisville."

"Lilly, I don't really know. Neither Mr. Thompson nor Major Culpepper gave me a firm date. I know the Secret Service has been told the Galt will be hosting a strategic planning session on General Sherman's planned *March to the Sea* in December. I also know President Lincoln's Inaugural will be around January 20th. The question appears to be whether the Generals will want to hold off their strategy meeting and combine it with a meeting with the Vice President when he passes through Louisville en route to the Inaugural. I think Mr. Culpepper will want us to reconnoiter the hotel sometime in early December."

Lilly said, "I sure hope Mr. Thompson gives us enough time to get caught up."

"Honey, perhaps Mr. Thompson will allow us some extra time on our trip down the Ohio. Who knows, perhaps we can go on beyond Louisville to St. Louis, Memphis, or even New Orleans."

Looking at Jacob and Lilly, Lucy commented, "My, aren't Lorenzo and I fortunate.

We have at least until you get back from Louisville to get caught up."

***

On December 1st while catching up on some amorous activities, Jacob heard a firm knock on his door. He told Lilly to stay in bed while he answered the knock. Approaching the door, Jacob inquired, "Who is it?"

"Jacob, it's Mr. Thompson. I didn't mean to inconvenience you but I have your tickets on the Queen City leaving from Cincinnati on December 3rd. Because of your status, I was able to get you a very nice stateroom with windows. I'll slide the tickets under the door. I'll also slide under the door your hotel reservations for the Galt and instructions on what information we'd like you to collect. Included also is a floor plan of the hotel."

"Mr. Thompson?"

"Yes, sir."

"Will all those things fit under the door?"

"Jacob. They will, I've done this before."

In less than a minute Jacob saw four envelopes slide under the door. Jacob reached down picked up all four envelopes and started to open the first one. Before he got it open, Lilly reached out, grabbed Jacob by his shirtsleeve and pulled him back into the bed. She commanded, "Not now Jacob, put those things down. Tomorrow is plenty soon enough."

# Chapter Thirty-Four

## *Journey to Louisville*

THE LAST week in November, Jacob and Lilly took a carriage to the Montreal train station and boarded a train that would eventually deliver them to Cincinnati. This early departure date insured their arrival in Cincinnati before the paddle wheeler *Natchez* departed for Louisville on December 3rd. Lilly's travel papers, identifying her as a French princess, allowed her to receive the kind of treatment expected by the royalty she was pretending to be. Everyone was at her beck and call. Jacob, too, enjoyed the special treatment he received traveling as the heir to the Jameson whisky fortune and fiancé of Princess De Conti. They were basking in all their glory.

When Jacob and Lilly arrived in Louisville, the Galt hotel sent their most luxurious carriage to pick them up at the dock and deliver them to the hotel. The hotel also sent a special luggage cart to the dock to pick up their bags and bring them to the hotel.

The first night the Concierge gave Ian and Princess De Conti a tour of the hotel. As they approached each area of the hotel, Ian would ask probing questions about security arrangements for dignitaries like himself and his Princesses. Obligingly, the staff answered each and every question, hoping to put their guests concerns to rest. It was clear the employees of the hotel were anxious to show Ian and his Princess just how much effort was being taken to protect them within the confines of the hotel.

About halfway through the tour, Ian asked the Concierge, "Have any famous people stayed here at the Galt."

With great pride, the Concierge answered, "Mr. Jameson, many important people have stayed here at the Galt, including several senior military commanders, government officials and the revered author Mark Twain."

"Really?" Ian asked with great interest.

Without hesitation, the Concierge continued, lowering his voice and looking around to see who else might be listening, "In fact, we have reservations for Generals Ulysses S. Grant and William Tecumseh Sherman for the last week in December."

Ian raised an eyebrow, waited just a moment, then asked, "Do you have any idea why General's Grant and Sherman are meeting in Louisville?"

The Concierge replied, "Since they asked for additional security both inside and outside the hotel, I suspect they're going to hold some kind of meeting on how to wrap up the war. The war department's already told us to expect a large number of sailors from gunboats and ironclads brought to Louisville to patrol the Ohio in front of the hotel."

"Have you ever had a president stay at the hotel?"

He promptly answered, "Yes, several.  President Lincoln often stayed at the hotel when he was in public office in Illinois." With a certain amount of pride, the Concierge added, "Sir, Vice President Johnson has rooms reserved for himself and his protection detail of Pinkertons for the first week in January."

Following up on the Concierge's comment, Ian added, "I suppose Vice President Johnson has several Pinkertons with him at all times."

"Yes, sir.  He's reserved 4 rooms, 2 men to a room."

Ian, although deeply interested, asked casually, "Why on earth would the Vice President be staying at the Galt in January?"

"Sir, it's to attend President Lincoln's second inaugural. Mr. Lincoln is to be sworn in on January 20th. Louisville provides a good overnight stop for him when he's heading to Washington."

After the tour, Jacob and Lilly retired to their suite. Once inside the suite, Jacob remarked about the room's remarkable size. Lilly, on the other hand, seemed particularly interested in the room's large and very comfortable featherbed.  Jacob asked, "Lilly, how long should we stay in Louisville."

"Honey, I think all we need to do now is confirm what the Concierge told us about the dates of General Sherman, General Grant and Vice President Johnson's visits. After that, I think we ought to treat this trip like a holiday and enjoy ourselves."

"I'm assuming you're going to tell Major Culpepper all this frolicking was done to preserve our cover."

"Of course, dear. But Major Culpepper could have preserved our cover a lot better by sending us farther down the river to Memphis or New Orleans." She laughed, then reached for Jacob. "Regarding frolicking, I think we should start right now."

Joining Lilly in her playful mood, Jacob asked, "How long do you think the frolicking should last?"

"I don't know. Does the hotel have room service?'
"I believe they do. Do you want to order something now?"
"Not now, we're going to be busy."

***

After three more days of following employees to identify their normal work routines and observing security measures being taken by hotel detectives and staff to protect visiting dignitaries, Jacob and Lilly boarded the paddle wheeler *Natchez* and headed upstream toward Cincinnati. There, Jacob and Lilly boarded a train to Montreal via Detroit and Toronto. Between Cincinnati and Detroit, they prepared a meticulous report on the routine operations of the Galt hotel, described the hotel employees and emphasized the special security measures the hotel would be taking to protect Generals Grant and Sherman while they were in Louisville. Between Detroit and Toronto, they prepared a separate report on measures the hotel has taken in the past to protect Presidents and Vice Presidents when they visited the hotel. Jacob and Lilly included with their reports arrival and departure schedules for trains and paddleboats passing through or docking in Louisville. Jacob and Lilly also prepared an annotated map of Louisville identifying the best routes north into Jeffersonville and the hills of Southern Indiana and south into the sparse regions just beyond the city. On the last leg of the trip, Lilly leaned against Jacob pretending to take a nap. She knew the number of days they would have together was diminishing rapidly. Soon she would be boarding the *Portofino* – without her lover and father of her child.

About halfway between Toronto and Montreal, Jacob looked to his right and saw a tear in Lilly's eyes. He whispered, "Honey, are you alright?"

"Yes, dear. When I'm with you I'm always alright."

Jacob pulled a handkerchief from his pocket and wiped away her tears. He pulled her in close and tenderly held her hand. Neither said a word until the train stopped at the Montreal rail station.

## *Return to Montreal*

As Jacob and Lilly stepped down off the train, Jacob Thompson approached and called out, "Jacob, Lilly. I'm over here! How did it go? Were there any problems?"

As Jacob and Mr. Thompson shook hands, Jake replied, "Sir, from an intelligence standpoint, I'd have to say we obtained a great deal of information. However, I'm not sure it tells us what we want to know. Generals Grant and Sherman have secured reservations at the Galt for the last week in December, and Vice President Johnson has reservations for himself and his Pinkertons for the first week in January. In both instances, the parties involved are bringing plenty of security. Additionally, the hotel, its detectives and local police all seem to be aware of the timeframes of the visits and have prepared accordingly. If we want to penetrate the hotel's security, we're going to have to be well prepared when we make our move."

As Jacob handed Mr. Thompson his reports, he told him he and Lilly would be at the *Hostellerie Pierre du Calvet* should questions arise later in the week."

After Jacob and Lilly returned to the *Hostellerie Pierre du Calvet*, their moods began to deteriorate into a sense of desperation. Everything they did was done with an intensity unimaginable to anyone who had never been so much in love. With every passing day, they found new and exciting ways to show each other how much they truly loved one another. Finally, the day came when Lilly realized she must think about returning to Marseille and her precious son, the secret one Jacob knew nothing about. Lilly wondered if she should tell Jacob. She even considered fighting for him and asking him to leave Annie, but there was no longer any time to think. Tomorrow the *Portofino* would sail—she knew she had to be on it.

Jacob planned a special goodbye supper with Champaign in their room the night before Lilly's voyage. They finished their meal, but neither really tasted it. One last sip of Champaign, and they tumbled into bed, pulling off their clothes desperately. The intensity of their lovemaking was beyond exhausting. It consumed them both. Although the night was not as long as some had been, when the light crept through the curtains at dawn, Jacob and Lilly found themselves bathed in a glow of ecstasy.

When the hotel staff came to wake them, Lilly was able to get out just one word—coffee. Jacob was famished and ordered a hearty breakfast. After they had finished and dressed, Jacob asked the Concierge for a carriage to take them to the Port of Montreal.

Lorenzo and Lucy decided not to say goodbye to Lilly at the ship—they would say their goodbyes at the hotel. They were waiting patiently in the lobby when Jacob and Lilly appeared. Knowing saying goodbye would be difficult for the two young women, Lorenzo and Lucy both hugged Lilly quickly and left for the dining room.

Before helping Lilly into the carriage, Jacob kissed her and they held one another for a very long time. Once inside the carriage, Lilly leaned

Figure 34.  The Port of Marseille.

affectionately against Jacob's shoulder and tried to rest. When they alighted from the carriage, Jacob asked the driver to stay and wait for him. Before walking up the gangplank, Lilly clutched Jacobs's hands and brought them in close to her swelling breast. She kissed them as tears flowed down her face.

Holding her hands tightly, Jacob said to Lilly, "You have been the love of my life." Hearing the finality of Jacob's statement, Lilly sobbed as her heart shattered, and she turned quickly and strode up the gangplank plank. She scurried across the deck to the hatch leading down to her stateroom. Jacob knew she would not be looking back. He turned around, entered the waiting hack and told the driver to take him back to the *Hostellerie Pierre du Calvet* where he expected to find Lorenzo and Lucy.

Just as the hack pulled into the hotel portico, Jacob saw Lorenzo and Lucy waiting for the doorman to hail them a hack. He invited them into his carriage where he rambled on about his precious Lilly. Lorenzo instructed the driver to take them to King's Pub where they ran into Jacob Thompson. After greeting the brothers and Lucy, Thompson found a table and made sure no one else could hear them, and then asked Jacob, "Would you be interested in helping plan the kidnapping of President Lincoln, Vice President Johnson, Secretary of State Seward or General Grant?"  Thompson added, "Should our kidnap attempt on Vice President Johnson fail, we might have to up the ante by kidnapping the President. As you know, the actor John Wilkes Booth has already volunteered to plan and execute the attempt of kidnapping President Lincoln."

Jacob asked, "You said at the meeting these attempts are to be held in the strictest confidence. How many people will be involved in Booth's conspiracy?"

"Perhaps as many as fifteen or twenty. We'll need at least four kidnappers, four individuals to hold the horses while the kidnappings are taking place; agents to bribe bridge guards, an owner of a small hotel who is sympathetic to the Confederacy, and local guides who can be bribed to escort the kidnappers and hostages through the bogs on the other side of the Potomac. Fortunately, we already have an Innkeeper who is willing to hide the kidnappers and their hostages and provide fresh horses for their trip out of Washington. The innkeeper's name is Mary Surratt, and she owns a small boarding house at 604 H Street, Northwest, in Washington. Booth is supposed to meet us here in just a few minutes."

Lucy interjected, "Mr. Thompson, why is he coming to Montreal?"

"He's coming to pick up a warrant for the release of $1,500 dollars in gold from the Confederate Treasury. President Davis signed it two weeks ago. I have it in my valise."

Lucy then asked him, "What can you tell us about this volunteer who wants to kidnap Lincoln?"

"He's well known and hates Yankees. I wouldn't be surprised if you recognize him."

As Mr. Thompson was finishing his sentence, a thin, well-dressed man with a flowing mustache entered the pub and approached Mr. Thompson. First looking at Jacob, Booth asked, "Mr. Thompson, is he alright? Can he be trusted?"

"He can be trusted, and so can his brother Lorenzo and his beau Lucy." Turning to the couple, then to Booth, Mr. Thompson said, "Friends, let me introduce you to Mr. Booth."

Lucy smiled broadly when she recognized him, "Mr. Booth, aren't you John Wilkes Booth, the actor? I once saw you on stage at the Dock Street Theater in Charleston. In fact, I think you stayed at our Inn during the run of your performance."

"Yes, I am one and the same, although on occasion I've used several aliases. I must say you've certainly grown up since then. Jacob, what do you and your bother do?"

"We're members of the 51st Virginia Infantry. Mr. Thompson was just telling us that you came here to get money to fund your conspiracy to kidnap the President, kill the Vice President, Secretary of State Seward and General Grant. Miss Lilly Cooper and I have already reconnoitered the Galt Hotel in Louisville for a possible kidnapping or assassination attempt on Vice President Johnson while he's en route to President Lincoln's inaugural."

Booth replied, "If the planned kidnapping attempt in Louisville is successful, perhaps I will only have to kidnap or kill three people instead of four. Mr. Thompson, did you bring the warrant with you?"

"It's in my valise, John. When you leave the pub, be sure to take it with you. I won't be needing it anymore."

Booth thanked Mr. Thompson and said goodbye to those sitting at the table. He picked up the valise and calmly walked out the door. Jacob said to Mr. Thompson, "Booth didn't act much like he wanted any help with his operation. He acts like he'd rather kill Lincoln than capture him. I'm not sure I trust him. Does he know he's supposed to kidnap President Lincoln and not kill him? It's hard to trade any dead man—including the President—for a thousand live ones."

"I placed a note inside the valise telling him to just kidnap him—not kill him.'

With Lilly gone, Jacob found little reason to stay in Montreal. He asked Mr. Thompson if he needed him further.

"No. Jacob. Not at this time."

Three days later Jacob, Lorenzo, Lucy and Captain Davis boarded the *John Jameson* and headed south for Charleston.

Figure 35.  Damage in Charleston.

# Chapter Thirty-Five

## *The End is Near*

ON THEIR way to Charleston, Jacob, Lorenzo, Lucy and Captain Davis discussed recent events that could lead to the collapse of the Confederacy. In November 1864, Union Brigadier General Edward Hatch landed 5,000 Army troops and 500 sailors at Boyd's Neck on the Broad River, just above Beaufort, South Carolina. He moved toward Grahamville with the objective of severing rail lines between Savanna and Charleston.

Confederate troops led by Colonel Charles Colcock Jones made contact with General Hatch's forces at Honey Hill, South Carolina, on November 30 and engaged them. After being reinforced by the 47th Georgia Infantry, commanded by General Beverly H. Robertson, Jones reengaged and dislodged Hatch's forces from their position. After nightfall, the Union troops withdrew to their transports. The Union sustained 764 casualties as compared to just forty-seven for the Confederates at Boyd's Neck.

During the six weeks of Sherman's *march to the sea,* little happened in Charleston. Union General Hatch, now on Morris Island, observed, "The battering of Sumter is, in my opinion, an idle waste of material." General Halleck in Washington then sent a dispatch to General Foster saying General Grant "wanted all shelling upon Charleston and Fort Sumter discontinued."

After General Robert E. Lee received a letter from South Carolina Governor Milledge L. Bonham asking him to reinforce the troops facing General Sherman with troops from Virginia, Lee responded, "If I send troops from my command south, I will have to abandon Richmond."

In December 1864, with Sherman troops close to Savannah, General Cooper wired Beauregard, he "hoped Savannah could be successfully defended but added the defense should not be protracted so much as to sacrifice the garrison." Cooper also remarked, "the same is true for Charleston."

Lieutenant General Hardee evacuated Savannah on December 21, 1864. Upon entering the city Sherman telegraphed Lincoln, "I beg to present you, as a Christmas gift, the City of Savannah with its 150 heavy guns, plenty of ammunition and 25,000 bales of cotton.

While in Savannah, Sherman received a letter from General Halleck in Washington.  Halleck stated:

> *Should you capture Charleston, I hope that by some accident the place may be destroyed, and if a little salt should be sown upon its site it may prevent the growth of future crops of nullification and secession.*

Having already decided to march on Columbia and not Charleston, Sherman replied:

> *I will bear in mind your hint as to Charleston and don't think salt will be necessary. When I move, the Fifteenth Corp will be on the right of the Right Wing, and their position will bring them into Charleston first; and if you have watched the history of that corps you will have remarked that they generally do their work up pretty well. The truth is the whole army is burning with insatiable desire to wreck vengeance up South Carolina. I almost tremble at her fate."*

## *Charleston, South Carolina - January 1865*

On January 15, 1865, Admiral Dahlgren dispatched the monitor *Patapsco* to look for harbor obstructions. Several hundred yards from Fort Sumter, the *Patapsco* hit a mine and sank, taking with her sixty-two of the one hundred and five souls on board.

On February 14, 1865, General Beauregard sent instructions to Charleston to evacuate the city by rail through St. Stephens to Columbia to reinforce General Joseph F. Johnson. Union signalmen on Morris Island intercepted several messages from Charleston to the harbor forts regarding the impending evacuation.

On February 16, Major Huguenin, Commander at Fort Sumter, received a telegraphic dispatch ordering him to prepare to evacuate his position. The next morning a new Confederate flag was raised at the fort. At sunset, the flag was lowered and a salute was fired, presumably from one of the surviving guns inside the fort. At 10.00 p.m. two steamers commanded by Lieutenant Thomas L Swinton arrived at Fort Sumter to evacuate the garrison. After roll call the troops were marched to two awaiting ships. Major Huguenin, the commander, Lieutenant White, the fort's engineer and Lieutenant Ogier, the Adjutant of the post went to the ramparts and relieved the evening's sentinels and sent them to the boats. Lieutenant Huguenin had been the last to depart Battery Wagner in 1863; and now he was the last to leave Fort Sumter. He recorded his thoughts about that night in his report:

*After visiting every portion of the fort with a heavy heart, I reached the wharf, no one was left behind but many a heart clung to those sacred and battle scared ramparts, I cannot describe my emotions. I felt as if every tie held dear to me was about to be severed; the pride and glory of Sumter was there, and now in the gloom of darkness we were to abandon her, for whom every one of us would have shed the last drop of his blood.*

Overnight the Confederate troops prepared to destroy everything of value they could not take to North Carolina. A large Blakely Gun at the corner of East Battery and South Street was blown up and the bridge across the Ashley River was set on fire. Volunteer members of the white fire companies had long since been converted to militia and left with the troops. This left only city ward engines manned by free blacks to fight the many fires breaking out over the city.

The next morning, February 18, several large magazines were set on fire and exploded. Meanwhile, supplies and ammunition were blown up at the Northeastern Railroad Depot. At the Cooper River docks, Confederate gunboats *Palmetto State*, *Chicora* and *Charleston* were blown up and the *USS Isaac O. Smith* was burned down to her waterline. Warehouses containing rice and cotton were also burned.

When the militia and troops defending Charleston finally boarded a train for Columbia, Jacob and Lorenzo were not on board. Instead, they rode inland and visited Miss Abigale for one last time. Miss Abigale prepared for them what likely would be their last warm meal before heading home. Jacob and Lorenzo's first inclination was to head west and try to make it home. Surely, no one would criticize them since so many regiments had already been captured or surrendered. Those soldiers not captured in major battles were often too confused to continue and walked into the waiting arms of Union patrols. With nearly four years of service under his belt, Lorenzo had the experience and training necessary to avoid Federal patrols. After a few days, the brothers began scavenging for food and supplies and, with the aid of a few prayers, made their way north to just outside Richmond. There, they started looking for any unit willing to accept them.

## Charleston, South Carolina

On the morning of February 18, the *USS Canonicus* unlimbered several shots at Fort Moultrie. Receiving no return fire. Major John A.

Hennessy, Fifty-Second Pennsylvania Infantry, departed Cummings Point on the tip of Morris Island in a small boat and landed on Fort Sumter. There, they raised their regimental flag, the first since April 14, 1861.

Colonel Bennett, Major Hennessy and twenty-five troops docked at Atlantic Wharf and were greeted by City Alderman George Williams. He presented Bennett and Hennessy with a note he was carrying from Charleston Mayor Charles Macbeth reading:

> *The military authorities of the Confederate States have evacuated the city. I have remained to enforce law and preserve order until you take such steps as you may think best.*

Two companies of the Fifty-second Pennsylvania and men from the Third Rhode Island Artillery landed in Charleston and accompanied Bennett to the Citadel where he made his headquarters. Bennett immediately instructed his troops to help fight the many fires burning across the city started the previous night.

A *New York Tribune* reporter, identified only as Berwick, described his arrival at the wharves and the city this way:

> *The wharves look as if they had been deserted for half a century – broken down, dilapidated, grass and moss peeping up between the pavement, where once the busy feet of commerce trod incessantly. The warehouses near the river; the streets as we entered them; the houses and stores and the public buildings – we look at them and hold our breaths in utter amazement. Every step we take increases our astonishment. No pen, no pencil, no tongue can do justice to the scene…And, all around this area of desolation are the ruined houses that still stand -- 'Gilmore's Town" as the negroes call it.*

As Union troops found their way to Broad Street, they found the offices of the great secessionist newspaper, the *Mercury*, occupied by a negro family. On the western side of the city a great tragedy occurred when children playing around burning cotton threw gunpowder at the flames and it exploded. More than 400 people were either killed or injured. It was described like this: "The miserable victims were seen tumbling about in agony, literally roasting alive; their wild shrieks were appalling – all help was impossible."

Eventually, the 127th New York Volunteers and the 21st United States Colored Troops were selected to establish a garrison to occupy Charleston. Their Commander, General Schimmelfennig established his headquarters at 27 King Street. This is the same house that served as the British headquarters in 1780 after the fall of the city.

By the 19th of March, the Union soldiers were running everywhere through the streets of Charleston looting homes, businesses and public buildings. Colonel W.H. Davis, 104th Pennsylvania wrote of their behavior:

*Not all soldiers participated in the plunder, but officers received a share. Their conduct in this particular was disgraceful, and should have cost the offending ones their commission. Some of them sent north pianos, elegant furniture, silverware, books, pictures, etc. to adorn their New England dwellings.*

General Schimmelfennig soon placed Charleston under martial law requiring citizens to take an oath of allegiance to the United States. Rations consisting of cornmeal, rice and salt were then distributed to starving Charlestonians.

On April 14, 1865, at a Gala event at Fort Sumter, Major Robert Anderson, former Union commander of Fort Sumter, raised the same Union flag that was removed from Fort Sumter April 14, 1861. Major Anderson was so moved by the event he had to have assistance raising the flag to the top of the 150-foot flagstaff as the band played on. After raising of the flag a gun salute was offered from the former Confederate batteries surrounding the harbor.

At 6:00 p.m., a grand dinner was given by General Hatch in Charleston. The final toast was reserved for Robert Anderson. After his introductory remarks, he raised his glass and offered:

*I beg you now, that you will join me in drinking to the health of another man whom we all love to honor, the man who, when elected President of the United States, was compelled to reach the seat of government with an escort, but now could travel all over the county with millions of hands and hearts to sustain him. I give you the good, the great, the honest man, Abraham Lincoln.*

The many people enjoying the gala evening, of course, did not know that as they toasted Lincoln, John Wilkes Booth would fire the fateful shot at the President's head at Ford's Theatre in Washington.

## Richmond

On April 3rd, word around the camp was that Richmond had surrendered. It was demoralizing and some troops began throwing their muskets on the ground, followed by their ammunition and anything else they considered too heavy to take with them. Jacob and Lorenzo decided to stay to the very end. They simply weren't ready to begin their long journey home. In spite of some desertions, most Confederate soldiers stayed and continued to fight mostly because of their loyalty to their individual commanders.

On the morning of April 9th, word started circulating around the camp that General Lee's Army was surrounded and cut off from its supplies in the town of Appomattox Court House. Everyone seemed to know nothing short of a miracle could prevent a surrender. That afternoon, Jacob and Lorenzo's adopted regiment received word Lee had surrendered to Grant and had been granted what could only be described as generous terms of surrender. Essentially, Grant told Lee to tell his men to put down all weapons, except those needed for self-protection and hunting… and go home.

After hearing the terms of Lee's surrender, Confederate officers told their men to lay down their arms. At this point Jacob and Lorenzo quickly realized nothing was ever going to be the same. The time they had spent with Lilly and Lucy would, in time, become just a memory to be recalled only when the time was right. The long walk home was filled with questions as to what just happened. Even though the battle of Petersburg had been over for more than two weeks the brothers still vividly remembered the men lying dead or dying on the battlefield.

The brothers began thinking about what lay ahead and hoped soon they would be in the arms of Millie and Annie. There were, of course, questions about whether the North would be merciful and just let them return home to their cabins and families or be punitive and try to take all or some of their possessions because they had lost the war. Nonetheless, Jacob and Lorenzo were glad the war was over.

As the men walked home, the further west they walked, the fewer and fewer men they encountered along the side of the road. Occasionally an unfilled train would be spotted offering the brothers an opportunity to ride and not walk a hundred miles or more. After four days, the brothers were able to jump a train heading south toward Bristol on the Tennessee and Virginia railroad. A few hours later, Jacob and Lorenzo saw a familiar sign they often took shots at when they were young boys. It read: "Wytheville - 5 miles." With the war over, the streets of Wytheville were nearly dead. The military regiments and whores who followed them were gone. The brothers walked into the nearest livery stable and asked if there were any horses they could rent for a few days.

The owner replied: "Haven't I seen you in here before?"

"Yes sir, we just got back from the war. We live in Burke's Garden and need a couple of horses to get us over Burke's Garden Mountain."

"These days I have plenty, just pick out the two you want. Since you're soldiers and all, you can settle up with me when you bring them back."

Once over the mountain, Jacob and Lorenzo began to see all the familiar sights they had missed so much. They saw the waterfall at Wolf Creek, Blue Spring, and the trail they would take to their cabins. They saw smoke coming out of one of the chimneys and turned their horses in that direction.

Their arrival caught everyone by surprise. The children were delirious and Annie and Millie could hardly contain themselves. The war was over and there would be no more fear about whether Jacob and Lorenzo would return. Most of the slaves stayed and became sharecroppers and Miss Mary and Janet accepted work in the Harris household as indentured servants with a seven-year contract. At this moment in the Harris household, everyone believed life would return to normal and be good for many years to come.

In May 1865, General Sherman visited Charleston and announced:

*Anyone who is not satisfied with war should go and see Charleston, and he will pray louder and deeper than ever that the country may in the future be spared any more war.*

The Siege of Charleston lasted 567 days, the longest of any siege during the Civil War.

Figure 36.  The fields of Burke's Garden.

# Chapter Thirty-Six

*Burke's Garden - After the War - March 1, 1882*

AS ANNIE was preparing lunch, she heard the creaking rumble of the family buckboard climbing the last one hundred yards to the house. Looking through the front window, she was reassured to see Jacob and Lorenzo walking toward the front porch. Time had been kind to both of them. Each had a few more wrinkles and each was a bit grayer, but they were still as fit and trim as before. As they entered the home, Annie asked Jacob, "How did things go putting a new roof on Miss Mary's cottage?" Miss Mary now lived in a small cottage behind the Harris home.

Lorenzo spoke up and reassured Annie, "The new roof will last a long time."

"How is Miss Mary doing?" Annie asked. They were all concerned about her since the passing of her late husband, Homer, last year.

Lorenzo, "I thought Miss Mary appeared nervous at times and acted somewhat unsettled."

Annie then suggested, "Why don't you boys go back and visit Miss Mary this afternoon to see if you can cheer her up some. Take her some of the blackberry jam I canned and put up last fall. I opened a can yesterday and it's still fresh.

"That sounds like a wonderful idea, Annie," Jacob said. "I'm sure she'll appreciate the gesture."

After lunch, Jacob pulled Annie into a big hug and said, "I think your suggestion to visit Miss Mary is a good one. When Lorenzo and I were teenagers, the three of us were almost inseparable. Perhaps reminiscing about the good ol' days will make her feel better."

On their way to Miss Mary's cottage later, Jacob and Lorenzo recalled Mr. Harris building the cottage for her and her daughter Janet when Janet turned twelve. With both spending so much time around the house, Mr. Harris felt they should have a place of their own offering some privacy. Three years ago, Miss Mary finally announced she was going to marry Homer Smyth, a man she had been seeing for over four years. Homer, a sharecropper on Mr. Harris' homestead, previously worked for Mr. Harris as a field hand. Before announcing her intentions to marry Homer, Miss Mary asked Mr. Harris for his permission. She told him, "Homer and I are very much in love. He's such a good man, but he said I should ask you before we marry."

"Miss Mary, you and Homer have been free persons for many years now, and you certainly don't need my permission to get married—but you do have my blessing."

Miss Mary was surprised when Jacob and Lorenzo came by for the second time in the same day. She greeted each at the door with an affectionate hug. Jacob was first to speak, "Miss Mary, how are things going? I know you must miss Homer a great deal. The accident was just terrible. No one expects to be hit by a tree limb during a storm. Is there anything Lorenzo or I can do?"

Winking conspiratorially at Jacob, Miss Mary quipped, "The thing I miss the most is illegal in this state for you and me."

Shocked just a little, Jacob's face flushed as he replied, "Miss Mary, I don't know what to say. That was a very long time ago. You're still a beautiful woman, but Annie would kill me."

"Oh, Jacob, I was just trying to lighten the moment." She laughed and hugged him again. Then turning serious again, she confided, "I still think of you every time I look at Janet." Then, realizing that Lorenzo was with him, she asked, "Should I not be talking about this in front of Lorenzo?"

"He knows everything. I told him during the war."

When it came time to leave, each brother put their arms around Miss Mary's waist and gave her a big squeeze. She blushed a bit and invited each to come back—any time. As they left, Miss Mary returned to her favorite rocking chair, picked up her needlework and sat down. She truly felt content for the first time in many months.


### *Harris Homestead - March 2, 1882*

Throughout the day, Jacob was preoccupied. He had just read in the Jeffersonville newspaper that congress was considering changing election laws to remove all poll taxes and allowing people to vote without passing a simple literacy test. He was clearly unsettled—at times almost angry. When Annie asked Jacob what was wrong, he attempted to explain to her he wondered if the apparatus set in place to establish of a new Confederacy father south was still in place. He also wondered if he could find remnants of the Knights of the Golden Circle or the Confederate Secret Service still active in the United States or Canada.

Annie tried to hide her annoyance. They had covered this topic so many times before but Jacob just would not let it go. She asked the same question she had asked him a hundred times before, "Do you really think there's anything you can do about it?"

"I can go talk to Jesse to see if the money's dried up. I can also send a telegram to Jacob Thompson in Memphis. General Beauregard told me he moved there after the war. Perhaps he has some idea what happened to the Confederate Secret Service money that was deposited in banks in Toronto and Montreal. Someone must know whose name is on those accounts, and who is authorized to withdraw funds. If that money's still in Canada, perhaps I can travel to Montreal to see if any of the officers who fled north to Canada are still there and willing to support a new fight for another Confederacy farther south."

"Jacob, those men aren't young men anymore and neither are you. Many of them have to be in their 60s or 70s. How are you going to get the word out in such a way you won't get arrested for treason?"

"Annie, I don't know. Near the end of the war, General Beauregard told me Captain Hines and Jacob Thompson had already moved to Memphis. He said during the war Union soldiers burned down Thompson's home in Oxford, Mississippi. General Beauregard said that Thompson was well off and had been appointed to the board of the University of the South in Sewanee, Mississippi.

"While he was in Memphis, Captain Hines edited the *Daily Appeal* newspaper and studied law. After passing the bar in 1867 he moved to Bowling Green, Kentucky, and started his own law practice. In 1878, he was appointed to the Kentucky Court of Appeals."

With a calmness that hid what she was really feeling, Annie asked softly, "Jacob, what about that girl in Charleston? Is she still around?"

Jacob froze, stunned by Annie's question. He could see the pain in her eyes. "What are you talking about?" he tried not to stutter. "I haven't been in Charleston in years. Don't you remember? Once the war was over, we started buying our canvas from textile mills in North Carolina."

Watching his reactions carefully, Annie said, "Jacob, that's the only reason I didn't bring it up. I figured whatever it was, it's over."

Now the pain reflected in his own eyes. "Annie, the last time I saw Charleston it was in shambles. Everything on the south side of the city was completely destroyed. There were no hotels, restaurants, banks or businesses still standing. The ground was filled with craters from artillery bursts, and fires started from shells containing an incendiary called *Greek Fire* were burning everywhere.  Most of the aristocracy had closed up their businesses and fled inland, to Canada or overseas to Europe."

"Jacob, I never thought I'd ever hear myself saying this, but somehow you have to get this war out of your head. I've watched it eat at you all these years. It's been over for the rest of us but not for you. You need to go to St. Louis, Memphis, Montreal or anywhere else you have to and prove to yourself the war is over. You should leave right away—tomorrow, if you have to.  I can't go on this way—and neither can you."  She placed her hand tenderly on his cheek.  "It's the only way you'll ever find peace. But I'm warning you, if you're not back in two months, I'm sending Lorenzo after you. I'll tell him not to come back until he finds you. Do you understand?"

He nodded wordlessly, knowing now just how well his wife knew him.

She wrapped her arms around him tightly, not wanting to let him go, but knowing she must.  "Since all the children are grown and gone, before you leave, I need you to love me the way you did before the war."

***

After spending the night showing Annie how much he loved her, Jacob finally rolled over and fell into a deep sleep. At five a.m. he rose, dressed, and packed his bags. Before leaving he wrote Annie a short letter, he kissed her tenderly on the back of her neck and placed the letter beside her on the bed.

He saddled up Daisy, his Tennessee Walker, and rode her over Burke's Garden Mountain to Wytheville where he left his horse at the Livery Stable. He told the young man watching his horse his brother would pick it up in a day or two.

When Annie awoke, she reached to her side hoping to find Jacob still there but she was not surprised to find his side of the bed empty—except for a slip of paper lying on top of his side of the bed. She sat up, picked up the letter and read:

*Dearest Annie,*

*I know the next few weeks or months will be hard for you.  I have asked Lorenzo to look in on you to make sure you are well while I'm gone. Yesterday, he told me you could stay at his new place in Ceres if it would make things easier for you. Of course, your sister would be there and, I know you will enjoy her company and the company of her two daughters still at home.  Needless to say, I have no idea of what to expect when I arrive in St. Louis en route to St. Joseph to find Jesse. I also have no idea if members of the Army or Secret Service, who fled to Canada after the war, are still there. Here is what I do know. I have to be sure, in my own mind, there are no avenues left to resurrect the glorious southern lifestyle we loved and cherished so much. Either way, I'm sure I will feel better when I return.*

  *Your Loving Husband, Jacob*

By the time she finished reading the letter, tears welled up in her eyes and began to flow. By now, she knew, Jacob would be passing by Wolf Creek on his way up the Burke's Garden Mountain Trail. By noon, he would be at the Wytheville train station catching the next train north, where he would catch another train headed west for St Louis and points beyond.

As she was planning the next leg of Jacob's journey from St. Louis to St. Joseph in her mind, she heard a tap at the front door. At first, Annie wondered why she had not heard the buckboard lumber its way up the last one hundred yards to the house. When Annie opened the door, she saw Lorenzo, arms extended, ready to hold her and comfort her.

"Just tell me what I can do, Annie. This isn't right," he said.

Opening the door and ushering him in Annie sobbed, "Lorenzo, it has to be this way. Losing the war has been killing him a day at a time. He has got to learn we can never go back to the days of chivalry and southern charm. Those days are over—and, they've been over for fifteen years. He has to find out for himself. There's just no other way."

Doing her best to stop the tears and regain her composure, she asked Lorenzo, "Would you hold me for a while? Afterwards, I'll pack my things to come and stay with you and Millie until Jacob returns."

"Of course, Annie, let's sit down on the couch and, when you're ready, I'll help you pack. Then we can load your things in the buckboard and head over to Ceres. By the time we get there, Millie and the girls will have lunch prepared. After lunch we can sit down and talk about what we need do over the next few days or weeks."

***

At Wytheville, Jacob caught a train heading north to Charleston, West Virginia. From there he took a westbound train destined for St. Louis via Huntington, West Virginia; Lexington, Kentucky; Louisville, Kentucky; and Mt Vernon, Indiana. When he arrived in St. Louis, Jacob was surprised how small the train station was. Looking in the direction of the boarding platform, he spotted a small sign reading: "Mills Depot." There was only one track at the depot and one wheeled luggage cart parked on the platform.

After stepping off the train, Jacob picked up his bag and walked inside the station where he asked the ticket agent when the next train was leaving for St. Joseph. The agent replied, "The next train for St. Joseph leaves from the Alton Depot just north of the city tomorrow morning around ten."

As the clerk wrote up his ticket, Jacob asked why the train station was so small. An elderly gentleman sitting on an inside bench offered the following explanation, "Sir, right now St. Louis doesn't have what you'd call a central train station. The city relies heavily on several smaller ones spread throughout the city. The main reason is because of the river. There are only two railway bridges, the Eads and Wabash that cross over the Mississippi so most people have to take a ferry across. Most of the train stations are owned and operated by railroad companies themselves. The Alton train station has been dispatching trains to Kansas City for a long time and has the best schedule."

By this time, Jacob was famished. When he asked the ticket agent where he could find a good place to eat nearby, the clerk suggested Nellie's Cafe three blocks down the street on the right. Once inside, Jacob took a seat at the counter and ordered pancakes and a cup of coffee. While waiting, he noticed a boy wearing knickers, a light green shirt and brown vest selling copies of the *St. Louis Post-Dispatch* in front of the restaurant. Jacob pulled out a coin, waved it high over his head to get the boy's attention and motioned for him to come inside. In less than a minute the boy stood in front of him, paper in hand. Jacob gave the boy the coin, folded the paper and tossed it on the counter.

Before he had a chance to pick up the paper and read it, the waitress brought his order to the counter and placed it in front of him. Looking directly at her, Jacob asked, "Is Jesse James still hanging his hat in St. Joseph?"

Surprised by Jacob's bold question, she answered, "Sir, I don't know quite how to answer your question. Can you explain?"

Jacob laughed. "Jesse once told me that everyone in Missouri, except the police and Pinkertons, know where to find him."

The waitress replied, "Yes, Sir. Have you read this morning's *Post Dispatch*?"

"No, I just bought one—It's right here on the counter."

"Sir, take a look at the front page."

As Jacob unfolded the paper he saw the headline:

"JESSE JAMES – SHOT IN BACK BY BOB FORD."

Shocked and stunned by what he read, Jacob suddenly felt queasy and he was overcome by a sense of despair. His emotions were running wild, but he struggled to remain calm. Eventually, when he had regained his composure, he asked the waitress in a steady voice, "Do you know of a good place to stay not far from the train station?"

"Yes, Sir. There's a decent hotel down the street to the right about four blocks. If you'd like to save a few pennies, Mrs. Lynch runs a good rooming-house four doors down to the left. The cost at the rooming house includes a hearty breakfast in the morning."

Jacob thanked the young lady and placed a silver dollar in her hand. The next morning, he took a hack to the river dock to board a paddle wheeler named *Southern Belle* heading south toward Cairo, Illinois. Jacob thought the long ride would give him time to collect his thoughts and reminisce about the last time he and Lilly were on a paddle wheeler from Louisville to Cincinnati. This trip would be very different. Jacob would be alone heading first downstream on the Mississippi and then upstream on the Ohio en route to Cincinnati—with a lengthy stop at the Galt hotel in Louisville. His plan was to stay at the Galt for three days hoping Jacob Thompson or Captain Hines could join him.

Figure 37. Jesse James.

At the dock, Jacob learned the *Southern Belle* would not be leaving for another three hours. Jacob sent a telegraph to Mr. Thompson at the University of the South in Sewanee. The telegraph read, "Mr. Thompson, this is Jacob Harris, we met in Montreal. It is important we meet in Louisville not later than 7 April."

An hour later, he received the following response: "Jacob, I am not sure I can make your 7 April 1882 date. Captain Hines is much closer as he now lives in Bowling Green, Kentucky. He is now a judge on the state's Appellate Court. At the moment, the Court is now in recess. I will ask him to meet you at the Galt on the 7th. The timing of this meeting could not have been better. Three days from now I am leaving for Montreal to make a withdrawal from my account in a local bank. Captain Hines is making a similar withdrawal from a bank in Toronto."

Not long after his departure, Jacob was overwhelmed with a longing for Lilly that he knew was not right, but the memories kept racing through his head, and he could not stop them. Sometimes, when he passed a familiar place along the river's edge, his memories were so strong he felt an urge to call out to her. For a while he could not sleep, but somewhere between St. Louis and Cairo he finally fell asleep.

As the ship approached the docks in Cairo, Illinois, the sounds of people talking, packing their bags, and lining up to leave the ship awakened Jacob. Some passengers, those exiting the ship to catch other paddle wheelers traveling downstream to Memphis and beyond were hailing porters on the dock for assistance transferring their bags to other vessels. For passengers ending their voyage here, they were now free to travel by horseback or carriage to destinations in and around southern Illinois or southeast Missouri. Passengers on the *Southern Belle* continuing upstream on the Ohio River would have a three-hour break before turning left and heading upstream on the Ohio River to Louisville and Cincinnati.

As Jacob walked to the front of the *Southern Belle*, another paddle wheeler pulled into the dock just in front of her. That ship, named *Queen of the River* was ready to take on passengers booked downstream on the Mississippi to Memphis and New Orleans. After the layover, the *Southern Belle* pulled away from the dock and headed upstream on the Ohio River.

After the passengers destined for Memphis and New Orleans left the ship, the *Southern Belle*'s Captain said to the remaining passengers, "Folks, our next stop is Louisville. There, we're going to take a three-hour break before continuing on to Cincinnati. In Louisville, there are several quality eating establishments along the waterfront including the dining room at the Galt hotel. For those leaving the ship in Louisville, we thank you for joining us on the *Southern Belle*."

After docking in Louisville, Jacob heeded the Captain's suggestion, and walked to the Galt hotel. After checking in he took in a quick lunch at the hotel's superb dining room and smoked a fine cigar. Afterwards, he walked around the hotel reminiscing about how much he and Lilly enjoyed their stay there.

Jacob then hailed a hack and toured downtown Louisville, seeing all the changes that had occurred since he and Lilly were last here sixteen years before. Many tall smoke stacks belched smoke high into the air. The city was putting in horse drawn trollies and installing gas lights throughout the city. Louisville was now prosperous with many new storefronts opening downtown.

Two days later, Jacob felt a tap on his left shoulder while sitting at the hotel bar. He turned quickly to see the familiar face of Captain Hines. Jacob was so pleased to find someone he knew, he was almost giddy.

"Jacob, is that you?"

"Yes, Captain." Jacob was surprised to see the toll the years had taken on Captain Hines.

"With the war being over I think it best you just call me Thomas or better yet Judge Hines. Mr. Thompson said he was very surprised to hear from you. How can we help you?"

"Thomas, is there any interest in following up on our plans to start a new Confederacy farther south than before?"

"You mean with slaves, plantations, chivalry and southern charm?"

"Exactly."

"Jacob, that ship has already sailed. Mr. Thompson and I are going to Canada to clean out all the old accounts that were under our names. I think the money should go to Confederate soldiers that need help in some way."

"So, there's no desire to see if we can regain the lifestyle we loved so much?" Jacob asked regretfully.

"It's been too long, Jacob. The surrender terms weren't all that harsh, and there's just no interest. Once the slaves were freed—well, you just can't put a genie back into the bottle. Do you really want to go back into battle over this? I sure don't. Why don't you come with me to Toronto and see for yourself? Who knows, perhaps from there you could travel to Montreal and catch a Clipper for Charleston and see how much it's changed since the war."

Jacob appeared to think about it for a moment, but he had already made up his mind. "Thomas, you've talked me into it. My ship sails tomorrow for

Cincinnati.  From there it's an easy train trip to Toronto via Detroit. The ship sails at nine. I don't know about you but if you want to continue this conversation I'll be in the bar around eight-thirty. I need a few minutes to take a nap and clean up."

Later, when Thomas walked into the bar, he found Jacob at a corner table with a bottle of Jack Daniels and two glasses sitting on the table. Looking up, Jacob asked, "Tom, I'm over here, care to join me."

"Having a bottle of brother Jack is enough motivation for me.  How has life been treating you since the war?"

Hearing Thomas' comment, Jacob braced himself for what he knew Tom's next question would be—whatever happened to that lovely Princess who accompanied you to the Gala in Montreal?

"Jacob, where is your Princess? She was the most beautiful woman I ever saw—and that's saying something here in the South."

"She moved to the south of France and now lives in Marseille. I haven't seen her since I took her to the *John Jameson* after our mission. We reconnoitered this very hotel for the planned kidnapping of Vice President Johnson on his way to Lincoln's inaugural. As you know, when our agents got to Louisville they realized the Vice President was protected too well to make the attempt.  Enough about me.  What happened to you? I heard you escaped the jail in Columbus, Ohio. That must have been quite a trick."

"It's not all that important. I don't think the guards were all that well trained to stop an escape from a little ole' county jail. After the war, Jacob Thompson and I went to Memphis and I entered law school.  After I passed the bar, I moved to Bowling green, Kentucky, started a law practice and eventually ended up on the bench."

"Mr. Thompson sent a telegram advising me that he could not be here by today. He added he would contact you and ask you to meet with me. If it's okay, I'd like to take you up on your offer to accompany you to Toronto."

"I'm glad you've decided to accompany me. It'll be interesting to see how much money's still there in the account I set up to hold Secret Service assets.  I don't expect to find a hell of a lot of money but even a few thousand could help the right people.  You know—people in need. I'm sure he told you he was going to Montreal to check on funds we had in a local bank there to pay for Secret Service operations ran out of Canada. I suspect Mr. Thompson is the only one who has any idea how much money's in that account.  Were you hoping to find a funding source for future operations against the government?" Captain Hines paused, but did not wait for a response. "Even if we have the money, I can't think of anyone willing to start another war over our southern lifestyle or slavery."

"Thanks for setting me straight," Jacob said, but he smiled to cover his disappointment. "I'm booked on a paddle wheeler to Cincinnati tomorrow. If you'd like to join me, I'd love to have the company. From Cincinnati, we can catch a train to Detroit and then on to Toronto. Are you interested or have you made other plans?"

"I am interested, and I've not had time to make other arrangements. If I recall, you said she leaves at nine."

"See you at then. I'm going to my room and see if I can digest all the information I have floating in my head."

At a quarter till nine, Jacob returned to the dock and waited to board his ship. Fifteen minutes before boarding time, a new paddle wheeler named the *Ohio Belle* tooted its horn alerting waiting passengers she would soon be pulling away from the dock. As he approached the boarding plank, Judge Hines joined him and together they walked up the plank and on to the main deck. Once aboard, Jacob and Thomas stood at the ship's bow until they felt the ship's paddles rotate causing the ship to lurch forward. Within minutes, the *Ohio Belle's* paddles were at full speed, leaving a wide wake trailing behind her. Once underway, Jacob returned to his cabin to take a short nap. Judge Hines remained on deck taking in some fresh air. Jacob was glad he had taken the time to walk around Louisville and see how it had changed since the war. He began to wonder. *Is now the time for me to accept a new reality regarding change? Has this walk around downtown Louisville taught me a new reality, one focused on "what is," instead of "what could be or should be."*

Approximately 10 hours after leaving Louisville, the ship's captain announced: "Attention on board. Our voyage will be coming to an end in Cincinnati—known to all as the Queens City. It's a lovely city with many fine accommodations. For those leaving the ship in the Queen City who wish to travel by train, I recommend you contact the concierge at your hotel and ask for the best railway station to get you to your final destination. At this time, Cincinnati does not have a central train station. If you are fortunate enough to get a good hack driver, he may also be able to point out the best station for you to use."

Since Jacob and Judge Hines had traveled this route before, they hired a hack to take them to the Hamilton county train station, just north of Cincinnati. There, they booked two seats on a train to Montreal via Detroit and Toronto. During the Civil War, he remembered Confederate spies and saboteurs telling him that this portion of the journey back into Canada was the most dangerous.  Jacob thought, *Today, I booked a seat on a train to Montreal with no fear whatsoever of being caught, captured, or hung as a Confederate spy.*

Figure 38.  At the train station.

# Chapter Thirty-Seven

*Lucy Rutledge & Lilly Cooper*

IN TORONTO, Jacob boarded a horse drawn streetcar from the train station to the Queens Hotel on Front Street between Bay and York. Four large trees graced the front of the large four-story high building. On the second floor, balconies at each room reached out over the sidewalks running along Front Street. At the height of the Civil War Union operatives in the city suspected the Queens hotel was the center of Confederate spy activity in and around Toronto. From this hotel two successful bank robberies had been planned and executed against a single bank in St. Albans, Vermont, each netting more than two hundred thousand dollars in cash. Jacob was hoping to run into one of the Confederates operatives at the hotel bar or a nearby restaurant.

After checking into the hotel, Jacob and Judge Hines asked a polite, aging bellman to take their bags to their individual rooms. Because they didn't have any small bills, they promised to leave his tip at the front desk. They proceeded in the direction of the hotel bar for a drink. As they were leaving the lobby, they heard someone call from the mezzanine, "Thomas…Thomas Hines—is that Jacob Harris with you?"

Turning, Judge Hines saw a tall, distinguished-looking gentleman whom he thought could be Jacob Thompson. "Why yes, I'm Thomas Hines and the man with me is Jacob Harris. Is that you, Mr. Thompson?"

"It is indeed. Are you headed for the bar?"

"We certainly are. Would you care to join us? Jacob is looking for some information."

"As you well know, I was in the information business for quite some time." Mr. Thompson seemed genuinely pleased to see Judge Hines and Jacob again.

In Mr. Thompson's presence again after all these years, Jacob was flooded with relief. Perhaps, now he might find the answers to the long-standing questions that troubled him for fifteen years. They found a small table near a window facing the front street and, as a tribute to their past, they ordered two Jameson's.  After exchanging pleasantries about their health and the wellbeing of their families, Jacob asked Thomas, "What happened to the members of the Knights of the Golden Circle, the Sons of Liberty, the Copperheads and the Confederate Secret Service?  Is there anyone out there still willing to pursue a new Confederacy further south?"

"The direct answer is 'no,' Jacob.  When Bob Ford killed Jesse, we lost all hope of additional funding.  Rumors have it that he buried a lot of gold and got the owners of the land to swear, into perpetuity, they'd never reveal where it was.  Apparently, neither Frank nor the rest of the James gang were there when the gold was buried."

"Are there any other operatives like yourself living here in Canada?"

"A few years back I saw Thad Culpepper in Montreal. He was help-ing the Canadian police develop codes for telegraph operations be-tween provinces.

Jacob spoke, "But you've stayed in contact with Captain Hines. He told me you both lived in Memphis for a short time."

"Near the end of the war, we did.  Thomas was captured by the Yanks in New York state. Although they couldn't connect him to his operation, they did connect him to the riots in New York City before the election and sentenced him to twenty years in prison."

"Ouch!"

Hines interjected, "It didn't last long. I escaped and that's when I went to Memphis. I studied law and passed the bar there before moving to Bowling Green, Kentucky.

Jacob asked, "Is there anyone else around?"

"Three days ago, I saw Lucy in Montreal. Since her parents are both gone, she was looking at her chandleries to decide which ones to keep and which to sell.  Apparently, the United States government offered to return them to the family if she promised to reopen them. Since the government couldn't prove a direct link between the Rutledge Inn and the Confed-eracy, they decided to return the Inn to her as well. The *John Jameson* was waiting at the port of Montreal to take her back to Charleston to see Lilly.

Stunned at hearing Lucy and Lilly's names mentioned in the same breath, Jacob was suddenly speechless.  The news was almost more than he could bear.  His thoughts were in turmoil.  If I can get to Montreal could I catch Lucy before she sailed for Charleston? Taking a deep breath, he stilled his thoughts and focused again on his conversation with Mr. Thompson.

When they finished dinner, Jacob shook Judge Hines and Mr. Thomp-son's hands and thanked him for the meal. Although deeply disappointed, he also thanked them for informing him that past patriotic organization like the Knights of the Golden Circle, the Copperheads, the Sons of Liberty and the Confederate Secret Service were no longer interested in creating a new Confederacy.

As Jacob left the dining room, Mr. Thompson waved his hand and asked for the check. He paid the waitress the full amount plus a little extra, knowing that at the end of the evening his waitress would accompany him to his room. Jacob headed towards the main desk and paid for his room in advance since he would be leaving early the next day. After Jacob left, Judge Hines asked the front desk clerk if there was a card room in the hotel. The clerk replied, "Sir, there's a card game in progress in Room 127 this very minute."

The following morning, Jacob packed his bags for the trip to Montreal He met Judge Hines in the foyer and a few minutes later Mr. Thomson joined them. They caught a hack for the train station and boarded the 8:17 train heading east for Montreal. Throughout the ride, Jacob was restless, wondering who else might also be staying at St. Lawrence Hall. Would he find former President Jefferson Davis or Thad Culpepper or General Pike's old friend Senator Bell? He remembered all had, at one time or another, taken up residence or visited Canada after the war.

As the train began to slow down, Jacob looked for a marker sign on the main platform. Soon, a small sign saying Montreal came into view. A bit later, the engineer put the wheels into reverse, and the train slowed and came to a screeching halt. As he stepped down from the car, Jacob was astonished to see Lucy standing on the platform waiting for him. Except for a few more laugh lines around her eyes, she looked just as he remembered her. Once on solid ground, he ran to Lucy and put his arms around her, lifted her up, spun her around and sat her back down on the platform. Breathless, Jacob spoke first, "How did you know I was on this train?"

"Haven't you heard of the telegraph?" Lucy grinned and hugged him again. "Mr. Thompson sent a message before he boarded the train telling me you were boarding the morning train to Montreal. Apparently, he assumed you'd want to see me before I sailed for Charleston." She clutched his arm and guided him through the station. "There's a quaint café near the chandlery. I know the owners and can check in on the chandlery on the way. I have a carriage waiting for us at the curb."

Once inside the carriage, Lucy looked Jacob over thoroughly and said, "You look wonderful, Jacob. How are things going with you?"

"You haven't changed at all, Lucy. You're as beautiful as I remember. As for me, not well. There are too many times I miss the way things were before the war."

"Jacob, you've to get over it. Our family lost a great deal—but time changes things. A year ago, the government gave us back our properties, and the Inn is already up and running."

Jacob was almost afraid to ask, but he couldn't help himself. He whispered, "What about Lilly?"

Lucy saw the pain in his eyes. She reached over and patted his hand. "She's fine. The government told her she could have the old Cooper Estate back if she wanted it. The government certainly doesn't want it. As you remember, it's kind of off the beaten path. A new lane will have to be built, and the house needs substantial work. The soundest structure on the estate is the guesthouse. I'm sure she'll be glad to see you."

"Lucy, what if she gives up on the place and goes back to France?"

"Ray passed just a few months ago. Elizabeth lives with her younger sister in Cannes. I don't think she has any obligations to keep her in France now, and she's still well off."

"Are there still any Confederate ties to Montreal?"

"Several Confederate leaders fled to Montreal near the end of the war, but most returned home after hearing Lincoln's terms for surrender. Most who stayed married Canadians and established families here or in Toronto. To the best of my knowledge, there's no one here remotely interested in creating a new Confederacy. It's just been too long." Lucy sighed with regret.

"What about you?" he asked. The look in his eyes was unmistakable. She could see that he was lost in the past.

"I'm going back to Charleston and run the Inn." She stated abruptly. "I've decided to keep all my family's real estate holdings and hire managers to operate them. I don't know much about Lilly's immediate plans. Until the house on the Cooper Estate is refurbished, she can live with me or in the guesthouse at her Estate. I suppose it's possible for her to return to France, but I think it's unlikely."

After stopping by the chandlery to tell Lucy's manager she was leaving for Charleston later in the day, Lucy and Jacob walked to the café. Once inside, Lucy ordered tea. Jacob asked for something a little stronger, but the strongest drink they had was cider.

Seeing the troubled expression on Jacob's face, Lucy touched his arm tenderly and said, "You're still very much in love with her, aren't you?"

Jacob rubbed one hand across his face slowly before responding. "Lucy, do you think a man can love two women at the same time?"

Lucy chuckled softly, "I do, but he'd better not get caught by either one of them."

"I'm in a mess. What do you think I should do?"

"Are you saying this Confederacy thing is out of your head?"

"I guess so. Suddenly I don't give a damn about the Confederacy, but I do give a damn about Lilly. I want to see her."

"If you are cured of your obsession with our former lifestyle, I suggest we go to the Port of Montreal, board the *John Jameson* and set sail for Charleston."

After an hour of catching up on old times, Jacob and Lucy left the café, leaving half-full cups on the table. They walked down to the chandlery where she asked her new manager to take Jacob and herself to the Port of Montreal. At the port, Jacob viewed, for the first time in years, the majestic three-mast clipper *John Jameson*. Turning to Lucy, Jacob asked, "Do you have any idea when she will be ready to sail?"

"She'll be able to hoist her sails in less than four hours. After getting Mr. Thompson's telegraph message, I sent a runner to the port to tell the *John Jameson*'s skipper, Captain Davis to be ready to sail by late afternoon."

"You mean Captain Joe Davis?"

"No! I mean Captain John Davis, Joe's son."

Jacob was astonished. "I didn't know Captain Davis had a son."

"He didn't either until one of those girls he keeps in every port announced he had an eight-year old son in Savanna. Joe sails with him just in case there is trouble on board. I heard Ray gave Joe and his son the ship provided Lilly gets first priority. Let's get on board and ask when he thinks we'll be in Charleston. I assume you have your bags with you."

"Lucy, I always pack light. When you're in combat, the last thing you need is anything heavy to slow you down."

As Jacob and Lucy stepped off the gangplank onto the deck, Joe Davis greeted them with a warm smile. With pride, he introduced his son as Sea Captain John Davis.

As a strong breeze nearly blew off his cap, Jacob said to Captain John Davis, "Young man, when do you think she'll be ready to sail?"

"Not long, perhaps an hour or two at the most. I still have to check my jibs to make sure they're not twisted and see to it there are no broken cross arms. I checked my sextant yesterday, and it seems to be working fine."

Joe Davis interjected, "During the war a working sextant was critical. You couldn't move in close to land to check your bearings using lighthouses, coves, etc., as reference points. John's better at navigating by land references than I am—but I can sure as hell run circles around him on a sextant."

John laughed and retorted, "Who are you kidding?  You can barely stand up.  Why don't you, Lucy, and Jacob go below so I have some room to work.  I don't want to have to navigate the river in the dark."

### *Charleston Seven Days Later – Aboard the John Jameson*

After a rough night at sea, Jacob said to Captain John Davis, "Young man, you did a marvelous job of getting us through last night's storm. For a moment, I thought it was your dad at the helm. Those winds must have been close to hurricane strength."

"I appreciate your confidence, Jacob, but the storm did put us a few hours behind."

Lucy reassured him, "Skipper, your schedule is my schedule."

At two p.m., Captain Davis dropped the main sail and used the jibs to steer the *John Jameson* through the west channel to Southern Wharf. When the ship gently floated side first into the wharf, Captain Davis asked his Boatswain to throw a line to a bollard where it was easily tied off by a dockhand. After the ship stopped, the Boatswain, with the assistance of two crewmembers, lowered the gangplank and rested it against a lengthy block of wood.

Within minutes, Lucy and Jacob walked down the gangplank followed by two members of the crew carrying their bags.  As they walked down the wharf, Captain Davis waved at the pair and called out, "Lucy, we'll keep her right here till we get further instructions."

"Thanks, Captain, I'll let you know sometime next week."

Looking at Lucy anxiously, Jacob asked, "What now?"

"You can either come with me and hope Lilly has stopped by the Inn, or you can hire a carriage to take you to the Cooper Estate.  If Lilly is there, she might be staying in the guest cottage till the main house is refurbished. If you go to the Cooper Estate and Lilly stops by the Inn, I'll tell her where you are."

Pulling a handkerchief from his pocket to wipe sweat from his face, Jacob asked, "How do you think she'll react when she sees me?"

Surprised by his question, Lucy answered, "I honestly don't know.  I do know she will not be expecting you."

"When you went to France, did she say anything about me?"

"She was really hurting—for a lot of reasons.  She and her family were leaving a place and a lifestyle they really loved.  She was also leaving a man she loved and knew she couldn't have. Your guess is as good as mine."

Hearing Lucy's comment, Jacob wondered if his decision to come to Charleston had been a good one. *Will seeing me again hurt her even more?*

"Lucy, I think I'll grab a hack and ask the driver to take me to the Cooper Estate. I promise, with or without her, I'll stop by to see you again."

"Jacob, can I ask you a question?"

"Of course. It wouldn't be about Lorenzo, would it?"

Lucy's whole demeanor softened. "How is he?"

"Lucy, he's fine. He still has two children at home—both girls."

"Jacob, don't say too much, but please tell him I still think of him—often."

"I'll tell him you still love him." Jacob gazed at her for a moment. "Isn't that what you meant to say?"

Longingly she admitted, "It is."

Figure 39. Lucy Rutledge.

Figure 40. *John Jameson* at the Dock.

# Chapter Thirty-Eight

## *Lilly and Jake*

JACOB asked the driver to hurry up so he could get to the Cooper Estate before dark. As he turned down the lane where he took out Union spy James Reynolds, Jacob looked for any indication that the house was occupied. Eventually, he saw a dim light coming through a side kitchen window. A minute later, faint shadows moved across the window. Even though daylight was fading, Jacob could see the house had sustained substantial superficial damage. As he got closer, Jacob was so nervous he began to shake in anticipation of what he would find.

Inside the kitchen, Miss Abigail whispered to Lilly, "Miss Lilly, don't be afraid, but I think I hear something outside. Did you hear it? It sounds like a carriage or a hack. Are you expecting any visitors? Should I get a gun?"

"Miss Abigale, the war ended fifteen years ago. Just look outside and tell me what you see."

"Oh, my! A man just stepped out of a hack and he's walking toward the front door. He's well dressed and carrying a bag and a small valise."

"Miss Abigale, I need to run outside and bring in the biscuits from the oven. You go ahead and answer the door."

Miss Abigale tiptoed to the entrance and waited expectantly for the knock. When it came, she opened the door slowly, and peered out from behind the door to greet the late visitor. Miss Abigale almost fainted when she saw who it was. "Oh, God! Mr. Jacob, I never thought I'd ever see you again."

Jacob laughed, "I never thought I'd ever return to Charleston either, Miss Abigale." Holding a finger to his lips to signal her not to mention his presence, Jacob asked, "Is Lilly here?"

"Yes, Mr. Jacob. Do you want me to fetch her?"

"I do, but first, let me step into the library so I can surprise her."

When he was in the library, Miss Abigale stepped outside and called, "Miss Lilly, there's a man here who says he needs to talk to you right away."

"Tell him I'll be right there.  Ask him to sit down. A moment later Lilly came back into the living room.  When she did not see a man there, she asked, "Miss Abigale, where is the man you saw outside?"

"He's right behind you, Ma'am."

She turned around, and there was Jacob standing two feet in front of her.  She began to quiver and nearly fainted. Tears sprang to her eyes and rolled down her face.  She was visibly shaken.  Jacob, himself overcome with emotion, asked cavalierly, "Are those tears of sorrow or tears of joy, my Dear?"

"Damn you, Jacob!" she cried.  "You know they're tears of joy.  Come here at once and hold me for as long as you can.  We have so much to talk about. Can you stay?"

"You know I'll stay.  Of course, I will."

Looking into Jacob's eyes, she said, "It's been too long for us.  I need you—I need you now."  Looking down for a moment, Jacob saw the wedding ring on the third finger of Lilly's left hand.  "You say you want to talk?"

"Honey, we can talk later—we can talk about everything.  But first, we need to show each other how much we still love one another."

After hours of holding each other, kissing and making love, Jacob and Lilly decided to break for a late evening meal. After dinner, they heard a horse ride up the lane and stop at the tie-up rail in front of the house. He glanced at Lilly, "It's kind of late.  Are you expecting anyone at this hour?"

"It could be my son.  He went into Charleston earlier today. He didn't know if he would stay at the Inn tonight or come home after picking up some carpentry supplies for the house restoration."

Jacob thought to himself, *Why didn't Lucy mention Lilly had a son? Had she forgotten—or had she forgotten on purpose?*

After seeing the wedding ring on Lilly's hand, Jacob was not surprised by Lilly's words.  Hoping to reassure her, Jacob said, "I'm glad you found someone and have a child.  It's important to have someone to take care of you and keep you company as you grow older."

"Jacob, I saw you looking at my wedding ring earlier. I think I'd better explain before my son comes through the door. I was never married. I wear the ring so my son won't think his father and I weren't married. I didn't want him to think he was a bastard. I'm going to have to take the lead when he comes in, and you have to follow and make everything fit. I know you don't wear a wedding ring, but for now take my daddy's ring out of the right drawer of his desk and put it on.  By the way, his name is Jacob Harris, but I call him Jake so I won't get the names mixed up in my mind."

Jacob, overcome with emotion, was unable to speak. "Jacob, haven't you figured it out yet? When I left Charleston for Marseille, I was pregnant with Jake.  He's your son."

Hearing Jake coming up the steps, she said, "I'd better get the door so he doesn't have to put down his bags to come in. Please sit down, and I'll take care of the rest."

As Jake walked through the opened door, he said, "Mom, thanks for getting the door.  Is someone here?  I saw a fresh carriage tracks on the roadway."

"Son, yes, someone is here.  Someone I thought I would never see again.  His name is Jacob, just like yours. He's your father. All this time, I believed he was lost at sea during the war. A Turkish frigate returning to Constantinople picked him up in the Mediterranean and, by the time he got back to Charleston, I'd already left for Marseille."

The young man whom Jacob had just learned was his son had Lilly's brunette hair and her dark brown eyes and easy manner.  Jake shook his head, not quite comprehending what his mother had told him.  He looked at Jacob and then back at his mother, "Mom, are you telling me Jacob is my dad, my real dad."  As the realization of what this could mean dawned on him, he said, "I never had a dad before. I want to tell him all the things I've done over the years and to have him around all the time."  He paused again, before asking, "Can I give him a hug?"

Delighted with his response, Lilly said, "Of course!  I'm sure he'd love a hug from you."

Jacob extended his arms, "Come here, son.  Even though I've only known about you for a few minutes, I'm already so very proud of you."

## *Ceres - May 3, 1882*

Every time Lorenzo picked up the mail at the post office he looked first for anything from Jacob addressed to him or to Annie.  When he returned home once again with nothing from Jacob, she said to Lorenzo, "I haven't heard a thing from Jacob since he left for St. Louis." Clearly more upset than ever, Annie said "I know it's hard to get away from the farm this time of year, with all the planting and such, but it's been more than two months. We need to find Jacob. I've saved some money.  I want to hire a couple of field hands for a month or two while you search for him. I seriously doubt the James Gang is still around now that Jesse is dead. I haven't read anything about any of those organizations he met with in Montreal either."

"Annie, you know I will do anything for you." Lorenzo was not surprised by the request—he had been expecting it for weeks. "I'll pack a few things and leave for Montreal in the morning. Don't worry about the farm hands. I've got two teenage daughters who can pick up the slack. What do you want me to do if I find him?"

Annie answered flatly, 'I want you to bring him back."

The next morning, Lorenzo filled a small bag with paper money and silver, a few sandwiches, some beef jerky and three changes of clothes. He rolled a horse blanket and tied it to the back of his saddle. After saddling his horse, he mounted it and let his boots settle into the stirrups. Nancy, the older of his teenage daughters, reached up so Lorenzo could pull her into the saddle in front of him. He eased his horse to the right and began the trip to the Wytheville train station fifteen miles east if you travel by road. There, they dismounted and Lorenzo went inside to buy a ticket to Richmond. Once he received his ticket, he told Nancy to take the horse home. Nancy hugged her father, scooted herself back into the middle of the saddle and left for Ceres.

Lorenzo, contemplating what exactly he was going to do, reasoned that a stop in Montreal would most likely be a waste of time. Most of the Confederates who had left for Montreal after the end of the war were senior government or military Officials. Lorenzo had been careful over the years to watch for any reference in local or Richmond newspapers indicating the Knights of the Golden Circle, the Sons of Liberty, the Copperheads or any other organization sympathetic to the southern cause were carrying out operations directed at the United States in any region of the country. Near the end of the war, General Beauregard told him and Jacob that William Norris, head of the Secret Service and the Confederate Signal Service, had burned every document in his files before Richmond was overrun.

It had been years since Lorenzo had seen anything in print about any of these organizations. Lorenzo attributed this lack of action to the reality that most senior Confederate officials were now too old to oversee the overthrow of even portions of the Federal Government. He also surmised that the assassination of Jesse James likely resulted in the drying up of funds needed to start up a new war effort.

***

As the train entered Richmond, Lorenzo felt at ease, quite unlike the nervousness he had felt riding through Richmond during the Wilderness

Campaign. He transferred to a train on the Richmond-Danville Railroad heading south in the general direction of Charleston. Two hours short of Charleston the train passed near Lake Marion and made its last refill stop in the town of Santee. The train waited for an hour while wood was brought to the train and stacked in the car behind the engine. At the same time, a large funnel tube was lowered from a water tank to top off the train's boiler with sorely needed water. Lorenzo stepped back into the passenger car, took a seat and waited for the engine to start making steam. As smoke began to rise from the stack, the train wheels began to spin, pushing the train forward. Thirty minutes later, just before reaching the town of St. George, the train slowed to make a steep turn. Lorenzo jumped off and walked to a familiar switchyard, one now void of any soldiers, on the Charleston to Memphis Railroad where he jumped the next train headed toward Charleston.

***

When Lorenzo entered Charleston, he was extremely pleased to see a city void of rubble and with new construction springing up across the landscape. At Charleston's train station, he hired a hack to take him to the port so he could see what, if any, ships were docked there. As he passed by the wharves, he half- expected to see the *John Jameson* docked in its usual spot at *Boyce's Wharf*, but it was not there.

As the hack continued, Lorenzo looked farther south and was surprised to see the *John Jameson* docked alongside Southern Wharf. Its presence suggested to him that Captain Davis, or someone else who might remember him, could be in Charleston. Thinking he might find someone he knew, he asked the driver to take him to 116 Broad Street where he hoped to find a newly renovated *Rutledge House Inn* open for business.

As the hack turned onto Broad Street, Lorenzo saw the new *Rutledge House Inn* ahead on the right side of the road. Being so close to St. Michael's church, the preferred aiming point for Union Parrott Guns on Morris Island, the Inn was nearly seventy percent destroyed by endless shelling from the sea and islands surrounding Charleston harbor. He instructed the driver to let him off in front of the Inn and wait for him until he returned.

Outside the large oak doors stood a doorman who provided hotel guests with any assistance they might require. Lorenzo stopped at the door and spoke to the doorman, asking if the Inn was still owned by the Rutledge family. The doorman answered, "Yes, Sir. But there's only one member of the family still here."

Figure 41. St. Michael's.

Lorenzo's heart skipped a beat, then he calmly asked, "Who might that might be?"

"Lucy—Lucy Rutledge," the doorman said and smiled, apparently holding Lucy in high regard. "Her parents are both deceased now. A little over a year ago the government returned the *Rutledge House Inn* to her on the condition she reopen it and agree to pay taxes at a reduced rate for the next ten years.  They also returned the family's chandleries with the same conditions. Since she returned to Charleston about a year ago, she spends most of her time at the Inn. She told me that the chandleries, other than the ones here in Charleston and Savanna were still in good shape. Some never closed even during the war."

"Sir, might I ask where she is today?" Lorenzo asked eagerly.

"You don't have to call me Sir. My name is Charles. I saw her a few minutes ago in the wine room. Do you know her or the family well?"

"Charles, I certainly do. If it's okay, I'd like to step inside and make my presence known."

As Lorenzo stepped forward, Charles opened the door for him, tipped his hat and said, "Welcome to the *Rutledge House Inn*."

When Lorenzo entered the hotel lobby, he was surprised to see the hotel had somehow managed to retain much of its southern charm. The outside dining area was still in the same place and looked much the same as it did the last time Lorenzo saw it. Just inside the front door hung a beautiful portrait of Lucy with a metal label saying Proprietor underneath. She was smiling down at him from the portrait, nearly stopping his heart.

Lorenzo was pleased that Lucy had managed to keep much of the character of the old Inn. Although the furniture, lights and other accessories were new, they were exact replicas of what they replaced. The outside covered eating area was still in its same place as was the sometime inconvenient wine room. Looking through the partially opened door toward the wine room, Lorenzo spied Lucy diligently counting each bottle of every kind of wine. The hallway was dim and would provide him with an excellent opportunity to open the door quietly and slip down the steps to surprise her.

Lorenzo moved silently down the eight steps to the wine room's entrance and opened the door, hoping Lucy did not hear the small squeak it made. He gently slipped his arms around her waist and squeezed her, just as he had done so many times before. Feeling his familiar arms around her waist and his gentle touch, Lucy's body tensed, and she began to tremble. Words formed, but she was unable to speak, and tears formed in the corners of her eyes. She was hesitant but finally turned around. She stretched her arms around Lorenzo's neck and held him tightly. She kissed him passionately, melting into his arms. When Lorenzo looked down at Lucy, he saw the tears streaming down her face, tears she made no effort to wipe away. "Lorenzo, have you any idea how much I've missed you? Tell me you'll stay the night?"

"I promise. I'll stay longer than one night, if you'll have me."

"Do you even have to ask? Stay here with me and make love to me."

"You know I will."

Not wanting to let him go, even for a moment, but curious, she asked, "What brings you to Charleston?"

"I'm trying to find Jacob. He left home about two months ago, saying he had to learn for himself whether or not there's a chance to form another Confederacy."

"I know that. I saw him. He came with me from Montreal to see Lilly."

Lorenzo was not surprised. "Lucy, did he see her?"

Lucy pulled back from Lorenzo so she could see his reaction. "He did, and he also saw his son."

Lorenzo was astonished. "Lucy, what son?"

"When Lilly left Charleston, she was pregnant." Lucy watched the expressions washing over his face as she continued, "Her boy was born in Marseille. That's why she couldn't write or do anything. She knew she was in love with a man she couldn't have. Her son Jake is very mature for his age. He spends most of his time at the Cooper Estate overseeing its restoration. I've offered him a room here at the Inn any time he needs a break. He's doing some of the restoration work himself."

Lorenzo dropped his arms to his side and turned away, suddenly nervous when what Lucy said sank in—Lilly had a son. When he did the math, he could not help but wonder: *Could I be the father? Whose name is on the birth certificate as the father? More importantly, why didn't she tell Jacob and me about this before now?*

"Lucy, where are they—isn't Jacob helping with the restoration?"

Lucy couldn't look at Lorenzo when she told him, "They died three weeks ago—it was the fever." She spoke a little too quickly, "I was in Montreal at the time and didn't find out till I returned to Charleston. Her son told me."

Still undone by learning about Lilly's child, the news about Jacob and Lilly was more than he could handle. Overcome with despair, he dropped into a nearby chair and buried his face in his hands.

# Chapter Thirty-Nine

## *Heartbreak for Lorenzo*

LUCY'S heart was breaking when she saw how the news of Jacob and Lilly's deaths affected Lorenzo. She went to him, knelt in front of him, and said, "They're buried side-by-side at the Cooper Estate. Their son is going to stay here in Charleston. I'll take you to meet him, and you can see the graves for yourself." She shook her head sadly. "Every time I think about it—I just can't believe it. It's so sad."

When Lorenzo looked up, struggling for composure, tears glistened in his eyes. He tried to say something, but could find no words to express his anguish. Lucy pulled him to his feet. "Lorenzo, I'm done with the inventory. Let's go to our old room. It looks the same as when we were together. I still remember the times you and I spent there. We had so much fun."

Lorenzo followed Lucy blindly to her room. Doing her best to distract him, Lucy began unbuttoning her dress, exposing an expanse of her swelling breast. Lorenzo's eyes followed the slow provocative movement of her fingers as she revealed more of her firm well-maintained body. To him her body looked much the same as it had fifteen years earlier. Stifling the grief that threatened to overcome him, Lorenzo let desire burn instead.

Lucy stepped behind a folding screen and asked Lorenzo to pick out a negligee for her from her wardrobe. After rummaging through the negligees in Lucy's wardrobe, Lorenzo selected his favorite, a black one. When he handed it to her, she said, "Honey, I just knew you'd select the black one."

Lucy removed the rest of her clothes, handed them to Lorenzo and asked him to put them on the chair in the corner. When she handed Lorenzo her clothes, he peeked over the screen to look at her full, fair-skinned breasts. Smiling, she scolded him coquettishly, "Not now, honey, you have to wait till we're in bed."

Lucy stepped out from behind the screen in the black negligee, extended her arms to him and said, "I'm more than ready, please take me to bed." By now thoroughly aroused and distracted, Lorenzo did exactly that.

After what seemed like hours of sensuous lovemaking, Lorenzo and Lucy were both exhausted. They held each other close for another hour as they talked and laughed about the many joys they had shared over the years.

Lorenzo picked up his shaving mug, dipped his wet brush inside and filled the brush with a frothy liquid. Once lathered up, he asked Lucy if she were hungry. Her response was immediate, "I'm famished!"

"Is there somewhere around here where we can get a decent meal?"

"Lorenzo, how can you even ask that? The Inn is known as one of Charleston's finest seafood restaurants. I think I can use my influence and have supper brought to our room. After we eat we can talk about why you're here and what you're going to say when you go back to Burke's Garden."

Lorenzo stopped midway through a swipe down his cheek with his straight razor, "What makes you think someday I'll have to return to Burke's Garden?"

"Jacob told me you still have two daughters at home, and I know you to be a good man. You'd never leave your daughters."

When Lorenzo finished shaving, he turned to Lucy and said, "Tomorrow, I'd like to go to the Cooper Estate and meet Jake and see Jacob's and Lilly's grave. After visiting the estate, I'd like for us return to Charleston to discuss what happened while you and Lilly were in France. Since I'm not on a schedule, how long can I stay with you?"

"Honey, you can stay however long you want. I'll be grateful for every day we have together.

"Would two weeks be too long?"

"Oh, no, not at all—it would be wonderful. Thank you."

After a quiet, intimate dinner in Lucy's room, they returned to their lovemaking. Lorenzo was amazed at how smooth Lucy's skin was everywhere. How could I have forgotten this? He loved running his hands up and down her body, feeling its firmness. Lost in each other's kisses as they held one another close, the night was blissful, and they were happy once again.

***

In the morning, they took Lucy's carriage to the Cooper Estate. Miss Abigale answered the door, appearing visibly shaken. She said, 'Mr. Lorenzo, I'm so surprised to see you again. Did you come to talk to Lilly's son?"

"Miss Abigale, I did.  How are you?  I always hoped that you would survive the war."

She smiled at his thoughtfulness. "I feel pretty good. Miss Lilly told me before she left for Marseille that some of the slaves who were here then could stay with me in the house as long as we wanted.  She left us a little nest egg, and her attorney sees to it we get money every month." She pointed toward the back of the house and said, "Jake is out back watching the carpenters repair the old porch.  I'll go get him for you."

"Miss Abigale, I'd rather just go out back alone and introduce my-self.  It's not like I don't know my way around the place."

Miss Abigale nodded, wringing her hands nervously.

As soon as Lorenzo stepped outside, he was greeted with, "Sir, may I be of some assistance?"

Lorenzo was intrigued.  He looked intently at the young man for any indication that he could be his son.  He could see a slight resemblance to Jacob—or himself!  It was obvious, though, with his dark hair and intense dark eyes that he was Lilly's son.  "Perhaps," Lorenzo answered slowly. "Are you Jake Harris?"

Conscious that Lorenzo was looking him over, Jake's curiosity was piqued as well, and he looked Lorenzo over right back, "I am.  Might I ask your name?"

Lorenzo smiled, recalling how much that attitude was like his and Jacob's in their youth.  "My name is Lorenzo.  I knew your mother and Jacob quite well."

"Really?  In what way?"

"Well, Jacob was my brother, and Lilly was a close friend."

Jake's face lit up, "Did you say your name was Lorenzo?  My middle initial is L, and mom wouldn't tell me why."

"Yes, my name is Lorenzo.  I'm sure you realize that a lot of people name their children after an aunt or uncle.  In fact, I named one of my sons after Jacob."

Jake nodded his understanding.  "Are you staying in Charleston for a while?  I have a lot of questions to ask about my dad."

"Lucy asked me the same questions not long ago. I plan on staying about two weeks."

"Would you like to see where mom and dad are buried?" Jake asked solemnly.

"I would. They loved each other so very much."

By this time, Lucy had joined them. "Follow me," Jake said. "It's down this path and into the garden.  Mom said the bench up ahead was her favorite place, especially when dad was in town." As they moved farther from the house, Lorenzo saw the bench facing the center of the garden.

"Mom told me she and Jacob used to come here and sit by the hour. I can see why. It's really peaceful here. Over there you'll see their markers under the big oak tree. It all happened so fast. They had each other and, for them, that was enough. Even though mom and I had been in Charleston only a few months, several friends stopped by to visit her and my dad. Captain Davis came and brought his Boatswain's Mate with him. Some of mom's school friends have been here, as well as some of the militia who still live here."

Lorenzo walked up to Jacob and Lilly's markers, lowered his head, prayed a moment and began to weep. With tears glistening in her eyes, Lucy stepped up beside Lorenzo and squeezed his hand. After looking at the markers one more time, Jacob and Lucy joined Jake and returned to the house—each lost in their own thoughts.

Once everyone's tears had been wiped away, Lorenzo cleared his throat, and to change the subject, asked Jake, "Do you have any idea what happened to General Beauregard?"

Relieved to talk about a less emotional topic, Jake replied, "Mom asked some of her friends the same question when we first got here. Someone in the militia told her that after he left North Carolina, General Beauregard ended up in Virginia trying to stop Sherman from reaching Savanna. He was asked to leave because of his frailty and ill health. General Johnson gave General Beauregard, who was his second in command, the distasteful job of surrendering his Confederate troops to Sherman at the end of the war. Many Charlestonians felt Johnson should have been man enough to do it himself."

"Jake, what was Charleston like when city officials handed the city over to the Yankees?"

"Some of mom's friends kept copies of the papers printed around that time and showed them to her. They said General Beauregard's predictions were absolutely correct. City officials handed over lots of rubble, fires and refugees. When the troops entered the city, nothing was left worth fighting for on either side. Some of mom's friends who stayed in Charleston after the war told me Union officers didn't even set up a perimeter. They were too busy finding food for the starving Charlestonians and rebuilding structures to make them habitable. Apparently, it was all very sad. One thing I can tell you, when the Yankees took down the Confederate flag, men and women alike wept in the streets."

Jake wanted to know more about his father, what he was like as a child, anything to fill in the gaps for him. Lorenzo did his best to answer his questions without revealing anything about his other life back in Burke's Garden.

Over the next two weeks, Lorenzo and Lucy were inseparable. They talked about everything. Every day they found moments of passion. One night after the oil lamp had been turned off, Lorenzo asked Lucy why she had never married. He was shocked by her answer. "Lorenzo, for some people there can only be one love. You were mine. Since I never felt I'd find another man better than you, I never tried. You're my love for now and forever. I'll never forget you nor stop loving you. You'll always be welcome here at the Inn—and in my bed. I love you so very much."

A couple of days before leaving for home, Lorenzo asked Lucy if she would mind taking another trip to the Cooper Estate to visit the graves of Lilly and his brother. Lucy understood, and the next day they went to meet Jake at the Cooper Estate. Miss Abigale again answered the door and hugged Lucy and Lorenzo when they came in. Then she called for Jake to come to the front door. When he arrived, the three of them stepped out on the front porch to say goodbye.

Afterwards, Lucy and Lorenzo strode down the front steps and around the house to the path they had taken to Jake and Lilly's graves a few days earlier. At the site, Lorenzo looked down at the two crosses and thought to himself they were both far too young to die. He said the Lord's Prayer and, at the end, followed it with a prayer for Lucy, Annie, Jake and the rest of Jacob's family. As they were leaving, Lorenzo turned to look back one last time at the estate. He was surprised to see Miss Abigale retreating toward the little cottage behind the house with two trays in her hand.

Lucy and Lorenzo stepped into the carriage for the slow ride back into Charleston. After a light supper, they took an open carriage ride up and down the colorful streets of the city. Lorenzo wanted to remember it all. When the ride was over, his thoughts returned to Lucy and the wonderful night they were about to experience.

Their love was as it had never been before. By midnight, their bodies were hot and sweaty, but that didn't matter. They touched and caressed one another till they could wait no more. By morning their limbs were entangled together, and the bedcovers were a tangled mess. Both knew this would be their last night together but neither could acknowledge it.

Lorenzo awoke at 7:00 a.m., as he did every morning. Next to him Lucy's naked body lay across the bed, her legs dangling over the edge. With one hand he stroked the full length of her body, stopping only occasionally here and there for an affectionate caress. Slowly, she became aware of Lorenzo's gentle touch.  Practically purring, she smiled and reached her arms around Lorenzo and pulled him back close to her. For more than an hour they playfully kissed and made love again, then slipped off to sleep exhausted once more.  At 10:45 a.m. when they both awoke thoroughly satiated, they got up and dressed.

"I'll go to the dining room and ask that lunch be served by 11:00 a.m., Lucy said.  "You have a train to catch, and we'll never make if we don't get out of the dining room by noon."

Neither of them could find the words to say goodbye.  They did not even try. As they left the Inn at 1:30 p.m. Lorenzo asked Lucy to drive by the port one last time. With Lilly's death, Lorenzo expected the *John Jameson* would have sailed on to its next destination.  Instead, it was still docked at Southern Wharf, with its masts empty. All sails had been brought down, folded and put away in their storage boxes. There was no activity visible on the main deck.  She looked as though she would not be sailing for another two to three weeks.

Ten minutes later Lucy and Lorenzo arrived at the train station. Before boarding the train to Richmond, Lorenzo kissed Lucy passionately and whispered in her ear, "I love you."  He placed his bags near the entry door and stepped into the passenger car.  Lucy struggled to hold back tears, but the intensity of the moment was too much. She waved at him as he walked down the center aisle to his seat.  Still crying, she turned abruptly and marched toward her carriage with her head held high. It was time for her to go.

Once on board, Lorenzo settled in and thought about all that had transpired.  Then he thought about what he had seen at the Cooper Estate. Something did not seem quite right.  He felt uneasy as he recollected Miss Abigale's trip to the cottage in back as he and Lucy were leaving. She seemed to be carrying something from the kitchen to the cottage He remembered that Miss Abigale always took her meals in the little room adjacent to the kitchen. She once told him she did not like walking out to the cottage because of the uneven surfaces on the walkway. Because of her advancing age, she was afraid she might fall.

A little later, Lorenzo thought about Lucy's statement that Lilly and Jacob had died only a few weeks earlier.  Unsettled by where his thoughts were taking him, he recalled Lucy had seemed relatively unemotional and her answers almost seemed rehearsed. He would have expected Lucy to cry her eyes out in telling him about their tragic deaths.  Then, she was so quick to distract him by taking him to bed. He recalled, too, that Jake was not very emotional or as moved by the loss of his mother and father as might be expected under those circumstances.

Lorenzo thoughts tumbled in a frenzy: *Was this all a setup? Did they want me to believe Jacob and Lilly had died in Charleston? Could they still be alive and living, at least temporarily, in the guest cottage behind the house? Was Lucy's comment about having a room reserved for Jake any time he needed a break some kind of clue to me that my brother and Lilly are still alive? A break from what?*

Lorenzo tried to make sense of all the pieces that swirled in his mind: Is the *John Jameson* waiting to sail until Lilly, Jacob and Jake finish remodeling the Cooper Estate? *My God! What am I to tell Annie? What if she wants to go to Charleston to see his grave? What if she discovers his son? Will I have to lie once again when I return to Burke's Garden?*

After changing trains three times, Lorenzo found himself quickly approaching the train station at Wytheville. A few hundred yards from where the train would stop Lorenzo heard the train's engine start to slow down. Lorenzo felt a mild jerk as the train's wheels started spinning counter-clockwise before coming to a screeching stop. Lorenzo was off the train running up the platform before the conductor had a chance to step down from the passenger car.

From the middle of the platform, Lorenzo could see his daughter Nancy standing between the train station's back door and the boarding platform holding the reins of two horses that would take them back to the Harris homestead. She rushed to him, gave him a big hug and handed him the reins for his own horse.

His mind still in turmoil, he did his best to appear calm as he asked about the rest of the family. Before heading to Burke's Garden, Lorenzo stopped by the general store to purchase a few things for the house, including lollipops for her and her sister. Handing the bag of lollypops to Nancy, Lorenzo asked, "How did you know I would be arriving today?"

"We received a telegraph message from some lady in Charleston saying you'd left and should be home in just a few days. I was also here yesterday, but you weren't on the train. I decided to come over every day till you arrived."

"That was very nice of her. Miss Rutledge owns the Inn where I stayed in Charleston."

After a tedious ride over Burke's Garden Mountain, Lorenzo and Nancy followed the worn path to the Harris homestead. Before Lorenzo could reach the house, Millie rushed out to greet them and all but pulled Lorenzo from the saddle.  Lorenzo embraced her fiercely and Millie clung to him, smothering him with kisses. Annie stepped out on the porch, watched a moment, then said, "Stop it!  Am I going to have to throw a bucket of water on you two?"

Seeing Annie standing near the front porch, Lorenzo knew he had to explain to Annie why Jacob was not with him.  She stepped in front of Lorenzo and asked softly, "Where is he?"

Lorenzo took a deep breath and let it out.  The last four days on the train he had been rehearsing what he would tell her.  "Let's go inside, and I'll explain everything."  When they were seated next to each other, Lorenzo took her hands in his.  "Annie, I looked everywhere.  I know that in Montreal he was told all those organizations, the Knights of the Golden Circle, the Copperheads, the Sons of Liberty and the Secret Service, all had given up on reestablishing a new Confederacy. Most of their leaders are dead or just too old to fight. Those that stayed married Canadian women and chose to stay in Canada."

Annie could not look at Lorenzo when she asked, "What about the girl in Charleston?"

Without actually acknowledging the girl, he said, "I did go to Charleston and, I can truthfully say, I never saw him." Lorenzo was careful to look at Annie when he told her that.   "In Montreal, I met Mrs. Rutledge, the owner of the chandlery there, and in Charleston and other cities on the coast. She told me nearly every businessman we knew in Charleston was either dead, had moved inland or relocated to Canada or Europe. She remembered Jacob and me from years ago when dad, Jacob and I shopped for canvas and sailcloth at her chandlery. I looked around some at the hotels in Charleston where we ate and slept. At the end of the war most were in rubble and had to be rebuilt. Looking at Charleston today, you'd never know how bad it'd been shelled. I checked the docks used by the paddle wheelers that travel up and down the Ashley River inland to Summerville and the ships docked at some of the plantations along the way. I didn't see him there either."

Annie was devastated. "Lorenzo, did you have any luck at all?"

Lorenzo took another deep breath, squeezed her hands and said, "I did, but the news is not good."

Annie held tightly to Lorenzo's hands.  She could barely speak. "Is he gone?"

"Annie, he died." Lorenzo paused for a moment, watching the shock and devastation wash over her. "It was probably a heart attack. Mrs. Rutledge explained what happened. He got sick on his way back to Burke's Garden. She said Jacob met a fellow Freemason aboard the train and asked the man to look after him on the way home. Somewhere in the Blue Ridge Mountains his condition worsened, and he just passed away, Annie."

She looked expectantly at Lorenzo, waiting for the rest of the story. "After a great deal of prodding by the train's conductor, several Freemasons aboard the train took his body and placed it in a carriage. The man looking after him took him to the nearest Masonic Lodge. The Masons there promised to hold a proper service and bury him in their Masonic cemetery."

Annie pulled her hands from Lorenzo's and rubbed her arms, rocking unconsciously. Lorenzo's voice was soft and soothing. "Apparently, as the train passed through the mountains, the weather had worsened. It was already dark when that man took Jacob off the train. After moving him into the lodge, the man drove the carriage back to the station. On the way back he was caught in a terrible storm, and rain fell with a vengeance. Within minutes the road between the train station and the Masonic Lodge became muddy and slick. He arrived just as the train began to pull away. Not wanting to be left behind in the mountains, the man ran like he'd never run before. He grabbed the train's slippery rear handrail at the last minute and he nearly fell. Finally, he found a more solid footing, and pulled himself up on the train's back step. When that man returned from his trip, he told Mrs. Rutledge that he found the Inn's address on a sheet of paper folded in Jacob's pocket. He told her, "All I know for sure is that Jacob died on the train somewhere in the Blue Ridge Mountains."

With tears spilling down her cheeks, Annie sobbed "Where? Lorenzo, tell me where!"

"Annie, that's all I know. The weather was really bad, and it was pitch dark. Mrs. Rutledge said the man didn't recall seeing a sign of any kind." Lorenzo paused, then added hesitantly, "Perhaps when the weather is fit, we can go back and try to find him."

"No, Lorenzo, No!" Annie was adamant. "He's dead—that's all that matters. I'll miss him, and the kids will miss him—but there's just no way I can ever get him back now."

Annie, looking forlornly at Lorenzo, thanked him for trying to find Jacob for her. "What am I going to do? I don't want to be a burden on anyone, least of all you."

He embraced Annie. "You can stay with us as long as you need to." Lorenzo lifted Annie's chin and looked into her eyes, "Annie, Jacob loved you. He'd want you to go on with your life without him." In his heart, Lorenzo knew that this, at least, was true.

# Chapter Forty

## *Millie's Passing*

LORENZO and Millie were almost dressed when a brood of grand-children rushed into their house in Ceres, Virginia, to help prepare breakfast on a fall day near the end of September 1902. Their parents followed carrying the makin's of a pitch-in dinner to include deserts of homemade cookies, cakes and assorted pies. Millie slipped fresh biscuits into the oven then pulled two large jars of homemade blackberry jam from the jelly cabinet in the cellar. While the biscuits were baking, Millie retrieved two cakes of freshly churned butter from the springhouse just north of the weathered barn-shaped house.

After breakfast, the women and children cleaned up the kitchen before grabbing their heavy coats to fend off the morning chill. While they waited inside the door, Lorenzo and his sons, Ballard and Lorenza, brought enough buggies and carriages to take everyone to Bethel church for the morning services. Once the vehicles were lined up in front of the house, the families boarded them and proceeded to the church. The younger grandchildren, most still in their teens, led their horses from the barn, mounted them, and headed down the road toward the church, passing their parents on the way.

After an early dose of Sunday school and a longer-than-expected sermon, everyone shook the pastor's hand and walked down the wooden front steps of the church and boarded their awaiting transportation to return to Lorenzo and Millie's house for Sunday dinner.

Millie fanned herself with a kitchen towel after putting a pan of fresh biscuits into the oven, and then told Lorenzo she needed to get some fresh air. Once outside on the porch, Millie took a deep breath, leaned over and placed her hands on her knees.

"Lorenzo" she said softly, "I feel a little dizzy, I need to lie down."

Lorenzo lifted her in his arms and took her to their bedroom where he placed her gently on the bed. Her forehead was warm when he touched it with the back of his hand.

By this time, the rest of the family had finished preparing lunch. From the doorway, Ballard asked his mother, "Mom, is there something I can get you from the table?"

"Just a cold glass of water, if you don't mind."

Before he slipped out, she added, "Son, I want everybody to enjoy Sunday dinner. Right now, I need to rest and try to sleep. If I need anything else, I'll ask your dad. I promise."

Over the afternoon various members of the family left the house, taking with them portions of the special deserts the women had prepared for the Sunday dinner. Around three, Millie said to Lorenzo, who had remained by her side, "If I don't feel better by tomorrow, you might consider chasing down Doc Thornberry's and asking if he wouldn't mind making a house call? "

Only mildly concerned before, Lorenzo was now more anxious and a bit troubled. "Tell me what's wrong, Millie?"

"It's really nothing. My arm feels a little numb, and I'm having trouble feeling movement in my left foot."

"Alright, Honey. I'll track down Doc Thornberry first thing in the morning."

The next morning, as Millie rested quietly, Lorenzo struck out to find young Doc John Thornberry, grandson of the elder Doc Thornberry. On his way, he stopped by his eldest son Ballard's house and asked him to check in on Millie and see to it that she ate a good breakfast.

Two blocks down the street, Doc Thornberry was coming out of Miss Hunsucker's house carrying a basket of fresh eggs, his payment for taping her ankle sprain. Lorenzo shouted, "Doc, wait up. I need you to come over and see if Millie is okay. She has a fever and doesn't seem to be able to move around like she ought to."

"Let me grab my bag, Lorenzo. Go home and keep her calm so she doesn't overstress her heart. Give me ten minutes."

When the doc arrived, he noticed immediately that Millie was virtually immobile on her right side. She was upset, complaining that two of her grandchildren would soon be coming over for quilting instruction. After checking her pulse, looking closely into her eyes, and assessing her mobility limitations, he said, "Now, Millie, for a while you'll have to let others take care of you like you did when they were small. You may have had an attack of apoplexy and need to slow down. I'll leave some medicine that should help. Even so, I'll stop by every few days to see how you're doing."

Before Millie could object, he continued, "I know you've been an active woman for many years, but you've had ten children and that's taken a toll.  For the next two weeks, I don't want you to leave that bed unless you have to.  I'm sure Lorenzo and the others will see to it that you rest.  I'll leave some medicine that should help.  And I'll be back," he assured her.

"Don't worry, Doc." Lorenzo said. "There are a lot of us close by, and I can promise you we will all chip in to take care of her."

After leaving the bedroom, Lorenzo asked Doc Thornberry, "How bad is it?"

"There's just no way to know," he replied. "I'm trying to determine how much damage her heart has sustained.  The attack of apoplexy limits to some extent what we can do to treat her condition.  More importantly, her age and physical condition are now larger factors than when she was younger.  She's near seventy and has had several more children than most women her age."

Lorenzo hung his head, "I know, Doc.  I feel terrible.  I feel responsible.  We shouldn't have had so many kids."

"Nonsense!  You can't blame yourself.  Every one of those children was a precious gift, and they're no less precious now."

"What if she doesn't get better, what then?"

"I suppose she could have another attack.  There's just no way of knowing."

Over the next week, Doc Thornberry stopped by religiously every day to check on Millie. He checked her pulse and listened carefully to her heart's rhythm with his stethoscope. As the days passed her heart rate became more rapid and irregular. Occasionally, she would drift in and out of consciousness. By the end of the week Lorenzo was genuinely concerned whether she would even make it to the beginning of the next week.

## *Tuesday, September 30, 1902*

The second Tuesday after Millie's attack, Millie's heart beat for the last time.  Lorenzo, their children, and grandchildren were by her side when she passed away. Lorenzo glanced at his watch, mentally noting that Millie had passed at 9:45 in the morning. He knew Doc Thornberry would need a time of death to report on Millie's death certificate. Grief stricken, Lorenzo decided recording her death in the family Bible could wait.

Lorenzo's middle son, Lorenza, told his father that he would take his horse, and ride to Bethel Church in Ceres to contact a local *shrouder* to come and prepare Millie's body for burial at the Church on Saturday.

"Be sure to tell the shrouder that we would like to have a viewing here at the house starting at seven this evening and continue through tomorrow.

"Dad, what is a shrouder?"

"Sometimes they are called *layers-out of the dead*, son.

"I think I understand."

By noon, the word of Millie's passing had spread throughout the county. Visitors from Ceres and Wytheville were first to arrive bringing with them sufficient food and drink to last for several days. An hour later, several local women came to the house to prepare Millie's body. Before they started, Lorenzo asked, "Will you please be gentle? She's so frail. We're planning to have her burial at the Bethel Church cemetery in Ceres. Is it okay to wait till Saturday?"

One of the ladies assured him, "We'll take good care of her. I promise you that we'll do everything right, and we'll have her ready in a little while for viewing. Is there a special dress that might be suitable for this occasion?"

"There is. I'll have one of my daughters fetch it right away."

"We don't need it right now. An hour or two will be fine."

* * *

Lorenzo asked Lorenza to ride back into town and ask Doctor Thornberry to prepare a death certificate for Millie. He instructed him to take the certificate to the Clinch Valley Newspaper in Tazewell so they could write a proper obituary for his mother.

Lorenza nodded and said, "Since I have to go to both Wytheville and Tazewell, I'll be a little late getting home. As I ride through Rocky Gap and Clear Fork, I'll pass the word about mom's death to our friends and family members there."

"Okay, son. I won't plan on seeing you till late this afternoon or early evening.

As he watched Lorenza ride out, Lorenzo thought of the future without Millie, his first real love. He was already lonely, and sadness was finding a home in his heart. As his mind began to drift, he recalled the woman he had also loved so much but gave up for Millie…so long ago—Lucy.

* * *

Unable to sleep that night with Millie gone, Lorenzo rose in the middle of the night and wandered into the small alcove next to the dining room and sat down at the writing desk in the corner. On impulse, he pulled out a sheet of paper, placed it on the desk and reached for his favorite quill pen. He dipped the quill into a small ink jar and began to write.

*Lucy*

*Although, I have often thought of sending you a letter or tel-egram, I was never free to make that choice. I'm sure you understand. Today, however, I can. This morning, I lost my wife of forty-one years. The doctor said her heart just gave out. Tonight, my own is   aching.  I will miss her, yet I know life has to go on. I'm not sure how I'll be able to do that.*

*My children are all grown now.  Even Annie went away back in '81, when she left with her son James and his family for Ne-braska.*

*I do hope you will respond. I doubt anyone here even knows about my trips to Charleston before and during the war. Should anyone ask, I will tell them the truth—you are a long-time friend who helped me escape Charleston when the Confederates aban-doned the city.*

*Lorenzo*

The next day, when a friend from his Confederate unit, Company F, came to offer his condolences, Lorenzo gave him the piece of paper and asked him to send a telegram with the words it contained to the Rutledge House Inn in Charleston.  He asked his friend to instruct the telegraph operator in Wytheville to be sure it reached its destination.  And Lorenzo made him swear not to mention the telegram to anyone.

## *Charleston - October 1, 1902*

When the boy who delivered the telegram to the Inn saw Lucy, he said, "I have a telegram for you, Lucy, but I don't recognize the address.  It's from Wytheville, Virginia. Do you know anyone there?"

"I do," Lucy replied, "but I haven't seen them since the war." The thought that it could be from Lorenzo almost took her breath away.

When the boy saw the change in her demeanor, he grinned at her, "Gosh, Miss Lucy! I can see how happy you are. You must be expecting good news."

"I do hope so!  Hand me the telegram at once.  Please!  I can't wait."

He handed her the telegram and laughed as he made his exit.

As Lucy read the telegram, tears glistened in her eyes and soon were flowing down her cheeks. She wiped her eyes, sat down, and poured her-self a glass of white wine.  She could feel her entire body tremble as she thought about her last days with Lorenzo. She knew what she had to do.

She grabbed her favorite cape and threw it over her shoulder, then told her staff that after stopping at home to pack a trunk, she was going to see Lilly and Jacob.  She just knew Jake would be there as well with his sweet wife Melinda. Jake met Melinda at a dance sponsored by the Carolina Yacht club in 1884.They were married three years later at the newly restored St. Michael's Episcopal church.

Lucy added that she was not sure how long she would be gone.  As an afterthought on the way out the door, Lucy instructed her manager to look after the Inn until she returned.

## Cooper Estate

When Jacob answered the door, he could tell from the streaks on Lucy's cheeks that she had been crying. "Lucy, are you alright? What's wrong? What can I do?"

"I have to go to Wytheville right away.  Lorenzo's wife has died. I want to be there for him.  I don't want him to go through this alone."

Realizing how upset Lucy appeared to be, Jacob quickly ushered her into the living room and asked her to sit down with Lilly.  "What do you mean alone?  If he needs help, Annie's there. So are his children and grandchildren."

"I know, Jacob, but I have to go to him. In Lorenzo's telegram, he said that Annie went with James and his family to Nebraska back in '81. When Lorenzo returned home from his last trip here, he told Annie you had died from a heart attack on a train while returning from Charleston.  Apparently, she bought the story lock, stock, and barrel and told everyone you were buried in a Masonic cemetery somewhere in the Blue Ridge."

Seeing her tear-stained face, Lilly rubbed Lucy's arm in comfort and asked, "Do you really want to go?"

"I do," she said.

"Then we'll take our train car.  Jacob, didn't I hear you say that Wytheville has a spur off the Tennessee to Virginia Line. We can be there in one day – two at the most."

Jake had just come in to see what the commotion was all about. Jacob asked him, "Would you like to see where your dad was born, Jake?

"Of course, Dad.  But do you think there'll be anyone there who'll remember you?"

"I expect the only person would be Lorenzo. I doubt he told anyone about our days here in Charleston, especially his children."

* * *

Before dawn the next morning, Lilly, Jacob, Lucy, Jake, and Melinda took a carriage to a nearby switching yard and boarded Lilly's train car. There, Jacob made arrangements to have the car coupled with the next west bound train headed toward southwest Virginia. For the return trip, Jacob made arrangements with the railroad to provide a dedicated engine to pick up their train car and return them to Charleston. Once aboard, Lilly spoke, "I hope everyone brought their best clothes. If we have to attend a funeral, I want everyone to look proper."

"Lilly, my dear," Jacob said, "I brought my best suit, a bowler, a vest, a watch chain and, of course, the gold watch you gave me. I should look just like I did when I was Ian Jameson during the war."

"Honey, I love you, but you'll never look as good as you did when you were Ian Jameson." Then she added wickedly, "I, on the other hand, will look every bit as good as I did when I was Princess Theresa De Conti."

"Don't you wish?" Jacob said as he pulled Lilly into his arms.

Jake quickly interrupted, "Just who the hell are Ian Jameson and Princess Theresa De Conti? Are they parts in a play?"

"No," Lilly replied. "They're people we played in a real-life espionage plot we executed for the Secret Service. Please don't repeat what we've told you. We don't want any problems over our counter-intelligence activities during the war. You," she said, pointing at him, "are sworn to secrecy."

"You mean you and dad worked for the Confederate Secret Service?"

"Yes, Son. Both your dad and I participated in several Secret Service Operations. Also, your grandfather was a major smuggler of guns from England to Charleston for the Confederacy. He picked up guns at the Whitworth factory near Liverpool and ran the blockade just outside Charleston Harbor. We decided not to tell you about these activities until now. We didn't want it to interfere with your status among the business community in Charleston."

Jake's jaw dropped at the stunning news. "Well thanks for finally telling me. I promise not to say anything. I'm sure Melinda feels the same way. When we get back home can you and dad fill in the details? We'll be anxious to hear more."

"Of course."

Late Thursday night, around midnight, a train with the Cooper train car attached rolled into Wytheville, parked its passenger car on the old side spur and continued on its way to Richmond. During the war, the side spur led to a water tank that refilled train engines destined for stops on the

Tennessee-Virginia line. After the war, the old water tank was torn down and hauled away. One leg of the tower had buckled, and the fall ripped a large hole in the side of the tank. The cords of wood formerly stacked along the sides of the track over time were cut up and used for firewood. When they arrived, the spur was used only as a side spur where freight cars could be parked until their cargo was removed.

Lilly suggested it might be wise to stay on the train overnight and find a place to eat in town the following morning. Everyone agreed.

Early the next morning, Jacob stepped down off the train and approached a teenaged boy who was looking at the private railroad car in awe.

"Excuse me, young man."

"Yes, sir."

"I'm guessing that you know your way around this place?"

"Yes, I do."

"I need a carriage or a buggy that can carry five people. Could you help me with that?"

The young man smiled broadly and he stood just a little taller. "Yes, sir. When I'm not in school I work part time at the Livery Stable. Sometime my boss has me take a carriage to pick up people in Tazewell or Bluefield.

"Would you like to make a couple of dollars?" Jacob asked.

"Yes, sir!"

"Do you have a horse?"

"Yes, sir. When my dad passed last year, I got his horse."

"I'm sorry to hear about your dad, son. Here's two dollars. Go to the Livery Stable – run if you have to – and bring back a carriage for five. Be sure to tie your horse to the back of the carriage when you come back this way. That way you'll have something to ride after you drop off the carriage. I'll give you another two dollars when you get here. Tell the owner of the Livery stable that I'll settle up with him when I return the carriage. Right now, I'm not sure just how long that will be."

Twenty-five minutes later, the young man showed up with a carriage for all five of them. As Jacob, Lilly, Lucy, Jake and Melinda stepped down from the train car, the boy untied his horse from the rear of the carriage and retook the rains to the carriage horses. Once the party boarded the carriage, Jacob stepped up into the driver's place, took the reins from the boy and proceeded to a small restaurant in downtown Wytheville. Once inside, Jacob casually asked the waitress if there had been any recent deaths in the area over the past two weeks. The waitress said, "Yes, sir. Last Tuesday

Mr. Harris lost his wife Millie. One of her sons told me the doctor said she likely died of heart problems."

Collecting his thoughts, Jacob asked, "Have they had her funeral yet?"

"No, Sir. I understand the funeral and internment will take be at Bethel Church on Saturday morning. Lorenzo, Millie, and the entire family have attended that church for several years. If you plan on going, you should get there no later than 9:30 a.m. The viewing was held on Tuesday and Wednesday."

"Thank you for the information," he said.

After finishing breakfast, they reboarded the carriage. Jacob took them on a tour over the back roads of Tazewell, Bland, and Wythe counties. On the road between Rocky Gap and Tazewell, Jacob turned left on the road over Burke's Garden Mountain into the valley where James and Christina had taken in the two brothers. He showed everyone Blue Spring where he and Lorenzo got fresh water for the homestead. From a distance, he showed them the Harris homestead, explaining he was not yet ready to run into his brother. After giving everyone a good look at Burke's Garden, he traveled back over the mountain and headed to Wytheville, returning to Lilly's train car. Along the way, they picked up assorted fresh fruit to supplement their supper. Once everyone was back to the train, Jacob returned the carriage. He asked the young man to pick up his party at the passenger car at 8:00 a.m.

"Yes, sir. Be glad to."

## *Saturday - October 4, 1902*

It appeared everyone in Wytheville knew about the newly arrived luxury train car parked on the side-spur a hundred yards from the train station. Gawkers had been walking or riding by all day to take a look the sleek, black, ornate passenger car.

That evening, the five of them took an evening stroll into Wytheville for an early supper. More relaxed now, Jacob began telling stories of his youth, his enlistment into the 51st Virginia Infantry, Army of the Kanawha, and his trips to Charleston with his brother to buy sailcloth and canvas for his father's wagon-making business.

Jake was surprised to hear so many stories that his dad had never told him before. Melinda was elated to see her father-in-law so relaxed and at ease in this environment that he had only occasionally spoken of while living in Charleston.

After supper, they returned to the train car and began preparing their clothes for Millie's funeral in the morning. Before they started unpacking,

Lucy told Lilly, "I'm not going to Millie's funeral.  I just don't think it's the right thing to do under the circumstances."

Lilly was not surprised, and she agreed.

"I did bring several nice dresses to wear at other occasions on the trip back to Charleston."

They unpacked their trunks and held their dresses to the light. They had survived the trip well.  Jacob and Jake opened their travelling bags, unfolded their trousers, and hung them across two matching winged chairs. Jacob offered to shine everyone's shoes, or in Lilly and Lucy's case, their lace-up boots.  At the same time, Jake brushed the dust off everyone's coats and his dad's silver-handled cane.

When they finished their preparations for an early start in the morning, Jacob slipped under the covers. Lilly noticed immediately that Jacob was holding her a little tighter than normal. She felt relieved.

Jacob was up and dressed before sunrise.  The rest were ready by 7:30. All said they wanted some of the fresh coffee Lucy had brought with her from the Inn.  Neither Jacob nor Lucy were hungry, but Jake, Lilly, and Melinda supplemented their coffee with the raspberries, black cherries, and apples that they had purchased the day before.

While the others enjoyed their second cup of Lucy's coffee, Jacob stepped outside onto the rear platform and took a sip of Jameson's Irish Whisky from a silver flask he had brought with him. After only one sip, Jacob returned the flask to his inside vest pocket. He had brought the whisky with him in case Lorenzo needed it to get through Millie's funeral.  While he waited, he thought about some of his past decisions. He knew the minute that he saw Millie, he would think about Annie. Is she happy? Had she remarried thinking she was a widow? Jacob, once again, removed the flask from his pocket and took two more sips before returning it to his vest pocket. He stepped inside the passenger car and said, "It's almost time to leave."

A few minutes later the young man from the livery stable pulled a carriage up next to the train and knocked on the side door. While Lilly, Jake, and Melinda took their seats in the back, Jacob gave the boy another two dollars and took the driver's seat. He quickly snapped the horses' reins, and the carriage moved forward toward the Bethel Church in Ceres.

* * *

When they approached the church, Jacob saw all the carriages parked outside and horses tied up at the front hitching rail. He thought to himself, I wonder if there's going to be enough room?  Once in front of the church, they all exited the carriage and headed toward the front door. When they opened the door, nearly everyone turned to stare at them. Jacob could see four unoccupied seats on the back row. Perfect, he thought as they scurried toward the unoccupied seats.

Compared to a usual Sunday morning church service, the funeral service was shorter. Besides the tributes given by Lorenzo and his children, many of their friends stepped forward to speak kind words of a woman loved by all. Traditional hymns were sung, and in his liturgy the pastor emphasized that the ceremony was a celebration of Millie's life and not of her death. At the end of the service, he invited those wishing to express their condolences or thoughts about Millie to come forward and speak to her family.

Jacob was the first in his row to stand, followed by Lilly, Jake, and Melinda. As Jacob approached Millie's casket, he was met by Lorenzo. At first, his brother didn't recognize him. When Jacob spoke, saying, "I was so sorry to hear about Millie," Lorenzo realized it was his brother standing in front of him. As they shook hands, Jacob leaned closer and whispered, "I hope we'll get a chance to talk. We won't be leaving till later on tonight."

Lorenzo at once knew the lovely lady offering him her hand was Lilly. He smiled and said softly, "Thank you so much for coming. You still look as ravishing as ever." Lilly blushed as the memory of their one night together flashed before her, but she looked him directly in the eye as she said, "I'm so sorry, Lorenzo."

As Jake and Melinda came forward to greet Lorenzo, Jacob stepped to the side and introduced them, "Lorenzo, this is my son Jake and his wife Melinda. They live with Lilly and me at the Cooper Estate."

Jacob said, "Since you're the only one here who remembers us, I think we will head out later tonight for Charleston via Bristol, Ashville, Greenville, Columbia to Charleston. It's a lot shorter than our old route via Bristol, Knoxville, Atlanta, etc. Jake has a city council meeting scheduled later this coming week that he has to attend. And there are still a few places we want Jake and Melinda to see on the way home. If you need to see us before we leave, we won't be pulling out till after eleven."

Lorenzo was more than a little shaken at the sudden appearance of his brother and Lillie after years of wondering whether they were dead or alive, but he recovered quickly.

"Lorenzo," Jacob asked, "would it be possible for you to take us to our train in Wytheville later today and drop off our carriage at the Livery Stable there? That way the ladies won't have to walk from the stable to the train in their long dresses."

"I'd be happy to," Lorenzo answered. "Moments ago, my oldest son Ballard told me there's plenty of food at the house–why don't you join us until you have to leave. I doubt anyone there will know who you are. If anyone does ask, I'll tell them you're a long-time friend from Charleston that we knew before the war."

Jacob, Lilly, Jake, and Melinda accompanied Lorenzo to Millie's gravesite. There, a short prayer was given before the casket was lowered into the ground. As it descended mourners threw flowers on top of the casket. Once it reached the bottom, everyone left the cemetery.

When Jacob, Lilly, Jake, and Melinda arrived at Lorenzo's home, he introduced them to his guests as long-time friends from Charleston. He did not elaborate. Although many were inquisitive as to the identities of his guests, Lorenzo refused to say any more about his relationship with them.

Jacob and his family stayed until the mid-afternoon exit of Lorenzo's guests when they climbed into their carriages and headed for home. Once the guests were gone, Jacob said to Lorenzo, "I think it's about time for us to return to our train car." He patted his vest pocket; "I brought a flask of Jameson's with me in case you still have the taste. After I drop Lilly, Jake, and Melinda at the train car, we can share a few sips sitting on the bench in front of the train station."

"I do still have the taste," Lorenzo said, with a hint of a smile.

Jacob whispered to Lilly that he needed to talk with his brother for a while. After dropping the others off at the train car, he took the carriage back to the train station and tied it on the front tie-down rail. They found a bench under a shade tree in front of the station and sat down. Lorenzo could no longer stifle the question that had been on his mind all day. "Tell me about Lucy. How is she?"

"She's fine. I'm sure she'll tell you that herself after we finish our drink." Pausing slightly, he added, "We brought her with us."

"Lucy is here?" Lorenzo asked, his eyes widening with surprise.

"She is! She didn't attend Millie's funeral because she felt it would be inappropriate, but it was her idea to come here."

"Oh! Jacob. I have to see her!"

"We'll go back to the train car just as soon as I drop off the carriage and the horses at the livery stable and settle up with the owner. After that you can lead your horse to the train car, and I'll walk beside you." After a short pause, he added, "And Lorenzo, you should think about coming back to Charleston with us."

On the short walk from the livery stable to the train car, Lorenzo's nervousness was obvious. He removed his slouch hat several times and wiped the sweat off his brow. His hands started to perspire, and he started to walk faster. He even stood a little taller. Jacob was overjoyed knowing he would witness the reunion of Lucy and his brother.

## At the Train Car

As Jacob and Lorenzo stepped up into the train car's rear platform, they could hear Jake, Lilly, and Melinda discussing their route back to Charleston.  Lucy's voice could not be heard. The brothers entered the car and sat on two wing chairs in the main area of the car.

Lilly knew why Lucy had brought some of her finest dresses for the trip. She heard Lucy whispering behind her, "Is everyone ready?"

When Lilly said, "Yes, indeed," Lucy emerged from behind the curtain dividing the car in half.  She was stunning.

"I hope you like the dress, Lorenzo."

"You look amazing."

Lilly, who could see they had eyes only for each other, suggested to the others, "We should leave these two alone for a while. Why don't we walk into town and take a carriage ride?  We can stop for something to eat before returning about six-thirty."

For a moment, Lucy was lost. Although wanting desperately to be in his arms again, she knew that Lorenzo had just lost his wife, so she held back, trying to steady her emotions.  Lorenzo wanted only to crush her body to his and never let her go. Instead, he struggled to maintain his composure.

Neither noticed when the others left. For a few moments, they were content to just look at one another. Then Lucy placed her fingers along Lorenzo's jawline and slowly brought her lips to his.  As they embraced, both were overcome by the powerful feelings they had held for one another these many years.  For now, they felt it would not be proper to make love. The passionate act that once accompanied their love would have to wait. This afternoon they would settle for the comfort they brought to one another after being apart for so many years.

WhenJacob, Lilly, Jake, and Melinda returned just before seven, they discovered both asleep, with Lorenzo cradling Lucy in his arms, her head against his heart.  Lilly and Jacob looked at one another.  "It's not what I expected – but I can understand it," Jacob said.

Hearing Jacob's voice, Lorenzo woke with a start. "I have to go home now and spend some time with my family," he said gently as Lucy drew away. "I'll return and share one last drink with you and Jacob before you head back to Charleston."

"We'll be heading out around eleven," said Jacob, "that's when the engine taking us to Charleston is due to arrive from Richmond. I hope you can give us an hour or two to say farewell before we leave."

"Alright, Jacob. I'll be back no later than ten."

Without looking back, Lorenzo stepped down from the rear platform, untied his horse, and mounted up for his ride home.

### Lorenzo's home

When Lorenzo arrived home, the family, including his three sons Ballard, Lorenza, and Jacob gathered around, asking questions about who his friends were and how they helped him and Jacob escape from Charleston after the city fell. He did his best to give them honest answers without revealing anything about his personal relationship with them.

Claiming a need for fresh air, Lorenzo asked his sons to join him outside for a good cigar. Outside on the side porch, he told them that his friends had asked him to join them for one last trip to Charleston.

"I'm sure I'll be surprised how different the city looks, compared with how I remember it last." He looked down at his feet as he chose his words carefully before continuing. "After losing your mother, I am seriously considering their offer." He then added, "Do any of you have an opinion as to whether I should go."

Ballard spoke up first and said, "Dad, I think you should do what you think is best. If you need to get away for a few weeks to rest, then I think you should take the opportunity." He looked at Lorenza and Jacob and asked, "Do either of you have a different opinion?"

Jacob, the youngest, added, "If that's what you want to do. Dad, you should go."

"I had planned on going back to the train car and spending perhaps an hour with them before they leave. I haven't decided whether I'm going to go to Charleston or not."

"When are you planning on going back to see them?" Lorenza asked.

"I'd have to leave soon, but I'd like at least one of you ride along with me. But if there are two of you, you could keep each other company till I decide whether or not to go. If I do decide to go, you'd be there to bring my horse back. Who wants to go?"

Ballard answered, "We'll all go."

* * *

At ten sharp, Lorenzo and his boys rode up next to the train car. Lorenzo dismounted and suggested to his sons that they take this opportune moment to visit a local saloon and enjoy a drink or two. He also reminded them to return to the side spur by eleven.

As they rode away in the direction of the saloon, Lorenzo stepped up onto the rear train platform and entered the passenger car. Everyone inside was pleased to see him, and for the next hour they swapped stories about their families and their days together in Charleston. The atmosphere in the car was remarkably calm and serene, and Lucy and Lorenzo were much more relaxed. This time, being among family, they felt free and easy and just a bit playful. They were totally at ease in showing their affection for each other.

Just before eleven, Lorenzo heard the sound of horse hooves approaching the train car from the direction of the train station. As he and Jacob walked by Lucy on the way to the rear platform, Lorenzo kissed Lucy tenderly, promising he would make the trip to Charleston after things settled down. Looking lovingly at him she said, "I'm going to hold you to that promise, Lorenzo."

On the platform, Jacob once again withdrew his flask from his vest pocket, took a sip, and handed it to Lorenzo. "Brother, I brought the flask to give to you. It has a short inscription on it."

Looking at the flask, Lorenzo read the inscription:

> *To my brother, we lived our lives as friends, fought our enemies together, and remained loyal to each other. What else is there. Jacob*

Nodding as he read it, he turned to Jacob and clasped his hand tightly, "Brother, you said it all in those words." Then he took the last swig from the flask. As he placed the flask inside his coat pocket, he saw his three sons riding up to the side of the train car. Lorenza had his father's horse in tow behind him.

"Jacob, let me have a few moments with my sons before I decide whether I should accompany you and your family back to Charleston."

"Of course. I'll step back into the passenger car."

Ballard asked what all three had been wondering, "Have you made up your mind about joining your friends on their trip back to Charleston?"

In that moment, Lorenzo made his decision. As he stepped down from the platform, he  responded, "Boys, would you be hurt or respect me any less, if I decided to accept my friends offer?"

Ballard spoke, "Of course not, Dad."

Without warning, the train's boiler heated up, belching small amounts of steam from its stack. As the pressure continued building, the wheels spun intermittently until they had a firm grip on the rails. Soon the wheels began to rotate at a steady pace, and the train started to move.  At that moment, Lorenzo put his foot on the step leading up to the rear platform, grabbed the handle next to the door, and pulled, swinging himself upward. Jacob saw him from inside the passenger car and quickly stepped out, grabbed Lorenzo's free right hand and pulled him up onto the platform. As the train rattled down the old track, Lorenzo's sons waved, turned their horses and rode back home.

The End